FAULT LINES

FAULT LINES

NATASHA COOPER

ST. MARTIN'S MINOTAUR ✻ NEW YORK

Library of Congress Cataloging-in-Publication Data

Cooper, Natasha.
    Fault lines / Natasha Cooper.
        p.   cm.
    ISBN 0-312-25316-8
    1. Women lawyers—England—Fiction. 2. Child abuse—England—Fiction. I. Title.

PR6073.R47F38   2000
823'.914—dc21   99-462108

First published in Great Britain by Simon & Schuster UK Ltd, a Viacom company

First St. Martin's Minotaur Edition: April 2000

10 9 8 7 6 5 4 3 2 1

ACKNOWLEDGEMENTS

As always I owe many people gratitude for advice, information, facts – and corrections. Among them are Robert Avery, Mary Carter, Gillian Holmes, Clare Ledingham, Sarah Molloy, and James Turner QC.

For Joanna Cruddas

AUTHOR'S NOTE

Kingsford does not exist; nor do its council, police officers, social workers, second-hand-car dealers or anyone else who figures in this novel. They are all imaginary and if their names bear the slightest resemblance to those of any real people, living or dead, that will be because, despite my best efforts, even the unlikely names I have invented have not been quite unlikely enough.

Natasha Cooper

PROLOGUE

Kara woke in a rage. The noise that had disturbed her had stopped before she was fully conscious, but she knew what had made it. She slid her legs from under the duvet and got up stealthily, reaching for the heavy iron she kept beside her crumpled laundry.

She paused for a moment to listen. There was silence, thick and menacing, but she knew they were there. Ever since she'd moved into the cottage they had been eating her food and biting neat round holes in her clothes. They left their hard black droppings to show where they'd been, and little puddles of urine too.

Kara had never thought of herself as a violent woman, but the mice had really got to her. As soon as she'd understood what the puddles were, she had been determined to exterminate them, whatever it took.

With the iron clutched in her fist, her ears straining for any sound that would betray their current feeding ground, she crept downstairs, only to stop five steps from the bottom, transfixed by the sight of her room as she had never seen it.

All the brightness had been leached out of the colours

by the full moon. In its uncanny blue-grey light the place looked drenched in peace. Kara's fury died as she saw that she had achieved what she had wanted for so long: a haven from all the angst and anguish of the past.

A board creaked and she remembered why she was skulking on the stairs. She tightened her fingers around the iron, gathered the skirt of her long white nightdress in her free hand so that she wouldn't trip, and moved down another stair. Her bare feet were so cold that the carpetless treads felt painfully rough against her skin.

A man's shadow slid along the far white wall. She stopped dead, blood battering at the inside of her skull and thudding in her ears.

The shape grew bigger, spreading like a stain up the wall to brush the low ceiling. Kara's hands began to sweat, even though the cold had reached right through to her bones. She pressed her body against the wall. Her breathing was too loud, rasping through the stillness of the air. She knew it had betrayed her already.

The shadow reached out towards her across the ceiling. She gasped. But she couldn't move. There was a panic button by her bed; it could have been a hundred miles away.

And then she saw him: thick-set, powerful and dressed in army camouflage with a black woollen mask over his head. His eyes glittered in the almond-shaped holes that had been roughly cut in the wool.

She started to back up the stairs, almost falling as her knees buckled and her left foot caught in the deep flounce of her nightdress. Pain shot from her wrist to her shoulder as she grabbed the handrail to save herself from pitching down towards him.

He came up after her. She saw his tongue move behind the black wool, pressing it out towards her. His breathing shortened and grew ragged. Excited.

Her heart was flinging itself against her ribcage and each breath she took was painful. There was a bitter taste at the back of her tongue. The sight of metal glittering in his right hand shocked her into remembering her own weapon, and she swung the iron at him.

He dodged with ease, catching the long flex and tugging until the plug burst out of her slippery fist. Then he laughed. He sounded very young, which made it worse.

Kara turned and fled towards the panic button. His gloved hand closed around her ankle. She kicked backwards to free herself, but she couldn't shift him. He began to pull. As her feet went from under her, her face hit the stairs. She could feel one of her teeth cutting into her lip as it was mashed against the rough wood.

He yanked her body round, pulling it down as her head bumped, stair by stair, to the bottom. A sticky wetness under her thick hair told her that one of the repeating blows had broken the skin.

As soon as she felt his grip lessen, she scrambled to her feet. Whatever he was going to do to her, she wanted to be standing, facing him when it happened. She opened her mouth to ask what he wanted – as if she didn't know – and felt the thick, horrible taste of wool against her tongue as he thrust a gag into her mouth.

His breath smelt of beer and vinegar, and his hand was tight as a wrench around the back of her neck as he stuffed the woollen mass deeper into her mouth. As she retched and tried to fight, he shoved once more and then grabbed her wrists to hold them high above her head.

At last her mind started to work. Driving her knee upwards, she tried to force it between his legs. But he dodged again, using one of his booted feet to scoop her other leg from under her.

He plumped down on top of her, winding her with one

heavy knee in her stomach and forcing the back of her tongue up against the gag. She couldn't breathe. He dropped the knife and she began to hope. But his right hand closed round her throat.

Fighting for air, bucking and rolling between his legs, she tried to get him off her.

As his hand squeezed tighter and tighter, her terror was shot through with the memory of an obligation she couldn't ignore.

Oh, Darlie, she thought. Darlie, I'm so sorry.

CHAPTER ONE

Fifteen-year-old Darlie Walker looked like every bully's victim as she stood, white-faced and trembling, in the corridor outside court number six.

Her solicitor and the latest of her many social workers stood like buttresses on either side of her. Her barrister, Trish Maguire, still breathless from an ungainly run between chambers and the robing room, saw how hard they were working to keep her upright.

Trish could have done with a few more minutes to get herself under control, but Darlie had recognised her instantly and was already waving. When Trish didn't respond, Darlie beckoned repeatedly with increasingly feverish gestures.

After a moment or two more to ensure that her breathing was as steady as she could make it, Trish moved across the lobby with a magisterial slowness that had nothing to do with her own harassed state of mind. It had been a bad morning and it looked as though it was going to get worse. She had slept through her alarm and emerged from an unusually clinging sleep an hour and half late, only to discover that she had her period a whole week early. Clumsy as ever on the first day, she put her thumb through her last pair of decent black tights, feeling sharp threads snagging her skin as the ladder shot up her leg.

Giving up all thought of breakfast, she dressed as fast as she could and burst out of the flat at a run. For once there were plenty of free taxis in Blackfriars Bridge Road, but she ignored them because the traffic was stuck in a resentful, heavily panting snake that reached well back beyond the Stamford Street turn. Even walking, she could have outstripped the lot. As it was, she ran most of the way across the bridge and up New Bridge Street to the nearest branch of Boots.

Rushing out of chambers fifteen minutes later with her files, wig and gown, she was caught by Dave, the senior clerk. Maddeningly he tried to talk her into accepting a piffling little brief for some man who was claiming unfair dismissal against his local-authority employers. As Trish snapped out a reminder that she never took employment cases, Dave's cadaverous face took on the familiar smirk that meant he'd guessed why she was so dishevelled and bad tempered.

Seeing Darlie's white face and shaking arms, Trish got a grip on her temper. It wasn't the client's fault that Dave had got up her nose – or that she herself felt thick-headed and in dire need of caffeine. With luck Darlie wouldn't notice and would see only a barrister: robed, wigged, calm and competent.

Thin and dark as she was, Trish was well aware that legal dress suited her, and that even the absurdity of the yellowing-grey horsehair wig perched on her own dark-brown spikes could not make her look as silly as some of the English roses of both sexes. She smiled. 'Good morning, Darlie. I'm sorry I wasn't here earlier.' The girl's snatched shallow breaths began to slow as soon as

Trish spoke in her steadiest, friendliest voice. 'The traffic was terrible and I had to run. But I'm here now. How are you feeling this morning?' Given Darlie's appearance, the question was pretty much redundant, but it was the one Trish always used to greet her younger clients.

'Where's Kara?' Darlie asked urgently. 'She promised she'd be here early to be with me. But she's not. I can't see her anywhere. I'd never of said I'd come if she wasn't going to be here.'

'She'll come.' Trish patted Darlie's thin shoulder, feeling a lot older than thirty-two. She could only just have been Darlie's mother, but she felt like her great-grandmother. 'She'd never let you down, and she knows how important the case is. As I say, the traffic's terrible. I expect she's just round the corner, sitting in the jam. She won't be long now.'

'She was coming on the train. Into Waterloo. That's what she said. It's the quickest way from Kingsford. She promised.' Darlie's full lips wobbled and her pale-green eyes filled. She sniffed as a large drop appeared at the end of her nose, wiped it on her hand and then rubbed that on her short skirt.

'She'll be here, Darlie. She cares about you very much, and she knows how important the case is. She's been working really hard on it for weeks and weeks now. You don't need to worry. Honestly.'

Trish was still smiling steadily, looking right into Darlie's damp, restless eyes, trying to will confidence into her. She was never going to be the ideal witness, but if she lost what little bottle she had left she would either start stammering as she presented her carefully practised evidence, which would make her look shifty, or else resort to outrageous – and obvious – lies.

Her eyes focused on something behind Trish's left shoulder and widened. She started hyperventilating again. Her freckled skin turned an ugly red under the makeup and the tears overflowed. A trail of diluted mascara melted the thin layer of foundation on her face.

Trish glanced over her shoulder and saw a squat, black-browed man dressed in a pale-grey suit. As she caught his eye, he looked up at the ceiling, his coarse skin flushing vividly. 'He can't do anything to you here,' Trish said, putting a comforting hand on Darlie's brittle wrist. 'Now, soon we're going to have to go into court. Can you remember everything I said about the procedure and how I'm going to deal with the case?'

'Yes. At least I think so. But what if Kara doesn't come? I won't be able –'

'She'll come. I know she will. And you'll be fine.'

Trish hoped she was right. It would be an ordeal for any girl of Darlie's age to stand in the witness box and accuse a man of forty-five, a man who had once been the most powerful person in her entire world, of physically and emotionally abusing her. For a girl who had been in care, fostered and then moved from one home to another, for as long as she could remember, it was going to be almost unbearable. And the defence were pretty certain to give her a tough time.

Like so many of the children Trish encountered in her work, Darlie had a terrible record. Her temper was legendary in the social services department, and she had had several police cautions. She was also well known for the fantastic stories she invented to explain away the evidence of her various misdemeanours, and for her habit of flinging herself against walls and floors at the slightest hint of opposition. The defence would undoubtedly claim, as John Bract himself had always said, that the bruises seen by independent witnesses on Darlie's body had been self-inflicted.

Trish was going to need Kara, who was was one of the

few people who had always believed in Darlie. In fact it was largely Kara's evidence that had made it possible to bring the case in the first place. Where the hell was she?

Eventually an usher appeared to summon them all into court. By then there was nothing for it but to admit that one of her chief witnesses had not arrived and ask for an adjournment. Trish walked into court with as much flamboyant confidence as she could muster. The Nurofen she had taken was softening her various aches, and adrenaline was beginning to sharpen her wits as it nearly always did when the time came to get to her feet and address the court.

'M'lord,' she began slowly, her mind racing to work out the best way of persuading the judge to postpone the case until Kara could be found to give her crucial corroborative and character evidence.

Why hasn't she come? Trish asked herself, as she spoke so carefully to the judge. Has something happened? Or is it the sodding trains again? But why hasn't she phoned?

Trish showed no anxiety as she finished her speech, hoping she had kept the tricky line between arrogance and creeping humility. She sat back to listen to her opponent explaining just why the whole case should be dismissed.

There had never been any satisfactory evidence, he claimed, and now that one of the principal witnesses had thought better of coming to court at all, there was very little point in his lordship wasting any more time. The proceedings should be dismissed forthwith and without any further waste of costs. He sounded righteously indignant.

To Trish's relief, and considerable surprise, the judge came down in her favour and granted an adjournment. The court rose, he departed, and she forced herself to wait long enough for one more attempt to reassure Darlie.

Her eyes looked bruised and she seemed unable to hear anything Trish said to her. It was as though, having been betrayed by yet another adult she had trusted, she wasn't prepared to believe anyone ever again, or even listen to them.

Trish could hardly blame her. She knew what Darlie's life had been and how much Kara's faith in her had meant. She also knew that Kara would never have stayed away from court voluntarily, but Darlie was much too wound up to accept that.

Later, as Trish hurried back to the Temple, she was frowning so ferociously that various acquaintances crossed the road to avoid her. She didn't notice.

Dave called out something as she swished past the open door to the clerks' room on her way to listen to her voice-mail. The words did not register, but his presence did. She looked over her shoulder to say; 'Has Kara Huggate left any message for me?'

'No, but –'

'Not now,' said Trish, her coat hissing against the walls as she ran down the long corridor to her small, dusty, book-lined room. There she stopped, staring at the two people sitting beside her desk, warming their feet at her tiny electric fire.

They were about her own age, or perhaps a little younger. Their clothes were too scruffy for them to be barristers, or even solicitors, and yet they didn't look quite like clients either, or their social workers. They got to their feet.

'Ms Patricia Maguire?' said the woman, who had tousled, mouse-coloured hair and an unmemorable, very English kind of face. Her intonation alone was enough to tell Trish she was a police officer.

'Yes.' Wariness made Trish's lively voice colder than usual.

'I'm DC Sally Evans. This is DC David Watkins. We're from Kingsford CID. We'd like to ask you some questions about your case this morning.'

'Yes?' Trish could feel the frown increasing her headache. She deliberately relaxed her eyebrows. Taking her gown out of the red brocade bag, she shook it and hung up both on the back of the door.

'You were expecting a witness, Ms Kara Huggate. Isn't that right?'

Trish turned back to watch them. The mixture of tension and sympathy in their expressions made her feel queasy. 'What's happened to her?' she said, when she could speak.

'Why d'you ask that?' DC Evans said, her voice quick with suspicion.

'Because she didn't turn up at court. I expected to find a message from her, but there's been nothing. Instead you're here, asking questions. That adds up to something pretty bad. What is it?'

'There's been a serious assault,' said DC Watkins reluctantly.

Trish wasn't sure whether it was the idea of giving up any information that worried him or the possibility that he might upset her. The queasiness turned to gut-twisting fear. 'How serious? Is she in hospital? In the nick? Is she dead? Come on . . .' Trish read that answer in their faces, too, but she could not believe it. 'She's not dead, is she?'

'Yes.'

Trish swung her chair round so that she didn't have to look at them. Her mind kept throwing up memories of Kara: sitting frowning over some written evidence, running her hands through her thick, dark-blonde hair;

looking up to laugh at a tension-busting joke with the amusement lightening her broad, serious face into something much livelier and more attractive than usual; sipping the extra-strong coffee they both used to see them through long evenings of work; enduring a ferocious set of arguments with steady grace; and talking, with unshed tears making her big grey eyes glisten, about the difficulty of living with Jed Thomplon and the impossible loneliness of being without him.

'It would help, Ms Maguire,' said Watkins from behind her, 'if you could give us some idea of the evidence she was going to give in court today.'

Trish blew her nose and swung her chair back to face them. She gave a crisp, professional description of the morning's case then added, 'Presumably you're trying to find out whether the defendant could have had anything to do with Kara's death?'

Watkins nodded.

'I can't believe it. Darlie's allegations were serious, but not that serious.'

Neither officer looked convinced.

'Look, as it happened, John Bract had a pretty good defence.'

They still looked obstinately incredulous.

'In any case, why would he do something to Kara so close to the trial? He's not stupid – he'd have realised he'd be bound to be a suspect.'

'Surely, doing work like yours, you've come across the concept of intimidation of witnesses,' said DC Evans, looking surprised by such ignorance.

'Murder would be a pretty exaggerated form of intimidation,' Trish said mildly. There didn't seem much point in challenging the woman, who probably meant well enough.

'Perhaps it just got out of hand. Perhaps whoever did

it was sent to frighten her but got carried away and went too far,' she said, with an earnestness that reinforced Trish's judgement of her brains. But that didn't matter in the face of what she'd said.

'"Carried away"? Are you telling me it was a sexual assault?'

'That's right.'

Oh, Kara, Trish thought, closing her eyes for a second. Oh, poor, poor Kara. 'What exactly did he do to her?'

'Take it from me, Ms Maguire,' said Watkins, 'you don't want to know.'

He showed none of the relish Trish had occasionally seen in officers dealing with assaults against women.

'Did you know her well?' DC Evans asked, watching her with sympathy. Trish shrugged and nodded. 'Then perhaps you can help us with something else.'

'If I can I will. Of course I will.'

'Great. So do you know Dr Jed Thomplon at all?' Evans was flipping through her notebook, looking for something.

'No, I've never met him. All I know about him is that he's a GP in Middlesex and that he and Kara lived together until about six . . . no, nine months ago.'

'Why'd they break up?'

'Because she got the job with Kingsford Social Services and he refused to move there with her.'

The expressions on their faces suggested that this was news to them.

'Why?' It was Sally Evans who had asked the question, not Watkins, who appeared to think Jed's refusal perfectly acceptable.

Trish remembered the day when Kara had begun to tell her about the quarrel. She'd been pretty sure that if it had been Jed who had been offered such a huge step up in his career, she would have been expected to follow meekly in his wake. 'But then,' Kara had said, with all the humour that had shone through her preoccupations, even when she was at her most miserable, 'he probably thinks that a wake is a suitable place for an adoring woman. And in Jed's life most women have been remarkably adoring. That was half the trouble.'

'Why'd she agree to take the job, then?' asked Constable Watkins, apparently reading something in his own notebook.

'Refuse the challenge of reorganising Kingsford Social Services after the scandal and all those resignations?' said Trish, amazed that anyone from Kingsford could ask. 'How could she? It was a big promotion for her. Look, have you got any more questions for me? If not, I've a lot on today.'

'Yes,' said Evans firmly. 'We have been told by Kara's mother that Jed Thomplon resented the parting and that he was "angry and controlling". Would that fit with what you know of him?'

Aha, thought Trish. So it was Kara's 'bloody mother' who told them about Jed. She took a moment to think, then said reluctantly, 'I suppose so, but . . .

'If you don't know him, why're you trying to defend him?' demanded Watkins.

Trish raised her eyebrows at the first hint of hostility. She had been on the wrong end of police questioning before and did not want to go through anything like it again.

'I'm not,' she said, pacifically enough. 'Look, anyone faced with the break-up of a relationship is likely to be angry. That doesn't mean that months later he's going to murder the woman who left him. If Jed Thomplon were ever going to get violent, he'd have done it months ago, when Kara first said she was leaving him.'

Something was nagging at Trish's memory, something she'd read. One of the officers was talking to her, but she was concentrating so hard on retrieving the facts that she heard very little. Then she remembered. 'Wasn't there a string of sexual assaults in your area a few years ago? I'm sure I read about the Kingsford Rapist in the papers. Two years ago, or three; isn't that right?'

'Yes.'

'Are there any similarities in the MO?'

'I haven't been told,' Watkins said, looking as though he'd licked an unripe lemon. Trish almost smiled as she understood the reasons for his hostility. How he must have resented chasing up red herrings in London when the real action was in Kingsford!

She got rid of them at last and tried to settle down to work. Before she'd got very far, the phone rang. She picked it up and gave her name.

'You wouldn't listen this morning,' said Dave, at his most peevish, 'but I have to give an answer to this solicitor from Kingsford in south-west London who wants you to represent his client, Mr Blair Collons, at an employment tribunal. Unfair dismissal. I heard what you said this morning and I know you don't do employment law, but for some unfathomable reason of their own . . .'

Trish felt faint amusement as she recognised one of the favourite phrases of the most senior silk in chambers, for whom Dave had always had a quite sickeningly exaggerated respect.

'. . . they want to brief you and no one else. Will you do it?'

'No,' she said, noticing the coincidence and dismissing it. After all, a lot of people lived in Kingsford. There needn't be any connection between Blair Whatsisname and Kara. 'It's not my field. I wouldn't be able to do a good enough job for the client.'

'I know, and in the normal way I'd never ask you to take the case, but they're adamant they want you. It's a simple enough business. You could do it standing on your head.'

'Then why can't the solicitor do it himself? Hasn't he got any bottle?'

'I've no idea. Neither he nor any of his partners has come to us before, but they're well thought of. I asked around. That's why I'd like to give them what they want. No bad thing to take a brief from them, you know. Could lead to a lot more interesting work in the future.'

'Look, Dave, there's no point mugging up the subject for one piffling little tribunal. Can't you get someone else to do it? Eric would be perfect. Let him cut his teeth on it.'

'They want *you*.'

'Sorry, Dave. Nothing doing. I've got far too much on already.' Trish put down the phone, glad that she had achieved a big enough reputation to be sure of getting plenty of work in the future, whatever Dave thought of her rebellion.

She found she couldn't concentrate so she started to excavate the paper ramparts of her desk, a nice, mindless task that had to be done some time. Filing, chucking, and putting as few things as possible in her pending tray, she came across the morning's post. It included an envelope marked 'personal', addressed to her in Kara's writing.

Trish sat looking at it, wiping her fingers on her black skirt. A strong scent of garlic and tomato wafted out when she eventually ripped open the envelope. Kara must have written the letter in her kitchen while something was cooking beside her. That brought her back into Trish's mind more vividly than anything else could have done. She'd never been to Kara's house, but once, after they'd been working late on Darlie's case, they'd gone back to Trish's flat with the solicitor for a working supper and Kara had volunteered to cook.

Unlike Trish, she'd been a brilliant, instinctive cook, and she'd moved around the strange kitchen, peeling and chopping, melting, stirring, caramelising, and amalgamating scent, taste and texture into one perfect dish. So at ease had she been that she hadn't needed to concentrate on what she was doing and had talked as passionately as Trish about the need for children to be protected against the awful damage that could be done to them by vicious or simply hopeless adults.

Trish bit her lip and tried not to think of the horror of what had happened to Kara herself. The letter might help.

Dear Trish,

I hope you're not going to be too cross with me, but I've given your name and phone number (chambers *not* home, of course) to a slightly pathetic chap – well, more than pathetic, actually – who's been sacked from the council here and is taking them to a tribunal. I'd have kept the news until we meet tomorrow except that I'm not sure we'll be able to talk privately for long enough and I don't want you faced with him without an explanation – as you'll understand when you do meet him.

He's called Blair Collons and he's an altogether sad case, and a bit difficult to like, but I think he's been very shabbily treated, even though I can't manage to believe in all the wild conspiracies he sees around him. Although I suppose he could well be a case of 'just because you're paranoid it doesn't mean they're not out to get you'.

Anyway, he needs a lot of help in general and just now a barrister to represent him at his employment tribunal. I know it's not your sort of work, but he needs someone kind as well as clever, if only to prove to him that not everyone in the world *is* out to get him. Somehow I feel sure that if you chose you'd be able to help him, even if you can't get him his job back.

And he needs help, Trish. He seems to have no one in the world and must be very lonely. I suspect that's half the problem in fact. If you could manage to squeeze the time, I'd be terribly grateful. And you'd earn yourself a lot of plenary indulgences for that great court up in the sky. If you see what I mean. Well, anyway, you will when you've met him, I'm afraid.

By the way, I'm sorry to have moaned so much about my love life that day. In fact it's been looking up recently. I've met someone. I'm not naïve enough to believe that this is happy-ever-after time, but it is wonderful at the moment. I haven't told you before because I wasn't sure it was real, but now I think it could be. There are complications, practical difficulties, if you see what I mean, but he's worth putting up with them. Well worth it. I'd love you to meet him in due course. I have a feeling that you'd like him and vice versa.

Love, Kara

P.S. Good luck tomorrow. I'll do my best for poor Darlie, and I won't forget any of your advice about behaviour in the witness box!

'Oh, shit,' said Trish.

CHAPTER TWO

The incident room at Kingsford was cold but nose-stuffingly airless. It smelt of stale smoke, coffee and bacon sandwiches. Four of the twenty phones were ringing and both dedicated fax machines were slowly cranking out sheets of paper as officers came and went, jeering, throwing mock blows, laughing at each other's jokes and scoring whatever points they could. None of them looked at the photographs of Kara Huggate's mutilated body that were pinned to the large cork board, or at the one of her in life, smiling gravely straight at the camera.

Chief Inspector William Femur, drafted in from the local Area Major Investigation Pool with a sergeant and two constables of his own, was waiting for them to settle down. The first half-hour in any local nick was always crucial. You had to establish your authority by the end of that time or you were done for. He was still surprised by the childish resentment his arrival could arouse in local officers, but he'd learned to deal with most of the stalling tactics they dreamed up.

Femur was in his early fifties. He'd done thirty years

and could have retired on a full pension, but he wasn't going until they pushed him out. It wasn't so much that he loved the job itself – although he did get a kick from building an unshakeable case against the sort of toe rag who beat up old ladies or raped and murdered social workers. No, he wanted to stay because he was good at what he did and someone had to do it. Besides, what else would he have done with so much time now that the kids had grown up and gone?

His hair was more grey than dark-brown, these days, but he was still fit: running and weight-training saw to that. To be fair, so did the gardening his wife nagged him to do at weekends. He certainly didn't look forward to spending more time on that, disliking her obsession with straight edges and her determination to poison everything that crawled or flew or grew where she thought it shouldn't.

As in so many things, Femur's taste in gardens was quite different from his wife's. He'd have preferred something more like a meadow, with a few real trees, full sized, here and there, instead of neat little pointed conifers in pristine beds cut into the edges of a lawn as flat and unrelieved as a snooker table. His grass would be longer and paler, with straw-like bits mixed in with it and seed heads, too. There would be flowers dotted about wherever they happened to grow, big daisy-like things and bluebells and something pink – or poppies, maybe. They'd be scented but not as overpoweringly as the paper-white narcissi Sue grew in bowls in the lounge, which made the room smell of sick all winter long. There'd be butterflies in his meadow and perhaps a river at the bottom, where he might dangle a line to catch a passing trout.

It was a pleasant fantasy, and thinking about it always made him breathe easier. He'd never have it. Still, it had done its work again and he was ready to get heavy with his new mob.

They looked a particularly unprepossessing bunch, these Kingsford officers, and Femur found himself thinking that it wasn't surprising they hadn't managed to catch their rapist. Then he suppressed the thought. It would do no good whatsoever if they picked up a blast of hostility from him. Firmness was crucial – humour, too – but no hostility. It would come across as weakness and, if they sensed that, they'd be on him like a pack of hunting dogs and he'd never get a result. That would be a win for them, a win they'd probably like even better than catching the killer.

'Right,' he said loudly, but not too loudly. Only one or two stopped talking.

Femur just stood there, his buttocks resting on the edge of the white melamine-topped table behind him, waiting, expecting them to settle down. After a while it worked and they began to pay attention. It probably took only a few seconds; it felt like minutes.

'Right,' he said again, when all but two were quiet and at least half were looking directly at him. There was one at the back who seemed a bit more co-operative than the rest, a young dark bloke with a lively eye and a hint of intelligence in his twisted smile. Good teeth, too, not that they had any bearing on his brains. Femur made a mental note to give him something interesting to do.

'We all know why we're here,' he went on. 'Forty-one-year-old social worker Kara Huggate, living alone at number three Laburnam Cottages, Church Lane, Kingsford, has been sexually assaulted and murdered. The killer's MO has some similarities with that of the Kingsford Rapist – he's been careful to leave no semen, for one thing, which means he's well aware of the risks of

DNA testing – so we'll have to look back at the old investigation to see where that leads us.'

'Nowhere fast, if you ask me.'

Femur couldn't see who'd interrupted. 'On the assumption,' he went on crisply, 'that we can do better this time.'

That didn't go down well but it was fair comment, and it wiped the grins off several smug faces.

'Right. Like I say, there are similarities, but there are differences too this time. We'll have a clearer idea of how many and how serious they are when we've got all the SOCO and lab evidence in, but there's one obvious difference already and that's the look of the victim.'

Femur pointed over his shoulder at the row of glossy ten-by-eight colour prints. He'd seen plenty worse in his time, but that didn't make these any easier to look at, or any less important. Even the thought of them made him sick and angry; so angry that he'd do whatever it took to nail the bastard who'd rammed a chisel up Kara Huggate for his own pleasure and then throttled her.

However hopeless or obstructive the Kingsford officers might be, Femur would use whatever skills they had between them to get a result.

'As you can see from the photographs of the earlier victims – that is, the five who lived and the one who died – they were all small women; in their late teens or early twenties, with pointy little faces and feathery dark hair.'

Femur saw one of the Kingsford officers sniggering with a mate as they mouthed the word 'feathery' and waggled limp wrists at each other. He ignored them. If that was the worst they could find to do to irritate him, he'd be on velvet for the whole investigation.

'Kara Huggate was bigger, older, blonde and notably square-chinned. Where the earlier victims were physically fragile, she was powerful. She could hardly have been more different. Why?'

'Could've been a different man wot dun it, sir,' suggested one of the local officers, with a yokel's earnestness.

It was so convincing a picture of stupidity that, if Femur hadn't been well aware that it took a certain amount of intelligence to get into CID, he might have taken the comment at face value and set about reminding them that he'd just raised the possibility himself. A few of the other locals sniggered.

'Or something could've happened to the Kingsford Rapist during the intervening period to make him select a new type of victim,' Femur went on. 'He's been inactive now for three years . . .

'As far as we know,' said the thin, dark chap from the back row. Femur suddenly remembered his name: Stephen Owler.

'He could've moved away from the area and been knocking off older women up in the north or somewhere and grown out of feathery girls, sir.'

'Good point, Owler. Get on to the central reporting desk at the Yard and find out what they've got on unidentified rapists operating anywhere in the country.'

'Or he could've been done for something else and spent the time banged up somewhere,' suggested Brian Jones, the younger of the two AMIP constables Femur had brought with him.

'Quite possible, Bri. And, if so, there might've been a probation officer who bugged him or a woman from the Board of Visitors, prison governor or what-have-you, who's given him a new blueprint for the ideal victim. See what you can dig up about any local men who've recently been released, will you?'

'Sure, Guv.'

'Right. Another possibility is that something happened to the Kingsford Rapist after his last known outing, when, as you will remember, he first killed.' Femur glanced behind him at the photographs and saw the head-and-shoulders shot of the nineteen-year-old who had died. He pointed to her to make them concentrate. 'Maybe the knowledge that he'd murdered someone shocked him into stopping for a while. Or maybe something in his life changed and gave him some kind of legitimate satisfaction that meant he didn't need to terrorise young women to make himself feel powerful.'

'Like what, Guv?' Jones sounded puzzled. Femur didn't think he was putting it on for the benefit of the local mob.

'I don't know, Bri. We'll have to go to the shrinks for that. But I think it's possible there was something, something that was reversed when he encountered Kara Huggate.'

'Maybe she sussed him, sir,' suggested Owler. He was frowning. 'She'd only recently moved to Kingsford, hadn't she? And she was a social worker, so she'd had the right sort of experience. Maybe she'd met him somewhere and realised who he was.'

There was an audible whisper of 'Teacher's pet' from the middle of the room. Femur ignored it and nodded at Owler to encourage him.

'Or maybe when they met she said something that spooked him.' Owler was beginning to look excited. 'Yes, Guv, couldn't it be that? He's been going straight since the first killing and thinks he's got away with it. Then he runs into Huggate somewhere around Kingsford, at work maybe or just socialising, and they talk. She says something casual about rape or women or murder that tickles him up and makes him think she knows what he's done, so he decides to get rid of her. Couldn't it be as simple as that?'

'I'd have said that's as likely as anything else at this stage,' Femur said, pleased that his snap judgement of Owler looked like being correct. He glanced around the room, bringing in all the others, who hadn't yet spoken. 'But don't forget, any of you, it's more than possible that this case has nothing to do with the Kingsford Rapist. The similarities could be coincidence, or we could have a deliberate copycat on our hands.'

There was a sudden coldness in the room, as though someone in the crowd disagreed powerfully. Femur was surprised. He couldn't see anything on any of the faces to account for it.

'That means we've got to follow all feasible lines of inquiry before the trail gets cold. Right?'

There were a few desultory murmurs of agreement.

'Right. So, what else have we got, Tony?' Bill Femur looked towards his AMIP sergeant, trying not to show too much affection – that was as sure a way as any to piss off the locals – and nodded encouragement.

'OK, Guv. Well, Sergeant Jenkins has been talking to the victim's next of kin – that's her mother. He's got details of a couple of people who could've wanted her out of the way. Jenkins?'

Femur watched a big bloke, rugger-player by the look of him, with a great thatch of reddish hair, get to his feet and prop himself up against the wall as though he was far too tired to stand up by himself.

'First there's the manager of a Middlesex children's home, sir. He was up in court this morning, where Huggate was due to give evidence against him. We think he could've paid someone to warn her off and it went too far. Or he could've had a go himself, and made sure she'd never do him any harm. Two constables, Evans and Watkins, are up in town interviewing the relevant people now.'

Tony Blacker pushed one hand through his smooth brown hair and tugged at his left earlobe as he watched Femur's impatient face.

'Then there's Dr Gerard Thomplon, known as Jed,' Jenkins went on, apparently unaware of any of it. 'He's a GP from the same area as the children's home. He and Huggate lived together for five years and split up a few months back. Her mother says it was a nasty break-up and he's an angry sort of bloke.'

'Yeah,' said Blacker. 'And the danger time for women who've escaped a violent relationship is now thought to be up to eighteen months, so that would fit. Or he could've been trying to get her back and lost his temper when she refused again. Someone'll have to interview him soon, Guv.'

'Right, Tony. You'd better take that one on.' Femur grinned around the room, inviting a laugh, and then looked back at his sergeant. 'You've always been good with men who've a beef against uppity women.'

'Yeah, I can slag off any feminist over a pint,' agreed Blacker, well aware of what Femur was trying to do and happy enough to play along. They'd been a double-act for long enough to know when they had to resort to blokery to get people on side. The atmosphere in the incident room warmed up enough to justify what they were doing, although one or two of the younger women looked pissed-off. That was a pity but only to be expected.

'And then, of course,' Blacker went on, in his usual voice, 'there're her clients, maybe an addict who hadn't had his methadone and thought she should've helped him, a schizophrenic who'd decided he could do without chlorpromazine and then got paranoid about her, an angry parent of some young scrote, lifer out on licence . . . Could have been any of the above.'

'Or none,' said a joker in the second row.

'Right,' said Femur, ignoring him. 'Thanks, Jenkins, Tony. Now, Kara Huggate had neighbours. Someone must have seen or heard something, even though the gardens in Church Lane are bigger than your average semi and might've given the villain some protection. I want exhaustive door-to-door in Church Lane itself and in the next two streets either side. I want her phone bills and answering-machine tapes. I want any letters found in the cottage. I want a list of all her clients and their whereabouts last night. Right.'

He looked at the officers' names listed on his clipboard and started to hand out the tasks.

'Owler!' he called, when he'd got to the end.

'Sir?'

'When you've finished with the CRD at the Yard, I want you to get hold of the old Kingsford Rapist files and cross-check the SOCO evidence, and the pathologists' and all the other lab reports with everything that comes through on Huggate. I want to know of every item that matches and all the discrepancies, too. All of them. Got that?'

'Yes, sir.'

'Right. Now, Jenkins, what was she doing yesterday? Who did she see?'

'Not sure yet, sir. We haven't had time to get a list from her office.'

'I've got her diaries here, Guv.' Blacker's voice was as soothing as warm black treacle, and it had a bite in it, too: just like black treacle. 'This year's and last.'

'Right. Somebody's got brains, then. Let's have a shufti.'

Jenkins looked bootfaced, as though he'd been personally bollocked.

Femur hid his contempt as he riffled through the

current diary, trying to get some fix on the kind of woman Kara Huggate had been and how she'd arranged her life. January and February were filled with appointments, mostly work-related from the look of them, but the pages were also decorated with little drawings, doodles usually, and also reminders to pay specific bills and buy more washing powder and milk. It looked as if she'd reached that stage in midlife when women begin to mistrust their memory, or perhaps she had so much to think about that trivialities like shopping lists and bills could not be allowed to take up any mental space. Femur sympathised. At last he turned to yesterday's page and sighed.

'So. Who's this "S", then?' Femur looked up at the local officers who were still hanging around not getting on with the jobs he'd given them. 'Anyone any idea? Jenkins? Owler?'

He'd get all their names straight in the end, but those two were already stuck in his short-term memory so he'd concentrate on them for the moment.

When no one said anything, Femur tried again: 'She's got him listed for what looks like yesterday evening. Who is he? Why –'

'Why should it be a he?' asked one of the women. The sulkiness of her voice made it quite clear to Femur that she, at least, knew why he was so impatient with them all. He'd better get her name soon.

'Good point. But not the most important. No one any idea of the identity of this character?' Femur asked again, thinking, dozy buggers. Why didn't they check out S the minute the body was discovered instead of waiting for us? If they've already talked to the victim's mother about her life and possible enemies, and sent two officers chasing off after the ex-boyfriend and some man she was supposed to be giving evidence against in court, why the hell haven't they bothered to find out who she was due to meet just before she died? He shook his head. If he hadn't known better, he'd have thought there was some kind of deliberate obstruction going on. But long experience told him that it was much more likely to be cock-up than conspiracy.

'No one's got any idea yet, Guv,' said Blacker, earning himself a few useful brownie points from the locals, who were drifting away to start doing what they'd been told. 'But we'll get on to it.'

Femur had picked up last year's diary and was leafing back to Kara's first months in Kingsford, looking for other mentions of S. 'She's had a fair lot of meetings with him, usually on Tuesdays or Wednesdays. Never weekends. No times are ever mentioned, only the initial. But it's always at the foot of the page, which suggests it's an evening date. Right, Tony. Give it number-one priority. Even if he didn't kill her, he'll be able to give us a better fix on the time she was last seen alive.'

'It must be a boyfriend, don't you think, Guv? Or maybe a client.' The sergeant was picking his ear again as he always did when he was worried.

Femur was surprised he'd started so soon, it was a habit that didn't usually appear until much later in an investigation. Perhaps he, too, was more than usually sickened by what had been done to Kara Huggate. 'Boyfriend sounds more likely to me,' Femur said. 'She's been drawing hearts and flowers round the initial here. And here, too.'

'Looks like she was sitting by the phone doodling as they talked, doesn't it?' said a jaunty voice from behind them. 'My sister does that when she's first in love. Little hearts when she's feeling soft and romantic, then houses, like that one there, when she starts working out how to get the poor bugger to talk engagement rings and wedding bells. She's never succeeded yet. I'd say Huggate was in love and thinking about how to get the bloke to commit.'

Femur and Blacker exchanged glances. It was a valid point, but the young constable hadn't been invited to make it, and in any case he should've been out of the room doing what he'd been told.

'Owler?' said Bill Femur, making himself sound surprised. 'You still here? Why aren't you phoning Scotland Yard?'

'On my way, sir. Sorry, sir.'

When he'd gone, Blacker said, 'If this S *is* a new boyfriend, that could fit with Owler's other idea, couldn't it?'

'That Huggate could have met the Kingsford Rapist socially and spooked him? Yes, it could. Either way we'll have to find out. In the meantime, Bri?'

'Yes, Guv?' said the AMIP constable.

'Get on to the lab and tell them to hurry up with Kara's address book. She must've had one. Get it as soon as you can and check out everyone with the letter S in the first or surname, wherever they are. OK?'

'Sure.'

'What about me, Guv?' asked Caroline Lyalt, the second of the AMIP constables. She was twenty-six and had already passed her sergeant's exam but hadn't yet got the promotion she deserved. If this case went the right way, it might do the trick, and that was another reason for Femur to pull out all the stops. Not that he needed another reason.

He had a lot of time for Caroline. In fact, he often thought that if she'd been his daughter he'd've been bloody proud of her: serious but always ready to see a joke, sensitive but never neurotic, attractive but not bothered about it, and a hard-worker. He didn't give a toss that she had a woman lover. In some ways, it made it easier for him, spending as much time with her as he did, but he knew Tony found it tough. Still, they were all old enough to work round that.

'Right, Caroline, I want you to make a start interviewing the five earlier victims who survived and the family of the one who died. I know they were all questioned three years ago, but there may be something that was missed then which might help us this time.' He smiled. 'If there was, you'll get it, even if no one else could. Pick one of the locals to take with you and I'll excuse her the house-to-house.'

Caroline laughed. 'Looking for a bit of easy popularity for me, Guv?'

'They've got to like one of us, Cally,' he said, ignoring Tony's disapproval. 'You're the obvious candidate. You have my permission to slag me off as much as you think'll help. OK. Now, hop it and leave Tony and me to a bit of man's work.'

Caroline made her favourite insulting gesture, laughed at Blacker's inadequately hidden disapproval, and went off to select her assistant.

'Is that wise, Guv? Caroline will pick one of the girls, you know, and you don't want her to start something . . .

'Oh, grow up, Tony,' said Femur, with rare irritation. 'Just because she's a dyke it doesn't mean she's a lunatic – or insatiable. She's much less likely to make a pass than you are, or Bri. She's sorted, settled. She's not looking for anyone else.'

'Oh? I thought . . . Have you met her, er . . . ?'

'Yes.' Femur was grimly amused at his sergeant's mixture of curiosity and revulsion. 'She's a ravishing actress you'd give your eye-teeth for. Take it from me. Besides which, she's got a will of steel and a mind like a razor.'

'Actress, Guv?' He looked astonished, presumably having expected a whiskery dungarees-clad activist of some kind. 'Anyone famous?'

'Yes. Even you'd've heard of her, but don't even think about it. I'm not going to tell you. She's Caroline's story, not mine. Now, let's do some work.'

CHAPTER THREE

Trish was lying on one of the two enormous black sofas in her converted warehouse flat. Her overcoat was slung across the back of a chair just inside the front door and her shoes and tights lay in a heap next to her briefcase. Hating the feel of tights biting around her waist and chafing her thighs, she always stripped them off as soon as she got home. She usually had a shower and changed into jeans, too, but this evening she wanted to write to Kara's mother first. In spite of the central heating, her bare legs felt waxy and very cold, but she paid no attention.

The letter was much harder to write than she'd expected. If she had ever met the widowed Mrs Huggate it might have been easier, but all she had to go on were Kara's guarded comments. They had left Trish with the impression of a savagely disappointed woman who had loaded her resentments on to her daughter and blamed her for them. That wasn't how Kara had seen it, but it had been Trish's interpretation of the little Kara had said. She had apparently believed, quite simply, that her mother detested her.

When Trish had protested, Kara had said that she had felt disliked from the moment she became properly conscious of having a separate existence. She had added, half-laughing, that she had long ago realised there was no point holding grudges, so she'd tried to mend things: to find some way in which she and her mother could learn to like each other. But it had never worked. Nothing Kara had ever been able to do had seemed enough to wipe out her lifelong shortcomings: her dreadful appearance, with hair much too long for a woman of her age; her frightful friends; her unsuitable job, working with 'deviants and criminals'; and her refusal to live a life that would have helped her mother meet the kind of people she deserved to know.

As she thought about the woman Kara had described, Trish wrote draft after draft. None of them could possibly have been sent. They were all far too cold. Reminding herself that any woman, however disappointed or disagreeable she might have been, must mourn a daughter killed as Kara had been, Trish tore up the fifth version and started again.

Having shaken some more ink down into the felt tip of her pen, which kept drying out and scratching through the paper, she settled for a short, formal note that couldn't offend anyone:

Dear Mrs Huggate,
Although we have never met, I wanted to write to say how sorry I am about Kara's death. She was one of the most generous and impressive people I have known. I shall miss her very much.

Yours sincerely,
Trish Maguire

PS Please don't even think of answering this letter.

Trish reread the letter and shivered, at last becoming aware of just how cold her legs and feet were. She stuffed them under one of the sofa cushions, rubbing one leg against the other. There was a mug of tea on the floor beside her, half drunk, but that, too, was cool. In a minute she would summon the energy to get hold of Mrs Huggate's address and then have a hot shower, but for the moment she just sat, thinking about Kara and what it must be like to face someone who'd come to kill you.

The sound of a key in the front door made Trish smile. Her shoulders relaxed and she rubbed both hands across her face and through her short hair.

'Trish?' George's deep voice was full of all his usual vigour and affection, and it satisfactorily filled the empty spaces of the flat.

'I'm in here.'

He appeared round the side of the great open fireplace she hardly ever used, and the sight of him – tall, powerfully built and, as always, alive to everyone and everything that happened around him – sent new energy streaking through her like an electric current. She got to her feet.

'George.'

Hi, Trish.' The pleasure in his face changed as he looked at her, and his deep voice quickened: 'What's wrong?'

'One of my witnesses was found murdered this morning,' she said, with an attempt at casualness that didn't work. Knowing that her voice had wobbled, she made herself explain: 'More than a witness, a friend.'

'The social worker you like so much? Kara Something?'

'Yes.' Trish had often thought Kara and George would get on, but there had never been an opportunity to introduce them. On the only two evenings when Kara had been able to stay up in London, George had been busy with inescapable commitments. Now they never would meet.

'Oh, Trish.' He said nothing more, just dumped his briefcase on the floor and put his arms around her.

Trish felt one large hand pulling her head against his firm shoulder. The first tears oozed out from between her lids, wetting the smooth bird's eye worsted of his expensive suit. He stroked her head. Self-control didn't seem to matter any more, and she let herself howl.

It was soon over. Trish loathed crying, and in any case, did not see why George should have his suit ruined, or why he should be bothered with her feelings before he had had a chance to recover from the stresses of his own day.

'Tea?' she said, in apology, as she pulled away from him.

He smiled and wiped her cheeks with his thumbs. She could feel a tiny callus on the edge of one scraping her skin. It made him seem all the more real. She leaned against his hands.

'Yes, but I'll make it. You ought to shower.'

Trish raised her eyebrows, about to ask whether she was particularly smelly, when he added, 'You feel freezing. You'll never get warm without hot water. I'll go and put the kettle on. D'you want a refill?'

'Great. Thanks. And then I'll think about what we might eat. I'm not sure what there is in the fridge.'

'OK,' he said, never one to make a fuss.

Since they had started to spend most of their free evenings together, Trish had tried to remember to shop more efficiently than in the old single days, but there were still times when there was nothing edible in the flat and they had to send out for a takeaway.

George hadn't needed to learn any new skills. As Trish

had discovered, when he first took her back to his house in Fulham, he seemed able to keep his fridge full of fresh food. Surprised, and even a little awed by the sight of meat, vegetables, three sorts of cheese and unmouldy bread, she had peered into his tall freezer and seen that it was stocked not only with luxurious ready-cooked dishes but also with all kinds of raw ingredients that could be defrosted and made into something delicious. He had turned out to be a much better cook than she was, too, nearly as good – if not quite as relaxed and imaginative – as Kara.

Trish went slowly up the spiral staircase to the shower, hearing him padding about her narrow kitchen brewing tea, and she counted her blessings. They had been together for nearly eighteen months, which was longer than any of her previous relationships had lasted, and they had left the first astonished, terrifying excesses far behind. The next stage of any affair, which had been one of perplexed, unhappy disillusion for her in the past, had been successfully negotiated and they were beyond that, too, into something that felt very like a safe harbour.

She stood under the shower, feeling the cold being drummed out of her, and admitted that once again he had known just what she needed. She didn't even mind that any longer, which was saying something for a woman as determinedly independent as she.

George looked up from his *Evening Standard* when she came down the stairs, dressed in loose black jeans and a soft scarlet sweater, and wondered what was making her look so cheerful after her unprecedented flood of tears. She saw him watching, and smiled at him with so much love that he almost dropped the paper. When she was lying again on her usual sofa, he knelt beside her, put his hands on either side of her thin, magnificent, still tear-marked face, and kissed her.

In the early days, her response would have led to a frantic rush back up the spiral staircase to her bed, with both of them wrenching off their clothes at every step. Occasionally George missed the passion of those days, but as he felt her lips moving softly against his he knew that their infinitely less frenzied, more communicative – altogether easier – life suited them both much better.

He loved Trish in a way that had surprised him from the start. He couldn't have defined what he meant by 'love', but if he had had to sum up what she had given him, he would probably have said that he had never once been bored in her company; she made him laugh; and when she showed that she trusted him, which was happening more and more often, she could move him almost unbearably.

She could also make him angrier than anyone else in the world.

'So, tell me about Kara Huggate,' he said, much later, when they had opened a bottle of Australian Cabernet Shiraz and shared the cooking of a mushroom risotto. Well, he had done the actual cooking, but Trish had chopped the onions and the garlic, soaked the *porcini* and offered plenty of helpful suggestions.

'What d'you want to know?' she asked, handing him the plate of Parmesan she had grated.

'What happened to her, why, what the police are doing about it, and what you feel – if you want to tell me. And anything else that's relevant.'

He poured more wine into her glass and watched her as she told him everything she had already told the police, adding a bit more about Kara and why she had come to matter so much and so quickly. Trish's occasionally harsh face grew soft as she talked, and George was surprised to feel a prick of retrospective jealousy. He'd always known from the way Trish had talked that she had liked the woman, but he hadn't realised quite how much. Not that it mattered now. It might as well have been a hundred years ago since the wench was dead, poor thing. And in unspeakable circumstances. Jealousy was idiotic. It always was, but especially now. He tried to stop feeling and start thinking again. That was the only way he was going to be able to help Trish. And that was what he was there for. Partly.

'OK,' he said at the end. 'I think I've got most of that – except this Jed character. I can't fathom him at all.'

'In what way?'

'You say he knew she longed to leave her old job, yet he tried to stop her taking the Kingsford one. Why? Just because he didn't want to move?'

'That was a bit of it. He said he didn't want to commute, which was fair enough, or leave his existing practice, which was less fair since he'd spent their whole time together complaining about how much he detested his whingeing patients. But there was more. Worse.' Trish felt the usual tug between her eyebrows that meant she was frowning.

'What was worse?' George asked, his own frown pulling down the corners of his mouth.

'It's pretty nasty.' Trish put both elbows on the table and propped her chin on her clasped hands. 'And you'll need a bit of background to understand why.'

'OK. I'm listening.'

'I know. You always do. It's . . . Anyway, Kara was never very confident with anyone except her clients, in spite of all her obvious talents, so she needed a fair bit of reassurance from wherever she could pick it up. Being offered the Kingsford job like that, out of a huge field of other candidates, gave her a lot.'

Trish paused, gathering her thoughts. Had Kara's

lifelong sensation of being disliked by her mother contributed to that lack of confidence? Had her care for the disadvantaged and hopeless had something to do with her own need to be valued?

'So?' George said, as his frown gave way to an expression of absolute benevolence laced with amusement. He was thinking that it didn't seem to have occurred to Trish that everyone needed shovelfuls of their own particular form of reassurance.

'And Jed didn't like that,' Trish said. 'She once told me that he found it much easier to be nice to her when she was feeling what she called "a bit pathetic".'

Trish's voice had taken on an edge as she thought of one of George's predecessors in her life, who, now she came to think of it, had shared Jed's taste for being surrounded by subordinates.

'What is it, Trish?'

'What? Oh, nothing, George. I was just thinking. In some ways Kara was a bit like you.'

He frowned again, but it was a different frown, not the worried sort, merely the prelude to the kind of question designed to amuse her. She waited.

'Would you really have said I was lacking confidence, Trish?'

She gave him his laugh then, shaking her head. 'Never. But there are lots of other ways you're like her. You *care* about people, as she did. And you stick with them, even when they annoy you.'

'Some people.' He was serious. 'Mostly you.'

Trish considered asking what it was she did that annoyed him, but then thought better of it.

'So, anyway, while Kara was feeling so boosted by the job offer, Jed just had to take her down. He told her she'd never hack it, and that if she believed anyone would offer her a job so much bigger than her current one unless they positively wanted her to fail, she must be even stupider than he'd thought.'

'Charming!' George poured more wine into both their glasses.

'Wasn't it? And there was plenty more on the lines of: "Given that you'll be out on your ear within twelve months, I'm buggered if I'm going to up sticks and move to an armpit like Kingsford, only to have to move again."'

'No wonder she left him.'

'Exactly. She said that she told him she hadn't realised he despised her so much, and she wasn't sure she could bear to live with someone who felt like that about her. He said she could do as she damn well pleased, that he'd fallen out of love with her years before and only stuck with her out of charity. Oh, yes, and he also told her that she bored him rigid in bed and out of it, that her bum was droopy and her tits were getting as wrinkled as pricked balloons.'

'Sounds as though she had pretty awful taste in men,' George said, too casually, as he helped himself to more risotto, scraping the rich brown burnt bits from the edge of the pan. Then he looked up. 'What's the matter?'

'You're making it *her* fault. That's not fair.' Trish could see that George had heard the stiffness in her voice and was irritated by it, but he couldn't have known that something that felt like an unpeeled lychee was stuck in her throat.

'You said yourself that she'd lived with this Jed character for five years, Trish,' he said, sounding infuriatingly reasonable, 'and he sounds unspeakable. She didn't have to stay so long. Ergo, she must have had poor taste in men – or a masochistic streak five miles wide, and none of your descriptions of her have ever suggested that.'

Trish drank some wine, concentrating on her glass. The lychee wouldn't move and she wasn't going to say anything else until she could be sure she'd sound normal.

'Oh, Trish, come off it.' George wasn't quite laughing at her, but he wasn't taking her seriously. 'I know she was a friend of yours and I know she's dead – and that's miserable for you and worse for her – but that doesn't mean you have to ignore the laws of logic and start claiming that she couldn't have contributed to anything that ever went wrong in her life. Now does it? It's not like you to be irrational and –

'I just can't stand it when people blame the victim,' she snapped. 'Like those judges who say that a skimpily dressed woman out on her own at night has invited rape.'

'After eighteen months you ought to know me better than that.' George's quiet voice sounded odd after Trish's unusual harshness. His eyes had gone blank. He looked hurt.

At once she reached across the table for his hand. After a moment he let her have it, although sometimes he still chose to reject such casually affectionate gestures, particularly when she'd made him angry. 'I do,' she said. 'But I suppose I can't always stop my subconscious making me afraid you'll turn out to be different . . . Don't *you* ever have doubts about me?'

'I don't go in for your sort of angst,' he said.

She was relieved to see that his lips were horizontal again and his eyes looking more lively.

'I trust you and I trust my own judgement. I wouldn't love you if you weren't who you are.' There was still something cold about him, withdrawn. Then he shrugged. 'Since I do love you, I know you're the sort of person I can love.'

'I wish I'd done a degree in logic or philosophy or something instead of law,' Trish said, relieved that his face was almost normal again. 'I don't think a circular argument like that works.'

'Pedant.'

'Aren't all barristers at bottom?'

George pretended to think about it. He was smiling. 'Well, on balance, I'd say that although you're about the worst pedant I've ever come across, even at the bar, your bottom's terrific.'

Trish threatened him with the sticky risotto spoon and all was well.

CHAPTER FOUR

'The ones on the left are the ones with first names that begin with S. There aren't many, so I've put down all the ones with S surnames on the right,' said Brian Jones, handing his boss a neatly typed sheet of paper, 'with everything I've been able to find out about them.'

'Right.' Femur took it, not sure whether S and the rapist were the same person, but determined to find him. He looked down the list, noticing how many of the names had either 'colleague' or 'client' attached to them. 'As you say, not many Simons and Stevens.' He thought of Caroline Lyalt and had another quick look. 'Or even Sallys. Who's Sergeant Spinel?

'Barry Spinel. Sergeant with the drugs squad here, apparently.'

'Where's young Owler? Get him in here, will you, Bri?'

The dark-haired young constable was obviously pleased to be summoned back and seemed unaffected by Femur's earlier brush-off, but he looked disappointed merely to be asked for nick gossip.

'Barry Spinel and Kara Huggate? No way. I mean, I

45

shouldn't have thought that was a runner, Guv. He couldn't have been a friend of hers.'

'Why not?'

'He's about a decade younger for one thing, and for another she was a social worker.'

'So?'

'Well, do-gooders aren't really Spinel's bag.'

'Why's that?'

Owler laughed. 'If he had a motto, it would be "Bang the scrotes up and bugger the evidence. They're sure to have done something you can use to scare them into talking or blackmail them into grassing up their mates." Social workers don't approve of that sort of thing.'

Femur raised his eyebrows, hoping he didn't have to point out that police officers shouldn't either.

Owler grinned at him, looking very young. 'You know what I'm talking about, Guv. People like Huggate see their clients as children who have to be saved from the rough boys in the playground. And they don't come much rougher than Spinel. He's even been heard to say he thinks social workers are to blame for most crime.'

'Right. It does sound unlikely they were friends, then.' Femur shuffled through the paper on his desk and picked up Kara's diary. 'Thanks.'

Working back from the day of her death through both diaries, he didn't find any entry for Sergeant Spinel until fourteen weeks earlier. Then there were three meetings marked on successive Mondays. It was soon after the last that the first clutch of evening appointments with S began to appear. Too much of a coincidence, or not?

Whatever young Owler had said, Spinel would have to be interviewed about his dealings with Kara Huggate. If they had had a thing going, it wouldn't be the first meeting of opposites Femur had ever come across. Spinel might have been giving Kara some kind of rough-trade frisson, and, if he did play as hard as Owler had suggested, he could have been softening her up for some nefarious purpose of his own.

She could have been lonely in Kingsford, perhaps regretting the break-up of her five-year relationship, in which case she'd have been easy prey for a sting of some kind. To Femur it seemed likely enough. After all, the initials fitted and the hearts and flowers started coming remarkably soon after Kara's three professional meetings with Spinel.

It was, of course, possible that the two had met and discovered in each other something that cut right through their prejudices. Cynic though he was, Femur had to admit that kind of thing did happen. It could have happened to these two. He'd have to see.

'Get a hold of Spinel for me, will you, Owler?' he said. 'I'll need to have a word with him.'

The young Kingsford officer turned away obediently to the nearest phone.

'Thanks, Bri. That was useful. Will you process the rest of the names on the list? Find out how well they all knew Kara and when they last saw her. OK? And talk to her colleagues. One of them may have been a confidant.'

'Sure, Guv.'

'Spinel's with his guv'nor,' Owler said, turning back from the phone. 'I've left a message for him to give you a bell as soon as he's free.'

'Right. Good. Anything from the CRD while you're here?'

'They're faxing a list of unidentified rapists through to us, but there's nothing that sounds exactly like our boy – in either phase.'

'Let me see the fax as soon as it comes in.' Femur smiled, Owler deserved it. He'd done OK. Not well enough to be called by his Christian name yet, but that'd probably come. He was a bright lad. 'Meantime, you'd better get back to the old files. It may be a waste of time, but we've got to be sure.'

Barry Spinel was almost spitting with fury. He'd always thought the DI pathetic, but he'd never been this hopeless before. It was more than time he learned the facts of life. Flexing his powerful thighs in their tight, faded jeans and hunching his big shoulders, Spinel said, 'What's the point, sir? Supposing they do get Drakeshill on receiving or theft, or whatever it is their Neanderthal brains have come up with, what good's it going to do anyone? He'd probably get no more than a slapped wrist, at the most a year or two inside. And we'd lose our best snout. He's been funnelling gold-dust information through to us for over two years now. We've intercepted three major deliveries of smack, we've picked up God knows how many small dealers, and one reasonably big one. To put him out of action for a few nicked cars – cars that there's no real evidence he had anything to do with himself – is just barking. Can't you keep them off his back?'

'I'm doing my best, Barry,' said Detective Inspector Robert Lydane, with an irritating whining note in his voice, 'but surely you can make him keep his nose clean and control those young men of his so that we can avoid upsetting our colleagues.'

'How many more times do I have to say it, sir? Can't you get it across to those brain-dead bozos that snouts are never model citizens? They wouldn't have access to any useful information if they were.'

'There's no need to take that tone with me, Spinel.'

It was a relief to know the man had balls of a sort, even if they were the size of sugar lumps.

'Sorry, sir,' Spinel said, loading the apology with contempt.

'Thank you.' It didn't sound as though the DI had noticed anything but the words. 'Now, Barry, think about it from their point of view. In some ways it would be easier if Drakeshill was into drugs fair and square. Then it would be only our own cases we'd have to pull to protect him, not theirs. It would be our trade-off. As it is, the crime squad see us messing up their operations after a lot of work and some expensive stake-outs and they get royally pissed off. You can understand it, can't you?'

Spinel shook his long curls, and rubbed his stubbly chin. 'Can't you just tell 'em it's hands off Drakeshill for everyone for ever? That way the crime squad won't waste time trying to make cases against him and we won't risk our best source of information.'

'I can try,' said the DI, sighing, 'but they're never going to be happy giving *carte blanche* to a known criminal.'

Carte blanche, Spinel thought. Must he sound so prissy? It would do him good to get back out on the street and face some real aggro. Wrapped in cotton-wool, sitting behind his desk all day, he'd forgotten what it was like out there – how violent.

'Have a word with him, Barry, and get him to cool it on the cars for a while. And do it soon. I mean that.'

Spinel said nothing and watched the DI flush as he understood what the silence meant. So perhaps he wasn't so thick, even if he was too pathetic to stand up for his own men.

'It's important, Barry.'

Spinel shrugged. 'OK, sir. But he won't like it. The information may well dry up and we'll be back to square one. Class A drugs coming into Kingsford is a lot more serious than a few old bangers nicked for an evening's joyriding by his mechanics, even if it was them that did it.'

'The thefts sound considerably more serious than that.

But it's important, Barry. I should like you to do it, and to do it now.' There was a surprising hint of steel in the DI's face at that moment, and Spinel, who had been intending to have a jar with Drakeshill in any case, decided he'd be too busy to do it until the next day at least.

He turned away and sauntered back towards his own desk without another word, every muscle in his hard-toned body expressing his feelings. That was probably a waste of time, too.

'Sarge, someone from AMIP wants to talk to you about the Huggate case over at the incident room,' said one of the woman constables, whose first name Spinel could never remember. She was Becky or Betsy Deal, plain as her surname and just as uninteresting: hardly even worth winding up since she took everything he threw at her and never reacted, just like a lump of uncooked pastry. He always thought of her as Doughface.

'Get him for me, will you, darling?' he said casually, still hoping for a rise one day but not prepared to put in much effort. She didn't answer back, she didn't even wince at the sarcastic endearment, or smile. She and the DI would make a good pair, Spinel thought, impervious to insult. Fucking boring.

When Doughface had put the call through to his phone, she picked up a file and appeared to block out of her mind not only him and his call but everything else that was going on around them. He wondered what it would take to crack her, but stopped thinking about her as soon as he heard the voice of the AMIP officer introducing himself and asking about his dealings with Kara Huggate.

Spinel took a moment or two. 'Yeah. I do remember her,' he said. 'She had a client whose nine-year-old son was sold a microscopic rock of crack by the school dealer. The mother wanted the dealer hanged – or at least castrated – and Huggate came to me with the name. It's one we knew well – we'd been watching the little toe rag for weeks, hoping to get on to *his* supplier – but we've had trouble getting enough evidence to go after either of them. Huggate and I had a couple of meetings a few months back when she tried to persuade me to make an arrest on the unsupported word of a frightened nine-year-old, who wouldn't have stuck by his story in court for more than five minutes. We had a bit of a fight – you could tell she'd not had many dealings with the CPS. Still wet behind the ears, like most of these do-gooders.'

'Right. I'd like all the details, as soon as possible,' said the chief inspector, with stupid politeness. It made him sound as though he was as much of a big girl's blouse as the DI, but that didn't square with the powerful voice that came so confidently through the phone. Spinel began to feel vaguely curious about the man. 'Names, dates, and so on. And your personal impressions of Huggate, too. Could you fax it all over? Or you could give the details to one of my officers over the phone, if that would be simpler.'

'Sure,' said Spinel, through his teeth. Why should he waste time helping their investigation? Of course, there would be compensations. He grinned to himself. It would piss off the DI if he spent so long producing information for this Femur bloke that he had to put off the drink with Drakeshill. A murder inquiry definitely took precedence over warning off an iffy snout. But Spinel was damned if he'd look too co-operative with the AMIP team, that would ruin his reputation with the local boys if they got to hear of it. And they probably would. Everyone seemed to know just about everything in this nick that wasn't protected with serious threats.

'If you think it's worth doing, sir,' he said, as though he was commenting on someone's urge to use doilies.

'Let me be the judge of that,' said Femur, sounding much more on the ball than the DI. He'd have to watch that. 'It sounds as though you didn't like Ms Huggate much, Sergeant.'

'She was all right, I suppose, as social workers go. But she had stupid ideas about what can be done to protect children who go out looking for drugs.'

'Right. Idealistic, was she?'

'You could say so. Or you could call it naïve. She once told me I'd never make a difference until I got over my cynicism. Cynicism!' Spinel was still outraged. Kara Huggate had been one of the few people he hadn't even tried to wind up, so she'd had no reason to give him aggro. Uppity cow. 'I told her if she'd seen the half of what I have to deal with on a daily basis she'd be cynical too.' Spinel laughed then, and after a moment Femur joined in, which made it sound as though they'd be able to work together.

'You want me to dig out my file and bring it over, sir? I've got plenty of time. Then you could ask whatever you want without waiting for your officers to get to it.'

'Would you, Sergeant? That's very good of you.'

Chapter Five

Trish's day had gone well. In court for the sentencing of a man she had helped to prosecute for living off the immoral earnings of under-age girls, she had got pretty much what she wanted. The trial itself had finished a couple of weeks earlier. The CPS had done their stuff and provided all the necessary witnesses; there had been no nasty surprises, and none of them had been broken in cross-examination. The silk who'd been leading her had performed brilliantly, and Trish had thoroughly enjoyed herself as she and her leader had wiped the floor with the defence evidence as well as counsel's arguments.

It had been particularly satisfying because there had been rather too many trials recently in which Trish had had to steel herself to argue an unattractive client's case or make witnesses look untrustworthy to the jury, even though she herself had believed what they'd had to say. This time, from the moment she had first seen the case papers and read what the defendant had done to keep the girls under his influence, she had wanted him behind bars for as long as possible.

Sentencing had been postponed for the usual pre-sentence reports, but she'd had few anxieties. And she'd been right. He had been sent down for the maximum of seven years, with a further sentence of five for unlawful wounding to run concurrently. Trish would have liked the sentences to be consecutive rather than concurrent, but she'd always known that was unlikely.

When it was over she emerged into Old Bailey and sucked in a great lungful of cold, exhaust-laden air then had to cough most of it out.

'You sound as though you're on sixty a day,' said a familiar voice behind her. When she turned she saw Michael ffrench, an old acquaintance at the criminal bar, whose case must have just finished. He, too, was looking pleased with himself. 'Share a taxi back, Trish?'

'I think I'll walk,' she said. 'I haven't much to carry. But thanks.'

'OK. See you.'

Hating gyms as she did, walking back to the Temple was almost the only exercise Trish ever took. As she emerged into Ludgate Hill she saw that some of the black clouds were grudgingly drawing apart to show glimpses of slightly paler sky, but the sun had set a good hour earlier so the only real light came from the street-lamps, glittering on the bumpers of cars and vans as they belched at the traffic lights. The orange glow made the faces of the hurrying people look even more ill than they did in full daylight, and most of them seemed to have chapped lips and dripping noses.

Ugh! A typical London winter. Trish shuddered. She didn't want to loiter in the freezing damp, but she didn't want to be back in chambers either. She was due to have a conference with Kara's weird-sounding protégé Blair Collons.

Trish knew she had to meet him since she'd accepted

the brief, but he'd sounded ghastly from Kara's letter, and the case itself wasn't of any real interest. Knowing she had a bit of time in hand, Trish decided to give herself a quick treat first. She turned back and took a short detour, crossing Ludgate Hill and walking down Carter Lane to Wardrobe Place, which was almost her favourite place in the City.

Built on the site of the King's Wardrobe, which had been destroyed in the Great Fire, it was an enchanting secretive courtyard with a short row of Georgian houses down one side and decrepit shops opposite. Trish had first stumbled on it years earlier, late one summer's night, and fallen in love with the place. One day it would probably be developed, but for the moment it was still the same as she'd first seen it. Pleased, she turned back towards the Temple, almost ready to face Blair Collons.

As she waited to cross Ludgate Circus, pulling her scarlet wool scarf higher round her neck to keep out the icy damp, Trish tried not to think too much about Kara. All the tabloids had been full of lurid details of what had been done to her, and to Trish they seemed to carry an insidious subtext of the kind of victim-blaming she most hated. Nearly all the articles had mentioned that Kara lived on her own, and several had included supposedly helpful hints about the ways other women in her situation could minimise the risks they took, which made it sound as though they thought Kara had almost invited what had happened to her.

One paper had even interviewed Jed Thomplon about the break-up of his relationship with Kara, eliciting, after the first routine expressions of horror and sorrow, several misogynist comments about the way feminism had destroyed women's chances of safety and happiness by making them discontented with the kind of life that would have been right for them. The journalist had quoted Jed as saying that large numbers of his female patients suffered stress-induced illnesses that could be put down directly to the fact that they were trying to succeed in two mutually exclusive worlds.

Trish had her own views about the unreasonable demands made on women who did paid work all day and still shouldered the majority of their family's domestic responsibilities, but she did not like the spin Jed had put on their difficulties. But then she wouldn't have expected much better from him after the few things Kara had told her about their life together.

Trish was interested that he had let himself sound so bitter and took that as a sign that he knew he couldn't be a suspect for the killing. Either he'd had an unbreakable alibi to give the police, who had clearly been all ready to suspect him, or else it had never even crossed his mind that anyone would think he could have been involved.

Like most of the journalists who'd written about Kara, Jed seemed to assume that she'd been the seventh victim of the Kingsford Rapist. Several articles lambasted the police for their incompetence in leaving him uncaught for so long.

The lights changed and Trish crossed Ludgate Circus. The traffic was even thicker than usual – there must be yet more road works higher up Farringdon – but there were also hordes of pedestrians, jostling, getting in the way, and not moving quickly enough. She pushed through eventually and made her way to Pret à Manger in Fleet Street for a cappuccino to go. With the tall cardboard cup in one hand and her briefcase in the other, her red bag slung across her back, she made her way across the crammed, noisy road into the peace of the Temple.

She stopped by the clerks' room to tell Dave what had happened in court and asked him to chase up some of her most outstanding fees. He looked hurt at the suggestion that he might not have done all he could to keep her income flowing in, so she reminded him that there were at least three cases she had done two and half years earlier for which she had still not been paid.

'Well, you know how it is.'

'Yes, I do, Dave. But I always have a lot of big bills at this time of year. It's when I moved into the flat so all the annual things like insurance come up this month, and the January tax payment has cleaned me out. I *hate* this new system of paying tax in advance. Do your best for me, won't you?'

'Don't I always? Now, you haven't forgotten the con, with Mr Collons, have you?'

'No, but I wish I could.'

'It won't take long and I know you'll do a fine job.' Dave was looking at her with qualified approval. That was rare enough to make her smile. As he opened his thin lips to smile back, his sharp teeth gleamed in the light of his cherished antique brass desk lamp.

He had once told Trish, in an uncharacteristically soft moment, that the lamp had come from what he called 'Churchill's bunker' in the Cabinet Office war rooms. She didn't believe the story, but Dave obviously did. She had occasionally seen him stroke the lamp when he thought no one was looking. Whenever he'd been particularly acerbic or difficult, it gave her a certain private satisfaction to think of his fantasising about being a great war leader, battling against the odds to get his troops to the front so that they could do their bit for King and Country.

She took her coffee back to her room and gave herself five minutes of self-indulgent relaxation before hanging up her gown, and tidying herself and her desk ready for her new client.

When he came, she was not impressed. He was a small

man, probably in his mid-forties, with a tight, round belly pushing out the waist of his brown trousers. They were so deeply creased around the crotch that the suit couldn't have been cleaned in years.

To be fair, Trish had to admit that he had done his best with the stains on the jacket. Even from across the desk she could see where the water he had dabbed on them had puckered the cloth and spread the grease way beyond the original mark.

He smelt faintly of stale sweat, bad teeth, and resentment, and he looked frightened. His thin brown hair was greasy and stretched across his scalp in unattractive strands. But he was hardly the first unappetising client Trish had ever had. She knew what she had to do.

Trying to look as though she was pleased to see him, she invited him to sit down and tell her all about his case. His solicitor, who was as clean and pressed as Collons was not, leaned forward to give Trish a crisp explanation.

'I think, Mr Bletchley,' she said, 'that it would be of great benefit if I could hear about it from Mr Collons himself first.' She turned to smile encouragingly at him again.

He stared back at her from under half-closed lids. Something in his eyes, the peculiar intensity, perhaps, suggested that he was trying to tell her something he couldn't actually say.

'Carry on, Mr Collons,' she said cheerfully, as though she had not noticed. 'How long had you been working for Kingsford Council before they sacked you?'

'Nearly four years. In the finance department.'

'As a bookkeeper?'

'That's right. I am . . . I used to be . . . I am an accountant, chartered, but bookkeeping's been my job at Kingsford from the beginning. Needs must when the devil drives, you know.'

Trish only just stopped herself from blinking. He didn't look like any chartered accountant she had ever seen. 'I see,' she said feebly, waiting for more. 'And what exactly is it that the council thought you'd done?'

'Falsified expenses, creaming off a slice for myself before paying out to the people who'd presented claims.' His voice was indignant. There was no attempt at justification, just outrage. 'When they showed me some of the dockets, it was easy to see that they'd been altered. It had been very clumsily done, but it hadn't been done by me.'

'Fine. Any idea who had done it?'

'None. And since these particular expenses were all for petty cash, there'd been no cheques paid in anywhere, which would have provided some evidence.'

'I see. And how much is involved?' Trish had read all the papers already, but she wanted to make sure that the story the client would tell at his tribunal tallied in every respect with the documentary evidence.

'The charge is that I'd been doing it ever since I arrived and had made something in the region of ten thousand pounds out of it.'

'That's a lot of money to be made out of claims for bus fares, even over four years.'

'There was a bit more to it than bus fares, Ms Maguire,' Blair Collons said pettishly, once more making peculiar faces at her.

Any minute now, she thought, he's going to start winking at me. She was beginning to understand why his solicitor might not have wanted to represent him at the tribunal. Quite apart from his unsavoury appearance, the facial tic – or whatever it was – wouldn't exactly enhance his credibility.

'And yet they haven't involved the police,' she said. 'Is that right?'

'Quite right,' said Bletchley, crossing his elegantly suited legs. 'Which makes it clear that they can't ever have had any hard evidence, which makes their sacking my client on what amounts to little more than suspicion quite outrageous.'

The phone on Trish's desk rang, which surprised her. Dave and the junior clerks were usually scrupulous in refusing to put calls through during a con. Assuming it was something urgent, she picked up the receiver.

'Ms Maguire?' said Debby, the much criticised and put-upon secretary who worked in the clerks' room. She sounded anxious. 'I'm sorry to disturb you, but there's someone on the line who says he positively must speak to Mr James Bletchley and I know he's in with you. Dave's not here at the moment, or I'd have –'

'Don't worry, Debby,' said Trish, anxious to hold back the flood of explanation. 'I'll tell Mr Bletchley.' She put a hand over the receiver, forgetting that modern telephones are too efficient to be so easily muffled, and asked whether he was prepared to take the call.

'Ah, thank you, Ms Maguire. Yes, I know what it is and it's important. I wonder if I might take the call somewhere else? The clerks' room, perhaps.'

'Fine.' Trish was not sure that she wanted to spend any time alone with the peculiar Mr Collons but she could hardly say so.

As soon as his solicitor was out of the room, he said, 'That's lucky. Now, we haven't much time, and I must speak to you alone. Kara told me all about you, and said she was sure you'd understand everything.'

So that's what the grimaces were all about, thought Trish. Help. 'I'm afraid,' she said, doing her best to avoid sounding patronising, 'that you'll have to wait until Mr Bletchley comes back. The bar's code of conduct means that you and I cannot discuss the case – or anything that might have a bearing on it – without your solicitor present.' Trish thought of her meetings with Kara and decided they had been quite different, and just about acceptable. 'But, as a friend of Kara's, you might be able to help me. D'you know if there's going to be a funeral? I wouldn't want to miss it, but I haven't heard anything about when it might be. D'you know?'

'No. But, then, they wouldn't tell me. It was only Kara who ever . . .' He produced a surprisingly clean handker-chief and blew his nose. 'But listen, Ms Maguire, it's not the case that we need to talk about. Not really. I don't mind Bletchley hearing about that, even though he thinks I'm guilty. You don't, do you?'

'No,' said Trish, surprising herself. 'No, I don't.'

'Kara said you wouldn't. She said she'd trust your judgement anywhere.' He smiled, revealing chipped, discoloured teeth, but also a saner, slightly more attrac-tive personality. 'That's why I said I had to have you in spite of all Mr Bletchley's protests that you weren't the right kind of barrister for me. Kara had recommended you, you see, and that was enough for me.'

'That was nice of her,' said Trish, still trying to keep him off the subject of his case. 'Had you known her long?'

'Not long enough. Not nearly,' he said, as his eyes started to water. Trish quite liked him for that. 'Only since she came to Kingsford. But she was wonderful to me. Really, really kind. I've never known anyone like her before.'

Trish nodded, wondering how much longer she could spin out the innocuous discussion.

'She thought you were wonderful, too,' Blair went on, his smile beginning to look a bit sickening. 'She was always talking about you.'

'Oh,' said Trish inadequately, wishing Kara had never mentioned her to this peculiar little man. 'I wonder when

Mr Bletchley's going to be back. I shall want to get everything clear then so that I don't have to trouble you again before the tribunal. I shall be asking you to tell me why exactly you think someone on the Kingsford Council staff was trying to frame you.'

'But that's what I've been wanting to tell you *now*. While he can't hear. It's not safe to involve him. I don't . . . You must listen, Ms Maguire. You must. Kara wanted you to. Really she did. There have been things going on at Kingsford Council that only she and I know about. That's why they tried to get me sacked and I'm sure it's why they killed her.'

Trish blinked.

'So you do see, don't you, why I can't trust anyone but you?' Blair Collons's breathy, excited voice did not help his ludicrous statements. 'And why I need you to help me now. I wouldn't be telling you any of it if I hadn't had Kara's word that you were pure gold.'

The door opened and Trish signalled her relief at the sight of the solicitor in a wider, warmer smile than she usually let any stranger see.

James Bletchley looked a little surprised but, having glanced at his client, who was sitting back in a resentful heap in his chair, nodded as though he understood.

'Now, Ms Maguire,' he said briskly, coming back to his chair and sitting down, 'how much more do you need to know from us?'

Trish scanned her notes and listed several points on which she wanted clarification. Collons fumbled his facts and couldn't get the right words out. In the end James Bletchley stopped prompting him and simply gave Trish the information. Even then, he stopped politely at the end of almost every sentence to check with his client that he had got everything right.

When everything had been said and all three of them

were on their feet, Collons came towards Trish with his right hand outstretched. She had hoped to get away with only verbal farewells, but it was clear she was going to have to shake hands with him. She knew exactly how his palm would feel: limp and clammy as a raw squid.

It did, but she could feel something else as well, something inanimate. As he pulled his hand away from hers, she realised he had left a folded scrap of paper in her palm, rather as the oldest and grandest of her great-aunts had occasionally left a five-pound note with her when she was a schoolchild.

As soon as she was alone, Trish unfolded the piece of paper and saw written on it a telephone number and the words: 'Please ring me. Please. I MUST talk to you about Kara *alone.*'

He'd had no chance to write it during the conference so he must have brought it with him. Trish shuddered. She couldn't think what Kara had seen in him. And she couldn't think what she herself was going to do about him and his bizarre fantasies.

CHAPTER SIX

Hundreds of miles away, on a balcony looking over the French Alps at Meribel, a fat man sat immersed in his newspaper. He seemed oblivious to the sharp icy peaks of the mountains that looked so dazzling against the blue sky, and to the only other occupant of the balcony, who watched him resentfully.

It wasn't that he was doing anything wrong, but Sandra thought it would have been nice if he'd paid her a bit of attention. She was bored out of her skull and longing to chat to anyone, even a man in his fifties who looked like he weighed twenty stone. She'd wrenched her knee when she fell off the drag lift on the first day of the holiday so she couldn't ski at all. The others wouldn't be back at the hotel till tea and she might just as well have been stuck at home in Kingsford waiting for Katie to come home from school and hoping that Michael wouldn't be in too bad a mood when he got in from work. She'd already written to Simon, who was staying with a schoolfriend because he didn't like skiing, and now there was nothing except her book, which was boring.

The fat man must have felt her gaze on him because he looked up quite suddenly, his face shocked. She smiled reassuringly. 'Isn't it a lovely day?' she said, hoping that might lead to something.

'What?' He sounded nearly as sharp as Michael on the worst of his bad days. 'Oh, yes. It is. But the news is *horrible*'

'Is it? I haven't seen a paper since we left London. What's happened?'

'Another rapist who's killed his victims.'

'Oh, no.' There was nothing forced about Sandra's reaction. 'We had one in Kingsford a few years back. For anyone like us with a young daughter, it was –'

'You'd better read this, then,' he said, in a weird voice, and started to heave himself out of his chair.

Sandra had to look away. It would've been too cruel to watch such a difficult, humiliating process. But he managed it in the end, after several painful grunts. She took the paper, which he'd folded open at the centre spread. It was the least she could do after he'd made such an effort. When he'd padded off for his usual afternoon swim, she opened the paper out flat to see a huge headline:

LONELY SOCIAL WORKER RAPED AND MURDERED IN
DREAM COTTAGE

Underneath it was a colour photograph of one of the houses in Church Lane in Kingsford. Sandra knew it at once, even before she'd read the caption, because she recognised the way the garden sloped down to the pretty white picket fence and the spire of St Michael and All Angels towering above the deep roof. She'd often hankered to live in Church Lane and always drove that way when she could. It was nearly as familiar as her own road, and less than half a mile away.

Below the picture of the house there were three photographs of a woman. The largest showed her business-like in a straight-skirted suit of some dark material with her hair tied back and a large pair of spectacles disguising half her face. She looked smart and in control, the kind of woman who always made Sandra feel a bit inadequate.

Flanking that picture was one that must have been taken on holiday: the woman was sitting squinting up at the sun, with her long hair blowing loose around her bare shoulders. Her bikini wasn't at all flattering. Sandra thought she should've known better – a woman of her age – and worn a black one-piece that wasn't cut nearly so high in the leg.

The last photograph must have been taken ages ago. It was clearly the same woman, with that great cloud of thick hair and the square chin, but she looked years younger and much thinner, and she seemed to be shouting into a microphone. In front of her was a huge crowd and behind her a banner with the words 'A Woman Needs a Man Like a Fish Needs a Bicycle' painted in straggly letters. Sandra started to read:

Who would have thought in the heady days of seventies' Women's Lib, for which Kara Huggate fought so hard, that there would come a time when she must have longed for male protection?

Two nights ago she became the seventh known victim of the Kingsford Rapist. He broke into her dream cottage some time around midnight, raped and murdered her. She was found only when her cleaner turned up for work the next morning.

Dr Jed Thomplon, her partner of five years, has told the *Daily Mercury* of his anguish when she left him just over nine months ago. He never wanted to break up with her. Even so he blames himself for not fighting harder to keep her. But, as he says. 'When you've been hurt by someone who values her career over every-thing you had together, it's all too easy to turn your back. If I'd been more tolerant then, she might be alive today. I'll never forgive myself for that.'

Sandra usually enjoyed reading the *Mercury*. Its mixture of gossip and features interested her and she agreed with what most of the columnists had to say about family values and the importance of making sure that children have a proper start in life and the right sort of up-bringing. But she didn't like the introduction to this piece one little bit. It sounded gloating and as though the poor woman had deserved what happened to her. And Sandra wasn't sure she liked the idea of Dr Jed Thomplon either. Why shouldn't his girlfriend have wanted a career just like he had?

Sandra hadn't had a paid job since her marriage, and she hadn't minded when the children were little and Michael still talked to her. But recently, once he'd started alternately ignoring and yelling at her, she'd been thinking that if only she had something of her own, some job where she was with other people, then it would've been easier to put up with him. He was hardly ever at home these days, but when he was he was snappy and impatient, always finding fault with her or picking on the children. She'd tried to tell him that was just the kind of behaviour to make Simon go back to his druggy friends again, but Michael wouldn't listen.

She'd come to expect so little from him that when he and Katie came back for tea she was amazed that he kissed her. He even told her he'd missed her, which made her think that perhaps the holiday would work the miracle, after all.

'Were you very bored, sitting here all day?' he went on, just as the waitress came out with the loaded tea-tray she'd ordered. 'Oh, aren't you clever to have guessed when we'd be back? That looks good. No, no, don't move, Sandra. We'll bring it to you.'

She sat in her basket chair with the sun on her face, waiting while Michael brought her the tall glass of lemon tea in its silver holder and Katie put a selection of cakes on a plate for her. She'd never eat so many, as Katie must have known very well, but it was a nice thought. Perhaps they were all going to be all right. She smiled at them both.

'So, what did you do with yourself?' Michael asked, stirring sugar into his glass of tea.

She told him a bit about the massage she'd had, trying to forget how awful it had been thinking about the Kingsford Rapist while the masseur was digging his hard fingers into her spine. Only when Katie had eaten two huge pieces of chocolate cake and gone off to have her bath, did Sandra tell Michael about what she'd read in the paper.

'What? Sandra, what *are* you talking about?'

'I read it in the paper,' she said, angry with him for treating her like a stupid child all over again. 'A man who was here lent me his *Mercury* and it was in that. A social worker has been raped and murdered in Kingsford – in Church Lane. It's making me really scared for Katie again.'

She wondered whether Michael had heard what she said. There was something funny about his face. It was looking white and pinched again, but it wasn't just that. He was staring past her as though she didn't even exist.

'It's all right, love,' she said, leaning forward uncomfortably to pat his knee. 'If I can't fetch her from school myself, I'll make sure one of the other mothers does.

We'll fix up some kind of rota so that all the girls have an adult with them all the time they're not in school.'

She rather wanted him to say that he was worried about her, too, but he didn't.

'Social worker?' he said, as though the words had only just filtered through to his brain. 'What social worker?'

'I can't remember her name. Higgins or something like that. No, Huggate, I think.'

'Where's the paper?'

'I threw it away.'

Michael sighed, closing his eyes, as though she was completely useless.

'How was I to know you'd want it? The fat man had finished with it and so had I, so I threw it away.'

'Where?'

'In the bin in the bar. It's probably still there if you want it that much. They don't usually empty the bins till just before drinks' time.'

Sandra was talking to the air. Michael had already gone.

CHAPTER SEVEN

The pub was quiet and not very interesting, which was just what Barry Spinel liked. Neither he nor Martin Drakeshill had ever been there before, and judging by the thin beer and limp crisps they'd never go again. No one showed any interest in them. With luck no one would ever remember seeing either of them.

The only problem was that the scrawny barmaid was as uninterested as the rest of the drinkers and kept refusing to catch Drakeshill's eye when he lifted his tankard to signal his need for a refill. Spinel could not imagine why he should want any more, but he understood how the difficulty of getting it made it matter.

Martin Drakeshill hated being beaten, especially by a woman. And she knew what she was doing, this barmaid. In the normal way, she would have looked in their direction at least once. As it was, she kept her back to them whenever she could and stared over their heads when she could not, or picked at her nails.

'Sod that. I'm buggered if I'm going to trip up to the bar and ask for the other half,' Drakeshill said. 'No tip for her.'

Spinel smiled sourly. He had seen too many waitresses and barmaids hiding resentment at the way Drakeshill stuffed hard, dirty banknotes into their cleavages with his sausage-like fingers to be sorry that this one wasn't going to get a tip. He'd been waiting for the day one of them fished the money out of her bra and hit Drakeshill with it. It had nearly happened once and Spinel had had to intervene and turn the whole thing into a joke.

Drakeshill was not the kind of man to take that kind of insult lightly. He'd probably have slugged the tart for real and then everyone in the place would have remembered them for all time, and a fruitful – if tricky – relationship that had taken years to build up would have been damaged.

It was quite a good kind of double-bluff cover, Drakeshill's behaving so like a fictional Essex gangster, Spinel thought, but there were times when it would have helped if he'd cool it a bit, and not fling his money about so obviously or surround himself with the tough 'boys' he employed as mechanics.

Spinel knew all about them, and in a way approved of Drakeshill's giving them work. After all it kept them off the streets – some of the time anyway – and there weren't many other jobs they could have done with records like theirs. Nightclub bouncing and minicabbing were just about the only things, and if the politicians had their way, even minicabbing would be regulated soon and ex-cons wouldn't have a hope.

The worst downside of Drakeshill's lot was that most of them looked like heavies. That tended to pose an irresistible challenge to anyone in the Job who came across them and they were always being picked up for this and that. Spinel had to spend far too much time dealing with the fallout.

He was always reminding suspicious colleagues that

the boys were real mechanics, in spite of their records, and that they did a good job with the rubbish motors people flogged Drakeshill. So far, the DI had believed him, or near enough not to make too much of a fuss too often. But once in a while, when stories of intimidation and baseball-bat injuries started circulating about the police station, one of the boys had to be picked up and made an example of. Spinel couldn't save them all.

There were times when he tried to make Drakeshill keep a firmer hand on some of the more excitable ones, but it didn't do to say so too often. Drakeshill was not a man to be criticised lightly.

'Could you fancy something as skinny as that, Bal?' he asked, watching the barmaid's flat, denim-clad bottom swaying as she slipped out from behind the bar to wipe a newly vacated table and smile at one of her more favoured customers.

'Not me. I like 'em more . . . more interesting than that,' Spinel said, looking at what he could see of the foxy little face with its hard eyes and thin-lipped mouth. 'More brains and less spiteful-looking.'

'I like bigger tits meself. Well, are you going to get the other half or am I?' Drakeshill knew better than to give Spinel orders, but they were both well aware of who most needed to keep whom sweet. Spinel stuck his long legs out from under the table, pushed himself upright in one easy movement and went to get his snout another pint.

'So, what've you got for me, Marty?' he said, as he brought it back. He stood for a while, knowing that Drakeshill found his much greater height annoying, even intimidating.

'Not a lot this time, old son.' Drakeshill ignored the tall figure looming over him and shook the heavy gold links of his identity bracelet down his wrist, removing the coarse dark hair it had pulled out of his arm. 'If I hadn't spent a fortune on this, I'd chuck the bloody thing out.' He scratched one pitted nostril. 'But there's talk among some of the lads of a lorry coming up from Dover with a biggish delivery of smack.'

'Name? Load?'

Drakeshill told him which haulage company was being used, he thought without its owners' knowledge, and said he'd heard the drugs were hidden in a shipment of dried fruit coming in from Turkey, but he couldn't swear to it. They could have been concealed somewhere in the lorry's structure.

Spinel was busy counting out the requisite number of twenty-pound notes when he said, as though it was a not-very-important afterthought, 'By the way, Marty, did you have to send your boys out to nick a load of GTIs?'

'Who says I did?' There was laughter in Drakeshill's voice, and his round dark eyes were alight with mockery.

'The crime squad. According to them you've been doing a Fagin and sending your team out to nick hand-picked cars.' Drakeshill laughed again and Spinel nearly lost it. 'What the fuck were you thinking of, doing it on your own patch? It's one thing to buy up stolen gear from the other end of the country, quite another to set up the thefts in a place where everyone knows who you are. You've embarrassed me and I'll have trouble keeping you out of the courts on this one.'

'You'll have to, won't you?' Drakeshill grinned. 'I'm not admitting anything, mind, but a man like me has to keep his hand in once in a while, Bal. If he wasn't known to be on the wrong side of the law he'd never find out what you needed to know, now, would he?'

'Which is the very point I made to my guv'nor, Marty.' Spinel was working to sound casual. It was important to keep the relationship easy. 'You'd better lay off for a bit.

It can't go on. You'll ruin everything if you draw attention to yourself.'

'Drawing the right sort of attention keeps the wrong sort off.'

'I know that's your theory, Marty, but this was stupid. Why d'you need to have cars nicked anyway?'

'Even I've got to earn a living, Bal,' Drakeshill said, with a winsome little smile, as though he were Oliver Twist asking for more. Then he let his face relax into the usual piratical leer. 'Everyone knows that.'

Barry Spinel shook his head. 'Used cars is a licence to print money even on the right side of the law, you old villain. Don't push it, Marty. I'm serious. Keep your nose clean for a week or two at least. Just till everything quiets down and the crime squad stop watching you. OK?'

'You giving me orders, old son?' For all his pantomime-gangster act, Drakeshill could sound remarkably dangerous.

'Friendly warning, Marty.' Spinel was not particularly bothered by the threat. 'Just cool it. For the moment.'

'I'll think about it. But you think about it, too. You need me.'

'Way I see it, Marty, we need each other.'

'Yeah. Well, don't you forget it.' Drakeshill drank some more of his ant's-piss beer and wiped his mouth on the back of his hand. 'So how're your colleagues getting on with the murder then? Doesn't sound from the radio as though they've got much yet.'

Spinel shrugged. 'Fat lot of nothing from all I've heard.'

Drakeshill nodded and a few minutes later they parted. Spinel decided to go back to the nick to have another crack at Doughface Deal. He'd been collecting the worst sexist jokes he could find and so far she hadn't blinked an eyelid at things even he thought were gross.

But he'd heard a really good juicy one from Marty, and he wanted to try it out. If this one didn't make Doughface wriggle he'd give up on her.

As he passed Drakeshill's forecourt and had to stop at the lights, he saw one of the newest and youngest mechanics moving down the slope. He was a gangly boy called Wes, who'd done time for ABH after his snooker cue had broken across a mate's face. Wes looked self-conscious, as though he had something to say. Spinel wound down his window and called out, 'Yeah? Wes? What is it?'

The boy jumped a mile, as though someone had poked him with a hot skewer, and looked all round him. Dozy bugger.

'Wes!' yelled Spinel. 'Hurry up. The lights are changing. What d'you want?'

'What? Want? Me? Nothing.' He looked like crying. Poor sod wouldn't last long with the rest of them if he went on like that. They were tough, Drakeshill's boys, and they had a reputation to keep up. They couldn't be doing with wimps or nerds.

Spinel shrugged and wound up his window. Some idiot behind him was leaning on his horn. The lights had gone green. So what? He'd have given the bastard the finger if he'd been sure he wasn't on the Police Committee.

CHAPTER EIGHT

Against her better judgement Trish had put the scrap of paper with Blair Collons's phone number in her handbag. Normally she wouldn't even have contemplated talking to a client on the quiet, but Kara had begged her to help him, and Kara was dead. It might be irrational to feel that that gave her plea extra force, but Trish didn't see how she could ignore it. The code of conduct was a problem, but she'd find a way to get round that if she had to.

She went up the spiral stairs to shower. The hot water gave her the usual pleasure, sluicing the frustrations and grubbiness of the day off her body and out of her hair. The ache that had settled down her neck and across her shoulders began to ease as wet warmth filled the big shower cabinet. Steam billowed around her and the water splashed up against her legs.

Rolled into a huge red towel, with her short hair looking like the pelt of an otter around her well-shaped head, she went back into the bedroom and lay down on top of the duvet to dry off and think about what she was going to do. After a while she reached for the phone and propped it on her damp chest.

Blair Collons answered after three rings. As soon as she had identified herself, he gasped and said, 'Give me your number and I'll call you back within five minutes.'

There was no way Trish was giving out her home phone number to a man like him. She'd long ago arranged to have it automatically withheld against all 1471 calls, so he wouldn't be able to get it that way. But she couldn't think of any good reason not to give him her mobile number.

'Thank you,' he said. 'Don't go away. I'll ring you back. Please wait.' The connection was cut.

Trish blinked. If she had to wait five minutes, she might as well dress and get herself a drink. She chose her loosest, sloppiest jeans and a long, soft cashmere tunic George had given her for Christmas.

She was just pouring out a glass of white wine from an open bottle in the fridge when the mobile rang.

'Thank you for waiting,' Blair gasped into her ear. 'I had to get to a callbox. They're bugging my phone.'

'I see,' Trish said, the frown dragging her eyebrows together across her nose. She drank some wine, grimacing at the sharpness, and waited.

'I know what you said about your professional ethics and I can respect that, but we have to meet, Ms Maguire. And soon. I think –'

'Mr Collons, I've explained why that's not possible.'

'No. We must. Listen. I have to talk to you about Kara. She trusted you. You can't let her down now. Not after what was done to her. It's too important.'

'Look, of course I'd like to know anything you can tell me about Kara,' Trish said, almost truthfully, 'but we can't meet, and I ought not even to be talking to you like this. I really mean it. I'm sorry, but any other conversation we have before your tribunal will have to include your solicitor.'

'It'll be too late afterwards. There are things you need to know *now* about what Kara was doing. They explain why she died.'

'Then you should tell the police,' Trish said firmly. 'At once.'

'I can't. You don't understand. They won't believe me. That's why I was sacked, to make sure no one would ever believe me. There's a faction in the town hall that's so frightened of what I might say that they had to make sure I'd look unreliable.'

So that's what all this is about, Trish thought, in some relief. He's invented a grand conspiracy to deal with the humiliation of being accused of a shabby little crime. Aloud she said kindly, 'Have you talked to your solicitor about this?'

'No.'

'But, Mr Collons, that's what he's there for, to protect your interests. He'd be able to contact the police for you and be with you while they interviewed you to make sure you were fairly treated and taken seriously.'

'He mustn't know anything about it.' The statement was more forcefully delivered than Trish would have expected. 'Not under any circumstances.'

'Don't you trust him?'

'No.'

'But why not?' Trish asked, quickly adding, as she realised she'd probably let herself in for a long paranoid saga. 'Not that it matters. What does matter is that you have a solicitor you can trust. I could probably recommend someone.'

She wondered whether she could sacrifice George, then decided that wouldn't be fair. He always had more work than he could comfortably handle and, in any case, life was more likely to remain tolerable if one of them stayed free of this peculiar client.

'You don't understand,' Blair said again. 'You see, Kara recommended Bletchley as soon as the council sacked me. She said he was the best solicitor in Kingsford.'

'Well, that sounds all right,' said Trish, in the tones of a games mistress urging her bored, cold charges to run out on to a muddy hockey field and do their bit for the school. 'So?'

'No, it *isn't* all right. I thought it was, too, up until yesterday when I went to his office before we came to see you. What I heard then horrified me.'

'But why?'

'Because it showed how dangerous it would be to let him hear what I've got to tell you. That's why I was in such a state when we met in your chambers.'

Trish could hear him panting and fumbling for more coins to feed into the phone.

'I still don't understand. What happened when you were in Mr Bletchley's office?' she asked patiently, when he had put in his money. She also offered to call him back if he was short of change, but he assured her he had plenty.

'It was while I was waiting for him, outside his office where his secretary sits. She took a phone call for him while I was there.'

'From whom?' Trish asked, wishing she didn't have to work so hard to winkle out a story she did not even want to hear.

'I don't like using names over the phone.'

'You must if I'm to understand what all this is about.'

'A man called Drakeshill. Martin Drakeshill,' Blair said, with a gulp. 'He's a local gangster, you see, who pretends to be just a second-hand-car dealer, so if he and Bletchley are working together, that means –'

Trish had to laugh. 'Oh, Mr Collons, every solicitor in the country who has anything to do with the criminal law has clients who are known to the police. That's one of the things solicitors are there for. And if yours is the best known in Kingsford and this Drakeshill character operates there, it's only natural that he should have chosen the same practice as you.'

Apart from a series of heavy, aggrieved-sounding breaths, there was silence on the phone. Trish tried again, having sipped a little more wine during the interval. 'Having criminal clients – if that's what this man is – doesn't mean that your solicitor is anything but squeaky clean, Mr Collons. Now, I think we ought to stop this conversation right here.'

'I should've known you wouldn't believe me. No one ever does, except Kara. But she told me you'd be different. She told me you'd help. *She* believed Drakeshill was in league with the council and –'

'What?'

'I shouldn't have said that. Please don't tell anyone I said that. You won't, will you? *Please.*'

'No,' said Trish, with complete sincerity. 'I won't tell anyone.'

'Thank you. Kara told me I could trust you, but I wasn't sure. You can never tell, can you?, until people show themselves to be trustworthy.'

Trish thought of Kara's letter and wondered whether, having listened to too much of this sort of thing, she had decided to shift the burden of Blair Collons on to someone else.

'Look, Mr Collons, why not write it all down – everything you suspect about what happened to Kara – and send it to me? That way I can concentrate properly.' And, she thought, if there's anything in it, I can involve James Bletchley and keep on the right side of the code.

'No. That would be far too dangerous. We can't trust the post any more than my home phone. They're watching me. They know I know too much. Please, Ms Maguire, please let me come and see you. I could get them off my tail long before I got anywhere near you so that no one would know. You wouldn't be in any trouble.'

Trish sighed. There was no way she was letting him come to the flat. No barrister would willingly allow any client, let alone one as weird as Blair Collons, to know where she lived. She tried again. 'As I said, the people you should be talking to if you're worried about anything to do with Kara's death are the police. I'm sure they won't be swayed by anything anyone on the council has said about you, but if you like I could have a word with them myself. I've already been interviewed, but if you'd rather not approach them in person, I could always phone them for you now and let them know that you were a friend of Kara's and might be able to help. How would that be?'

'It would be a disaster.' His voice was tragic. 'You must promise not to talk to them until you've understood everything. And then you must promise you won't ever say that it was me who told you. Not now; not ever. Please. Say it. Say you promise.'

'All right. All right. If you don't want me to talk to them for you, I won't. It's all right, Mr Collons. You don't need to be so het up.'

'You don't understand. If you'd only let me tell you all about it, you would. And you need to understand in case they come after you, too. They probably will, you see. They'll know you were a friend of Kara's, just like I did. And they'll be afraid she might've talked to you, too.'

'Now, calm down,' said Trish, sounding nearly as tetchy as she felt. 'Mr Collons, you really mustn't get hysterical.'

'But *why* won't you listen to me? Oh, Christ! I feel like Cassandra.'

'I will listen. I *am* listening,' Trish said, surprised by the reference. 'We can't meet, but I will listen to anything you want to tell me now, while we're on the phone.'

'It's not safe, even on a mobile. People have scanners to eavesdrop with.'

Trish sighed again and thought of asking whether extra-terrestrials ever sent him messages through his television screen, but the man sounded desperate. It might be wildly unethical – no, it *was* wildly unethical, but she was beginning to think she would have to meet him, if only to shut him up. Without Kara's letter, she would never have done it but, as things stood, she did not see that she had any option.

After some to-ing and fro-ing, they arranged to meet the following evening in an obscure pub near Waterloo station. It sounded anonymous enough and quite unlike the sort of place where anyone she knew might drink, particularly on a Friday evening.

Having got rid of him at last, Trish had a look in the fridge to see what she could cook for George. There was a chicken, which she had forgotten about but which, amazingly, had three days to run before it was no longer fit to be eaten. She set about dealing with it.

The following evening when Trish reached the pub, she peered through the smoky gloom, hoping that Blair Collons had had second thoughts. He hadn't. He was sitting without a drink at a table about fifteen feet away from the door. As he saw her, he got to his feet and waved furtively before tucking his hand deep into his trouser pocket and looking over his shoulder to see who was behind him.

He was no longer wearing the dreadful suit. Instead he had on a pair of relatively clean cords and a crumpled shirt that was fraying at the collar and cuffs.

'Hello,' she said. 'What. . . ?'

'I was afraid you weren't coming after all. Thank you. It's really good of you. I'm *so* glad to see you. You can't imagine –'

'That's all right. Now, we'd better have a drink. What would you like?'

'Anything soft. I don't mind. A Coke? Thank you.'

Trish fetched his drink and a half of lager for herself. 'Now, what exactly is all this about?' She put the glasses down on the smeared table, wishing she had a cloth to wipe up the spilled drink and ash.

'Kara wasn't killed by any rapist, whatever the papers say.'

Trish blinked.

'They're only repeating what the police have told them, and *they* want everyone to believe it was the rapist. It's in their interest that the truth should never come out. But there was no rapist involved. Kara died because of what we were doing together. I've been worried sick.'

Trish put on what she hoped was a sympathetic face and relatively credulous expression. 'I see. And what exactly was it that you and she were doing?'

'I . . . She . . .' He fell silent, biting his lip and then the edge of his left thumbnail. His eyes kept flicking left and right and once he even turned to check whether anyone was listening to them.

'How did the two of you meet in the first place?' Trish asked, more gently.

Collons's terrors might have been no more than products of his own imagination, but they were obviously real to him. He drank some Coke then coughed, neatly covering his mouth with his hand like a well-behaved child. Then he took another clean handkerchief from his pocket and wiped his lips.

'When she came to the finance department. She

wanted information on the costs of the social housing Kingsford Council is going to build on some waste-ground near the high street.'

For the first time since Trish had met him, Collons sounded normal. At that moment she could – just – believe he had once worked as a chartered accountant.

'She told me a little about the scheme,' Trish said. 'It's to deal with difficult families who need a lot of super-vision, isn't it?'

'That's right. It's going to be so different from any other public housing scheme that, as soon as she heard about it, she was determined to be part of it. That's why she wanted the job in Kingsford so much.' He smiled and sat more proudly on his stool. 'She told me so when we had a drink once in her house. She invited me there. To her home.'

As she saw how even remembered approval trans formed him, Trish began to understand why Kara had come to feel so protective of him. 'And what exactly did she think was so special about the scheme?'

'Well, to cut a long story short, the council was – is – going to build small blocks of flats, some two-storey houses and some bungalows for the elderly and infirm, all together in a kind of complex. There are going to be safely enclosed gardens and a health centre on site and plenty of wardens and care workers. It's to have a very high carer-to-client ratio. Oh, yes, and there's going to be some kind of children's home, too, and maybe facilities for children with special educational needs, but they're not sure if they can afford that in the first phase. It's going to be a long-term project.'

'I see. It all sounds admirable. Expensive, too.'

'Well, that's just it, you see. That's how it started. Part of the total cost has to come out of the social services budget, and that's been seriously stretched for months.'

Collons paused, looking speculatively at Trish. 'I don't know how much you knew about the detail of Kara's job?'

'Not a great deal.'

'I thought not. Bear with me, will you? I'll have to tell you or you won't understand. One aspect of her brief was to make quite big savings in the budget. If she couldn't get what she needed from greater efficiency and less waste, then she was going to have to cut jobs and services. And she didn't want to do that, you see.'

'No, I can imagine that would go against the grain. So, she came to you to see whether her department's share of the building costs could be reduced. Is that it?' Trish was frowning again, unable to believe that Collons had been in control of anything as important as the financing of a major construction project. But if she didn't pin him down, she'd never find out what was really bothering him.

'Oh, no. She just wanted information. She'd already tried to get it from the chief finance officer, but he didn't have any time for her. He sent her to me, and told me to talk her through the estimates. Even he would admit that *that* was within my capabilities.'

'And could you satisfy her?'

Collons's plump cheeks turned a rich cochineal. He looked so embarrassed that Trish realised what he must have thought she'd meant. Watching him, it struck her that his fantasies might have gone beyond paranoia to include some kind of erotic fixation on Kara, which would have explained a lot.

'We worked out,' he said, with a resumption of his official manner, settling his shoulders with a series of tiny shudders, 'that the estimates were so much higher than they should have been because the land on which the housing is to be built is heavily contaminated with chemical residues from the factories that were once operating there. Cleaning it up is going to be costly. Very costly indeed.'

'Then why on earth,' asked Trish, 'did Kingsford Council ever pick such an unsuitable site?'

'That's the sixty-four-thousand-dollar question,' Collons said, beginning to look happier. 'Kara and I both asked each other the very same one over and over again.'

'That wouldn't have done much good,' Trish said, forgetting that she had meant to be supportive, 'since neither of you had any answers. Didn't you ask it of anyone else?'

'Well, of course we did.' He sounded pettish again. 'Both of us, separately. And when they saw that we weren't going to be fobbed off, they had to get rid of us. One way or another.'

'Oh, come on.'

'It's true. First they made sure that anything I ever said would be taken as spiteful revenge for being sacked. And then, once I was out of the way and no more risk to them, they stopped her too. *Now* can you see why I'm so worried?'

Trish took a moment to think how best to deal with him. He was obviously serious and believed every mad word he'd said. Somehow she was going to have to persuade him that local council officials just do not go around raping and murdering people who ask inconvenient questions about building overspends. But she was worried about how he might react to the demolition of his grandiose fantasies. Facing up to the reality of his own pathetic situation might cause all sorts of problems, and he clearly had enough of those already.

'Mr Collons, you can't really expect me to believe that Kara was killed because she was trying to reduce the social services' contribution to the costs of a housing project,' she said at last. 'Are you sure that your quite understandable distress at the loss of a friend isn't making you see enemies where there aren't any?' At the sight of his face, she added, still more gently, 'I expect that her death has left a big hole in your life. And I can understand exactly why you want her killer caught. I do, too. But we have to leave it to the police. It's their job and they have all the resources.'

'We can't leave it to them. It's far too dangerous. They have their own agenda.'

Trish tried not to roll her eyes to heaven. She sipped her lager and gathered her patience. She wished that she had the deep wells of kindness that Kara had apparently been able to draw on at will.

'Is it this Martin Drakeshill you mentioned who's frightening –'

The colour drained out of Collons's face. His hands clutched the edge of the table. He was mouthing words soundlessly. Trish felt seriously worried that he might faint, or worse. She did not want to be responsible for an unconscious man whom she ought not to have been with in the first place.

'You mustn't –' he gasped. He put one hand to his chest. 'You mustn't tell anyone I ever said anything about him.'

'Of course I won't, if you don't want me to. But it would help me to understand, Mr Collons, if you could tell me a little more about what's frightening you so much.'

'I've told you all I can. Kara was killed because of the questions she and I were asking about the social housing so we both had to be silenced. That's all I can tell you. And you have to believe it.'

Trish detested being told by anyone that she *had* to do anything. She would have liked to explain to Blair Collons that she was under no obligation whatsoever to believe anything he told her or to take any kind of action. But she didn't. Instead, hanging on to her temper with difficulty, she said, 'but I don't understand what you expect me to do about it, given that you don't want me to talk to the police.'

He looked at her as though she had been deliberately obtuse, and cruel with it. 'Not the ones on the ground because they're in it, too. I'm sure they are. I want you to find out why our questions frightened them so much that they had to kill Kara.'

'Mr Collons . . .'

'And then I want you to use that information to persuade someone really senior in the police, who's well above all the local corruption, that her death has to be properly investigated. And then I'll get my job back.'

It was absurd. He must see that.

'I'm your barrister, Mr Collons, not some kind of private eye. I'll do everything within my remit to get you your job back, I promise, but I can't investigate Kara's death. The police are doing that at this moment. I have neither the facilities nor the skill to compete with them. Nor the time.'

'Someone has to do it,' he said, sighing deeply, as though all his blood were being drained out of him, 'and I can't. You're the only person who's in a position to do what has to be done.'

'It's a job for the police,' Trish said again, feeling sorry for them. Still, they must be used to dealing with people like Collons.

'Even though the victim was Kara, your great friend? Isn't this the least you can do for her after everything she's suffered?'

He stood up. His hands were trembling and his eyes were nearly as full of hurt as Darlie's. Trish thought he needed a doctor not a lawyer.

'I'll think about it,' she said, as a way of helping him leave the pub peacefully.

'Don't take too long. It's desperately urgent. We have to stop them before they do any more damage.' He bent down so that his face was so close to hers that she flinched. She couldn't help it. Lowering his voice, he added, 'And you must promise not to tell anyone – at any time – that it's me who alerted you to what's been going on.'

'I won't.' Trish wiped his spit from her cheeks, hoping his peculiar appearance and hoarse, desperate whispers weren't making too many people look at them.

He turned away at once and scuttled out through the crowd of drinkers, some of whom moved aside as though he might infect them. Trish gave him plenty of time to get away then left the pub herself, ignoring everyone who looked in her direction.

That night Collons lay in bed with his prick in his hand, talking to Kara. Her photograph was stuck on the wall at just the right height so that he could see her as he lay on his side. It wasn't the same as talking to her when she was still alive, not as thrillingly wonderful, but not nearly as difficult either.

She always understood him now and he wasn't clumsy with her any more. She knew him very well, and loved him, and she gave him all the right answers. There weren't any more of the equivocations that she used to go in for. Now she was all reassurance as she smiled at him and loved him.

'I hope you're right about Trish Maguire, Kara,' he said to her. 'She seems bright enough, and I know you think I can trust her. But she didn't believe me and I didn't see any of the warmth you talk about. She didn't seem warm to me at all. Just hard.'

Kara smiled at him with her wise, gentle smile, the one he loved most of all, and told him he was right to be careful. She advised him to wait a bit more and test Trish, watching her carefully, before he told her the rest.

And then Kara kissed him as she had every night since her death. And a few minutes later he came. And slept.

CHAPTER NINE

By Sunday, Sandra's knee was better so she and
Michael spent all morning together while Katie was
at ski school. He was more affectionate than he'd been for
ages, and Sandra knew everything was about to come
right again. In a sudden surge of happiness, she realised
that in spite of everything she was going to be able to
forgive him for making her life hell.

He chose a very expensive restaurant for lunch and
ordered a bottle of white wine instead of the usual beer.
The food was lovely, and so was the way he listened to
her instead of snapping and sniping. Her face began to
ache she was smiling so much. When he'd paid the bill,
he even put his arm around her, kissed her cheek, and
said that he felt so knackered he thought he'd go back the
hotel for a snooze. Sandra smiled secretly and pressed
herself against him.

In the early days of their marriage, when Simon was
tiny and woke them at all hours, they'd usually been
too tired to make love at night. But at weekends, after
lunch, they would put him down in his room and shut
the curtains in their own, pretending they were young

lovers having an affair in Paris or somewhere.

'Why don't I come with you?' she said luxuriously. 'I'm quite tired, too.'

She looked up at him, smiling, to make sure he knew what she meant. His handsome face closed up as though he was a woodlouse rolling up at the touch of a broom.

'Better not,' he said, pulling away from her and walking towards the massed skis in the rack outside the restaurant. 'You've missed three days already and you need to work on your turns. You'll be fine so long as you stick to the runs I've shown you. I'll see you out here later if I wake in time, or else at tea.'

Sandra couldn't believe it. She stood open-mouthed, watching him collect his skis from the rack and leave her without another look. Her goggles were all misted up, not because she was crying – she wasn't really – but because her eyes were hot and the plastic lenses were so cold. She took them off to polish them, squinting in the sudden dazzle.

She couldn't see properly and didn't know what was happening when a child smashed into her at what felt like a hundred miles an hour. She picked herself up, expecting an apology, but all she got from the horrible child, who looked like an insect in his huge goggles, helmet and bright red salopettes, were furious shrieks in some foreign language. Seeing that she did not understand, he gave up in the end and flew off down the mountain, shaking his fist as he went.

Sandra couldn't bear it. Whether Michael wanted her or not, she was going back to the hotel after him.

The compacted snow in front of the hotel had brown stains all over it, like a baby's nappies that hadn't been properly washed in hot-enough water. Sandra shuddered. Tiredness hung on her legs like lead anklets and made the climb up the outside steps to the balcony almost more of an effort than she could manage.

The first thing she saw on the balcony was Michael, sitting beside the fat man and reading his newspaper. She couldn't believe it.

'Michael, what *are* you doing?'

The fat man looked round at the sound of her sharp voice, his face almost comically frightened.

'Sandra!' Michael said, with a snap that meant: how can you embarrass me like this, you awful woman?

'You said you were too tired to ski,' she said, more quietly. 'I thought you'd be in bed.'

'I'm on my way. Mr Watford here has kindly lent me his paper and I've been catching up on the news before I go up. What *is* the matter with you?'

She couldn't tell him, not with the fat man there, anyway. So she shrugged and then, to save face, asked whether there was anything interesting in the paper.

'Not a lot,' he said, folding it up and putting it on the floor under his chair.

Somehow that made Sandra even angrier. He looked shifty and embarrassed enough to suggest he was hiding something. She bent down to pick up the newspaper. It was easy to see he'd been reading about the Kingsford Rapist because the pages were all wrinkled from his sweaty fingers.

'Don't read it,' he said quickly. 'The police haven't got him yet so it'll only worry you.'

'Then why were you reading it?' She looked up from yet another big photograph of the victim, trying to understand. 'Why are you so interested?'

'Kara Huggate was a colleague,' he said, turning away. 'I need to know what's happening in the case.'

'A colleague?' Sandra was amazed. 'She couldn't have been, Michael. She was a social worker, nothing to do with the planning department.'

'We're both employed by the council. That makes her a colleague. And we're working with social services at the moment.'

Sandra looked at the photograph again and then up at Michael. 'D'you mean you *knew* her?'

He nodded, still not looking up.

'Did you know her well?'

'Not really.'

'Then why are you in such a state?'

He didn't answer.

Sandra looked at the picture of Kara Huggate in the paper, wondering if the incredible suspicion that had just occurred to her could possibly be true. There was nothing glamorous about Kara Huggate, in fact she looked quite old; but perhaps some people might find her attractive, if they weren't bothered about her awful thighs.

'*How* long have you known her?'

Michael shrugged, staring down at his boots. 'Two months? Three? It must be about that.'

In other words, Sandra thought, just about the length of time you've been extra specially sulky and difficult. You must have met at the same time as you stopped wanting to touch me. She'd never been particularly good at maths, but the sums in front of her weren't exactly difficult to add up. 'You must have thought me very stupid,' she said slowly. He did look up then, surprised. 'What were you planning to do, the two of you? Just have an affair till you got bored? Or were you thinking of something more permanent? When were you going to tell me – and the kids?'

'Don't be ridiculous, Sandra.'

The fat man, who was looking ill with embarrassment, at last managed to get out of his chair so that he could leave them alone.

'I've been wondering for weeks why you've been so difficult,' she went on, feeling as though her mouth was full of cotton-wool, 'but I never thought it could be something like this. I believed every lying word you said, all those evenings about how you'd been working late or having a drink with Barry Spinel and the lads. And all the time you were with her. How could you?'

'Sandra, don't be ridiculous. Kara Huggate was a colleague, an acquaintance, no more than that, but she's been killed in horrible circumstances. Anyone who'd met her even for an instant would be upset.'

'Not like this,' she said, staring at his lying face. 'I've been married to you for nineteen years, Michael, I know you. This is more than just being sorry a colleague's dead. You're feeling really guilty. And so you bloody well should.'

'What's the matter?' said Katie, from behind her parents. Her voice was shaking.

Sandra wondered how much she'd heard. 'Hello, Katie,' she said brightly, trying to ignore the frozen expression on her daughter's face. 'Good ski school? Where did you have lunch?'

'It was OK, but what's the matter?'

'Nothing. Don't you worry. Your dad and I were just having a disagreement.'

'No, we weren't,' said Michael, coming back to life. 'Your mother's gone mad. Temporarily, I hope. What are you doing with all that makeup on your face, Katie? You look revolting. Go and wash it off at once and put some sunscreen on.'

Katie burst into tears. 'I hate you, Dad.'

Sandra did not try to stop her rushing off. Instead she rounded on Michael. 'So, not content with ruining our marriage, you have to go and upset Katie, too. Why do you always have to spoil everything?'

Like the good mother she'd always tried to be, Sandra didn't wait for an answer but followed her daughter, knowing that she would have to spend the next half-hour calming Katie and reassuring her that everything between her parents was fine. Sandra's own pain, the real searing hurt at what Michael had done, would have to wait.

CHAPTER TEN

Trish was not in court on Monday and had long ago booked a rare lunch with a friend, Anna Grayling, who had recently set up her own small television production company. Living on opposite sides of London and moving in very different circles, they did not often meet, but they kept up with each other's news on the phone and lunched on the few occasions when they were both free in London on the same day. Anna always gave Trish the feeling that she swam in a sea much wider – and sometimes even rougher – than the legal one Trish knew so well.

As they sat down at a small table in the Chancery Lane wine bar Trish favoured, she was tempted to ask Anna's advice about Blair Collons, not about her legal and ethical obligations to him as a client, but about his likely mental state and what she could – or ought – to do about that.

If Kara were still alive and had seen him as he was in the Waterloo pub on Friday, Trish was sure she would have done something to help him. Even though he must have invented the story of a police and council conspiracy as a way of dealing with the shame of being sacked for gross misconduct, it had run away with him now. He was definitely frightened. Trish had the uncomfortable feeling that Kara would have taken him home with her and allowed him to believe that she understood him, perhaps even shared his fears, so that she could have guided him towards the right kind of psychiatric specialist. But Kara was dead and Trish couldn't pretend to be her, or even to be like her.

Collons's idea that she should start poking around in Kingsford looking for evidence to back up his claims was absurd. Even if she had believed his story, she was far too busy and, in any case, it wasn't her job. On the other hand, she found she couldn't forget his bitter little question at the end. Was it really the least she could do for Kara?

If Kara hadn't begged Trish to do her best for Collons, she'd have sent him packing without the slightest hesitation. As it was, she thought she might have to go a bit further than the usual duties of counsel to a client, even if it was only as far as making sure that his suspicions of his solicitor were as unfounded as they seemed.

Eventually, half listening to Anna and making all the right noises to keep her talking, Trish decided that if she spoke to James Bletchley and got some idea of what he thought about Collons, then pumped a few reasonably accessible sources for background information on Bletchley himself and some of the other targets of Collons's suspicion, she would have done enough. She might even pick up something that would prove to Collons that his fears were groundless, which would help them both.

'So, Trish, how are things with you? You seem a bit pre-occupied,' Anna said, as she looked up from the menu.

'Oh, work, you know. A tricky case I can't quite see my way through.'

'Oh, God, don't I know what that feels like?' The waitress appeared with her pad at the ready. 'I'll have the goat's cheese salad. Trish?'

'What? No, I think it's too cold for that. I'll have *penne al arrabbiata*. Thank you. And we'll have a bottle of the Chianti. So, Anna, what is it you can't see your way through?'

'The financing of my bloody company. But I'll get there.'

Trish smiled. Anna's vivid face, which only the most charitable would have described as anything but pudgy, took on an expression of almost pantomime horror as she started to tell Trish about the struggles she had had to raise the money she needed to keep afloat. As she talked it became clear that she was so full of her own affairs that she wouldn't have been able to concentrate on anything much else, even if Trish had decided to raise it.

Trish, who admired her guts in going it alone, asked all the right questions. But even as she listened, throughout the hour and a half they spent together, part of Trish's mind kept reverting to Kara and Collons.

'So I think we'd better get the bill,' Anna said, breaking into Trish's thoughts. 'Alas.'

'It's on me,' Trish said, hoping that Anna had not realised quite how distracted she was. 'No, no, honestly. I haven't got any huge debts to all those smoothly sexist venture capitalists.'

'Well, I have, so I'll accept with pleasure – if you're sure. It's sweet of you, Trish.'

'Not at all. Look, it's been great seeing you, Anna. It always is. An inhabitant of another world. I love hearing about it, and I can't tell you how impressed I am with what you've achieved.'

'Then that makes two of us.' Anna's round freckled face was alight with the kind of affection no one could doubt or question. 'I don't know how you keep going, having to spend all your days with child abusers and murderers.'

Trish handed her credit card to the waitress, laughing and fully back in the present. 'It's not quite as bad as that, you know. What I actually do is spend my days with like-minded friends, most of whom I've known ever since I was called to the bar. Sure, we're often dealing with some pretty unsavoury – or desperate – clients, and occasionally it all gets too much, but for a lot of the time it's really stimulating, fun, too.'

Anna looked at her with the kind of speculation a judge might show towards a defendant who had just changed a not-guilty plea at the last possible moment and at great cost to the public purse.

'What?' Trish asked warily.

'I'm just thinking that George Henton must have some amazing secret. I can see I shall have to pay much closer attention when we next meet.'

'George? What *do* you mean, Anna?'

'Well, when you and I last had lunch on our own – what is it? Nearly two years ago? – you spent most of the time telling me how ill it made you to be dealing all the time in human misery and watching children being punished for their parents' inadequacies and angers. George is the only thing that's different in your life now, as far as I can see, so it must be him.'

'I suppose you're right in a way,' Trish said. 'Being happy these days, it is easier to keep a space between me and what happens to my clients.' She was struck all over again by how much she owed George and made a mental note to tell him so. 'And Seb, Anna? How're things with him? You haven't said a word about him.'

'There's nothing very interesting to say.' Trish frowned in quick concern. Anna noticed and smiled as she shook her head. Then she shrugged. 'Honestly. We're OK.'

'I'm glad.' Being five inches taller, Trish had to stoop to kiss Anna goodbye. 'Really glad. Good luck with the big series.'

'And you with the next case. It's been great, Trish. Thank you for lunch.'

'See you soon.'

Back at her desk, feeling better and more decisive for the distraction, Trish rang the clerks' room to ask for Blair Collons's solicitor's phone number. She got through without trouble.

'Mr Bletchley? It's Trish Maguire here. Look, I've been thinking about our client, and I realise I need to know a bit more about his background.'

'I see. What exactly is it that you wish to know?'

There was something extra-careful in his voice that made Trish's antennae twitch. 'Whatever there is.'

'I don't think I quite understand.'

'Oh, I think you do,' Trish said, hoping she sounded lightly amused instead of intensely curious. 'I've heard that tone from solicitors before, and I know what it means. Look, you badgered my clerk to get me to represent your client in a case that, on the face of it, does not require the attentions of counsel. I want to know why. And I think the least you can do is give me everything you know about him. What is it you've been hiding?'

'Hiding? Ms Maguire, what can you be thinking of?'

'Oh, come on. What's the snag? Has he got a record?'

There was a pause and then a dry cough.

Now we're getting somewhere, she thought. Perhaps that explains Collons's peculiarities – and his terrors.

'In a way. But please do not think, Ms Maguire, that I have been concealing anything. It is simply irrelevant and I didn't want to bother you with it. His past difficulties have no bearing on this case. There was no question of fraud or dishonesty, you see. Naturally I'd have told you if there had been.'

'So what was there, then?' Trish was feeling for a pen so that she could take proper notes.

'A few years ago he had a rather unfortunate experience with a young woman,' Bletchley said, his voice taking on a distant tone Trish had not heard from him before. It made him sound self-conscious, almost guilty, which couldn't have been his intention. 'Not so young, in fact, now I come to think of it.'

'What kind of experience?' In the long silence, she remembered Collons's exaggerated reaction to her question about satisfying Kara. 'Something sexual? Assault of some kind?'

'It wasn't exactly assault.'

'So something like flashing then? Or was there physical contact?'

'Some. Not much. And it was all a mistake.'

'Oh, come on, Mr Bletchley, for heaven's sake. This is like drawing teeth. And it only makes him sound worse. Why not just spit it out?'

'He once formed an affection for a woman he hardly knew. She lived in the same block of flats as he in Balham. It was a genuine misunderstanding. He believed that she cared for him, although they had never been introduced and had hardly ever spoken to each other. You see, they travelled on the same tube to work every single morning and after the first year or so, she tended to smile at him and occasionally greeted him or commented on the weather. No more than that.'

'The kind of thing most commuters do,' Trish agreed, remembering with a shudder the daily trauma of being squashed between other people's bodies in a dirty train that sat in airless tunnels for minutes at a time. Living within walking distance of chambers was worth an incalculable amount. How George could stick with his Fulham house, she couldn't imagine.

'Yes. Unfortunately, our client, who – as you will have realised – is a little short on social skills, built up the relationship in his mind into rather more than it actually was. He, er, took the woman's friendly courtesy as a sign that she had fallen in love with him.'

'I see. And what did he do?'

'To begin with he just followed her through the block of flats to her front door whenever they returned from work at the same time, and once or twice he loitered outside her windows to catch a glimpse of her. She had a ground-floor flat. I have talked to him at some length about all this, you see, and realised how innocent he was.'

'There's innocence and innocence, of course,' Trish commented drily.

'Indeed. Every time the young woman left a gap in her curtains, he was sure it meant that she knew he was there and wanted him to see her . . . well, undressing. And so he occasionally, er, took down his trousers to show that he "understood" her messages. Either she did not see him or she did not realise who he was. Having inter-preted her actions or lack of them as encouragement, he began to touch her surreptitiously in the underground, during the rush-hour, and when she did not protest, he took it as another signal that she knew what he was doing and enjoyed it.'

'Poor woman. She was presumably either too embarrassed or thought it was just the crowd pressing in on her.'

'I fear so. But our client deserves sympathy, too. One day on the underground, she smiled particularly kindly at him over her shoulder and all his inhibitions were overcome. He put both hands on her hips and dragged her back against him, grinding himself into her and whispering something lewd into her ear.'

Described in the solicitor's precise, chilly voice, the scene seemed almost funny, but Trish could well imagine how the unknown woman must have felt at the time. 'So presumably she went to the police,' she said, as a tadpole of suspicion wiggled into her mind.

'She did. At first they did not believe her because she was not exactly a thing of beauty and a joy for ever.' The solicitor sounded regretful rather than contemptuous. 'But there was very little doubt that she was still unravished.'

What is it about solicitors, Trish wondered, that makes them bring poetry into their everyday conversation? George did it, too. She quite liked it from him in their private lives, but in Bletchley, talking about a case, it irritated her.

'I don't understand,' she said stiffly, as though she had never read 'Ode on a Grecian Urn'.

'She was in her late thirties, unmarried, rather plump and very dowdy. This was some time ago, don't forget, and they assumed in their misogynist way that it was she who was fantasising. That is, until they interviewed our client.'

'He confessed, did he?'

'Immediately. As soon as they asked him about the incident, he poured out the whole story. He was so puzzled by her reaction that he wanted them to understand and told them everything he had done and why. There had been more, you see, silent telephone calls and so on.'

'Pretty much a classic stalker, in fact.'

'That is what it sounds like, isn't it? But in those days

no one knew about the forces that drive such men. He was merely cautioned for the indecency.'

'You mean he wasn't prosecuted?' The tadpole in Trish's mind was growing legs.

'That's correct. If he had been, I should have told you. Naturally. But the whole episode rocked what little confidence he had. He had genuinely believed the woman thought of him in the terms in which he had been dreaming of her. He became very depressed, started drinking, lost his job, stopped paying his mortgage, and ended up on the streets.'

'I see.' Trish was beginning to see quite how unfair Collons had been to his solicitor. James Bletchley sounded remarkably tolerant and very much on his client's side.

'I hope you do. He's been quite a hero in his way. You see, he pulled himself together, found his way to a Salvation Army hostel, kicked the drink and eventually he began to look for a job again. And then a flat.'

'Which is why he's been working as a lowly book-keeper despite having been a chartered accountant.'

'Precisely, Ms Maguire. I do not suppose he would ever have set the world on fire, even the world of accountancy, but if he had been able to talk to that unfortunate young woman in the ordinary way and invite her to eat with him, go to the cinema perhaps, enjoy some normal social intercourse with her, he might well have behaved acceptably and none of it would have happened.'

'Maybe.' But if he had been able to approach her like that, thought Trish, he wouldn't have been the man he was, so the point was academic.

'As it is, he has shown considerable courage and has never offended again. Indeed, he positively keeps his distance from women. This unfair dismissal is giving him exactly the kind of stress that could throw him right back. It was truly unfair, Ms Maguire, and I am determined to have it rescinded. You do see, do you not, why he needs your help?'

'Yes, I do.' Trish thought of Kara's letter. She, too, had seen Collons's disadvantages principally in terms of the help he needed. Clearly both Kara and James Bletchley were better people than she was herself. 'As a matter of interest, why didn't you tell me all this before I met him?'

'I felt it would not be fair. I thought it better that you should have the opportunity to form your own judgement of him.'

'I see. Well, I'd have preferred to know it all first. We'll have to work out a way round it, if it comes up.'

When Trish had put down her phone, she realised that the tadpole of suspicion had turned into a full-grown frog. She knew all about the way some sex offenders progress from voyeurism and minor crimes, such as the theft of knickers from a washing line, to harassment, assault, rape, and ultimately murder.

If Collons were one of them, and if he had once believed that a woman who had merely smiled at him on the tube had wanted a relationship with him, how much more might he have misinterpreted Kara's kindness?

Had he gone to her cottage the night she died in the belief that she wanted to make love with him? If so, she would have rejected him. Trish had no doubts whatever on that score, just as she was certain that Kara would have done it gently. But could anyone have done it gently enough? If Collons had moved up the ladder of serious offences, any rejection could have triggered real violence. Well aware that most rapists were motivated by power rather than desire, Trish also knew of cases in which an inability to relate normally to women did impel men to try to take what they couldn't ask for.

Something was nagging at her memory, something the two young police officers had said when they came to her chambers the morning after Kara's death. Then she remembered: they had told her that Kara had been assaulted 'with an implement of some kind'.

Trish's mental pictures became increasingly vivid as she thought of Collons in the grubby pub near Waterloo, his face glowing like a peony after her unintended suggestion that he might have failed to satisfy Kara.

What if he had tried to have sex with her against her will, been unable to sustain an erection, grabbed something he could use to punish her for his failure and then in an excess of humiliation and fury killed her?

But why, if he were the killer, would he have risked arousing suspicion by forcing himself on Trish and banging on and on about how she must investigate Kara's death?

A knock on the door made her blink. Debby's anxious face appeared round the jamb. Trish forced herself to concentrate on the present. 'Yes, Debby? What is it?'

'It's this opinion I'm typing for Mr Hogwell. I can't work out what he's getting at and I can't read his writing.'

'Debby, why come to me?' Trish, who had done all her own typing for years, found some of the other barristers' refusal to learn to use a laptop quite infuriating. She saw Debby flinch at her impatience and made herself smile as she explained, 'It's not my writing you can't read, is it? Or my opinion you're typing. Why should I be able to answer your questions?'

'No, I know it isn't,' Debby said, twisting her long curly hair around her index finger and looking about ten years younger than she could possibly have been. 'But Mr Hogwell gets so angry when I ask questions, and looks at me as though I'm stupid. I thought you'd know, you see, what he was getting at here, so I wouldn't have to ask him. Sometimes he tells Dave to make me concentrate better if I've asked too many questions, and you know what Dave can be like when he's angry. I'm really sorry if I'm disturbing you.'

'That's OK.' Trish could not remember ever being as young and frightened as Debby. 'Bring it here.'

The problem was easily solved and Debby went off more happily. Trish's difficulties were less tractable. Her own advice to Collons was ringing in her ears. If he had information – or even simply suspicions – about Kara's death then he should go to the police.

But it wasn't so easy for her. This time it wasn't the code of conduct that held her back. Collons hadn't told her that he'd had anything to do with Kara's death so there was no question of contravening the rules about client privilege. But there were other considerations.

Trish knew from her own experience how it felt to be the target of unjust police suspicions and she would not wish that on anyone, particularly not on someone with a personality as fragile as Collons's, and a past like his. The stress of being taken in for questioning again, having his flat searched, even just living under suspicion, might be more than he could take.

If he had killed Kara, then he deserved pretty much anything that happened to him, but if he was innocent, he had to be protected, as Kara herself had asked.

Trish pulled forward a sheet of rough paper, trying to remember all the things Collons had told her or hinted he might tell her. As she wrote them down, the frog started leaping around in her mind again and she wondered how much he had understood of the client-privilege rules. If he hadn't been aware that they covered only things a client had actually told his counsel, then he might have thought the very fact that she was his barrister would neutralise her.

He had always known that she was a friend of Kara's; perhaps he had been afraid that Kara might have told her something about him that would incriminate him if it were passed to the police. If so, his determination to persuade her to take him on as a client could have been an attempt to make sure that she would not be able to tell them anything.

Or perhaps he had simply been trying to establish himself in her eyes as someone who desperately wanted to know what had happened to Kara so that she would ignore whatever information he was afraid she might have.

Oh, come on! Trish said to herself. You're over-complicating this. If Collons knows anything about client privilege, he must know it applies only to things he's actually told me. And he hasn't said anything damning about himself in connection with Kara or her death. It's really only his appearance that seems so prejudicial.

But it was not only that, as she had to admit a moment later. There was also his past, his paranoia, and his peculiar reaction to her unfortunate *double entendre*.

She decided to talk to George about it. He was absolutely trustworthy and totally discreet, and he had a clear, logical mind. She knew she could tell him anything without worrying that it might leak out, and simply putting her suspicions into words might help her decide what to do about them.

Having got that far, Trish deliberately put Collons out of her mind and reached for the papers for the next day's case, in which her client was suing her husband for a share in the profits of the business they had set up together.

By seven thirty, she had had enough. On her way out, she was surprised to see a light still on in the clerks' room. Hoping that Debby was not crying over her word-processor, Trish looked round the open door. Dave was there alone, writing something in the soft yellow light from his cherished desk lamp. The brass seemed even shinier than usual.

'Why are you still here, Dave?' Trish said, thinking a little maliciously that perhaps he was suffering from domestic difficulties. 'Everything OK?'

'Naturally. The wife and I are meeting friends up West tonight. No point going back to Croydon first.'

'No, I suppose not. Look, Dave, I'm glad you're here. I was wondering if you could do me a favour.'

'Were you, Ms Maguire?'

'Yes,' she said, ignoring his provocative smirk. 'I wondered if you could ask around for any gossip there is about James Bletchley.'

'Blair Collons's solicitor?' Dave was immediately serious. 'Why? Is there a problem?'

'No. But I've heard a few odd things about him, and about a client of his called Drakeshill. Martin Drakeshill. I just wondered whether, if there were anything iffy about either of them, you could let me know. It's not likely to affect our brief, but I always like to know if I should be watching out for elephant traps.'

Dave's harsh face softened as it did on the rare occasions when one of the juniors impressed him. 'It's stood us in good stead, that caution of yours, Ms Maguire. Yes, all right, I'll put the word out among the clerks.'

'But without saying who wants it or why?'

'Naturally.' Dave stroked his Churchillian desk lamp and puffed out his narrow chest. 'You can rely on me.'

Trish left him and pulled up her coat collar as the cold hit her. Even so, she paused half-way across Blackfriars Bridge as usual, to look back over the muddle of Puddle Dock and the Mermaid Theatre to the dome of St Paul's sitting magnificently solid above them. It would have been lovely if the light had been white and the sky inky blue and splattered with stars, but that night it was nothing but a murky pale-orange blur.

She was just turning off the Blackfriars Bridge Road into her own small side road when it struck her that she had automatically believed James Bletchley's story about Collons's past without so much as asking for evidence. She should have known better.

CHAPTER ELEVEN

Bill Femur was staring red-eyed at the mess of pizza boxes, sandwich wrappers, butt ends, and half-eaten remnants of his officers' latest working meal. He wished he could call it a day, but there was still far too much to do.

The team was working reasonably well, and Caroline Lyalt was doing her usual good job of welding the separate parts together, but there were a few glitches yet to be sorted. Still, it could have been a lot worse.

At times he thought they were beginning to get somewhere; at others, like now, he felt thwarted and thick, which always bugged him. Particularly when there was a scrote out there who enjoyed terrifying and mutilating women before he killed them. The lab reports had made it clear that Kara's killer had played with her for some time before he had finally strangled her, maybe even as long as an hour.

What that hour must have been like for her was something Femur wasn't going to let himself think about. It wouldn't get him the result any quicker, and that was all that mattered. Whether it was the original rapist or a copycat, they had to get him soon. More than anything else at the moment, Femur dreaded hearing that there'd been another body found.

He rubbed his sore eyes and tried to think what he might have missed. He was almost sure that S and the killer were the same man – otherwise why was S being so sodding elusive? – but as yet he'd no idea whatsoever who S could be.

Between them, the team had spoken to every single person in Kara's home and work address books whose first or last names began with S. None had admitted to any of the appointments listed in the diary or seeing her on the evening she died. No letters from any S had been found in her cottage, and none of the messages on her answering-machine tape were any use either.

'Could it be a nickname, sir?' said a muffled young voice from the shadows at the far end of the room.

Femur stopped digging his fingers into his eyes and looked up. Young Owler, who, to do him credit, was a bloody good worker, was eating yet another cheese-and-pickle sandwich as he tapped at his keyboard. The boy had an inexhaustible capacity for food, and yet he was as thin as knitting needle.

'Could be, of course,' said Femur. He put his hands in his pockets so that he couldn't do any more damage to his eyes. 'Or it could be a place. Like the hotel.'

'You thinking of a love nest of some kind, Guv?'

Femur turned to see Tony Blacker standing in the doorway, taking off his old mac to shake the wet off it. He'd been following up the leads provided by the house-to-house officers and looked as though he hadn't got anywhere useful. He'd been in a bad mood ever since he'd interviewed Jed Thomplon and learned that even though he hadn't a good word to say for Kara he had an unbreakable alibi for her murder. Thomplon had been driving back from a long weekend in Scotland with his latest girlfriend for most of the night.

The story might not have been enough to get him off the hook, except that the girl, the restaurant where they'd stopped for dinner off the motorway, and the credit-card receipt for the petrol he'd bought at the Leicester service station on the M1 all confirmed his story. Blacker had checked it extra carefully because he'd taken a strong dislike to Dr Thomplon and would have loved to have him in an interview room for a few hours, putting him through the hoops. But no dice.

'Right, Tony. How'd it go?' Femur asked, ignoring his question.

'Not well, Guv. The neighbour is sure it was a man she used to see hanging about in Huggate's garden. He was probably in his thirties or forties. Or maybe older. But, then, maybe younger now she comes to think of it. Brown hair, or maybe black, but as it was raining she can't be sure. Quite a big man, she thinks, although he wasn't much taller than the weeping cherry in the front garden.'

'Which is?'

'Five six, according to my tape, Guv.'

'Right. A real giant, then.'

'Exactly. Not her fault, though, poor old duck,' Blacker said, with more tolerance than Femur had expected. 'She hasn't got good eyesight, it was always in the dark when she saw him; and she didn't like the look of him, so she didn't stay any longer than she had to when she was putting the rubbish out or whatever else took her out of doors after dark.'

'Did she ever report him?'

Blacker raised his eyes and his shoulders. 'Three times, apparently, and the nice man she spoke to at the police station said she wasn't to worry too much as the man wasn't breaking in anywhere or shouting or making a nuisance of himself, but a patrol car would come and have a look as soon possible. So nice he was, the man on the phone, so nice and so reassuring.'

'Right.' Femur produced a smile at Blacker's faithful impersonation of a worried witness, trying to be helpful and failing. 'And did they ever send a car?'

'Yes. Once. After the first call. But there wasn't anyone there and no sign that there ever had been. They even rang Huggate's bell and asked if she'd been bothered by loiterers and she looked gobsmacked, said she'd never had any trouble at all. So whenever the poor old duck rang again, they just soothed her and ignored her. Dotty old ladies seeing men in the dark . . . You know how it is, Guv.'

'Right. But you'd have thought someone would've remembered after she was killed and told us. God! They are a bunch of dozy buggers, aren't they? D'you think your dotty old woman would be any good at identifying the man if we ever pick anyone up?'

'We could try, but I doubt it. She couldn't stick by any description she gave for more than two seconds, always contradicting herself or adding something and then taking it back.'

Tony Blacker blew out his frustration in a gusty breath and shook his head. His hair was dark with rain and he looked as tired as Femur. He started to pick savagely at his left ear.

So, it's like that for him too, is it? thought Femur. What is it about Kara Huggate that's got under our skins? I've never had it this bad before.

'What was it you were saying about a love nest, Guv?' Blacker asked, eyeing the remains of the sandwiches.

Femur shrugged. 'Kara's phone bill shows she twice made calls to a hotel at Gatwick on days when she was supposed to be meeting S.'

Owler reached for the other half of his sandwich. Femur watched him, thinking that he couldn't possibly still be hungry. Perhaps he found eating eased the frustration. Or perhaps he didn't even notice what he was doing and just put any food he saw into his mouth.

'Aha! Any idea who she was calling?'

'Nope. The calls went through the switchboard at the hotel and none of the operators can remember her voice – Jenkins has played them all tapes of her speaking – so we've no idea which room she wanted. But why should they remember? Operators like them get thousands of calls a day.'

'No, but the very fact that it's an airport hotel gives us a clue, doesn't it, Guv?' Tony Blacker began to look excited. 'S must be a foreigner, staying over at the airport. So if he flew out straight after he killed her . . .'

Femur raised his eyebrows.

'I know, Guv,' Blacker said, putting up both hands in surrender. 'I know you'll have thought of it too.'

'Right. But I don't think he *is* a foreigner. For one thing there are no foreign numbers in her address book, apart from a US law firm, an Australian publisher and a gîte in the Dordogne, and they're not going to give us anything useful.'

'So what *do* you think then?'

'That S is a married man, who wanted to meet her in the most anonymous place he could think of. And what could be more anonymous than a big airport hotel?'

'And if he's married, that's why he's being so hard to find and didn't leave any evidence of himself in her cottage or on her answering-machine.'

'Right. I think she must've kept his number some-where else . . .'

'Or learned it by heart?'

'Maybe. And called him from the office, where the

system isn't sophisticated enough to show which extension called which number. There are no calls on her home phone bill that were to him – as far as we've been able to establish so far. Anyway, Jenkins is back at the hotel now, questioning the night staff about any guests who arrived late or dishevelled or behaved in any suspicious way on the night of the murder. There had to be a lot of blood on him, whoever he was. Kara's drains show no sign that he washed there, so he must've done it somewhere else. But it could've been anywhere. I can't say I'll be surprised if he didn't go back the hotel looking like an abattoir slaughterman. Why would he?'

'He wouldn't, particularly if he only used the place to meet her. And if she was deliberately keeping the relationship secret, we're going to have the devil's own job finding him.'

'Right. And we've got to. He could be setting up some other poor woman at this very moment.'

'Still, the hotel's the first chink of light, isn't it, Guv?'

'Maybe,' said Femur, sounding as depressed as he felt.

'Any joy on the list of discrepancies in the SOCO evidence with the old cases?' asked Blacker as he picked up one of the half sandwiches to inspect it. He made a face and put it back on the big platter. He pulled a Kit-Kat out of his suit pocket and started to peel off the silver paper.

Femur sat back in his chair. Now that Blacker was back and asking all the right logical questions, his need to get out of the filthy incident room seemed less urgent. He could hear the cleaners in the background and decided to stick it out until they came to deal with the mess. Then he'd get out and clear his head one way or another.

'Definitely. You tell him, Steve.'

The young constable grinned, perhaps in pleasure at the rare favour of being addressed by his Christian name.

He abandoned his desk and the last corner of his sandwich and was wiping his hands on his jeans as he reached Femur's big table. He waved at the photographs on the cork board.

'OK, Sarge. Apart from the physical differences in the victims, which we've all known about from the beginning, there's not all that much, but what there is looks quite significant.'

He spread out a stack of yet more glossy photos on the table.

'Now, the sock he used to gag Huggate is just like the ones the Kingsford Rapist used. See.'

'Sure.' Tony Blacker exchanged weary smiles with Femur at the boy's enthusiasm.

'We know he took his screwdriver, or chisel, with him when he went, just like the original rapist did, but the pathologist thinks it's a slightly different tool this time, wider and a bit longer.'

'That doesn't mean much. With a three-year gap, he might well have needed to buy a new one and not been able to find one exactly the same.'

'I know. But the screwdriver's only the beginning. It gets better. Now, look here, Sarge. Here's the lab's shot of the gloved-thumbmark bruises on Huggate's wrists and neck. And these are some of the original ones from the earlier victims. I know they look much the same, but they've been measured and the Huggate ones are a millimetre smaller in both directions.'

'Couldn't that just be the way she bruised? Older women mark much more easily than young ones, and Huggate was a good twenty years older than the first dead girl.'

'Could be, except for these bits here and here.' Owler picked up two glossy prints of the marks. 'It's hard to see, but they've blown up the detail for us and you can just see the marks where his nails pressed extra hard even through the gloves. They make it reasonably sure that the size of the thumbs was different. The new ones are narrower than the first, and I don't believe anyone's thumbs get smaller over three years, whatever they've been doing.'

Femur stood up, yawning. 'You're spinning it out too long, Steve. We're all knackered. Give him the crucial bit.'

'OK, sir. Look, Sarge. Look at the way Huggate's lying. And now look at the only other victim who was killed.'

By then all of them had seen the photographs of the body so often that their shock value had lessened. Even so the contorted expression on Kara Huggate's face, as much as the blood between her splayed legs, made Femur look away. He thought again of the hour she'd lived while the animal was amusing himself with her.

'Just the same position,' Blacker said, squinting up at him as though he was afraid his boss had lost it.

Femur shook his head. 'No, but look, Tony. Here and here. Don't you think Kara looks more *arranged*?'

'Ah. Yeah, perhaps. Yes, I do see what you mean. Could be coincidence, though.'

'Right. But look at the elbow here, the right elbow. It's quite stiffly bent. The other victim looks as though she was left exactly as she fell. But someone's taken the trouble to match Kara's position to hers, and you can see from the blood marks on the floorboards that she was dragged away from the original spot where she fell. He tried to wipe up the blood, here and here, but enough had soaked into the timber to show up easily. There's no doubt that he moved her. But why, if it wasn't to make her look like the first victim? There was no sign that that one was moved.'

'So, you do think it's a copycat.'

'We both do, Steve and I. Cally, too. But whether it's just another rapist, or someone with a quite different kind of motive, we're still not sure.'

'I see Caroline's been clockwatching again. What time did she knock off this evening?' Blacker asked stiffly.

Femur frowned. He couldn't be doing with Blacker's childish resentment of any discussion with Caroline Lyalt that did not include him. 'She's back talking to the surviving victims, trying to find out who else was given details of what was done to them. They've all admitted to being counselled, so the information could have come out that way, though it's unlikely, but so far they've all sworn that they obeyed police instructions and didn't give even their counsellors precise details.'

'You see, the screwdriver and the sock were deliberately kept out of all the press reports,' Steve Owler said helpfully, 'so that if anyone came forward to confess, we could weed out . . .' Blacker silenced him with a look. 'But, Guv, even if one of them did tell someone about the sock and the screwdriver, there's no way any of them would've had access to photos of the body of the girl who didn't make it.'

'Exactly,' said Femur. 'So while Cally's doing her bit with the victims, and Jenkins is down at the Heathrow hotel with Sally Evans, we've been checking up on everyone who could've seen the files or heard about the SOCO evidence that was withheld from the press.'

'And so far, Sarge, there's been no one who wasn't on the team,' said Owler.

'Are you certain that none of the published reports included any details or drawings, or photos?'

'Dead certain, Sarge. And I had a go at the Internet, too, just in case any of those true crime websites had details. But there's nothing there that I can find. Though there may be sites I haven't seen yet.'

'So who exactly did know what the body looked like?'

'All the officers on the investigating teams. The photographer, the SOCOs, the lab technicians. That's it.'

Femur felt as though his brain was beginning to crank up again.

'Right, Steve, I want a list of their names, and when you've got it, you'd better cross-check them with Kara's address books and diary. OK?'

'Will do.' Owler sounded so bright and wide awake that Femur sighed in envy.

'What about a pint, Guv?' said Blacker, putting a hand under his elbow. 'There's nothing more you can do tonight and you look all in.'

'I'm fine, but a pint's not such a silly idea. You'd better knock off, too, Steve. Or you'll addle your brain and be no good in the morning.'

'OK, sir.'

Femur smiled. 'Good lad. See you tomorrow. Coming, Tony?'

CHAPTER TWELVE

Trish had hardly got through the door and kicked off her shoes when she heard George's unmistakably heavy tread on the iron staircase that led up to her flat. She leaned back to open the door for him.

As he hugged her, she thought how lucky she was to be with him instead of a man like Jed Thomplon. There was something she'd meant to say to George, but for the moment she could not think what it was. He kissed her, tasting of peppermint.

'Oh, sorry,' she said, pulling back and thinking how typical it was of him to have got the taste of the day out of his mouth before he breathed on her. 'I had a lot of garlic for lunch.'

'Good one?'

'Not bad. Filling. That must be why I forgot to buy us anything to eat. I've just remembered there's nothing in the fridge. I'd meant to get something on my way home. Shit. George, I *am* sorry.'

'It's fine. We can go out.' He kissed her again, heroically ignoring the stale garlic. 'Or would you rather have something from the Village Tandoori?'

'Oh, what a good idea! I'm not sure I've got the energy for a restaurant, and anyway I'd quite like to ask you about a case I've got, which I ought to do in private. Would you mind?'

'Of course not. I'll go and get the Village T's menu.'

He passed Trish's answering-machine on his way to the kitchen and called back over his shoulder. 'Looks like you're well in demand – eight messages.'

'Help.' Trish dreaded finding that Blair Collons had somehow got hold of the number. 'I suppose I'd better find out what they are. D'you mind?'

'Course not. Carry on. I've got my mobile, so if you choose what you want first, I can ring and order while you're getting your messages. D'you need the menu?'

Trish laughed. 'Nope. I'll have veg samosas, Lamb Pasanda, and a Peshwari naan.'

'Trish, one of these days you're going to have to live a little more dangerously.'

'Why?' she asked, walking up behind him and putting her arms around his big body. He smelt deliciously of himself and a little of petrol. 'You know perfectly well that whenever I try anything else it's revolting – or dull.'

'Still . . . Where's your spirit of adventure? Go on, get your messages and I'll deal with this.'

She retreated reluctantly to the answering-machine and pressed the relevant buttons, hoping that she was not about to hear Collons's voice.

'Hi, Trish. This is Emma, suffering from pizza-withdrawal. I wondered if you were interested in going to Casa Roberto this evening – if you're not doing anything else. Hope all's well and that you and George are flourishing. See you soon. 'Bye.'

A click, a beep, then a short pause, and then her mother's voice reporting the time of her call and adding,

'Nothing urgent. I just thought it would be nice to chat. When you've got time.' Beep.

'Miss Maguire. This is Simpson's Garage. Your car will be ready on Tuesday evening. We'll be fitting the new brake shoes tomorrow. Otherwise it's just the regular service. The total will come to two hundred and fifty pounds.'

'Shit,' said Trish, wondering why she kept a car since she hardly ever used it and it cost a fortune to maintain. Walking over the bridge to chambers, taking taxis in the evening if she was planning to drink anything alcoholic, and going to most other places with George, it hardly seemed worth it. On the other hand, at her age and earning her income, it would be absurd to be carless. And anyway she sometimes needed it for out-of-London cases.

'Ms Maguire,' said a crisp female voice she did not recognise, 'you don't know me, but my name's Maggie Roper. I was given your name and number by Anna Grayling this afternoon. I'm researching a sixty-minute documentary about women and the law. I wondered whether you'd be prepared to talk to me? I'm particularly interested at the moment in this secret dining club for important women lawyers. I don't know whether you're a member?'

Trish raised her eyebrows at that one. She assumed the researcher was talking about SWAB, the Society of Women at the Bar, which had always sounded like the most civilised of organisations to her. Said to be devoted more to dining in seriously good restaurants than any kind of dreary institutionalised networking, it wasn't precisely secret, but members tended to avoid talking about it. Occasionally one would list it in her *Who's Who* entry, but such publicity was frowned on by the others. Trish was not yet a member, but she cherished a private hope that it would not be too long before the founders decided she could be invited to join. She certainly wasn't going to jeopardise her chances by talking to any television researcher about it, even a friend of Anna's.

Click. Beep. A man's voice, older than any of the others, and with an Irish lilt in it. 'Trish, m'dear. I know you don't like answering letters, so I'm phoning instead. Are you there now? If not, will you give me a ring? My number's in the book. Will you ring, Trish? It would be nice to talk. We've a lot to say to each other, one way and another. And we don't have to meet if you –'

Trish cut off the voice and the remaining four messages. Her hands were shaking and she felt very cold.

'Trish,' George said quietly, from behind her.

'Don't say it.' She did not look round. 'I know what you think. You've told me three times already. But I don't want to have anything to do with him. He's only getting in touch now because he read about me in that article in *The Times*. It's always the same: if I'm ever quoted or mentioned in the press, he starts pestering me again. It'll stop eventually, it always does. Until the next time.'

'But why not see him?'

'Why should I? He never wanted to have anything to do with me when I was a child, when *I* needed *him*. Now that I'm successful, he wants a piece of me. Well, I'm not prepared to give it to him.'

'He's your father, Trish. You really ought to make peace with him.'

She stared at the silenced answering machine, gathering her patience and all her skills of advocacy. It wasn't fair to have to use them at home as well as in court.

Then she turned, feeling as stony and calm as any cemetery statue, to say: 'He lost the privileges attached to fatherhood when he abandoned my mother and me.'

'Well, I think you're being melodramatic and rather silly.'

She felt the anger spreading through her brain. It was an old fury, uncontrolled and frightening, which she thought she had conquered long ago. He opened his mouth. 'Don't say it, George. Whatever it is, don't say it. This is none of your business.'

'But –'

'No. You have no right to tell me how to behave to my father.' There was a knock at the door. They both turned towards it, George feeling in the inside pocket of his suit for his wallet.

'I'll do it. This is *my* flat,' said Trish, not forgetting that George often paid for the takeaways he ordered when they were in Southwark, just as she often paid in Fulham. In the middle of such a quarrel she could not bear the thought of his buying her food.

Knowing that he was nearly as angry as she – and hurt, too – made her clumsy as she scuffled in her bag for the necessary money. In the end, she gave up and handed over two twenty-pound notes. The young man in the motorcycle helmet gave her the change and a large brown carrier-bag.

Without another word to George, Trish walked straight past him to the kitchen, where she assembled a trayful of plates, glasses, cutlery and bottles of cold lager, which she then brought out to the large dining-room table. Still in silence, she fetched another tray and laid out all the foil boxes and bags, putting a serving spoon beside each. When she saw the number of dishes that George had ordered for himself, two kinds of vegetables and rice as well as the meat-filled naan, main course and starter, she wanted to tell him what she thought of his eating habits, on the basis that if he could give her orders about the way she should behave to her father, she could give him orders about protecting his arteries. But she didn't because that wasn't how she operated – and, besides, she knew she'd already hurt him.

She could feel an urge to apologise for that, but the words were going to stick in her throat unless he admitted he'd been in the wrong first.

'It might be different,' she said, in a voice that vibrated with the effort of keeping it under control, 'if my father had ever apologised for leaving us. But no. All he does is make demands.'

George looked at her. His eyes had none of the warmth or the amusement she was used to. They looked hard and very dark. 'It's difficult for some men to apologise, Trish. It goes against everything they've learned since the nursery. But it doesn't mean they don't feel apologetic.'

'Well, they should have the guts to come out and say so. Like the Japanese.'

He did not comment, so she silently picked up her fork. They both started to eat and later made polite conversation, as though they had only just met. They commented on the food they were trying to swallow, and asked each other questions about the day's work. Trish almost expected one of them to ask whether the other had been abroad recently or seen any good films.

She gave up eating when she was only a quarter of the way through her naan and there was more than half the lamb untouched.

'Is something wrong?' George asked, putting down his own fork.

Surprised by his choice of words, because he must have known precisely what was wrong and why, Trish answered coolly that she had found she was not particularly hungry after all.

'Nor me,' he said, wiping his mouth on the napkin she had provided. 'In fact, I think I'd better be getting home.'

130

Trish, who was longing for him to tell her he understood how he had made her feel and was sorry for it and would not infringe again, nodded. 'Yes, that might be best.'

'Thank you for my supper,' he said, getting up.

'Not at all.' She stayed sitting at the big, pale wood table.

When he had let himself out, closing the front door with scrupulous care, Trish put her head in her hands. How could he not have understood?

She had told him all about her father soon after they had first made love and he had seemed to understand then. She could not remember the precise words he had used, but she could re-create the warm safety she had felt as she listened to him.

In an unprecedented orgy of talking it all out, she'd told George everything about how hard it had been to pretend not to mind her father's desertion so that she did not add to her mother's burdens. George had said then that he could see why she had grown up determined never to be at any man's mercy. Why couldn't he remember that now?

Trish looked at the sticky remains of the highly spiced Indian food in disgust and leaped up to take it all out to the kitchen bin. Scraping plates, running them under the almost boiling water from the tap before putting them in the dishwasher, she couldn't understand what had made George think he had the right to tell her what to do.

The flat felt very empty without him, and cold with memories of the anger that had spread between them, like water from a melting iceberg.

But there was nothing she could do about it until George apologised.

Kara would have understood, she thought, having

been through much worse with Jed Thomplon. But Kara was dead.

'Oh, fucking hell!' Trish shouted, to the echoing space around her.

Lonelier than she had ever expected to be, she reminded herself that there had been seven more messages on her answering-machine and that she did have other friends besides George and Kara.

As soon as she had finished clearing up, she opened some of the big windows to get the smell of curry out of the flat. She hoped it was just the smell that was making her feel sick. Then she went back to the phone and rang Emma Gnatche, who had left the first message.

'Hi. It's Trish,' she said, when Emma answered. 'Look, I'm sorry to be ringing so late. Did you get your pizza?'

'No.' Emma's voice was warm with laughter. 'No, I thought of my expanding waistline and made do with cottage cheese instead. It was a good thing you weren't in or I'd be a thousand calories fatter. Were you working?'

'No. I had George here.' Trish's voice wobbled on his name, but Emma did not comment. 'We had a bit of a fight and he's gone early. I . . .'

'Shall I come round?'

'Oh, no need for that. It's not that serious. In fact I'm fine, Emma. I just thought . . .'

'No, you're not. Let me come, Trish. You've scraped me off the floor over and over again. It's my turn to be solidaritous. I've got a smashing bottle of wine here, which I could bring to cheer us both up. I could be with you in about twenty minutes. Let me come.'

It was irresistible.

CHAPTER THIRTEEN

Blair was sleeping badly. He and Kara had had the nearest thing to a quarrel since her death. She was still smiling at him off the wall, but she wanted him to tell Trish Maguire everything.

'It's not safe, Kara,' he kept saying, as she refused to touch him. 'You thought she'd be on our side, but I don't think she is. I've told you over and over that she's hard, but you won't believe me. She's not like you, not like you when you're kind. You're loving, but she isn't. She's so full of anger that I can't trust her.'

Kara told him in her softest, most adoring voice that she knew he wanted to tell Trish everything, that she understood how badly he needed to tell someone.

'Yes, because it's too much to carry on my own, now that you're . . . now that you can't help me any more. But I don't think she's safe.'

Kara told him that nothing was ever absolutely safe and no one completely trustworthy. She reminded him that she had once thought she could trust him and then discovered that she could not.

Crying, Blair turned away from her picture. That night

he couldn't come. So he couldn't sleep. It was all Trish Maguire's fault.

CHAPTER FOURTEEN

'Oh, Ms Maguire!'

'What is it, Dave? I'm in a rush.' Trish's arms were full of papers. Her red brocade bag had somehow swung round and got itself caught up with her suit jacket as she halted in her dash for the door. She tried to straighten it and ricked her neck. If Dave didn't hurry up, she was going to be seriously late. One day she might have enough time to do everything without running anywhere. In her dreams.

'I just wanted to let you know that your client's solicitor has come up smelling of roses,' Dave said. 'James Bletchley has some criminal clients, but why shouldn't he? Most of his work is protecting the interests of people who have been arrested. Nothing odd *there*.'

'It sounds as though you're telling me there is something odd somewhere else,' Trish said, well aware of Dave's pleasure in making his employers wait. She still didn't know what they did – or had done – to him to make him need to take such an exasperating kind of revenge.

'Well, there is just a suggestion that one of his other

clients, the one whose name you mentioned to me in point of fact, Martin Drakeshill, might have some interesting friends.'

'Interesting how?' asked Trish, almost forgetting the risk of being late as she thought of the terror in Collons's face when she had asked him about Drakeshill. 'Mafia? Money-launderers? Drug-dealers? What?'

Dave looked as though someone had just farted in court. 'Of course not. Nothing like that. Just people who can make inconvenient cases disappear.'

'Is that all? Dave, you know as well as I do that it doesn't even take friends to make files disappear, just sloppiness.'

He looked so pissed off that, mindful of her likely need for future favours, she added quickly, 'Did your source have any idea who the friends might be? If you can, tell me fast. I haven't much time.'

'I'm coming to that. A year or two ago this Mr Drakeshill was arrested for GBH, along with a much younger man who was probably employed by him in his used-car business. It was a baseball-bat job, debt-chasing I should think, but I didn't hear any details. The CPS were up in arms about it . . .'

Trish looked at her watch and ran, muttering an apology to Dave. She put him, Drakeshill and even Kara right out of her mind as she set about the day's work, proving that her client deserved at least fifty per cent of the profits her ex-husband had made out of her ideas and groundwork in the business they had started together. Trish was rewarded for her careful preparation almost as soon as she embarked on her opening remarks.

The husband began to look uncomfortable and later started whispering to his solicitor. He shook his elegantly brushed grey head and calmly turned back to face the judge, but Trish knew enough about him and opposing counsel to read what lay behind their air of confidence. She completed her remarks and sat back to wait for Charles Bishop to unpick the damaging information she had stitched together.

He did it quite well but things got stickier and stickier for him, and when the court rose for the day, Trish was not surprised when Charles strolled towards her and asked if she and her instructing solicitor would mind waiting while he had a word with his client. She smiled understandingly, which she was pleased to see annoyed him, and settled down to wait.

In the end it was an hour and a half before an acceptable settlement had been hammered out. She and her late opponent parted from their respective clients and went down the stairs together on reasonably good terms, swapping all the usual stories about impossible briefs and pompous judges, only to find that the main hall of the Royal Courts of Justice had been turned into a badminton court. Trish stopped on the stairs, amazed. She did vaguely know that it happened, but she had never seen it in use before.

'Energetic little buggers, aren't they?' said Charles Bishop.

'Aren't they just? Who are they?'

'No idea. Staff here, I should imagine. I don't think counsel use it much. I must dash. See you around, Trish. El Vino's sometime?'

'Probably,' she said, without thinking. 'It's been a pleasure doing business with you, Charles.' She skirted the badminton court, amused at the unexpected frivolity, and walked back to the Temple, huddling in her Burberry as a few clammy snowflakes flopped on to her face and melted down her chin.

Dave was still in his room. When she stopped by his desk, she became aware that the leather soles of her neat black court shoes had let in the wet. She wiggled her toes to warm them, but it didn't help. There was a tiny toaster-like electric fire in her room. As soon as she had finished with Dave, she could hang her feet over it and watch the steam rise as they dried out.

'You were going to tell me about Martin Drakeshill's magic friends,' she said.

'So I was, but you ran off before I had a chance to finish what I was saying.'

'I could hardly be late for court.'

'You need to leave yourself longer to get there.' Trish narrowed her eyes at that typical example of clerkly sanctimoniousness. 'Yes, well, as I was saying, Drakeshill's friends are said to be in the police. I got the impression that the lost files might have been a reward for information received.' Dave sounded disapproving, but Trish was interested.

Minor cases, and sometimes even relatively important ones, could be dropped as being 'not in the public interest' if the defendant were in a position to give the police good-value information. If that were known to have applied to Drakeshill, it might explain a lot. To Trish, the idea of a violent second-hand-car salesman being a police snout was a lot more convincing than Collons's hints of a player in a major conspiracy that encompassed not only council building plans and the local police, but also rape and murder.

'Thanks, Dave. You've been a help. I owe you one.'

'I'll remember that.'

As he spoke, looking much more cheerful, Trish grimaced. Dave's way of collecting debts tended to include unwinnable legal-aid cases that involved inordinate amounts of work at no notice and took you to courts so remote that the brief fee hardly paid for the train fares. She told him that her debt extended only as far as Bristol.

'We must fight them in the Old Bailey, Miss Maguire; we must fight them in the provinces, we must fight them wherever they appear.'

Trish glanced back to see him standing even straighter than usual and laying his right hand on his lamp.

'I know, Dave, and we must never surrender.' She laughed. 'I do my best, but I draw the line at North Wales.'

She did not wait to see his reaction to her teasing but dumped her papers in her room, decided to ignore the fire and wait to dry her feet at home. Half-way across Blackfriars Bridge, she remembered how empty the flat was going to be without George.

Hesitating, she looked back at St Paul's and then on down towards Southwark. It seemed even darker than usual and bleakly uninviting. On the other hand her feet were wet and cold. But she needed friends that night even more than dry shoes. She turned back to walk up Fleet Street to El Vino's.

As she had expected, plenty of people she knew were drinking there. She was hailed at once by Simon Hogwell, and joined the table he was sharing with five others.

'So! Not cooking tonight, Trish?'

'Not tonight. And my case settled, so I thought I might celebrate.' '

'Did you indeed? Careful, chaps. Sounds like Trish is going to be an expensive drinker tonight.'

'Bugger off, Simon. I always buy my fair share of bottles, as you very well know.'

'You could've changed. We haven't seen you here for years.'

Trish turned round to look for someone from whom she could order another bottle and a basket of biscuits. It was true, she thought: since she and George had taken

139

up with each other, she hadn't spent many of the long, shop-talking, wine-drinking evenings that had once provided most of her social life.

The bottle was brought and poured, and she sank back into her comfortable leather armchair to enjoy herself. As always the jokes were good and the stories around her grew wilder and wilder as more bottles were opened. Some of her group drifted off, but their chairs were always refilled by newcomers, a few of whom she had almost forgotten. Lots of people commented on how long it had been, and Trish began to feel as though she were Rip van Winkle, coming alive again to a world she had not seen for decades. Her feet were drying out, too.

It wasn't, she told herself, as she sipped her claret, that George had trapped her or deliberately prevented her seeing her friends, it was just that she had chosen to spend her evenings with him. Finding that her colleagues bore her no malice and that she could pick up her friendships where she had left them eighteen months earlier was cheering.

'Trish, my only love,' called a rich voice from the door.

She turned to see Jeremy Platen, a criminal silk who had once been one of her pupil masters. There was the usual mocking smile on his otherwise cherubic face. She had enjoyed her six months with him and been sorry when he left chambers to join a different set.

'Where have you been hiding yourself?'

'Jerry,' she said, getting to her feet. He enfolded her in a huge and affectionate but in no way passionate embrace. 'Lovely to see you. How are you?'

'Flourishing. But what about you? What *have* you been doing to yourself?'

'What d'you mean?'

'You're all pale and miserable-looking. Trish, quite frankly you look as though you've crawled out from a dripping, rat-ridden cellar somewhere. Has someone been horrible to you? Not that fat solicitor of yours? I always said you should never sleep with the enemy. Why did you spurn me? Didn't I tell you you were missing out on a good thing?'

'Oh, shut up, Jerry. Of course he hasn't done anything to me. And he's not fat, anyway. He's a big man, in every sense of the word.'

'Fat!'

'No, he isn't. And he hasn't done anything to me. I've been a bit busy, that's all. And one of my witnesses was murdered the other day.'

'Ah, yes, I can see how that might take the edge off your pleasure.' For a moment Jeremy's bright black eyes softened with concern, but then he grinned again, buffeted her shoulder and asked why she hadn't offered him a drink yet. She made sure that he knew all the other people around her table then turned away to order yet another bottle.

'By the way, Jerry,' she said, when he had commented on the generosity of her choice and said how sensible she had been to spend some of her time on chancery cases instead of slogging away with the criminals as he had been doing, 'have you ever heard of a man called Martin Drakeshill, who operates somewhere in south-west London?'

'Drakeshill? No, can't say I have. But have you heard the story about the drake who went to a grand hotel with his best beloved duck and asked room service for a condom?'

'No,' said Trish, dragging out the vowel into an auntly sound of disapproval and resignation. She could vividly remember Jeremy's laughing himself into choking fits over the most childish jokes, most of them involving smut or lavatories, and sometimes both. For a man as sophisticated and clever as he, it was an odd quirk.

He understood her tone and stuck out his tongue. 'Well, all right then, Smarty-pants. I won't tell you.'

'Oh, go on. How could I resist?'

Like most barristers, he was an excellent raconteur, playing the part of each character in his mildly grubby story and giving them all the appropriate voices and gestures. In the end it was quite funny. Trish gave in and laughed with the rest. 'Did that come from your junior clerk?' she asked.

'No. My son. He's eight now, and the funniest thing ever.' Jeremy looked preposterously proud, and Trish had a moment's knife-like envy. 'He collects jokes for me from the school playground. I thought that was nearly as good as Napoleon and his armies.'

'Yeah, yeah, yeah. We've all heard that one,' said Rosie Boxwell, a hard-faced woman from the commercial bar, whom Trish had never much liked.

'But what about the man who was dying of thirst in the desert and met a genie?' called somebody's pupil, a young man Trish had never met before and whose name she had not heard properly.

Jeremy said, with tremendous dignity, that he'd heard that story long ago and that it was quite as old as his Napoleon joke, and not nearly as funny, besides being racist. The challenge proved too much for everyone and soon they were all at it, offering strings of madder and madder stories, as though they, too, were showing off in a school playground.

It was all very silly and great fun. Trish eventually reeled home across the bridge, as usual stopping halfway to look down the river, which was particularly romantic in the moonlight. Leaning on the edge of the bridge, unaware of the cold, she gazed at the piled buildings on either side of the river. White and silver with the black water rushing down to the sea between them, they made her wish she could paint – or even take good photographs.

Her elbow slipped off the metal and fading common sense told her she had better get herself home while she was still on her feet and drink at least a pint of water before she went to bed.

The water seemed to have had no effect when she woke at three-thirty in the morning with a dry mouth, boiling eyeballs and a thudding in her head as though devils in football boots were prancing about inside her skull. Getting up felt like a serious mistake as the floor swayed under her, but she needed some Nurofen.

She thought of Rosie Boxwell and the moment at which she had become just too irritating to bear. Trish had drunk enough by then to let her feelings show and she had roused a gale of laughter from everyone except Rosie with her neatly aimed insult.

Oh, shit! What a mistake! A woman like that wouldn't forget.

Trish closed her eyes and laid her hand across her aching forehead, wishing she could forget her idiocy. Later on, she had even started talking about SWAB. It was clear enough that hard-faced Rosie hadn't been invited to join yet either, but it had been mad to make it seem as though she herself had. Rosie must know some of the members quite well and she was enough of a cow to check whether Trish was a member. Oh, hell! That was probably the end of her chances there.

God, she was thirsty! Two pills and more water might help. But she didn't deserve to feel better. What a fool! And she wouldn't sleep for hours. Not now that the drink had tickled up her liver and made her brain think it was daybreak. Shit.

It was at that particularly awful moment that she

remembered George telling her that in his experience just about every barrister in London was incapable of keeping his or her mouth shut. Trish had furiously denied it at the time. Now she put her hands over her hot face and groaned. What a fool she'd been! Rosie would tell everyone what she'd said and they'd all laugh at her. Oh, shit.

When she came back from the bathroom, she dug around in the pile of half-read books on the floor by her bed for the one that usually solaced her insomniac hours. It looked boring. She tried another and then another and eventually got out of bed to find *Presumed Innocent*, which could always hold her attention. That was better. She drank some Badoit from the bottle and tried to believe she was a human being.

Turning the pages, she realised that some good had come out of the evening. Her physical sensations were disgusting and all those bottles she had shared had been quite unnecessary, but she felt younger, years younger, than she had for ages. Maybe it had something to do with the fact that George was past forty, and life with him had been getting a bit middle-aged recently. Perhaps a gap was no bad thing. And she still had a lot more friends than she'd realised. Good friends. They'd got tight too, most of them. It hadn't been only her. Lots of them had made fools of themselves, as well. She wasn't unique. And they'd mostly forget everything she'd said. Another swig of water and another chapter of Scott Turow and she'd be right as rain.

And somebody had said something useful about Drakeshill. Trish frowned, picking through her memories. Yes. Someone she hadn't met before who'd done a fair bit of criminal work in the furthest reaches of south west London had heard a rumour from a boy he'd been defending that Drakeshill was thought to be a dangerous man to cross. Trish had tried to pin the barrister down, but he either didn't know any more or was protecting his source. He'd just said that the word was that if Martin Drakeshill asked you to do something you either did it or got right off his patch before he could do you a serious mischief.

That made him sound a bit more of a player than the small-time informer Trish had imagined, but it was still some way short of Collons's major conspirator. As sleep continued to seem impossible, she began to wonder whether she ought, after all, to go to Kingsford herself and try to find out more about Drakeshill and whether he had had links of any kind with Kara.

Chapter Fifteen

When she woke again, soon after nine, Trish felt a lot better than she deserved, and after a long, hot shower almost well. There was no need to hurry because even Dave could not have drummed up some unwinnable case hundreds of miles from London in such a short time, and Kingsford and Martin Drakeshill could wait for an hour or two.

She could potter about in the kitchen, making herself some real coffee, instead of her usual mug of instant. While the kettle was boiling, she dug in the freezer for some bread and came upon a bag of brioches she and George had made as an experiment one weekend. Her pleasure in her renewed freedom faltered.

They had spent most of the morning in her kitchen, surrounded by the warm sexy scents of yeast and flour, discovering that they could share even the narrow space of her galley kitchen without falling over each other, except when they meant to. The whole enterprise had developed into an act of love almost as devastating as the real thing.

Trish could remember the way her fingers had slid into

the barely resilient dough that had felt so soft and smelt so evocatively of welcome and plenty. George had been standing behind her with his arms around her waist as she worked the dough. Every so often, he would lower his head so that his lips could lie on her bare neck.

Her eyelashes were wet as she opened the bag and levered two of the icy rolls away from the rest. They resisted her efforts and she picked up the breadknife to push between the rock-hard surfaces that seemed superglued together. Eventually one leaped away from the knife blade and ended up skittering across the hard studded rubber of her kitchen floor. She brushed the first brioche on the seat of her jeans and put it on a dark-blue pottery plate with the second, which had let go with less violence.

When she opened the freezer again to put the rest away in their plastic bag, a chunk of granular ice fell on to the bagged evidence of innumerable meals she'd shared with George. Neither of them liked waste so they tended to freeze the leftovers, meaning to use them up later. But they never had. She ought to throw them out, but not just now. She'd been getting rid of too much recently.

Having slammed the freezer door, she reached to the shelf above for her favourite French porcelain breakfast cup and a matching plate. She had bought them in Provence on a holiday before she had ever met George and he had never liked them. The thickness of the sticky dust lining the cup showed how long it had been since she had drunk out of it.

When she had washed and dried it, she took butter from the fridge and found a jar of particularly special macadamia nut honey, which he also disliked, and carried the whole lot to the dining table. She rarely breakfasted in such style, it was either a cup of instant on the run or a frolic in bed at the weekend with George. This kind of stately, private celebration was something new.

The first mouthful of black coffee tasted powdery, with hints of chocolate and a rich bitterness. Trish kept it in her mouth until she had decoded each separate flavour, amused to find herself behaving like the kind of wine critic who talked of delectable wet-nettle noses and tobacco-scented cedarwood notes with tarry overtones. She and George had often read out the wilder descriptions from the weekend papers, laughing at the thought of the earnest oenophiles licking wet nettles and cigar boxes to test their comparisons.

George. Why couldn't she get him out of her mind?

She was angry with him, and with reason, so it couldn't hurt this much to be without him. It couldn't.

'I won't apologise till he does,' she said aloud. 'I won't.'

A crash in the middle of her front door provided a useful distraction. The metallic clang of the letter-box being forced up was followed by the savage ripping of thick paper. She got up to fetch her mangled newspaper as it dropped on to the front-door mat.

There wasn't much in the paper about Kara, only a small paragraph on page four of the main news section, announcing that the police were pursuing various leads in their search for the Kingsford Rapist. Trish wished she had some kind of line into the investigation to find out whether they had ever considered Collons among their suspects, or even knew of his existence.

A second crash of the letter-box in the front door presaged the arrival of the post. There was the usual collection of exasperating mail-order catalogues, several bills, a postcard from a friend who was skiing in Italy, a thank-you letter from her favourite godchild, whose birthday Trish had managed to remember for once, and two other handwritten letters.

One was addressed in her father's writing. She put that on her desk unopened. The other proved to be from Kara's mother.

My dear Miss Maguire,

How very kind of you to write about my daughter's death. I do not know how you knew her, for she never spoke to me about you, but I am glad that you valued her so highly. I was so proud of her as she grew up and I loved her very much.

Her death has been the most terrible shock to me, and I sometimes feel as though I shall not be able to sleep again until the police have found her murderer and allowed me to put her to rest. They are doing their best, I know, but it is very hard not to be able to give her a funeral.

Forgive me for writing at such length, but I'm alone now except for some cousins in Australia whom I never see. There are very few people who can understand what I mean when I talk about Kara. Your kind letter made me think that you might be one of them. I do hope that when I am allowed to have a funeral for her you will come.

Yours sincerely,
Katherine Huggate

The tone of the letter was so surprising after what Kara had said about her mother's dislike that Trish had to reread it twice to make sure she hadn't misunderstood the first paragraph.

She pushed her hands through her hair, trying to understand, well aware that she was a relative innocent when it came to mother-daughter conflicts. Her own good relationship with her mother had always been part of the underpinning of her life, but she knew she was unusually lucky. Nearly all her friends had horror stories of argument and insensitivity to swap whenever they started talking about their mothers. Kara had complained much less than most, but the little she had said had been enough to tell Trish that Mrs Huggate had made her daughter feel not just unloved but unlovable.

Trish was increasingly sure that it must have been Kara's childhood experiences that had left her with such a profound need to make other people happy – or, at least, happier than they had been before she met them. Whenever she failed, her instinct was to withdraw, as though she couldn't believe herself worth liking unless she was doing something useful.

It was ironic that her mother was not only the one person she had never been able to help but also the one she could never have abandoned. Perhaps that explained the contradiction. The criticism that had so distressed Kara might not have originated with her mother in the first place. If Kara had been sending out signals of failure or dislike from some kind of emotional sonar, they could have locked on to her mother's unhappiness and come pinging straight back to Kara.

On the other hand, Trish reminded herself, the letter need not have been genuine. Mrs Huggate could have drafted that first paragraph out of guilt or simply as a way of rewriting history to make herself feel better about what she had done to her daughter.

'God! You're such a cynic, Trish,' Kara had said to her once, and it was true. But at least cynicism was safer than naïveté. As a cynic you could take a certain miserable satisfaction when you discovered that people were quite as treacherous or cruel as you'd feared. If you'd believed in them – trusted them – and they let you down, you were stuck.

Kara had been like that, believing that everyone she met was fundamentally good until she was forced to admit the opposite. She'd once told Trish that she was sure there was something likeable in everyone in the world and that if you were careful enough – kind enough – you could bring it out. She'd also believed that no one could consistently meet kindness with cruelty, so that if she could only hang on long enough she would get the response she wanted in the end.

Was that why she'd died? Had she been pouring out warmth and affection on to someone who was beyond help? Collons? Or someone even more damaged?

Trish put Mrs Huggate's letter in the basket where she kept things she didn't want to throw away but did not have any particular use for, and looked at her father's unopened letter. There could be no comparison. Kara might have been wrong about her mother, although that still wasn't certain, but it didn't mean that Trish had misjudged her father.

Whatever Mrs Huggate turned out to be like, Paddy Maguire was a treacherous louse, and his daughter had every right to avoid him.

Unable to destroy his letter without reading it, Trish put it in one of the drawers of her desk, along with all the others he had written whenever he read about her cases in the press. Having to think about him made the prospect of going to Kingsford to gather evidence to support or banish Blair Collons's suspicions into an alluring distraction instead of a dreary chore.

The road was dreadful, full of bottlenecks and in-adequate signs, inconsiderately parked delivery vans, and buses sitting panting while long queues of slow-moving passengers embarked and paid for their tickets.

Oh, for the days when all a driver had to do was drive, thought Trish, and buses could move off as soon as the waiting passengers had boarded.

She got to Kingsford eventually and was pleasantly surprised to find parts of it thoroughly attractive. Once a town in its own right, it had long ago been overtaken by the inexorable spreading of the suburbs, and its original seventeenth-century brick houses with their deep white cornices and sloping slate roofs were surrounded by streets of Edwardian half-timbered semis and over-looked by the ugly concrete towers of sixties housing estates.

The High Street was still alive and lined with branches of most of the usual chain stores and building societies. Trish drove into the car-park of Sainsbury's, not wanting to risk infringing unfamiliar parking regulations and find the car clamped or towed away.

Even though she had come to Kingsford to suss out Martin Drakeshill, she found that she wanted to see the place where Kara had died. It wasn't prurience, just a need to make some kind of contact with her friend.

Church Lane proved to be a pleasant quiet street on the edge of the recreation ground, well away from the bustle of the high street. All the cottages in the row were built to the same model and they had quite big gardens. They'd probably once been home to agricultural workers, but must have been gentrified several generations ago.

Each of the sloping front gardens was divided by a flagged path that led up to a plain painted door in the middle of a two-storey plastered building. There were two windows on the ground floor, three above, and the roofs were steeply pitched with working chimney-pots at either end. All the gardens were well kept and the walls and window frames recently painted. Most of the cottages were white or cream, but a few were the unsubtle pinks and greens of the Neapolitan ice cream that had been one of Trish's childhood treats.

Caring neighbours, she thought, and wondered why none of them had heard what was happening to Kara and come to help her or at least called 999.

It was easy to identify Kara's cottage by the white tapes tied around the boundary and the police notice stuck to the front door. As Trish stood at the bottom of the garden, looking up at the house and thinking of what had happened inside it, she was overwhelmed by a tide of anger that pushed aside every other feeling.

Whoever had killed Kara had to be found before he did any more damage. Then, whatever his private torments or inadequacies, he had to be punished as harshly as the law allowed.

At that moment Trish couldn't have cared less about understanding or rehabilitation; still less about forgiveness. She wanted to know that Kara's killer was suffering.

A movement caught her eye and she looked up. In the cottage to the left of Kara's a curtain was twitching. A moment later Trish was ringing the bell.

An elderly woman, very short and with a distinct dowager's hump, opened the door and tried to appear surprised as she twisted her head up to look at Trish.

'I saw that you were in,' Trish said, with a smile, 'and I wondered if I could talk to you about Kara Huggate. She was a friend of mine, you see, and I . . .'

'Oh, you poor thing,' said the woman, backing away, her head still painfully twisted to allow her to see more than her own feet. 'Come in and sit down. You look very tired. I'll put the kettle on.'

'My name's Trish Maguire,' she said, worried that anyone was prepared to let a complete stranger into her house, particularly a woman as frail and unprotected as this one. 'I'm a barrister, and Kara and I met over a case for which she was to be a witness. I'm sure I've got some identification with me. Hold on.'

'Don't worry about that.' The woman patted Trish's hand. 'I can tell you were a real friend of hers. You've got an honest face. You saw me looking at you, didn't you?'

Trish nodded.

'Well, I could see you, too, and I could tell how sad you are. Come into the kitchen while I make tea. I didn't know her well. She only moved in last autumn and we don't mix much in Church Lane. We keep ourselves to ourselves.'

'Although I see that you do have a Neighbourhood Watch,' Trish said, following her down a dark passage towards the kitchen, which looked out over a neatly dug vegetable garden. Her hostess must have help – or perhaps a younger, stronger person living in the house.

'Well, yes, we do, but we don't like to pry, you see.'

'No. I can imagine that. Do you . . . ? I can't go on calling you "you". May I know your name?'

'Of course.' She put the lid on the kettle and wiped her hands on a red and white checked tea towel. 'I'm Mrs Davidson.'

They shook hands. Trish gestured to the garden. 'D'you do all this work yourself, Mrs Davidson?'

'Oh, no. I've a man who comes in once a week. He's just done the winter digging. It's something to do with the frosts. I've never understood, but I let him get on with it. Kara was planning to do all her own gardening, but I don't think she had enough time, really. I mean, look at the weeds. I tried to persuade her to use my Jake, but she wouldn't, said she couldn't afford him.'

Trish stepped closer to the kitchen window and saw that there was an excellent view into Kara's back garden, which didn't seem to her unaccustomed eyes to be particularly untidy.

'You are quite close, aren't you? Did you hear anything on the night she . . . on the night it happened.'

'Well, no, I didn't.' The kettle was boiling and it was not until Mrs Davidson had made the tea that she added, 'but I don't sleep well these days without a pill, and then once I've taken one, a train could come through my room and I wouldn't wake. I'd had one that night, you see, and I didn't hear a thing. If I'd known she was in danger, I'd never have taken it.'

'Of course you wouldn't,' said Trish. 'I understand that.'

'And I haven't dared take any since. Not with him still out there.'

Mrs Davidson put a knitted cosy over the tea-pot and stood with her hands clasped around it, and her head on one side again so that she could stare out of the window. Trish would have liked to reassure her, but she couldn't. On the face of it, it seemed unlikely that anyone would risk returning to the place where he had committed murder, but you never knew. If the killer suspected – or had been told – that there had been a witness, he might well decide he had to silence her.

'So I lie awake thinking about what happened to her. It's awful knowing she suffered like that while I was asleep, that there was no one to help her when . . . Her other neighbours were away skiing, you see.'

Mrs Davidson turned and Trish saw that there was nothing ghoulish in her face, just fear and a bottomless sadness. 'She was a very kind woman.'

Trish nodded. 'Did she have many friends visiting her here?'

'A few. But she was considerate. If she was expecting anyone who might stay late or be noisy, she'd always warn me. Or if she was going to have workmen in or anything. So that I'd always know what any odd noises might be.'

'A good neighbour, in fact.'

'Very good, although sometimes we didn't speak for weeks. I hadn't seen her for several days before she died. I'd heard her sometimes, coming home in the evening when I was in bed, and I saw her to wave at one morning when she was going to work, and I was putting out the milk bottles. But we didn't meet so I never had a chance to tell her.'

'Tell her what?'

'About the man who was hanging around her garden in the night.' Mrs Davidson poured the tea and pushed forward milk, sugar and biscuits. 'If I'd known I wasn't going to see her, I'd have written her a note, but I kept thinking that one day soon we'd meet, and it would be easier to explain it face to face.'

Trish felt her eyes widening.

'He'd done it before, you see. I suppose it might not have been him who killed her, but I can't help being afraid it was. If only I . . .' Mrs Davidson sat with her hands on the tea-cosy, unable to go on.

Eventually Trish supplied a gentle prompt 'You said "before". Does that mean you saw him that night as well? The night she died?'

'Yes.' Her eyes were full of horror.

'And how often had you seen him before?'

'Twice. At least, I think it was twice.'

Trish smiled and willed her voice into even more gentleness. 'Have you told the police about the man?'

'Oh, yes. And I rang them each time I saw him. Straight away. But he went off before they came the first time and when I rang them again they didn't come at all. You see, I don't think they believed me.'

'That must have made you angry.'

Mrs Davidson nodded painfully. 'I told the constable who came round asking questions the morning after they'd found her, and then I said it all over again to the plain-clothes man who came later.' Her smile wavered. 'But I don't see so very well, these days, and when he started to ask for all those details and I got flustered, he was angry. And then I couldn't remember anything.'

'What do you remember about the prowler now?' Trish asked, wishing she could have given the interviewing officer a few lessons in making witnesses feel comfortable enough to do their best for you.

'Well, not really anything more than I told the police. He was middling height and I think he had brown hair, but it was dark and raining, so I can't be sure of anything. And I never saw his face. But he looked furtive, if you know what I mean?'

'Yes, I do. What did he do exactly?'

'Well, I don't know that he did anything. Except watch. I used to see him if I was putting out the rubbish or calling Suet – he's my cat and he's rather fat, a tabby. He – the man – would just be standing in the shadows inside her hedge and looking up towards her windows. She didn't always draw her sitting-room curtains, you see, so anyone could watch her moving about, reading, listening to music. She did that a lot when she was on her own.'

Trish drank some tea. 'You say he was of middling height. Did he seem to you to be thin or fat?'

'I'm not really sure. The police asked that, too. My impression is of a bit of stoutness, not real fatness, but something rounded about him. And furtive.' That seemed to be all she could remember for certain and so she was clinging to it. 'He was scuttly.'

Collons, thought Trish. It has to be Collons. There couldn't have been two scuttly, furtive, middle-aged men in Kara's life.

'What else did the police ask you?' she said aloud.

'Oh, whether poor Kara had any enemies, that sort of thing.'

'And had she?'

'Some of her clients were rather unpleasant.' Mrs Davidson dabbed her lips with a wisp of a lace handkerchief and tucked it back up her sleeve. 'One of them even put something disgusting through her letter box after she had had to take his children into care.'

'Did he? What was it?'

Mrs Davidson shuddered and had recourse to the handkerchief again, before whispering, 'Dog mess.'

'And you told the police that, too, did you?' asked Trish, thinking, Poor Kara.

'Oh, yes. I told them everything I knew. And they wrote some of it down.'

'Well, that's all right, then. They'll know how to take it further.' Trish hoped she was right. 'And you've been very kind, giving me tea like this, but I shouldn't really take up any more of your time.' As she got to her feet she watched Mrs Davidson push herself out of her chair, leaning painfully against the edge of the table. She didn't let go until she was sure of her balance.

'There. I'm up. The police were kind, you know, but I don't think they listened to me very hard or believed me.'

'They should have,' Trish said, holding out her hand. 'You're a good witness. One more thing: do you happen to know whether Kara ever had any dealings with a Kingsford man called Martin Drakeshill?'

'Oh, I shouldn't think so, my dear. He's not a very nice character, and Kara could never have bought such a nice car from his garage. No, I think it's most unlikely. Whoever could have told you that?'

'A man called Blair Collons.' The calculated indiscretion didn't provoke any reaction.

'I don't think I've heard of him. Was he a friend of Kara's?'

'Yes, although I don't think they were very close.'

'No. It doesn't sound like it. Not if he thought she'd ever have had any dealings with Drakeshill. He's a really rather dreadful little man. What Jake, the gardener, calls a "real slimeball".'

Trish couldn't help smiling at the relish with which the insult was delivered. 'Dreadful in what way?'

'They say half the cars he sells have been stolen or else been written off as too dangerous to drive, and his garage is such an eyesore in Station Drive. Why the council haven't closed him down, I'll never know. I write at least once a year to complain, and I'm sure I'm not alone, but no one takes any notice.'

'I see. Well, it doesn't sound likely that he knew Kara, then. I'd better leave you in peace. Thank you so much for the tea.'

'It was a pleasure.'

Trish knew that Mrs Davidson was watching her all the way down the garden path. She deliberately turned as she reached the road and waved. Mrs Davidson waved back and went indoors. How bad was her sight? Nothing she'd said about the man in Kara's garden had ruled out Collons but, then, nothing had positively identified him either.

If it had, Trish would have gone straight to the Kingsford police to point them in his direction. As it was, she didn't see how she could risk it. She set off for Drakeshill's Used Cars.

The first person she stopped in the high street knew exactly where it was and gave her precise directions to Station Drive. She was interested that he showed no surprise at her wish to go there, which suggested that there was nothing too serious generally known against the owner, whatever Collons or the barrister in El Vino's had suggested or, indeed, Mrs Davidson herself.

Station Drive was only about fifteen minutes' leisurely walk from the High Street, and Trish was soon wandering about among the gleaming cars parked in the forecourt. After a while a tall thin boy with the uncoordinated look of someone who doesn't know his own strength shambled out to ask if she wanted any help. He had a badge on his overalls, which gave his name as Wes Jones.

Trish smiled, hoping he wasn't the boy who had been in trouble for assaulting one of Drakeshill's customers with a baseball bat, and told him she was looking for a car for her mother, a nervous driver who wanted an easy little runabout that wouldn't cost her a bomb in servicing and new brake shoes. You know the sort of thing.

'Oh, yeah. Right. Well, you'd better ask the boss. I'll get him. Will you wait?'

'Yes, I'll wait. How kind of you to bother. Thank you.

He looked puzzled by her politeness, but he scuffed his way over the concrete to the one-storey building at the back, in front of which flew huge red-and-black flags with DRAKESHILL'S embroidered on them in gold letters. There was another youth outside it, looking like a much tougher proposition than Wes. As she watched he hauled up the bonnet of an ancient battered Sierra. He was too far away for her to be able to read his name badge or even see his face clearly, but as he bent into the engine then emerged to forage in a large metal tool box for a spanner, she had the impression of taut muscles and considerable strength. 'Hey, Wes,' he called, without bothering to look up from his work, 'how many times you been told not to leave customers alone?'

'I'm not,' Wes said, sounding scared. 'I'm going to get the boss for her. OK, Chompie?'

'Who said you could call me Chompie?' Even from a

distance, Trish could hear the menace in the question.

'Everyone else does,' said Wes resentfully.

The other youth emerged from under the bonnet, wiping his hands on a rag. Wes took a step backwards.

'You've a long way to go before you can.' He laughed. 'Go on, get him for her and tell him from me you need someone to wipe your bum for you.'

He bent into the car through its open window and turned on the ignition. The engine roared into life. Leaving it running, he walked back to stand in front of the bonnet, apparently examining the working parts. He paid no attention whatsoever to Trish or to poor Wes, who hurried, stumbling, into the office.

Charming, thought Trish.

A few moments later a man of not much more than five feet eight with a big paunch and a lot of gold jewellery waddled out of the doorway between the flags. Trish waited where she was.

'So,' he said, when he was within comfortable range. 'My lad says you're looking for a nice little mover for your old lady. That right, is it?'

'That's right,' Trish said, putting on her ditsiest, girliest smile, which was neither very ditsy nor girly. 'I'm looking for a new . . . well, a new second-hand car for my mother, probably one with that kind of opening back and costing not more than about two thousand pounds. Is that possible? Anyway, I don't really know what to get. I've been told by a man who works for the council that you'd be just the man to advise me if I was coming to Kingsford.'

'Oh, yes? And what's your mother driving at the moment?' Drakeshill said, apparently unmoved by the mention of the council.

Trish hadn't exactly expected him to fall on his knees and confess to being part of Collons's great conspiracy, but she had thought he might show a little interest in the identity of the person who'd recommended him. As it was, he looked supremely uninterested. That proved nothing, but it was a useful pointer.

'A Metro,' she said truthfully. 'She likes it but it's very old now and it keeps needing things mended. She's just had new brake shoes, and on her pension that sort of thing gets too expensive. And, well, I just don't think she's getting the best value out of it any more. But she doesn't know anything about cars, and she seems to think that I must know more. I can't think why, because I don't. But she's so scared she's going to be ripped off, and since you were so highly recommended to me, I thought it would be worth coming along to ask you what you thought would be the best kind of car for her.'

Trish wished that she had hair long enough to scoop behind her ears or a string of pearls she could twiddle. She did not think she could have kept up the prattle for much longer, even if she had had enough breath, and so she was glad to see from Drakeshill's impatient eyes that she had made her point. She blinked and smiled expectantly.

'You've come to the right man, love,' he said with a fatherly air that was no more convincing than her own act. Trish could well imagine him going after a defaulting buyer with intent and a weapon, probably with the unpleasant Chompie at his side. She blinked at him and smiled again. 'I know more about used cars than you know about your kitchen sink, love, and I'll see you and your old lady right. You won't have to worry about a thing.'

Trish heaved a sigh, suppressed the itch to smack his complacent face, and tried another wide smile. 'That's just what I hoped you'd say. If only I knew more, I wouldn't have to be so hopeless.'

'Don't you worry now. Ladies shouldn't never have to worry about cars.' He leered at her. She thought she had no right to take exception to that, if anyone had led a man on, she had. She smiled even more flutteringly and told him that it was such a relief to deal with an expert.

'Now, how about this one, then? Nice little Fiesta. Good little runner. A Ford's just what she'd like. Good reliable cars and easy serviced wherever you are.'

'I'm not sure she'd be happy with a yellow car. And respraying's awfully expensive, isn't it?'

'Can be. Or there's this Panda. That's a nice little motor, too.'

'Yes. It does look good, and such a pretty blue. Does the heater work?'

'Oh, sure. Come and have a look.'

Half afraid that he was about to suggest a test drive, Trish obediently sat in the driver's seat and tilted the mirror so that she could look at her own reflection, smoothing her eyebrows. She noticed Drakeshill smiling to himself. It was lucky she'd read that article the other day about the way some women chose their cars. He handed her the key and when she had switched on the ignition he showed her how to turn on the heater.

'I wish I could take you out for a spin,' he said, 'but I'm short-handed just now and I can't leave the boy alone. He's new. Doesn't know his arse from his elbow yet.'

'Oh, I see. Goodness. No. That's OK. There wouldn't be any point, would there? I mean, since it's not me who's going to be driving it. I'll tell my mother what it costs and that it's . . . You are sure that it's safe and in good condition, aren't you?'

'Sweet as sweet can be. Listen to that engine.'

'Yes,' said Trish, hearing an unmistakable rattle. 'It does sound powerful, doesn't it? Now, has it got a full service history, and a – what do they call it – a log book?'

His eyes narrowed for a moment. Trish kept the silly, inquiring look on her face. Then he patted her arm, and made it clear that he wanted to help her out of the driving seat.

'You don't want to worry about log books and service histories, love, whatever your boyfriend in the council's been telling you. That sort of thing is only used by poncy dealers up West to bump up the price of their motors. All you need is an engine that sings like this one and tyres with a good bit of tread.'

Trish thought of asking what 'tread' meant but she didn't think she could make the question convincing. Instead she asked him where he got his cars.

'Part-exchange mostly,' he said fluently, beaming at her. 'My punters have been coming back to me for years every time they want a new motor.'

'I see. Well, look, I think the best thing would be for me to tell my mother about the Panda. Then, if she likes the idea, I could get the AA to come and do a survey, and if they OK it, I can bring her here for a test drive and you could see her Metro to work out how much you could offer her in part-exchange. How would that be?'

'That's fine, if you want to have a survey. But you'd be wasting your money, love. I'll get Chompie over there to give the engine a good going-over. He's my best lad. Then it'll be ready for your mother to come and have a look. When shall we say? Tomorrow morning?'

'I'll have to ask her how she's fixed. I wasn't sure I'd find anything here so I haven't even mentioned that I was coming to look. I'll phone her when I get home and then let you know. What's your number?'

Drakeshill handed her a flamboyant card with a gold sports car embossed at the top and his name printed in flowing script beneath.

'Thanks. Have you got a pen?'

He handed her a gold-plated biro and watched sourly as she said she'd just write down the registration numbers of the Panda and the bright-yellow Fiesta so that her mother would know exactly which cars she was supposed to be looking at. Then she tucked the card into her Coutts diary, murmuring that she could not possibly lose it if it was in there.

'That's great.' She gave him back his pen. 'I'll be in touch.'

'You'd better give me your phone number in case something comes in that's even more suitable for your old lady,' he said, still with the sour expression in his eyes.

'Oh, of course, how silly of me,' she said. Remembering the baseball bat, she told him that her name was Sarah Tisbury and she made up a phone number. She thought she could see derision in his eyes and hoped that it had been provoked by her performance rather than the name she'd just invented.

CHAPTER SIXTEEN

Barry Spinel arrived at the new pub as nearly worried as he ever got. Drakeshill had asked for an urgent meeting. They'd set up the code for that months ago, but Spinel had never expected either of them to have to use it. Something must have happened. And it wasn't likely to be a huge delivery of drugs coming into Kingsford. Drakeshill usually had much more notice of things like that.

Pushing open the door and peering through the fug of smoke and dust, Spinel saw him in a corner near the fruit machines. He looked bad tempered, which was re-assuring. It couldn't be anything too serious. Spinel caught his attention and waved, then pointed to the bar. Drakeshill's face took on an 'at last' kind of expression. Spinel started shouldering his way through the mob at the bar to buy the drinks.

'So what've you got for me that's so rushed, Marty?' He dumped the two pints on Drakeshill's table then reached into the pocket of his leather bomber jacket for the crisps he'd bought. Sometimes biting things helped Drakeshill deal with his temper.

'I haven't. I want you to do something for me.'

Spinel was much too old a hand to ask any questions. He watched Drakeshill over the rim of his glass as he took a swallow of the bitter. Then he took another. It wasn't bad. No wonder the crowd at the bar was four deep in this dingy pub.

Drakeshill reached for the crisp packet and ripped it open. The whole thing fell apart and the contents shot out in all directions, covering the table and falling into both men's laps. Spinel started to shovel together the crisps on the table.

'Leave it, Bal.' Drakeshill's voice was edgy and rough. 'And tell me, why'd a scrawny bitch called Sarah Tisbury be sneaking round my place asking questions?'

'Who?' Spinel abandoned the crisps and, feeling foam on his lip, wiped the back of his hand across his mouth.

'Sarah Tisbury. She was round at my place today asking cheeky questions about log books and registration documents.'

'Doesn't ring any bells with me. Sarah Tisbury? What's she look like?'

'I told you. Scrawny. Five ten or eleven, thin, dark hair sticking up all over her head. Pleased with herself. Fucking pleased with herself. Poncy voice. Not the sort to buy cars from a place like mine. She's a snooper for sure. The question is, Bal, what sort of snooper?'

'I haven't a clue. The Revenue? The VAT? Could be anyone. Or no one. Are you sure she wasn't just trying to buy a car?'

'Yeah. She said she'd been sent by someone from the council.'

'Did she? Then it must be Trading Standards after you for selling dodgy motors.'

'Why? I've been in the game thirty years and more. Why'd they want to have a crack at me now?'

'How should I know?'

'Well, find out. And get it stopped whatever it is. OK?'

It was odd how dangerous Drakeshill could sound, Spinel thought. He'd better get him to cool it.

'Come on, Marty, it could be anything that's triggered an investigation. Half of Kingsford must've heard what happens to customers who complain too loudly when their new car's died on them and, these days, most of them know it's not worth trying to get you into court.'

Drakeshill's face softened, and he punched Spinel on the shoulder.

'Yeah, that's one of the better things you've done for me, Barry-boy, getting that GBH case dropped. Saved me a lot of bother one way and another.'

Spinel looked around to make sure they weren't being overheard, but there was no one within earshot who wasn't absorbed in his own conversation. 'Cheap at the price, Marty,' he said, tapping the side of his nose. 'Even the DI could see the point of keeping you on the street just then. That was a spectacular bust you gave us that time.'

Drakeshill grinned. 'You can tell him there'll be plenty more where that came from if you find out what this Tisbury bitch wanted and get it stopped.'

'I'll do my best, Marty.'

'You better.' Drakeshill laughed suddenly. 'Whoever she was, she made a piss-poor fist of her cover story. She tried to make me believe she wanted a two-grand max automatic mini-hatchback for her mother, when she was flashing a Coutts diary and driving an Audi herself.'

'So what? Just because she can afford an expensive bank account and a decent motor for herself, that doesn't mean she has to buy one for her mother as well. She could've been kosher.'

'Then why'd she take such care to park a good mile

and a half away from my place? I sent Chompie after her when she left, and he had to track her right down the High Street to Sainsbury's.'

'Why'd you do that, Marty?' Spinel drank some more of the surprisingly robust beer. 'Just because you thought she came from the council?'

'Partly. And then, like I say, she was asking cheeky questions about log books and service histories. But it was when she started taking down registration numbers, bold as brass, that I knew she had to be a snooper. I don't like to see that sort of thing, Barry. That's pushing it, that is.'

'It's Trading Standards, Marty. It must be.' Unless it's the crime squad, taking this route because I stopped them having him arrested. I'll break their sodding necks if it is. And the DI's.

'Anyway, the boy got *her* registration number.' Drakeshill handed over a folded piece of paper. 'Like I say, I want you to find out who she is and where she comes from and stop it. I don't want any nosy parkers around the place just now. OK?'

'Sure.' Watching Drakeshill's face as he tasted the beer, Spinel grinned and raised his own glass. 'I know. Amazing, isn't it? We should come here more often.'

Drakeshill settled himself more comfortably against the padded chair back and stretched his legs as though to signal that business was over.

'Maybe, old son. It's certainly better than that horse-piss you made me drink the other day. So, how's your murder coming along?'

Spinel shrugged. 'They're killing themselves with overtime and crashing every budget in the place, but so far they've got a whole lot of nothing.'

'Who're the suspects?'

'Far as I know, most money's on the old Kingsford

Rapist, with an outside each-way bet on some new man in Huggate's life who was playing copy-cat.'

'Oh?' Drakeshill looked intrigued. 'Who's the new bloke, then? I saw a photo of her in the paper. She was no oil painting, was she? Was he blind?'

'They don't know anything yet.'

'Piss-poor work, if you ask me. They've had how many days?'

'Seven.'

'Hopeless, the whole mob of you, Bal. How can it take seven days to pin down one murdering bastard?' Drakeshill laughed and drank some more, practically smacking his lips before he wiped off the foam.

'So, what's the news on the street, then, Marty? Anything for me to feed the DI with?'

'Funny you should ask that. I did hear a handy whisper the other day.'

'Oh, yeah?'

'Yeah. Another load's due to be delivered to our friends the week after next. They say this lot is coming in a container of rugs from the east somewhere. Want me to find out more?'

'Is the Pope a Catholic?'

Barry Spinel spent the drive back to the nick trying to remember whether he had ever heard the name of Drakeshill's snooper before, but he couldn't place it.

The only person in the office when he got back there was Doughface, looking as dull as ever. He asked her if she had ever heard of anyone called Tisbury. Her mind worked in its usual laborious fashion. He could almost hear the wheels cranking.

'No, Sarge. Can't say I have. While you're here, you wanted a report on all the successful drugs busts in schools last year.'

Was she stupid or did she do it to bug him? He looked at her fat face and saw that there was nothing behind her eyes. Not deliberate, then. Still, it made him want to hit her. At least she'd have to react if he did that. His fists tingled. 'I asked for the names of all known school-age dealers, Cloth Ears. Don't you ever listen?'

Still she didn't react. All she did was say calmly, 'You didn't, actually. You asked for the figures I've produced. If you want the names of the dealers, I can abstract them for you. It won't take long.'

Abstract them, indeed!

'Well, get on with it, then. You must've known that's what I wanted from the reports. TITS, Cloth Ears.' At that moment he wasn't trying to wind her up, but suddenly it seemed a good idea so he said it again: 'TITS, Betsy. Becky. Whatever your name is. TITS. You know what I'm talking about?'

'Think it through, Sunshine,' she said, as calm as if she was asking for a pound of potatoes. 'And my name is Bethany, Sarge.'

He couldn't have been more surprised if she'd taken her clothes off. Looking into her eyes again, he saw something moving, like a camera lens had suddenly opened. And it wasn't machinery he could see either. It was laughter. If he'd been a man to feel uncomfortable, it would have happened then. As it was, he stood back on his heels and looked her up and down as though she was a prize heifer.

'Well, well, well . . .'

'Said the policeman to the man with three heads.'

He snapped his mouth shut. A moment later he laughed aloud. 'Talk about finding a gold nugget in a load of ball-bearings! You do surprise me, Bethany. Bethany? I can't use a name like that. Anyone ever call you Beth?'

'No,' she said, with a coolness that made his eyes open even wider. 'Cloth Ears will do fine, though, Sarge. Or Doughface.'

Once again he had trouble keeping his teeth together. He was back at his desk before he realised how much more fun it was going to be winding her up now that he knew she had balls. At last life was looking up.

Refreshed, he thought he'd better check out the owner of the Audi for Drakeshill before he did anything else. It was never a good idea to keep the man waiting when he was angry. He reached for the phone.

CHAPTER SEVENTEEN

Back in her flat, Trish was still trying to decide what to do about Collons. The trip to Kingsford hadn't really helped. She'd learned nothing about Martin Drakeshill, except that his manner and appearance fitted the picture she'd already got of him.

It was easy to imagine the man she'd met beating up someone who'd crossed him then wriggling out of the charge by trading favours with the police, but she still couldn't see him as the influential conspirator of Collons's terrors. On the other hand, she had no difficulty whatsoever in seeing Collons as the furtive, scuttling watcher in Kara's garden on the night she was murdered.

Almost irresistibly tempted to phone the police, Trish made herself reread Kara's letter. By the end, she knew she had to go on until she had something concrete to prove to herself that Collons's stories were as mad as they seemed. Then she'd be justified in reporting what she suspected.

His main contention was that Kara had died because of the questions they had both been asking about the contaminated land on which the council's social housing was to be built. It should be easy enough to find out more about that.

Trish rang round her contacts in the environmental pressure groups and was eventually given the number of a small outfit called the Kingsford Green Brotherhood, who might be able to help.

'KGB. Roger here. How may I help you?' said a brisk young voice over the phone. It sounded amused enough to suggest that the name had been no accident.

Trish sat more easily in her chair. 'With a bit of information, I hope. If the KGB ever hands that out.' Roger laughed. 'This version does. It's what we're here for. What is it you want to know?'

'I heard a rumour about some land plumb in the middle of Kingsford, which the council is going to use for housing dysfunctional children. I've been told that it's poisoned with chemical residues of some kind. Can that possibly be right? As a site for children?'

'It's not quite as bad as it sounds. Though we were worried, too, when we first heard about the scheme, given that so many behavioural problems are caused by environmental pollutants. Or food additives. Did you know . . . ?'

'So it *is* true.' Trish did not want to hear again about E numbers or particulates or benzene derivatives. She wanted as much real information as she could get and as quickly as possible.

'In a way. But we've been assured by the council's planners that the land will be fully decontaminated before any building starts. Before the foundations are dug, in fact.'

'And d'you believe them?'

'On balance, yes.' Roger's voice had lost its laughter, but Trish couldn't hear any doubt in it, just concern and calculation. 'They've promised to allow us to take soil samples before they bring in the diggers for the foundations. There'd be no point in offering that if they were lying.'

Trish thought of Drakeshill's saying that it would be fine for her to bring in the AA to check one of his cars if she wanted, even though he thought she'd be wasting her money. Kingsford Council could easily be playing a similar game with the KGB on the assumption that giving them permission to take samples would persuade them that they didn't have to do it.

'And will you take the samples?'

'Of course. And we won't let them get away with any lick-and-a-promise kind of clean-up, I can assure you.'

Trish wished that she had a videophone. She wanted to know what Roger looked like. He sounded as though he could not be more than about twenty-five, and yet 'lick and a promise' was the kind of phrase her grandmother would have used. It seemed an odd choice for a young man, even for someone who enjoyed calling his green pressure group after one of the most repressive organisations on earth.

'And in any case,' he was saying, 'they've accepted Flower Brothers' tender for the decontamination work.'

The admiration in his voice seemed to invite a response. Trish wasn't sure exactly what it should be. 'And they're good, are they?' she said at last.

There was a short pause, then Roger said, 'Who exactly are you?'

So, it had been the wrong response. Trish decided to lie. If by any remote chance there turned out to be something in Collons's wilder suspicions, she would not want her name linked to any questions about the decontaminated land.

'Oh, my name's Sarah Tisbury. I'm a freelance

journalist looking into contaminated-land scandals for a possible article.'

'You should have said before, and I needn't have wasted your phone bill. There's no scandal about the chemical contamination.'

'You sure about that, Roger?'

'Positive. The scandal's in the damage to King's Park, and the fact that Goodbuy's were ever given permission to build a megastore there.'

'I'm sorry?'

'You haven't been doing your homework, have you, Sarah? Goodbuy's, the supermarket chain.'

'Look, I know who Goodbuy's are.'

'Well, that's a relief. OK. So, Goodbuy's owned the contaminated land and they gave it to Kingsford Council in return for permission to build on part of King's Park.'

'Oh, planning gain, you mean. Isn't that fairly normal?'

'Planning gain, indeed.' Roger sounded outraged. 'It's corruption, that's what it is. Not at all pure but very, very simple. And very, very nasty. Goodbuy's, who already make gigantic profits, are so greedy they want more every year. There's no point in trying to build in the middle of a place like Kingsford, these days – no room for container lorries or a big car park for the customers, and there are too many listed buildings all around for the kind of demolition they'd need to make it work.'

'I see. So where's this King's Park, then?'

'Just on the edge of the borough. Although it's called a park, it's mainly trees and scrub now, what's left of the original sixteenth-century deer park. There's never been any restricted access so we always assumed it was common land, but it isn't. It stayed in the royal family until Charles II left it to one of his bastards. Now it belongs to someone who lives in Argentina, and he couldn't care less about flogging off a couple of acres to Goodbuy's.'

The outrage in his voice sounded a bit exaggerated and so Trish said, 'But that seems fair enough. If he owned it, I mean. Why should he keep it for public access when it was his?'

'Yeah, there's nothing wrong with that. Just with Goodbuy's getting permission to build. They'd never have got it if they hadn't bought off the planning department. And since even Kingsford Council wouldn't accept cold cash – too obvious – and they already have all the swimming pools and libraries they can use . . .'

'They're unique, then.'

'All the swimming pools and libraries they can afford to keep open,' Roger amended, with the laugh back in his voice. 'So Goodbuy's had to think a bit more laterally and discovered that they did have one asset the council needed. They knew of the plans for the new social-housing unit, and that the council didn't have the necessary land. Goodbuy's had owned the site in the centre of the borough for years, knew they couldn't use it themselves and offered it.'

'So everyone was happy,' Trish said, thinking that whoever had brokered the deal had been pretty prag-matic and not done too bad a job. But perhaps there was just enough nefariousness about it to have given Collons the idea of a hidden scandal to use for his own fantasies. Or perhaps as a smokescreen for what he had done to Kara.

'Everyone at the council and Goodbuy's might have been happy,' Roger was saying, 'but it's a disaster for the borough. If the building goes ahead, and we won't be able to stop it for much longer, Kingsford will lose a lot of its one naturally wild space. Trees will be felled, there'll be even more pollution, greatly increased traffic, more high street shops going to the wall, and the end of all the small food retailers. Can you think of anything much worse?'

'I'm new to the subject.' Trish made herself sound humble. 'I can see I've a lot to learn.'

'You're telling me, Sarah. But you will write it up, won't you? The more people who get to hear about this sort of sleaze the better.'

The word 'sleaze' made Trish wonder for a second whether Collons could have been right. But it seemed impossible. No one was going to set out to kill Kara to stop her talking about a deal that wasn't really even corrupt.

'Are you still there, Sarah?'

'Yes, yes, I am. I was just thinking about the best way to go on from here.'

'Well, do your best for us,' said Roger. 'We can do with all the publicity we can get. There'll be plenty once they send the bailiffs in, but by then it won't do us any good.'

'Bailiffs?'

'Yeah. We've got people in the trees already in King's Park, and the contractors will need to get them shifted before they start felling. That'll get on the TV news, but it's always too late at that stage. Look at Newbury.' Roger's voice was roughening, perhaps with suspicion. 'What did you say your surname was?'

'Tisbury.' Trish assumed that as soon as she got off the line he would be checking with Goodbuy's head office – or Kingsford Council – to find out whether they had employed the mythical Sarah Tisbury to ferret out details of the KGB's plans to disrupt the building work. She was quite glad she had lied about her name.

'Will you send me a copy of anything you write? We like to photostat any useful pieces and circulate them to all the interested groups.'

'Yeah, sure. If I manage to place it.' Trish congratulated

herself on remembering a journalist friend talking about placing articles rather than selling them. She hoped it would add a hint of verisimilitude and soothe Roger's suspicions. 'Look, while I've got you, can you tell me anything about a colourful Kingsford character I've been hearing about? A man called Ducksmount or something like that. Something to do with dumping ancient cars and maybe CFC pollution.'

'You mean Drakeshill,' Roger said, sounding cheerful again. 'Martin Drakeshill. I doubt if there's any bother with CFCs unless he's fly-tipped his own fridge some-where. No, he's a straightforwardly bent second-hand car dealer.'

'Really bent?'

'I'd have said so.' Roger laughed. 'But perhaps not quite as bent as he likes to pretend. He's been flogging cars in Station Drive for as long as I can remember, and he's a bit of a joke round here, what with the huge red and gold flags he flies all round his forecourt, and his gold bracelet and air of "what a bad boy I am".'

'Would you buy a car from him?'

'I wouldn't buy a car from anywhere, Sarah. Would you?'

Silly question. Of course not. He'd use a bike.

'But I've known people who have bought from him,' Roger went on, in a fair-minded way, 'and, as far as I know, they were no worse than anyone else's.'

'I see. Look, you've been very helpful.'

'It's what the KGB is here for. Let us know if you need anything else.'

Trish put down the phone and thought about calling George's office. It would be so easy. 'Kingsford,' she said aloud, to stop the rot before it could eat into her determination to hold on until he said he understood why she had been so angry.

The phone began to ring. Absentmindedly she picked it up and said her name.

'Ah, Trish, it's you now, is it?' said her father. 'Trish, are you there? All I want to do is talk. Trish? Trish?'

'I can't talk now. I'm sorry.'

'That's OK. Tell me a time that would be better. I know you're very busy. I rang your chambers and they said you'd be working at home.'

'Well, they shouldn't have.' She gritted her teeth as she realised how childish that must have sounded. 'I'm sorry to be churlish, but I really am very busy. I can't talk now.'

'Fine. I'll try again later another day.'

'No, I . . .' But Trish was talking to the air. Her father had gone. Bloody man. Why couldn't he leave her alone? She dialled the number of the doctors' surgery where her mother worked.

'Hi, Meg?' she said, when they were connected.

'Trish, love. Has something happened?' Her mother's voice, usually so calm and matter-of-fact, had an edge of anxiety.

'No. No, I'm sorry to have worried you. No, it's just that my case has settled and I wondered whether you were busy tonight or might like some dinner?'

'No, no, I'm not busy.' Meg's voice was back to normal, apart from a residue of surprise. 'I'd love to see you, but I don't get off till eight tonight, and it would take me another forty, fifty minutes to get up to town, so . . .'

'I've got time for once. Why don't I come and pick you up at the surgery at eight and take you to the Black Bear?'

'Well, that would be lovely, if it won't make you too late back. I can't stop to talk now, but if it's really all right I'll see you here at eight. 'Bye.'

'Well, that's all right, then,' Trish said aloud, as she put down the phone.

CHAPTER EIGHTEEN

'Where's Owler?' called Bill Femur into the clatter and blather of the incident room.

'Checking out someone called Bob Smith, who had a drink with Huggate when she first came to Kingsford,' said Caroline Lyalt, turning round to smile at him.

In spite of the smile, she looked dispirited and rather grubby from spending too long indoors and eating too many sandwiches and takeaways. They all did. In a way she'd had the worst job of all, forcing the five known survivors of the Kingsford Rapist to go back into their old traumas in case there was any useful information that had been missed in the original interviews.

Some of the survivors had worked through what had happened to them, she reported, and been able to talk relatively freely, but one was driven to anguished, unstoppable tears as Caroline had probed too far into what had happened when she was pinned down on the floor by a masked man who drove a screwdriver up inside her.

No wonder Caroline looked so unhappy. Femur hoped her actress was giving her enough support and not whingeing about the long hours that kept her away from home. That had happened once or twice before. If he'd been one to interfere, he'd have gone round to their flat and read the Riot Act. But he wasn't. You never knew what you might upset if you started poking your nose into other people's relationships. And he'd have been outraged if anyone had talked to Sue on his behalf.

The cork board was much fuller than it had been. There were photographs of all the different types of chisel and screwdriver that could have been used on Kara; there were huge blow-ups of the bruises on her body beside the slightly bigger marks left on the earlier victims. And there were more close-up photographs of Kara's internal injuries.

Femur had a few new prints put up every day to keep the team's anger hot. He looked further along the wall to the whiteboard in case anyone had contributed anything new. It was still covered with red and blue scrawls, mostly his and Tony Blacker's. There were rows of dates, times, and names, half of them crossed out, and lists of questions with ever bigger question marks. But there was nothing new except that some joker had been playing noughts and crosses in one corner. Femur couldn't believe any of the local officers were still farting around when they had a vicious sex criminal on the loose.

'Can I help, Guv?'

'Not really, Cally. When you see Owler, will you tell him I want him?'

'Sure,' she said, with all the simple acceptance that made her so easy to work with. She had none of Blacker's resentment at the thought of the boss keeping from her things he was discussing with someone else.

'Any joy from anything your victims gave you?' he asked, thinking, What a stupid phrase! Joy is the last thing Caroline's had anywhere in this investigation.

'Not yet.' She stood up, holding both hands to the small of her back and stretching. Femur knew the ache she was feeling. He had once thought it was caused by working too long at a desk; now he knew that it came from holding the anger too tight inside you.

'Like I said, Guv, they all swear that they said nothing to anyone about the sock or the chisel. But, you know, I'm not sure how reliable that is. They're all still . . .' she paused, then said temperately '. . . troubled by what happened, and each of them has blocked bits out in her own way. Any one of them could've talked at the time and got no idea now what she actually said.'

'Right. Well, tell me if anything comes up. And by the way, Cally, you might find out who's buggering about with the whiteboard and get them to grow up.'

She looked over to the messy board, frowning. Then her face cleared as she focused on the noughts and crosses. 'I'll handle it, Guv.'

Femur went back to his desk and the confidential files of all the officers who had worked on the original rape cases. The one that interested him most was Barry Spinel's. None of the other officers had any connection whatsoever with Kara, but Spinel had met her at least three times, and maybe many more.

It was only a week or two between the last certain meeting they'd had and the first time she'd drawn hearts and flowers around the letter S in her diary.

And that wasn't all. Femur had disliked Spinel from the moment they'd first spoken on the phone, and when they met the dislike had grown. Femur had never admired the kind of cocky air of half-suppressed violence that Spinel exuded, or the lack of conscience.

He also had a very odd record with a lot of questions in it. His file was the kind Femur had seen often enough to make him go cold as he read it.

There were no disciplinary offences recorded against Spinel, but there was a whole string of complaints: from the public; from fellow officers; and from the CPS. There had been accusations of brutality, of sexism, of prisoners' property going missing, and files and evidence as well.

None of the complaints had ever been substantiated, but Spinel had changed jobs and forces rather too often for Femur's liking.

He tried to be fair and reminded himself that making complaints against arresting officers had always been some villains' favourite way of delaying proceedings and discrediting prosecution evidence; and there were some officers whose spectacular success made lazier colleagues resentful enough to invent internal difficulties. A mass of complaints against one man could be no more than coincidence, but it could also flag a bent officer more clearly than anything else except too smart a car, long-haul holidays and too many designer clothes.

Some of the senior officers' names recorded in the file were familiar to Femur from his own past, and he decided to ring up a few of them informally to get an off-the-record flavour of Spinel before he tried the Complaints Investigation Bureau. Once you let them in on an investigation they tended to take it over. Femur wanted to nail Kara's killer himself. He reached for the phone and rang the first on the list.

The exercise was as frustrating as everything else about the damn case. No one Femur wanted was in. He left messages all over the country and sat drumming his fingers on the desk waiting for someone to ring back or for Steve Owler to reappear. Eventually he cracked and sent a fax to the private house of an old mate who was now with the anti-corruption squad, asking for a confidential note of any information they might have on Spinel. At the foot of the fax, he scrawled in black felt-tip:

'Don't worry too much about slander, but keep the inquiry to yourself, will you, and phone me at home with the results? Bill.'

'You wanted me, Guv.'

Femur turned back from the fax machine, keeping his face blank. Bugger it! He felt like a PC on his first day who'd been caught with his finger up his nose.

Owler, who was chewing something as usual, seemed to notice nothing wrong.

'Yes. Steve. Right. We'll go into my office.'

'D'you want a cup of tea first, Guv? If you don't mind me saying so, you look as though you could do with one. And a sarnie?'

'A cup of tea would be great. But hold the sandwiches, unless you're going to faint from hunger.'

Owler laughed as he slouched over to the kettle and waved the half-eaten roll he'd been carrying in his left hand. Femur shook his head. Talk about hollow legs! The boy must be hollow right down to his little toes.

Femur went back to his office. A minute or two on his own would give him a chance to get rid of the original of the fax. If there were anything in the Spinel theory, everyone would get to hear of it in the end, but he didn't want any word of his suspicions reaching Spinel until he had something more solid to go on.

Three minutes later, he was stirring sugar into the depressing caramel-coloured liquid Steve Owler had brought him in a bendy white plastic cup and listening to an account of what a good copper Barry Spinel was.

'Always gets a result, Guv. The drugs squad have done much better since he went over there. He goes after every suspect, whoever they are, unlike some who think if you're rich enough you can do what you want. Spinel's clobbered a lot of nasty little public-school boys who've been dealing on the side, and he's put up with a good bit of flak from the great and the good trying to defend their little darlings. He's not one to mind making enemies, however many friends they've got on the Police Committee. And he's got good informants, too. There's been a steady stream of mules and minor dealers arrested.'

'But no big importers,' Femur said. 'Is this what you're telling me?'

'Well, yeah, maybe. But no one else has got them either, and at least Spinel gets the mules and the runners. Everyone thinks he's great. Except the DI that is, and that's only because Spinel shows him up.'

'Right.' This wasn't the moment to lecture Owler on the proper respect due to a senior officer. 'But Spinel didn't do much good when he was working on the Kingsford Rapist, did he?'

'No one did,' said Owler quickly, adding after a moment, 'S for Spinel? No, Guv. Honestly. I told you before. You're barking up the wrong tree there. It couldn't be him. I know he's in Huggate's diary, but he'd never have been the kind of man to make her draw hearts and flowers. And, anyway, why would he want to knock her off?'

Femur laughed. He'd never been much of a one for amateur dramatics, but he thought he'd done it quite well. Owler's tight jaw muscles relaxed visibly, so it must have been fairly convincing.

'I can't imagine,' he said, keeping a jolly smile on his face and thinking he deserved an Oscar nomination for that, too. 'No, I've just been wondering how far to trust his judgement. He seems to have known Kara better than anyone else here, even though he didn't like her. You were right about that. And he's come up with some interesting ideas about her and who her attacker could've been.'

'Oh, I see. Well, I don't know, Guv. I wouldn't have put

him down as the sensitive type who sits down and listens to women much, or cares what they're thinking.' He frowned, thinking hard. Then he shrugged. 'On the other hand, he has got a rich wife, and so . . .

'Rich wife?' The best possible disguise for a bent copper with more money than he should have from pay-offs and kick-backs. 'Has he? Have you met her?'

'No. She's not the type to mix with the Job. She's a headhunter in the City. Bit of a success story, they say. Earns a fortune. I can't see why she'd stay with him if he didn't have something other than, well . . .'

Femur, whose mind was beginning to work faster as he thought of the implications of the rich-wife story, looked up as the boy paused and was amused to see him looking self-conscious. Caroline must have been regaling the incident room with Femur's unparalleled dislike of smut. There was very little that bonded a disparate team as well as sharing surprise – and contempt – at the guv'nor's shibboleths.

'A good big lunch-box,' he supplied, smiling. Owler smiled back in relief. 'OK, Steve. Take that as read. A rich wife could do a lot to stop you worrying about making enemies on the Police Committee. Has anyone ever suggested that his mind's not totally on the Job?'

'Spinel? Fuck, no. Sorry, Guv. If anything, the opposite. He's got more people banged up than anyone else. He gives it everything he's got, whatever you've heard. He may bend the odd rule about dealing with suspects – I dare say he's even laid a finger on one or two in the past. But it's all been in a good cause.'

'Great. Thanks, Steve. Just what I wanted to know. Now, how're you doing?'

'Not so bad. Although Bob Smith isn't any good to us either. Hasn't seen Huggate in three and a half months and, anyway, he's got an unbreakable alibi.'

Femur raised his eyebrows. 'How unbreakable?'

'Totally. He was in hospital, Guv. Having an operation on his knee. Cartilage. According to the nurse, he couldn't stand.'

'That's him out, then. How many more on your list?'

'Another six.' Owler sounded bored.

'Still, it's got to be done. Stick to it.'

'Cool, Guv.'

Femur watched him go, thinking, If Spinel is involved in Kara's death, then the connection must be drugs. Nothing I've heard about her suggests she'd have liked him unless he was pretending to be someone else – decent, even gentle. He'd only have bothered with that if it was worth his while. And the only thing Femur could think of that would make it worth Spinel's while was drugs. After all, they only met in the first place because an underage client of hers was having trouble with a drug-dealer.

The idea seemed to be slipping out of his grasp, like a wet tumbler in the sink, but he held on, trying to work through the few facts he had, checking the logic of his suspicions as he went.

'Caroline!' he yelled through the open door a few minutes later.

'Guv?' She had her hand over the telephone receiver, and was obviously busy.

'How about a change from interviewing rape victims?'

'I wouldn't say no.'

'Right. When you've finished your call, then.'

There was a faint smile on her face as she came into his office and closed the door. She sat in the chair opposite his desk and sighed as she took the weight off her feet.

'We'll get there in the end, Cally,' he said.

'We nearly always do. But it's a tough case.'

'Sure it isn't more than that?' It was worth taking a

moment out to make sure she wasn't unhappy. Her well-being was essential to the team – and to him. 'Trouble at home, maybe?'

'Jess is having a tough time right now,' she admitted, rubbing the space between her eyes. 'And she needs more than I've got to offer at the moment. Her agent's giving her the runaround and her confidence is a bit iffy. I do what I can. But this is *my* job and she needs to under– Sorry, Guv. You don't need to hear this. We've been here before. We'll sort it. Now, what d'you want me to do?'

'A while ago Kara was after a schoolboy crack dealer,' Femur said, respecting Caroline's decision to keep her life private. 'A Sergeant Spinel from the drugs squad told me that they were well aware of the dealer's activities over there and have been watching him, presumably to get enough evidence for a successful trial. I want you to find out – discreetly, mind, and not from Spinel himself – whether they know where the boy got his supplies.'

'Sure.'

She never asked stupid questions or tried to show how clever she was, she just did as she was told; and if she thought what you wanted was right off the wall, she'd say so without making herself unpleasant – or sulky – about it. And then if you told her to stuff her objections and get on with it, she would. As he watched her leave his office, he decided she was worth her weight in bacon sandwiches.

God! He was hungry. Steve Owler's appetite must have infected him, after all. He drank the cooling tea the boy had brought and thought about getting away from the incident room for a proper meal that evening. Tony Blacker might be back and they could go out together and see what Kingsford could offer them. Meanwhile, Spinel.

Femur was well aware of the temptations of drugs squad officers everywhere. It was so easy to siphon off a half-kilo of this or that when you'd made a big bust and go into business on your own account. And then there were a lot of big dealers willing to spend 'twenty or thirty large' on making evidence of their crimes disappear before the CPS lawyers could see it.

If Spinel were in the pay of a big dealer, say, who'd been employing the schoolboy who'd sold the crack to Kara's client, he could well have been told to block her questions before they did any damage to the dealing network. And it was just possible, if she'd been persistent enough and got close enough to the identity of the original supplier, that he'd decided she'd be better out of the way.

Would Spinel have agreed to that?

Femur thought about the man he'd met, flexing his thigh muscles, thrusting his physical strength in your face, telling you with every gesture he made just how tough he was and how little he cared about your opinion. He was probably fairly free with his fists under the right provocation, but murder was a different matter.

Of course, he needn't necessarily have known anything about the murder plans. He could have reported Kara's intransigence to his Mr Big, handed over her address and whatever he knew about the layout of her cottage, and her likely movements, and the job could've been done by someone quite different.

Femur smiled sadly as he recognised the temptation. He'd always hated finding that any copper was bent, even one as dislikable as Barry Spinel, so he'd invented a scenario that would let Spinel off the worst of the hooks. But it wouldn't do. If anything in the scenario was true, Spinel would have had to know about it all. Otherwise, his Mr Big wouldn't ever have known enough about the

Kingsford Rapist's MO. Sod it! Either Spinel had nothing to do with Kara's death at all, or he was right there in the frame.

If so, this would be the first time in Femur's direct experience that anyone had paid a copper to set the scene for murder – or to carry it out. Still, it could have happened. There'd been whispers for years of contract killings fixed by police officers and at least one death within the force itself that some people believed to be the work of coppers with too much to hide.

The more Femur thought about it, the more it made sense. Spinel could so easily have set Kara up by having an affair with her. He was well pleased with himself and would probably be quite happy to seduce anyone, just to prove he could do it, even a woman ten years his senior. Whoever Kara's killer had been, he had known exactly what he was doing and how to get into her house without making enough noise to wake the neighbours – or give her time to push her panic alarm. True, there had been signs of forcible entry through the back door, but they could have been made after she was dead, as a distraction.

And Spinel would've known just how to distract the SOCOs from anything he didn't want them to see.

If he had done it, or told someone else how to do, it was a pity, from his point of view, that his knowledge had been so precise. If the killer hadn't moved the body into the exact same position as the first dead victim, Femur would've been much more likely to believe in the scene.

'Keep an open mind next time, lad.'

Femur could remember his first CID sergeant telling him that after he'd buggered a case completely by charging towards a suspect he was sure was guilty and trampling over some crucial evidence on the way.

'That way you won't make a flaming arse of yourself again and I won't be tempted to kill you myself.'

As though that remembered voice had sharpened his wits, Femur remembered that Spinel had had no first-hand knowledge of the case in which the Kingsford Rapist's victim died. He had dealt only with the first, in which the victim had been damaged – and traumatised – but had lived to tell Caroline Lyalt all about it.

Still, he must have had enough contacts left in CID and the labs to pick up whatever information he needed. He couldn't be ruled out yet. Femur decided he'd better get Tony Blacker on to all the possible sources of the relevant crime-scene photographs and find out whether any had been borrowed or gone missing, and whether any of the people who worked there was particularly friendly with Sergeant Spinel – or had an expensive drug habit they shouldn't have been able to afford.

CHAPTER NINETEEN

Trish got home from an exasperating day in Gloucester, paying her debt to Dave with a tiny unwinnable legal aid case that should have been handled by the youngest tenant in chambers, to find a heap of envelopes on her doormat. She made herself some tea and took them to her favourite sofa.

Her cleaner was not due for another two days so the red and purple cushions were still hollowed into the shape of her long body, ready for her. She sank into them and let her head fall back against the softest of them all. She realised that she had a headache, had had it in fact for most of the day, but she didn't have the energy to go in search of painkillers. The tea would probably help.

As she drank, the warmth spread down through her chest like an internal poultice. After a while she started to rip open the envelopes. Bills went into one heap on the floor, circulars and empty envelopes into another, and letters that needed answering into a third. There didn't seem to be anything very interesting. Even the bills were what she had expected.

The last envelope was large and brown with a printed

label addressed to her as Miss Patricia Maguire and it carried no stamp or postmark. Assuming that it must contain more rubbish she didn't want, and surprised that anyone had bothered to deliver it by hand, she was tempted to throw it away.

Something stopped her and she ripped it open, then shook the contents on to her chest. A red plastic folder filled with newsprint fell out, releasing a shower of cuttings that fluttered round her like feathers after a pillow fight.

Swearing, she got up and picked one small piece of paper out of her tea, shaking the drops off it and laying it to dry on the edge of the fireplace. The headline caught her eye:

WOMAN'S BODY FOUND IN CANAL

Trish read the short paragraph to discover that the naked body of a woman had been found in the Kennet and Avon Canal and was so far unidentified. Puzzled, she looked for a date on the cutting, but there wasn't one. The paper was thin between her fingers and brownish-yellow. Quite old, then. She smoothed it out and put it back on the edge of the fireplace before searching among the rest of the cuttings for a note to explain them.

She shook each of the coloured cushions in case it had floated behind one, then pulled the heavy square black ones off the seat so that she could feel down all the sides of the frame. There was a collection of pens, paperclips, crumbs and coins, and even – shamingly – some eggshell fragments, but there was no letter.

Puzzled and wary, she bent down to collect the rest of the cuttings and carried them to the dining room table, where she spread them out. The heavy black type of the violent headlines made a sinister patchwork on the smooth tabletop. She pulled out a chair and started to read.

CANAL BODY IDENTIFIED

Police say the body found in the Kennet and Avon Canal yesterday is that of Janet Peasdown-Jones, 29. She had been raped before being strangled. An unemployed man is helping with enquiries.

DOG DIES TO SAVE OWNER IN CANAL KILLING

Police are appealing for information on anyone seen with severe dog bites on his face and arms. Forensic evidence shows that black Labrador Bluejohn fought bravely to save his mistress, Janet Peasdown-Jones when she was attacked.

Before the dog was strangled and thrown into the canal, he must have marked his killer's arms and face. Anyone with anything to report should call the incident room on the following number . . .

There were twenty cuttings in all, some clearly from broadsheets, others from the more hysterical tabloids. They followed the case from the discovery of the body, through various arrests, and on to a long, expensive and ultimately fruitless search for a local man whose DNA matched samples recovered from the victim's body. There was also a retrospective article from one of the most serious weeklies, arguing the case for a national DNA register that would have enabled the police to narrow down their suspects to perhaps five men in the whole country, who could then have been thoroughly investigated.

Trish stared at the cuttings, trying to work out who could have sent them to her and why. She had never met anyone called Peasdown-Jones; she had never even been near the Kennet and Avon Canal, as far as she knew. There was no connection of any kind between her and the case, and yet someone had bothered to collect accounts of it and deliver them anonymously to her door.

There were only two likely reasons: one, that someone who knew – or guessed – that she was trying to find out more about Kara's killer believed there was a connection between him and the man who had murdered Janet Peasdown-Jones and wanted Trish to have the information; the other, that someone was trying to frighten her.

There were few people who knew of her interest in Kara's death: George, who would never have sent the cuttings in a million years, however angry she might have made him; Kara's mother, who could have had no more reason to do it than George; Kara's elderly neighbour, Mrs Davidson, who was just as unlikely; and Blair Collons.

Trish thought of his warning that the people who had killed Kara would soon come after her, afraid that Kara might have passed on to her dangerous secrets about the Kingsford conspiracy. Could he have sent the cuttings to try to make her believe that she, too, was a target for the conspirators?

It was, of course, possible that the cuttings had no connection with Kingsford or Kara. Whoever had sent them must have known that they would worry Trish, coming like that out of the blue, anonymously, and with no explanation. Perhaps someone she had annoyed had wanted to give her a bad evening.

But who?

There must be plenty of candidates, she told herself drily. My father, for one. Although I don't suppose even he could have sunk that low.

An idea slid into her mind, an idea and a memory. She was not sure quite what they were at first. There were no distinct details, only a powerful feeling of security and a fuzzy mental picture.

Her work had made her familiar with most of the techniques used for counselling disturbed adults and children and she knew that one of the questions often asked to release their memories was: 'You're in a room: who else is there?'

In her particular room the light was dim and she was warm and tightly held. More details become clear as she concentrated. The tightness around her came from cream-coloured cellular blankets, tucked firmly between her mattress and bedstead. There was a tear in one of them, making the neat square holes big and round. She was wearing soft, almost downy pyjamas. Suddenly she saw them with pinpoint accuracy, and felt them too. They had been made of Viyella: pale blue with pink roses, piping and buttons.

Trish would never have considered herself a child with a taste for pink or rosebuds, but she had been proud of those pyjamas. She couldn't have been more than four, five at the most.

She was in her bedroom, in her bed. Her father was there, reading her a story, and she was playing with his cufflinks.

They had been lovely and round with smooth edges, like Smarties made of gold. There were two for each cuff, joined together with a fascinating chain. Her father used to let her take them out of his cuffs and play with them while he read to her.

It had been hard to get them out of his shirt, pushing and tugging them through tightly stitched buttonholes. But it was always worth it. The metal felt warm against her skin and caught the light as she poured the two pairs of chained golden blobs from hand to hand. She would listen to her favourite books, and play with her father's cufflinks.

Her memory-blurred vision sharpened as she focused on the pile of cuttings in front of her again. She knew that the man who had sat on her bed and read her those stories could never have sent them. She also realised that he couldn't have been quite the louse that she'd thought for so long, but that was too much to take on board just then.

She slid the cuttings into the red plastic folder and then into the envelope, hating the feel of them under her fingers because of the other hands that must have touched them. She stowed the envelope in the bottom drawer of her desk and locked it, as though that might contain the fear that was growing in her. Then she went to have a shower.

As the hot water needled her skin then flowed softly down over her face and body, other memories surfaced from the emotional sludge in her brain.

One afternoon in a baking summer her father had bought a sprinkler for the garden. He had set it up and switched it on. Trish, even younger than the child with the cufflinks and the bedtime story, had sat on the lawn laughing up at the drops that splattered down over her.

She thought she had been plump then, and she had definitely been sitting in a pair of voluminous red and yellow bathing pants and nothing else. She had been laughing, and so had he as he bent to pick her up and swing her round and round through the spray.

It had fallen on her hot body with a thrilling kind of sizzle and they had both shouted with laughter and squealed at the cold. Her father had been fully dressed, and Meg had appeared in the kitchen doorway, wiping her hands on her apron to tell them both to come in out of the wet and stop being so silly. The two of them together.

Trish turned off the shower and shook the water out of

her eyes. George had once told her that she was like a vengeance-obsessed harpy in her stubbornness against her father. Was that true? Was it self-indulgence to have wanted to protect herself against the kind of damage he had once done to her?

She started to rub her legs with a clean towel. When she looked down minutes later, wondering why her legs hurt, she saw that the skin was bright red with the friction.

The safety her father had once given her had been a lie. The child who had played so trustfully with his cufflinks had been thrown away without a second's thought. Wasn't she justified in taking this small revenge for what he had done to her and her mother?

'So, George was right,' her inner voice said, with irritating satisfaction. 'It *is* vengeance you're practising here, not self-protection.'

'Oh, shut up!' she said aloud, and tried to turn her mind to more useful thoughts.

She suddenly thought of someone who might well have been angry and cruel enough to send her the cuttings: Darlie's tormentor.

He was not a stupid man, and he must have known – or been told by his solicitor – that Trish would be making the most of all the written evidence Kara had left to present to the judge. He might well have wanted to frighten her into dropping the case. Having read newspaper accounts of Kara's death, he might have thought descriptions of another woman's murder might do the trick.

'Really?' The derisive inner voice in Trish's mind sounded very like George at his most provoking, but she knew it was right.

She also knew that she had only one real suspect for the sender of the package and that was Blair Collons. But whether he was trying to threaten her or warn her that Kara's assailant had killed before, she could not be certain.

Sliding her bare feet into a pair of butter-soft leather shoes, she pulled a heavy sweater over her head. As she emerged from the steamy bathroom, she decided she'd been a fool to think that the difference in the way Janet Peasdown-Jones and Kara had been assaulted meant that their attackers must have been different, too. If Janet had been his first victim and he had read the press reports, he would have learned of the importance of keeping all traces of semen away from the bodies of any future victims.

Could it have been Collons?

Although Trish could imagine him killing Kara in the dark, driven by a frenzy of shame, self-hate and fury, she had great difficulty picturing him standing up to an angry black Labrador in full daylight and putting up with its bites long enough to kill it.

CHAPTER TWENTY

Sandra had no idea that she and Michael were blocking the way to the main chair-lift. All she knew was that she had to get him to admit he'd been having an affair with Kara Huggate. It was the lies he'd been telling that hurt most. There she'd been, worrying about him for months, trying to think of ways to help him and still put up with his snapping, and the only thing that had been wrong with him was a guilty conscience!

'So what was it about that middle-aged cow's rear end that made her so much more attractive than me?' she said, trying to goad him into dropping his stupid pretences.

This time she succeeded. He spat out two simple, cruel, words: 'Her intelligence.'

Sandra flinched and her skis slid away from her. Hauling herself upright on her sticks hurt her arms. She could feel the ligaments in her wrist stretching, and in the backs of her legs.

'Unlike you,' Michael said, with deadly coldness, 'she didn't spend her days having oil rubbed into her pampered body and using the organ that passes for a

203

brain in some women to work out petty revenges for imagined slights.'

The skin around his eyes, where his goggles stopped the sun getting to him, was white and hard, like a toilet pan, Sandra thought, as she tried not to cry.

'She used everything she had – her brains, her emotions, her strength, her warmth – in the service of the most miserable, least attractive members of the human race. She thought other people's needs were always more important than any of her own. She was brave and kind and clever, and worth ten of you. And now she's dead.'

I'm glad she's dead, Sandra thought. Glad. Her teeth were clamped together, making her jaw hurt, but she didn't dare open them to let out any of the words that were gushing up. Then she saw that Michael was crying.

He just stood there like a six-year-old, with tears pouring down his handsome face, *in public*, making them both look ridiculous.

'You're pathetic,' she said, and turned away. Her skis got tangled with each other and she fell heavily on her right hip. Trying to get up, she fell again, this time with her face in the snow. She hadn't realised how sharp it could be, like a cheese-grater rasping the skin off her face.

Later, when she was back in their room at the hotel, looking at the big bed where she'd thought they might make love again, she knew she never wanted to have anything to do with him ever again.

CHAPTER TWENTY-ONE

There was another fat brown envelope waiting for Trish on Friday evening. Only the possibility that it might contain some explanation – or a hint of who had sent it – forced her fingers under the flap. The paper seemed thicker than before and she had to wrench through it, bruising her knuckles as she tore it.

WOMAN CHAINED TO PIPE IN ABANDONED HOUSE
The naked body of a woman was found by police today after reports of a disturbance last night. She was so thin she must have been starved for several weeks, and she had been beaten. The wound that killed her was a slit wrist. She bled to death over many hours. On her chest . . .

Trish was not prepared to read any more. She glanced at the rest of the cuttings for just long enough to see that they were all about the same case.

She felt hated. Whoever he was, he wasn't sending the cuttings to give her useful information that might lead to Kara's killer: he wanted her terrified. That was clear enough. But it was the only thing that was. She knew she needed help.

George would have given it to her without question if she had asked him, but she couldn't do that. She'd bollocked him for giving her orders and telling her how to run her life. She couldn't go whimpering to him now, wanting protection, just because she'd been scared. She had to tough this one out without him.

Her hands felt so clumsy and swollen that she was surprised to see them still as thin as usual when she reached above her desk for the phone book. They worked well enough and she soon had the number for the main Kingsford police station. The phone rang and rang. Things began to move more quickly once she'd got through and said she had some information on the Huggate murder.

'Incident room, DC Lyalt,' said a pleasant female voice, a moment later. 'How may I help you?'

'My name's Trish Maguire. I'm a barrister. I don't want to bother you with something that may be irrelevant, but I . . .'

'If you have any information that may relate to Kara Huggate's death, please give it to me. It doesn't matter if it turns out not to be important.'

'Look, it's just that Kara was a friend of mine and she was due to give evidence in one of my cases. Two of your colleagues came to talk to me the morning after she died.'

'Oh, yes? Have you remembered something you wanted to tell them? Would you like to speak to one of them now?'

'No,' Trish said urgently. 'No. You'll do fine. I told them everything about that when they came to chambers. This is something different. I just wanted to explain the background.'

'I see. Carry on.'

'I've been down in Kingsford, asking a few questions – because I needed to know more about what's going on than I can read in the papers – and . . .'

'Oh, yes?' This time the pleasant voice was much harder. 'And what did you discover?'

'Very little. I'll tell you in a minute. That's not why I'm ringing. Please listen.'

'I *am* listening.'

Trish blinked and tried to sound as professional and sensible as she was. 'Since my trip to Kingsford I've had two envelopes stuck through my door, full of press cuttings about murders of women. Not Kara, but other women. I've tried to believe that there's no connection, but I can't.'

'Ah. I see. Yes. You'd better tell me exactly what it is you've been sent.'

Trish described the contents of the two envelopes in minute detail.

'Right,' said DC Lyalt. 'I've got all that. Now, who did you talk to in Kingston, and what did you say to them?'

Blair Collons, thought Trish. How much can I say? Oh, Kara, if only you hadn't landed me with this impossible responsibility.

'Ms Maguire?'

Trish pulled herself together and told DC Lyalt every-thing that Mrs Davidson had said about the prowler in Kara's garden, adding that she assumed he must be someone Kara had encountered through her job and explaining everything she'd worked out about Kara's need to help people. That was as far as Trish could go.

'Yes, we know all about the prowler,' said DC Lyalt. 'Who else did you see in Kingsford?'

Trish went on more happily to describe her visit to Drakeshill's Used Cars.

'And why exactly did you go there?'

'Because I'd heard gossip that the owner is known to be violent and that he might have had some connection with Kara and with Kingsford Council, which, after all, was her employer. I couldn't find any evidence of such a connection, and I must admit that I'd never personally heard her speak about him.'

'Who told you that they knew each other?'

'I can't remember.' Trish knew the statement must sound as weak as it was, but she couldn't help that.

'I see.' DC Lyalt sounded as though she had picked up a pretty good idea of what Trish was thinking. 'You were quite right to phone. We'll need to see the cuttings you've been sent and the envelopes they came in, and I'm sure my guv'nor would like to talk to you. There may be things you knew about Kara Huggate that will help us. Could you get down to the incident room?'

'Yes. Tonight?'

'I don't know whether he'll be able to see you tonight. I'll have to let you know. Where are you based?'

'Southwark,' Trish said and gave her mobile number.

'Thank you. Either Chief Inspector Femur or I will get back to you as soon as we can. In the meantime, don't handle the envelopes or cuttings any more than you need to and take care.'

'OK. But I'm afraid I have touched most of the cuttings already, if it's prints you're thinking of.'

'Pity.'

'Look, if your chief could see me tonight, I'll come straight away. The sooner the better, from my point of view.'

'He's very busy, but I'm sure he'll see you as soon as he can. Before you go, do you happen to know the name of Kara Huggate's boyfriend? Not Jed Thomplon, I mean, the new one.'

'No,' Trish said, surprised. 'Although she did tell me

that there was someone. She said, I think, that there were complications. Practical complications, were the words I remember. But she also said she thought it was going to work out.'

'Didn't you ask her his name?'

'I'm afraid I couldn't. The first I heard of him was in a letter she wrote to me just before she died.'

'Ah. Too bad. Well, someone will get back to you as soon as possible.'

'OK.'

'And, Ms Maguire, thank you for calling. You were quite right to do so.'

I hope so, thought Trish, as she replaced her receiver. But what am I to do about Collons? I can't leave it much longer.

Eventually she decided that when she went to Kingsford to talk to DC Lyalt's guv'nor she would drop in on Blair Collons first, as though she were casually passing through, and somehow persuade him to go with her to the incident room. They had to know about him; she couldn't betray him and still keep faith with Kara; he would have to give himself up. That was all there was to it.

With the phone so near, Trish couldn't resist trying George's number, but there was no answer, not even from the machine. He had never switched it off in all the time she'd known him. He must be furious.

Trying not to mind too much, she made herself an omelette and ate it in front of the television, watching a video because there were no programmes she wanted to see. It seemed odd, wrong in some way to be alone like this. Usually, she rather enjoyed the evenings when he was doing something on his own. They gave her a chance to catch up with herself. But this was different.

When it was time to go to bed, she went round the flat checking the locks on all the windows and the front door, trying not to feel quite so abandoned.

CHAPTER TWENTY-TWO

Sergeant Spinel was playing it very cool. Femur thought he looked like a man acutely aware of danger but determined not to show it. So far they had been covering what Spinel could remember about the Kingsford Rapist's first known victim, and whether he might have inadvertently passed on any details of the scene to an outsider. He didn't think it likely, but the whole case was so long ago that he couldn't say for sure.

Caroline Lyalt had already established with the woman herself that Spinel had interviewed her soon after she'd been seen by the doctor on the night of the rape, and that she'd told him everything that had happened to her. At first she hadn't liked Spinel, Caroline reported, but after a bit she'd warmed to him. She appreciated the way he'd been so angry with the rapist, she said.

Some of the other officers, even some of the women, had been lovely and sympathetic, but they hadn't seemed to feel much either way about the man who'd attacked her. Spinel, Constable Spinel he'd been then, had let her see his fury and told her how he'd wanted to beat the man to a pulp. She'd liked that. It was how she'd felt. She thought she'd probably told him exactly what had happened, but he was police, so that was all right, wasn't it?

Remembering most of Caroline's almost verbatim report, Femur listened to Spinel's account of the various interviews he had conducted at the time, always watching for unnecessary slickness, over-elaboration, or any other sign of discomfort.

'So why did you switch to the drugs squad?' Femur asked casually, when they had covered everything Spinel had said to, and heard from or about, the Kingsford Rapist's first victim.

Spinel stuck out his lower lip like a child thinking up a new story to tell and shrugged his big shoulders. The oversized leather jacket he wore looked expensive; not the sort that came by mail order or from the wrong end of Oxford Street. To be fair, it could've been a present from his rich wife.

He was sitting with his legs spread on the chair opposite Femur's desk, doing his best to dominate the room. Not that it was necessary. In comparison, Femur knew himself to be a mingy physical specimen, barely five eleven in his socks and as grey and wrinkled as an old elephant, too broken down to challenge the younger bulls.

'Mainly because we didn't get a result on the rapist,' Spinel said with a grudge in his voice. 'I found I couldn't take it, not after what he'd done to that poor little bitch. Someone out there knows who he is, has known all along, but you don't get snouts for that sort of crime. At least, I couldn't, nor any of the rest of the squad. I thought I'd rather work with crimes people will talk about.'

'Drugs?'

'Yeah. Over in the drugs squad, I can pick up a small-time dealer and lean on him to give me the dirt on the bigger ones, and do something that makes a difference in the end.' Spinel shrugged again, but he looked more honest and a scrap less unlikeable. Take it or leave it, said his body language. Believe me or don't: I don't care.

'And you do make a difference, from what I hear.' Femur forced a sycophantic note of admiration into his voice. Spinel spread his legs a little further apart and thrust his crotch forward. Femur suppressed a comment on the lines of, yes, I can see it's bigger than mine. Instead he said, 'Tell me, have any of your snouts said anything to you about Kara Huggate or her death?'

'No more than the bloke in the pub. I mean, why would they? That's what I mean: you don't get people talking about those sort of crimes. They're too frightening, too upsetting, maybe. Dangerous. I don't know.'

'There's been the suggestion of a drugs connection in the killing.'

Spinel didn't move. He didn't blink. But there was a change in the atmosphere. Femur felt it as a slight chill, a withdrawal of attention, like the effect of someone going to sleep beside you. Suddenly they're not there any more: you're on your own. Like death, really.

Bingo! he thought.

'What kind of connection?'

Spinel slowly crossed his legs, all casual, so that he didn't look too defensive. He must have been on courses: the sort about projecting yourself and management by mimicry. Femur hadn't, but he'd read about them and decided they were a right load of cock.

'We're not sure yet. That's why I wanted to talk to you.' He smiled again, hoping he didn't look as fake as he felt. 'An expert.'

'All I know about her and drugs is she had these

unrealistic ideas about what we could do with classroom dealers. But I told you all that last time you had me over here.' A hint of irritation in Spinel's smooth voice with its faint Essex twang made Femur nod.

'Right. What I – Yes, what is it?' he asked irritably, as the door opened and Caroline Lyalt looked in.

'Sorry to disturb you, Guv. I've just had a call from a friend of Huggate who's got some potentially useful information. I thought you ought to know straight away.'

'Will you excuse me a moment, Sergeant?' Femur didn't wait for an answer, but followed Caroline out into the main incident room, furious that she'd interrupted just when he was getting somewhere. 'This had better be good. What is it?'

He saw she'd registered his tone but she didn't bridle or apologise, just gave him her answer as direct as ever. 'Trish Maguire. She's the barrister that Evans and Watkins were interviewing when we first got here. It seems that Huggate was more than just her witness, they were friends. And now she's being harassed with bundles of newspaper cuttings about murdered women and she thinks it might have some connection with Huggate because she's been down here in Kingsford recently, asking questions.'

Femur ground his teeth. That was all he needed. Some lawyer who fancied herself as Miss Bloody Marple. They'd checked out John Bract, the defendant in the case Maguire had been running, and he'd come out clean. That should've been the end of Maguire as far as the case was concerned. Bloody women.

'I said you'd probably like to talk to her and would ring her either tonight or first thing in the morning,' said Caroline calmly.

'I don't suppose you thought of asking Maguire about S.'

'Well, I did, actually, Guv. But she doesn't know his name.'

Femur let his taut shoulders go. He shouldn't have doubted Cally. She always came through. Still it was a pity she'd chosen to do it just then.

'Although she did confirm there was someone new in Huggate's life. Apparently there were some practical problems involved, but Huggate thought they were being sorted.'

'Sounds like a married man to me,' Femur said, jerking his head back towards his own office. 'It's all stacking up around Spinel, isn't it? I'd better get back to him.'

'But, sir,' Caroline said with unusual formality. 'Maguire's being harassed. Like I said, someone's sending her – anonymously – newspaper cuttings about particularly unpleasant murders of women. I think we ought to do something about it.'

'Like what?'

'Talk to her and follow up some of the people she interviewed when she came down here. She went to Church Lane to talk to the neighbours, heard the story about the man in Huggate's garden. It sounds as though it could be more important than we thought.'

'Tony's already dealt with that and established that the witness isn't reliable and couldn't remember whether she'd seen him in the garden on the actual night of the murder or a week earlier. I'll talk to him again when I've finished with Spinel to double check, but if there was anything there he'd have got it. He's no fool.'

To his amazement Caroline raised her eyebrows. It was as near as she'd ever got to making a comment about Blacker. What the hell was happening to everyone in this case? It was fast becoming one of the worst he'd known.

'Right, if you've got the time and nothing better to do, you can have another go at the witness yourself, but talk to Tony first. I don't want you treading on his toes.'

'Very well, sir.' She turned away then added over her shoulder, 'Don't forget Maguire, will you, sir?'

Femur gritted his teeth. It must be the actress, he thought, making her so tetchy and naggy. She's not herself.

'Sorry about that,' he said, as he sat down in front of Spinel again. He decided to give the man a chance to relax, then hit him with the real suspicions again. That sometimes did the trick. 'It's beginning to look as though the murder might have had nothing to do with Kingsford after all. Did Huggate ever tell you about a man called John Bract?'

Spinel uncrossed his legs again and the muscles beside his mouth softened. Good. 'Not that I remember. Why would she? Who is he?'

'He's the manager of a children's home who was up in court on some kind of brutality allegation. Huggate was going to give evidence against him so he could've wanted to shut her up. Hangover from her old job. I thought she might've told you because it all blew up around the time you were meeting her on a weekly basis.'

'Sounds possible to me.'

'And me. You knew her better than most other people in Kingsford, didn't you?'

'Can't say I did, sir. We had our three meetings before Christmas, and in the end she accepted what I'd said all along, that we were already on the case of her schoolboy dealer and that harassing me on the phone wasn't doing anyone any good. She left me alone after that.'

'Right. It's a pain, though. We need someone who knew something about her private life. And we're not getting anywhere.'

'Sorry. Can't help.'

Femur looked at him, wondering how much to believe. 'Then we'd better get shot of this possible link with the drugs world while you're here. What I want from you is an introduction to your chief snout. I gather from the register of informers that he's a man called Drakeshill . . .'

Once again Spinel's muscles tightened, and this time not only beside his mouth. His meaty, well-toned thighs twitched. Perhaps to cover it, he slowly raised his left leg again to lay it across the right knee.

'No can do, Guv. Sorry.' Spinel raised his eyelids and transferred his attention from his shoes to the right of Femur's face. 'Too risky. And Drakeshill's a tricky bugger, not likely to play ball.'

'I could force it and pick him up myself,' said Femur mildly, watching Spinel's eyes. They seemed clear, but there was a tiny fluttering under his left eye. It looked a bit like an infant crocodile beginning to break out of its egg. Femur had seen that once in slow motion on some natural-history programme. 'Murder takes priority.'

'Not in my book, Guv. Like I say, I'd help if I could. But it wouldn't get you anywhere and it might dry up the only real source of drug intelligence we've got in Kingsford. Let me ask him if he knows anything and get back to you. OK?'

In the end Femur had to pretend to let it go. Spinel had something to hide, but he still couldn't decide what or how serious it was. Just as he couldn't make up his mind whether Spinel was S or not.

He fitted all the clues: he was married, and he had his hard-man reputation to keep up, both of which would've meant keeping an affair secret; he'd met Kara at about the right time; and he was the only link so far between her and the original rapes.

Femur knew he had to give it more time. Something

would crop up that would prove it one way or the other. And Spinel wasn't like an ordinary witness. Femur could lay hands on him any time he wanted. If the worst came to the worst, he'd put him under surveillance and bug his house.

CHAPTER TWENTY-THREE

Trish was asleep when the phone rang. Wrenched out of a dream that made her feel washed in light and kindness, she reached out a hand for the receiver and knocked something off her table. Whatever it was did not seem to matter, not with everything going so beautifully behind her eyes.

'George?' she said sleepily.

'No, it's not George.' The voice was male and full of malice. 'Who's he anyway? You live on your own.'

'Who is this?' Trish's eyes were now fully open; her breathing was quick, shallow. The dark space around her seemed enormous and full of threat. Her arms and neck were rigid, as though steel spikes were holding her head on to her neck.

'You know who I am. You've been getting my messages.' The man's voice was higher than George's, with an accent she couldn't quite identify.

Shadows seemed to bulge and advance from the distant corners of the room. Trish switched on the light. Nothing was moving, and no one was trying to hide in the corners.

'Patricia?'

No one ever called her that. No one she knew.

'Yes?'

Her clock had disappeared from the bedside table. Someone must have taken it. For a sickening moment Trish felt as though she were in a lift that had plummeted out of control from the top of a skyscraper. Then she remembered she'd knocked something off the table and the lurching in her guts eased.

The clock had rolled on to its side almost out of reach. The brass edge was gleaming, just beyond the circle of brightest light. She leaned out of bed to reach for it, with the receiver gripped between her shoulder and her ear. The man said nothing, but she could hear his breathing. Her stomach muscles stretched painfully as she pushed her free hand towards the clock. The metal felt very cold under her finger ends. As she tapped it, pulling it round and round towards her until it was near enough to pick up, she almost fell out of bed and had to prop herself up with her hand flat against the floor.

'You're still vere, aren't you, Patricia?' said the voice in her ear. 'You can't fool me. I can hear you breaving.'

So, she thought, whoever he is, he can't say 'th'.

'Why're you keeping so quiet? You've got my messages, haven't you?'

There was a tiny feeling of achievement as she pulled herself back against the pillows with the clock in her hand. It was three forty-five. No wonder it was still so dark outside. And so cold.

'Patricia? I'm talking to you.'

She could feel hatred all round her, but she wasn't sure whether it was hers or his.

'So you are,' she said, trying to make her voice contemptuous. 'By messages, d'you mean those brown envelopes full of press cuttings?'

Her thighs were bare where the T-shirt she wore instead of a nightdress had ridden up around her waist as she reached for the clock. Hastily she pulled the soft cotton down, stretching it to make it seem much longer than it was, and then she hauled the duvet over the top as though the man could see her. It did not provide any warmth. Her legs began to shake. She crossed them, like a child desperate for a pee.

'Yeah. You've been getting vem, haven't you?'

'Yes, I've been getting those.' That was better: her voice was beginning to sound better, more controlled, perfectly articulated.

She caught sight of her reflection in the cheval mirror that stood against the far wall and quickly looked away. There was no control whatsoever in her face or eyes. Above the pale grey of the round-necked T-shirt, her skin was dirty white and her eyes enormous. She was too short-sighted to have read the slogan on her T-shirt in the mirror, but she knew all too well what it said: 'DO YOUR WORST. I CAN TAKE IT.' Some hope.

'I knew you would have,' said the hateful voice. She tried to kill the fantasy that he could see her. 'I've been putting vem in your letter box myself, so I knew vey hadn't got lost. Like vem, do you?'

'I've got them.' Trish's breathing was steadying with each word she said. She tried to remember that she was a cool professional, capable, and unfazed by aggressive anonymous callers. She rubbed her legs against each other under the duvet. A faint warmth spread up from her calves. 'But I don't understand what they have to do with me.'

'Vey show what happens to slags who interfere. Not nice, is it, what happens to nosy slags? You want to stop getting in ve way, like, before it happens to you too. Slag.'

Trish bit back questions, fear, and protests. She tried

not to cower against her pillows. She tried to feel powerful.

'And it gets worse. Wait for Monday. You'll see ven, slag.'

There was silence and then a whine and then a mechanical voice telling her to replace the receiver. She unclamped her fingers with difficulty and obeyed. Perhaps if the call had come during daylight, when she was already wide awake and ready to work, she wouldn't have hated it so much. She made herself pick up the phone again to ring 1471 and got the infuriating sing-song message: 'You were called at three forty-five. We do not have the caller's number to return the call.'

So, she thought, pleased to find that panic had not completely dried out her brain cells, not 'the caller withheld the number'.

That meant it was either a private exchange belonging to some big organisation, a cellphone (although some of their numbers did register with the 1471 system), or perhaps a phone box. And that, of course, was the likeliest.

Trish sat with her arms round her knees. The duvet made a soft platform for her chin, but there was nothing around her back except the thin T-shirt, and that didn't keep out the cold.

Had Kara sat like this, too, trying not to believe that a rapist was outside her door waiting to break in and kill her?

Trish tried to be rational. She was shivering, but that could have been because of the icy air that filled the room. Or it could have been fear. She reminded herself that British Telecom could trace malicious calls from any kind of number.

Her teeth began to clatter against each other. She'd never known a night as cold as this. A hot shower might help. And so would George. If the fear was as bad as this once she was warm again and had had more sleep, she might have to ring him. He'd help. She knew he would. However angry she'd made him – however much she'd hurt him – he'd never leave her to face this alone.

The goosepimpled skin of her arms looked like seersucker. She knew she had to get warm. There must be some hot water left in the tank even after the long shower she'd had before she went to bed.

It was hard to force herself to get up and walk across the empty expanse of floor to the bathroom. There were windows to pass that looked out over the back of other buildings. What if the caller were in one of those? Waiting for her. Watching for her lights. She thought of the man who had watched from Kara's garden in the dark.

'Stop it, Trish. Get a grip.'

She said it out loud several times and eventually shamed herself into moving. The bathroom blind was already pulled down over the black glass of the window so it didn't matter even if he were looking in. He wouldn't be able to see anything. She turned on the hot water, stripped off the lying T-shirt and was soon standing under a flood of heat.

As her skin flattened and became the colour of raspberries, she turned her face up to the water. It drummed down, pushing her eyelids into hard little spots against the eyes themselves, getting up her nose, making her choke. But still she wasn't hot enough. Disgustingly she blew her nose with her fingers, shook them and then held them above her head to wash them in the strongest jets.

After a while the water began to cool. She knew she had to get out before all the warmth had gone and she was freezing again. The big red towel had dried on the hot pipes since her last shower and as she tightened it around her breasts, tucking the loose end deep into her cleavage, she felt a faint sense of security.

But it was nothing like the security she would have felt if she had had George with her. She wished he'd answered his phone when she'd tried to ring, or that she'd been able to leave a message. She needed him very badly.

Perhaps it wasn't anger that was keeping him silent. Perhaps he'd become bored with her and grabbed the excuse of the quarrel to get rid of her.

Her forehead was tight. In the mirror she saw that the skin and muscles were corrugated like a ploughed field. George used to smooth out wrinkles like that whenever he saw her frowning. He had done it first before she had understood what she felt for him – or he for her. She could remember the unexpected touch of his fingers, and the effect it had had on her.

Oh, grow up! You can smooth out your own forehead, she told herself. Don't be such a wimp. And don't start mooning about the past. If he doesn't come back he wasn't worth it anyway.

But she didn't believe it, and she longed for him to come back. As soon as her hair was dry enough to sleep on, she went down the spiral staircase to check that she really had double-locked her front door and all the windows. Back in bed, she turned out the light and lay on her right side with her hands tucked between her thighs, determined to sleep.

Ten minutes later, she flopped over on to her other side, trying to smooth out the pillows as she turned. She tucked her hands back between her thighs and forbade herself to think about the man on the phone. When the efficient-sounding DC Lyalt rang back in the morning, she could tell her what had happened and it would be sorted.

Unless it's Collons, Trish said to herself, as she turned over on to her front. But if I don't tell the police about him, and he breaks in here one night . . . Oh, stop it!

The softness of the pillows against her face was a comfort, even though breathing in brought a smell of dusty feathers to the back of her nose, but after a few minutes the position hurt her back so she turned on to her side again.

In her memory Collons's voice had always sounded more substantial, deeper and less whining, than the one on the phone, and much more powerful than his mien suggested, and he had never had any trouble making 'th' sounds that she could remember. But it was perfectly possible that he'd disguised his voice, or even got a friend to call for him.

Trish rolled over on to her back and turned her head to look at the clock on her table. It was already four forty-five. She must sleep again or she'd be no good to anyone in the morning.

Half an hour later she put on the light once more and picked up *Presumed Innocent*.

When the sun broke into her twitching dreams, it seemed as though she had only just shut her eyes. They felt puffy. She rubbed them and realised that her bedside light was still on. The lump under her breast proved to be the paperback novel. She felt worse than she had after the El Vino's orgy, and this time she hadn't even had any fun to pay for.

The phone started to ring. She rather hoped it was him again. If so, she'd give as good as she got this time. She sat up, cleared her throat, and reached for the receiver, noticing that it was still only seven thirty. No wonder she felt so awful.

Her greeting came out in a snarl and was answered by

someone who sounded no happier, telling her that he was Chief Inspector William Femur and understood from Constable Lyalt that she had important information to impart about the Kara Huggate case.

Trish caught hold of her temper, apologised for the way she had answered the phone and repeated what she'd said to DC Lyalt. Femur listened without interrupting, then said that although he'd be busy for most of the day, he could see her at the incident room at about six thirty. If the traffic was bad and she got held up, would she give him a bell to warn him so that he could reorganise his time?

Trish longed to go straight to Kingsford and pour out a hysterical account of everything her caller had made her feel, but she hung on to her dignity and embarked on a sober account of what had happened. Femur cut her off before she had said more than three words, telling her that he was urgently needed elsewhere and would listen to everything she had to tell him in Kingsford at six thirty that evening.

Barefoot, Trish went down to the kitchen in the hope that breakfast would make her feel stronger. She watched the coffee dripping through the buff filter paper and tried to work through her fears and do something useful.

If Chief Inspector Femur couldn't see her until six thirty, she'd have plenty of time to talk to Collons first. She was familiar enough with criminal investigations to know that as a chief inspector involved in a murder inquiry, he must be the leader of a team from the local Area Major Investigation Pool, in which case he was unlikely to have the kind of local connections that had so frightened Collons.

This might be the lever that would move Collons in the right direction. Trish could tell him that she had investigated Drakeshill, that she was on her way to talk to Femur, who was just the kind of senior police officer who would be above any local corruption. She would say that she was going to warn Femur about the conspiracy Collons had uncovered but that she thought it would be more convincing coming directly from him.

If he were recalcitrant, she would face him with the report of the prowler in Kara's garden, a prowler who looked just like him. With luck that would shock him into telling her the truth.

'Of course, if he did kill Kara,' said the derisive voice in her mind, 'you might also shock him into attacking you. Have you thought of that?'

She told the voice to shut up. She'd already worked out that she couldn't expose Collons to the police without evidence. And she still didn't have any. It was a risk she was going to have to take.

Carrying a mug of the strong black coffee in one hand, she rummaged among the papers on her desk with the other until she found the piece of paper on which he'd written his phone number. She pushed the relevant buttons on the phone, her fingers rebounding off the plastic in a good punchy way. She was definitely feeling better. Taking action usually helped, whatever mood she was in.

Collons had his machine switched on and she listened to his outgoing message with more than usual care, measuring it against her memory of the other voice. The taped message was not quite long enough for her to be certain, but she did not think the voice she heard could have been disguised into sounding like the night caller's.

After the beep, mindful of the professional risk of giving her name on to a tape, she said, 'Blair, this is me, Kara's friend. I have to be in Kingsford around six this evening, and I was thinking of dropping in to see you first. I'm not quite sure what time I'll get to you, but if you're not going to be in anyway, don't worry. I'll catch up with you some other time.'

She took her coffee up the spiral stairs and had another stinging shower, which completed her return to full consciousness. Later, warm, dry, and pulling on a new pair of jeans, she tried to feel that it was a relief not to have to warn George that she'd be out that evening or worry about what they might eat. She did not convince herself.

Her belt was still flapping unbuckled around her waist when she succumbed to temptation. With the receiver tucked under her chin, she did up the belt and waited for him to answer his phone. He, too, was out, but at least his answering-machine was on again.

'George, it's me. Trish. Can we stop this? I hate it. You're probably as cross as I've been. But don't let's throw away the good bits. I'm sorry for what I did, for what I made you feel, I mean. I've got a late meeting and I'm not sure what time I'll be back, but could we speak? I miss you so much.'

CHAPTER TWENTY-FOUR

Trish rang Collons for the fourth time when she was half-way to Kingsford, but she got his machine again. She couldn't think why he was playing so hard to get. There was no particular reason why he shouldn't have gone out or even be away for the weekend – but he hadn't given her the impression of a man with much of a social life.

When she eventually reached Kingsford, after an exasperating journey of traffic jams, potholes and kamikaze pedestrians, she drove straight to the address she had taken from the papers James Bletchley had left with her.

Collons's flat proved to be one of fourteen in a block of raw red brick barely softened by miniature evergreen creepers. She rang his bell and waited. After a long silence she tried again, putting her ear close to the intercom speaker, in case she'd missed his answer. Still nothing. She pressed the bell nearest his and within a couple of seconds a crackly male voice said, 'Hello.'

'Blair?' asked Trish brightly. 'Is that you?'

'No. This is John Barker. Who d'you want?'

'Blair Collons. Flat five. Have I rung the wrong bell?'

'This is flat five, but he's flat four. He's out.'

'Oh? D'you know when he'll be back?'

'I'm not his sodding secretary. I heard him go about half an hour ago. OK?'

'OK. Thanks. Sorry again.'

Trish went back to her car, sure now that Collons must be deliberately avoiding her. The first message she'd left had told him she'd drop in before her six-thirty meeting. It seemed a bit rich for him to have gone out deliberately after the way he'd forced her to see him and listen to his hysterical theories. Could he have guessed that she'd heard about the prowler? Or had he just assumed that her meeting in Kingsford must be with the police?

With no answers and no possibility of getting any until she'd managed to talk to him, Trish was stuck. The frustration was so distracting that she got lost three times and had to make tricky and illegal U-turns into fast oncoming traffic.

She could not find a way of letting herself off the hook of Kara's concern for Blair Collons, and it was driving her mad. Only if she betrayed everything Kara had stood for and everything she herself had so much admired in Kara could she tell Chief Inspector Femur what she suspected. But if she didn't say anything, her silence might allow Kara's killer to escape. And perhaps not just Kara's killer.

The Kingsford Rapist had been operating at about the time Collons had first moved to the area. He had raped six women and killed one within the space of a year and then, just as Collons had begun to find some renewed self-respect in the job he'd managed to get with the council, the Rapist had stopped. Only when Collons had been sacked and most deeply humiliated, had another rape and killing taken place.

She found the police station at last and was greeted

with enough suspicion at the main desk to reinforce her feeling that an innocent man with Collons's difficulties might not survive a police investigation intact. Once she had shown the sergeant her driving licence and told him three times that Chief Inspector Femur had phoned her at home that morning to make the appointment, he deigned to ring through to the incident room to check. Whatever he heard made his scowl thicken, but he grudgingly told his constable to take her to the incident room.

The constable, who looked as though he had hardly started to shave, took Trish to a big, smelly, untidy room furnished with rows of desks and battered chairs. There were only three people, each hunched over the keyboard of an ancient computer.

'He'll be through there,' said her guide, pointing to a scarred brown door. He knocked and announced her to a grey-haired man, who had an expression of reined-in irritation on his pleasant, weary face.

He was wearing a nondescript, crumpled dark-grey suit over a plain white shirt, and his blue and grey striped tie had worked its way round so that most of the loose knot was hidden under the shirt collar. He looked as if he'd slept in his clothes and hadn't had a very good night. His eyes were the only remarkable feature: almost diamond-shaped and of a clear hard grey. He got to his feet, holding out one large, dry hand.

'Chief Inspector William Femur,' he said, as Trish took his hand. 'Right, what have you brought to show me?'

'These,' said Trish, pulling the envelopes of cuttings out of her capacious shoulder bag.

'So?' he said coldly when he'd had a chance to look at them.

She reminded herself of the stress he must feel, but she could have done with a little human warmth, even a scrap of sympathy. When she had told him briskly how the cuttings had come into her possession and why they frightened her, she described the night's phone call. His expression softened marginally, but even so she kept most of her terror to herself.

'Right,' he said again, but this time the word carried overtones of 'oh, I see, I'm sorry I snapped', instead of 'you're a boring time-waster and the last thing in the world I need right now'.

'I can see why you're bothered,' he added, 'but what makes you think the caller was referring to Kara Huggate's murder?'

'Because he said he'd sent the cuttings to show me what happens to women who interfere.'

'And my case is the only thing you've been poking your nose into, is it?' Femur might as well have added, 'I don't believe it,' because that was written all over him.

'Yes.'

'Right.' He sighed and pushed back his thick grey hair with both hands.

Now that she looked more closely, she could see deep lines around his mouth, dragging its corners towards his chin. The skin around his lips was roughened too, as though he hadn't been getting enough vitamins. Or perhaps it was just chapped by the cold.

'Let's take it from the top.' Femur pulled a pad of paper towards him and wrote her name on it with the date and time.

Was it designed to intimidate? Trish wondered. Or was he merely being efficient? Be fair, she told herself, you always make notes of important interviews.

'Now, who could want to scare you into silence about your friend Kara?'

'That's just it. I don't know,' Trish said. It was almost impossible not to mention Blair Collons's name, but she had to do it. 'But, as I explained to the officers who came to see me in chambers, Kara was due to appear in a case for damages against a man who could well have wanted to stop first her and now me. He's called John Bract and he might have thought he could intimidate me into –'

'We know all about him, and we've eliminated him from our inquiries.'

'Why?'

'You don't need to know that, Ms Maguire, but you can take it from me that we're satisfied he had no involvement of any kind.' When Femur saw that *she* wasn't satisfied, he sighed. 'Did your caller sound like him at all?'

'No,' Trish said, certain that Bract himself couldn't have produced the voice she'd heard. But, then, she'd never thought that he would have attacked Kara himself, only paid someone else to do it. So he could've paid the same person to intimidate her.

'Right. So, who else could it have been? DC Lyalt told me you've been down here asking questions.' The tone of his quiet voice was quite enough to tell Trish that he was absolutely furious with her intervention. She was glad that she was not one of his suspects. 'Who did you talk to?'

'One of Kara's neighbours, a Mrs Davidson. I was standing in the road looking up at Kara's house when I saw her watching me, and I thought it too good an opportunity to miss.'

'Because you thought we might've forgotten to talk to a murder victim's neighbours?' Femur said, pretending to sound puzzled but actually showing every bit of his fury.

'No,' she said firmly. 'I needed to talk about Kara and find out what had been happening to her just before she died for some emotional reason I don't quite understand.

Look, Chief Inspector, Kara was an extraordinary woman, and I liked her so much that I had to do something.'

As she saw his face soften a little, Trish cleared her throat and sat up straighter to tell him everything she had heard and thought about the prowler, except for the name she thought he bore. She saw that none of it was news to Femur. 'And so I suppose what scared me when I got the cuttings and picked up the phone last night is that somehow, whoever he is, he found out my identity and has been trying to scare me off.' She saw that Femur wasn't convinced.

'I don't see how he could have heard anything about you, do you? He's hardly going to go banging on the doors of the Church Lane houses asking whether the owners have told anyone that they saw him loitering with intent. Who else did you talk to?'

'I went on to have a look at a man called Martin Drakeshill, a second-hand-car dealer in Station Drive here in Kingsford.'

There was a very slight stiffening in Femur's shoulders.

Ah, then, maybe there is something sinister about Drakeshill, Trish thought, working to keep her face clean of both surprise and satisfaction. Could Collons possibly have been right? If so, then I *was* right to keep his name out of it. There was a little comfort in that.

'Now, why would you do a thing like that, Ms Maguire? Did Kara tell you something about Drakeshill?'

Trish was tempted to lie because it would have provided such a convenient excuse for her questions, but she couldn't do it, not to a man struggling to find Kara's killer. She might withhold her suspicions of Collons in order to protect him for Kara until she had some real evidence against him, but she would not tell any actual lies unless they were forced on her. Instead she told him about the legal gossip she'd heard about Drakeshill.

She was relieved to see that Femur was looking more interested than angry.

'All right, I can understand *that*, but why did you go to see him?'

'I thought I might learn something. But I didn't. His appearance suggested that he could be capable of all sorts of things, and one of the mechanics on the forecourt looked easily tough enough to take on anyone with a baseball bat, but that isn't proof of anything. I have to admit that I didn't see anything to suggest any wrong-doing beyond, perhaps, fencing stolen cars.'

'I see.' Femur had written down Drakeshill's name, but that was all. 'And who else have you approached?'

She told him about Roger and the KGB, and the council's deal with Goodbuy's, and he wrote that down, too. It all seemed pitifully inadequate. 'You're not telling me everything, are you?' Femur said. He still sounded impatient but now there was something hard and dangerous in his voice. 'What d'you know about Kara's private life?'

'Not a lot,' Trish said, 'although, as I told DC Lyalt, Kara did tell me that she was in love again. But I'm not sure that's the most relevant thing.'

'Oh?'

'No.' She told Femur her theory that Kara's need to see good in everyone and bring it out by kindness could have led to her death, if the person she had been trying to help had been psychotic or psychopathic.

For the first time there was a hint of approval in his professional smile as he listened. It wasn't much, just a flicker in the tight muscles around his mouth, but it seemed to signal a definite weakening of hostility.

'You're talking about the Kingsford Rapist, I take it?'

'Yes. He's never been found, has he? And from the papers it sounds as though what happened to Kara was very like what happened to the other victims. He could have been a client of hers, couldn't he? Or simply an acquaintance.'

'Anyone particular in mind?'

'No,' she said, in a casually firm voice, glad that her ten years at the bar had taught her to speak to a hostile audience without betraying her own emotions.

'Right,' he said, after a long examination of her face. 'Now, what else can you tell me about this new lover of hers?'

'Nothing more than I told DC Lyalt. Kara never told me anything else. No, it's true. I'm not stalling, and I'm sorry I can't help you. I would if I could. The only hint I got was in a letter she wrote to me just before she died, and she didn't tell me his name or anything about him. By the time I got the letter she was already dead, so I couldn't have asked her anything even if I'd wanted to.'

'May I see the letter?'

This time she was going to have to lie if she was to keep Collons out of it, so she told Femur she had destroyed it.

'Now why would you do that? The last letter of a woman who you say was such a friend that you had to go gawping at the cottage where she was murdered and talking to her neighbours.'

'I'm not sure.' Trish looked him full in the face. It was no worse than trying to persuade a suspicious jury of the truth of her client's case. 'Ever since I got rid of it, I've regretted my impulse, but it's too late now.' I'm not under caution, she thought.

They went on round and round the letter, Jed Thomplon, the rest of Kara's private life, what she had said to Trish about it, what else she might not have said, and whether Trish had ever heard her talk about anyone of either sex with the initial S. Gradually Femur began to seem convinced that she didn't know who the person could be.

As he thawed, Trish relaxed too, but there wasn't much more either of them could do for the other. Femur told her that if she had any more threatening phone calls she should ring her local station to report the caller and get them to pass the information on to him. Or she could ring the incident room direct if she preferred. He gave her the number. She picked up her bag, leaving the envelopes of cuttings on his desk.

This time she did get an answer when she rang the bell of Collons's flat, but he refused to let her in when she said who she was. Left standing on the step, she was wondering what on earth to do next when she saw him running down the corridor towards the glazed front door. His short figure was rippled and distorted by the ridges in the glass but unmistakable.

When Trish opened her mouth to greet him, he thrust a piece of paper at her, pushing her backwards off the shallow brick step. Gagging on the almost feral smell that rose from his clothes, she opened the note and read the backwards-sloping writing: 'I must talk to you. I've got something important to tell you about Kara. But not here. It's not safe. Can we go somewhere in your car? That can't be bugged. It's important.' The last two words were underlined four times in thick black ink.

'I haven't long,' Trish said, exasperated by his dramatics. She was also deeply reluctant to let herself be trapped in her car with him. 'I have to get back to London.'

'I know,' he said, as he turned away from her to

double-lock the front door. It seemed a redundant gesture since any intruder could have broken the glass.

Those two words helped confirm her suspicion that he couldn't have made his voice sound like the one that had threatened her over the phone, but she still had to be convinced.

'Will you tell me, Blair, why –'

'Not now,' he said frantically, urging her down the slope to the small car-park.

She led the way reluctantly to her Audi. He stood there, waiting for her to unlock the door, his impatience so obvious that he might have had flags proclaiming it sprouting from his ears. Trish looked at him in the pallid light shed by the opaque white globes that stood on poles, like severed heads, at intervals around the fore-court.

For the first time she noticed that there were very few lines on Collons' face. In a man of his age that seemed sinister, but she could not work out why.

He was wearing the corduroy trousers she had first seen in the pub and a saggy old tweed jacket with fraying cuffs and ink stains in the corners of the right-hand pocket. There was debris of some kind sticking to his lapels. He looked weak and pathetic, but she had far too much experience to believe that the weak couldn't be dangerous. She thought of the little she had read in the papers about Kara's injuries and wondered whether he had a knife hidden somewhere in his clothes.

He had his hand on the passenger-door handle and was nodding urgently towards the bleeper in her hand. Not wanting an undignified scene, Trish released the locks and allowed him to get in.

'Now drive,' he ordered, with the surprising force he occasionally showed.

Trish gritted her teeth and briefly turned to see what he

was doing. He looked a lot less powerful than he had sounded. His hands were in his lap, trembling and glistening with sweat. Catching her eye, he clutched them together so that they stopped shaking.

'Please drive, Ms Maguire. We need to get away from here.' His voice was shriller than it had been, but it still did not sound anything like the one on the phone.

'Please. Oh, please, Ms Maguire.'

Trish turned on the ignition and backed carefully out on to the road. It was not a particularly busy one and she wanted to be somewhere where other people would be able to see her.

A large garage appeared on the left, positively glittering with bright yellow light. It was the sort of place that had not only banks of petrol pumps and automatic washing and vacuuming devices, but also a small supermarket at the back. Eight cars were being filled with petrol and several more queued behind them. It would do. Trish parked in the gutter, right under the oil company's enormous sign. Light spread over her windscreen and filled the car. Even one of the notoriously passive British passers-by would probably intervene if Collons started to assault her in such a public place. And she could always slam her fist on the horn if she needed help fast.

'There are too many people,' Collons whispered, as though the drivers filling their tanks would be able to hear him. He pressed himself back against the seat, trying to get out of the light. 'Far too many. We must go somewhere quieter, darker.'

'No,' said Trish firmly. The last thing she wanted to do was go anywhere dark and private with him. 'Look, Blair, there are no microphones here and no one who could recognise my car or know who either of us is. If you don't want to talk to me here, you'll have to go to the police or let me take you. There isn't any third option.'

'I can't go to the police.' There was hysteria in his voice. 'I told you. I wish you'd listen to what I'm saying.'

Whatever he had or hadn't done to Kara – or anyone else – Trish found it hard to believe he could be the kind of rapist driven by rage and a longing to make women cower in front of him. But it was impossible not to see him forcing himself on Kara because he believed she'd wanted him. If she'd fought him, perhaps screaming, showing how much she hated what he was doing to her, could the shock of it have made him angry enough to kill her? Or perhaps he'd just needed to keep her quiet.

'You *must* go to the police,' Trish said quietly, pushing down her own fears, hoping he couldn't sense them.

He looked as though he had just had confirmation that the whole world was against him. His cheeks were trembling and his slightly protruding lower lip was wet. And then he moved his head and the light caught his neat little round brown eyes. Trish thought she could see anger behind the creepy, pleading misery they always showed, anger and hate.

'Blair, you must,' she said, as steadily as she could.

'It's just that Kara . . .' His voice broke on her name. His eyelids covered the anger and whatever else his eyes might have betrayed. Coughing, he pushed his clasped hands between his tightly closed thighs and leaned forward over them. 'Try to understand, Ms Maguire. Kara told me only a few days before she was killed that she'd seen Martin Drakeshill having a surreptitious meeting with Michael Napton.'

He looked round at Trish, as though he expected her to know what he was talking about. '*Now* do you see?'

'No,' she said. 'Napton? Who's he? Blair, I don't know what you're talking about.'

'He's the chief planning officer of Kingsford Council. I've told you about him before.'

'So you have, but not by name.'

'They had a much younger man with them,' Blair went on, his voice now straining with the effort of persuading Trish to take him seriously. It only made him sound constipated, and his contorted expression didn't help. 'She recognised him too, you see, and she told me she thought he'd seen her and must have told the others who she was. It's at that point they realised she was on to them and would have to be killed.'

'On to them about what? I don't understand.'

'About the drugs,' he shouted. Trish recoiled, frowning. She felt as if she had hold of an eel that kept squirming out of her grasp.

'Kara said the young man with Drakeshill and Napton was Sergeant Spinel, an officer in the drugs squad she'd had dealings with. When she saw them together it all fell into place.'

'What did?' As soon as she'd said it, Trish remembered Femur's questions about the name of Kara's lover and whether she'd ever mentioned anyone with the initial S in his name.

Collons turned on her a look of such icy fury that he didn't seem remotely pathetic.

'I'm not trying to be difficult,' Trish said quickly. 'Just trying to understand what you think they were doing together.'

Her calm voice seemed to have some effect. Collons's thighs relaxed and he removed his fists, laying his hands almost flat in his lap. He leaned back against the seat, sighing.

'I'm also trying to understand,' Trish went on, still carefully, 'why on earth you didn't tell me all this when we were first talking if it's so important.'

His face blurred in front of her as a torrent of questions about him and Kara, and about Kara and the drugs-squad sergeant spurted into Trish's mind.

'I didn't know then that I could trust you,' he said. 'In spite . . .'

Trish made her eyes focus on his face again. His expression was curious so she smiled slightly, and saw an answering movement of his wet lips. He leaned closer. She flinched before she could stop herself and felt the back of her head touch the car window. Collons leaned even further out of his own seat.

'In spite of everything Kara always says about you.'

Trish felt a sickening lurch in her gut as she noticed his use of the present tense. Was he conducting seances or merely imagining Kara giving him instructions? Either would fit with his history. Or could he be like one murderer Trish had heard about, who had cut off his girlfriend's head and kept it to chat to for months. Oh, God! What should she do?

Stop it, Trish, she ordered herself. He hasn't got Kara's head in his fridge or anywhere else. No one has ever suggested that her body was dismembered. Calm down, grow up and concentrate.

She controlled her face, keeping a fairly easy smile on her lips. As she corrected her posture so that she no longer leaned backwards, Collons moved jerkily back into his own seat and plucked at the knees of his soiled trousers. A peculiar smile made his lips move. Trish thought that he was about to say something until she realised that the words being shaped were never going to be said aloud, and that she was not the intended recipient.

He clearly had a vivid fantasy life and, equally clearly, Kara played a huge part in it. Trish began to see what might have happened. If Collons had been in Kara's garden to collect material for his fantasies of their life together and seen her with S, his dreams would have been smashed. Had he decided then that if he couldn't have her, no one would? Had he waited until S had gone and then broken in to kill her? And if S were this Spinel, had Blair turned the story round to make S the villain?

Blaming S for Kara's death would have been a way of getting her back in his fantasies. But he must have known, at some level, that it was he who'd killed her. Perhaps inventing the conspiracy between S and a well-known local criminal had been an elaborate attempt to avoid that unbearable truth. If so, his desperate attempts to persuade Trish, not only a friend of Kara's but also a barrister, to believe it could have been a way of helping him to believe it was real.

'You see, it must be something to do with drugs, Ms Maguire,' Blair said, jerking her out of her pre-occupation. His staring eyes were watering. Everything about him seemed damp.

'Kara hated drugs. Everyone in the council knew that. She thought they were at the root of most of the problems she had to deal with. She was always talking about finding ways to penalise people who were known to be dealers, and she'd run up against Spinel several times as she tried to force him to do his job. She thought he was slapdash at best.'

'Did she?' Trish couldn't think of any more useful comment, and Collons was looking at her as though he expected something.

'Yes, and "dangerous" at worst. Dangerous. That was the word she used. He and Drakeshill and Napton were somehow linked with the supermarket land deal so when we started to ask about the costs they got frightened, and then when they realised Kara had seen the three of them together, they had to make sure she couldn't tell anyone.'

'Blair, there's no evidence for *any* of this. They could have been three friends chatting together. Come on, you must admit that.'

He said nothing. He just looked at her as though he hated her.

'Now, I've got a question of my own,' Trish said, in a voice that sounded astonishingly confident. 'I want to know what you were doing in Kara's garden after dark several times in the week before the murder.'

'You don't understand,' he said, beginning to whimper. 'I knew you wouldn't, but Kara keeps insisting that I talk to you. Tell you the truth. I knew it wouldn't do any good.'

Trish lost patience. 'Blair, she's dead. She can't be insisting about anything.'

He shuddered, his whole squashy little body juddering in the seat beside her.

'Blair . . .?'

'I'd never have guessed you could be such a bitch,' he said. 'For the first time I'm glad she's dead. It would have hurt her so much to know what you're really like.'

Trish felt behind her for the door handle. She needed to know she could get out of the car fast if she had to. And she laid her free hand casually on the horn in case she needed it. Then she said, 'I think you'd better go now.'

Collons swivelled on his seat so that he was facing her. His lips began to work. A bubble of spit appeared in one corner.

The effort involved in keeping her expression calm and friendly was making Trish's scalp itch and her throat ache.

'I can't. Not yet. You've got to help me stop Kara's killer. She told me you're like a terrier when you're fighting for what's right. And this is. He's got to be found and stopped. The police aren't trying to find him. They know who he is and they want him shielded. You've got to do it. No one else will. He's dangerous. You've got to stop him before he does it again.'

He was edging ever closer to her, almost crying. Trish kept her right hand on the door handle behind her.

'You've got to help me. I can't do it alone.'

She could feel the pressure of his breath on her skin, smell the baked beans and cheese he had eaten for his last meal – and the decay of his teeth. She tried not to recoil.

'He's got to be stopped. And only you can do it now. Kara can't. She tried, but she didn't know enough about him to understand the threat.'

'And you do,' said Trish, almost certain that he was talking about himself. 'It's not up to me to stop him, Blair. If he can't stop himself, the only people who can are the police. You must talk to them and tell them everything you know. The investigation's being run by Chief Inspector William Femur, who isn't a local man. He's been drafted in from another area. You'd be in good hands with him. I've just been talking to him myself and –'

'You promised you wouldn't,' Collons cried, fumbling with the door handle.

Trish could see that the sweat on his fingers was making it impossible for him to grip the metal. He pushed the door open at last and ran.

She didn't know what to do as she got out of the car. Leaning against the cold wet metal, she breathed in great lungfuls of the delectably petrol-scented air and tried to think.

Chapter Twenty-five

Bill Femur was sitting quietly in the one armchair in Kara Huggate's small living room, trying to get a handle on the person she had been: not the social worker, or the victim, but the woman. Trish Maguire had obviously had a lot of time for her, and he'd been impressed by Maguire, impressed and bloody angry too.

For one thing she should never have interfered in his case; for another, he was sure she'd been holding something back. He still couldn't decide whether it was Kara's lover she was protecting or someone else. He'd let her go – he hadn't had any choice given that he had no grounds for an arrest – but he'd have another crack at her soon. The one thing he had believed was that she'd cared for Kara.

Everyone who'd known her had been the same, except for Spinel. They'd nearly all talked about her warmth and the way she treated people as though they mattered. However disadvantaged, dispossessed, demented or damaged they'd been, she'd listened to them with the same respect she showed the great and the good. One of her colleagues had said, in a tone that was more puzzled than anything else, as though it was something he'd never come across before, that Kara had somehow seen through all the mess that life dumped on you to the person you really were inside – and the one you wanted to be. Which was much the same as Maguire had said.

Were she and Steve Owler right? Could Kara have met the man who'd been the Kingsford Rapist, penetrated his mask of normality, and scared him into killing her?

Femur shook his head in exasperation. They had to be wrong. If the Kingsford Rapist had killed Kara, the thumbmarks on her body would have matched the ones on his first dead victim, and they didn't. And even if the lab had made a mistake about the thumb size, the original rapist would never have arranged Kara's body to mirror the position of her predecessor. That first victim hadn't been laid out, Femur was sure; she'd been flung down when the bastard had finished with her. It was only Kara who had been moved after she died, dragged and *placed* in that apparently casual heap with one arm under her head and the other half twisted behind her back.

Femur just couldn't buy it. He hadn't in the beginning and he still didn't. This was a copycat killing of the nastiest sort and somehow he was going to prove it.

He looked around Kara's room as though her possessions could give him the clues he wanted. Everything had been meticulously searched by the SOCOs already. There was no evidence here. He knew that. But still he hoped that some essence of Kara would be there to tell him what had happened in the last agonised hours of her life.

With its whitewashed walls and two quiet sunny semi-abstract landscape paintings, the room was like an indoor version of his imagined meadow. The pale beech bookshelves were untidily crammed with novels and psychology textbooks. Only one basic kilim, in a mixture of buffs and russet colours, softened the hardness of the polished floorboards, and there were none of the china bits and bobs that Sue stuck all over their lounge and cursed him for breaking.

He started thinking, half embarrassed, about a film he'd once watched with Sue one Saturday evening. He didn't reckon much to watching old black and white films, but there hadn't been any sport on that night so he'd watched this *Laura* with her.

It had been a fairly silly film, but Sue had enjoyed it and, although bits of it had made him laugh, he'd got caught up in the story in the end. There'd been an American cop sitting in the apartment of a murder victim, falling in love with her portrait.

Well, he wasn't in love with Kara Huggate, but by all accounts she had been a woman he'd have liked a lot, and she shouldn't have died.

He told himself it was only a matter of time before he got her killer. All he had to do was take it step by step, go on asking the right questions, and never let himself get sidetracked.

There was a CD player on the low bookshelf by the chair he was sitting in and he gave in to temptation and pressed the buttons to listen to the last piece of music Kara had ever heard. The icy sound of a pure soprano was let loose into the room. According to the label she was singing a sixteenth-century lament.

Femur wondered why Kara had been listening to anything so sad, and then decided that it must have been peace she'd wanted in her music, the detachment of this singer's passionless, perfect voice. To him it sounded as though it was all about acceptance of sorrow and he was angry all over again: a woman like Kara shouldn't have had to accept anything.

Looking towards the foot of the stairs, he thought of the photographs of her body and wished he hadn't had to know exactly what had been done to her there. The thought that she could have been put through all that extra horror just to disguise her killer's identity and real intentions made him burn up. It was one thing for a mad psychopath to terrorise and murder a woman because of his own incomprehensible urges, but quite another for a cynical bastard to do it to cover his own tracks.

When the phone rang Femur almost shouted. He'd been so deep into his reconstruction of Kara that if he'd been one to believe in ghosts, he might have thought her spirit had been with him in the room, only to be frightened away by the noise. Feeling fooled by his own sentimentality, he waited for the answering-machine to cut in.

The caller was probably only a double-glazing salesman. Femur's officers had been checking the tape every day, just as they had collected Kara's mail to read, but so far there hadn't been anything useful in any of it. The machine clicked and there was silence, presumably as her message was played to the caller, and then a strong, masculine, American voice: 'Kara? It's me. Great news! I *am* coming over to the UK again next week. I should hit Heathrow Tuesday at ten after six. I'll call you from the airport and come straight on over unless I hear. I got your letter, honey, I just haven't had a moment to answer. There's so much I have to say. I wish you were there. Goddam, I'm missing you. Sorry I couldn't call before, or even write. It's been hell here with Mandy and the kids. I can only call from the office now, and even there it's hard. She has spies everywhere. She can't wait to get me out of the house, but her attorneys are nailing me to the floor, and my people don't want me to give them any ammunition – like you. I can't wait till it's over and we can be together. If there's a problem about Tuesday, will you call the hotel and leave a message? I . . .'

Moving slowly and with an effort, as though the air was resistant, almost viscous, Bill Femur reached out his right hand to pick up the phone.

'Good evening. This is Chief Inspector William Femur of the Metropolitan Police.'

'What? Who?' The pleasantly deep voice had sharpened, but with suspicion not fear. 'Why're you picking up Kara's calls?'

'There's been a serious crime in the area. Who am I speaking to?'

'My name's Dale Waters. How serious? Is Kara OK? What's happened?'

'I regret to have to inform you, Mr Waters, that Ms Huggate is dead.'

'What?' he said, in an explosion that sounded as though he'd been punched in the gut. 'What happened?'

'When did you last see her, sir?' Femur asked, letting some sympathy leak into his voice, but not very much because he was so angry with his team for failing to find this Dale Waters, and with the man himself for being so secretive.

'Tuesday of the week before last. How'd she die? Goddammit, man, tell me what happened! She was my –'

'She was murdered, sir. What time did you leave her?'

'Murdered?'

Femur sighed. He felt sorry for the man – if he was innocent – but they had to move the conversation on.

'Yes, sir, murdered. Now, will you please tell me what time you saw her that Tuesday?'

'We spent the evening together in her cottage, then I drove to the airport, Heathrow, slept at the Balkan Hotel there –'

'What time did you get to the hotel?'

'About midnight, I guess, having left her around eleven fifteen, maybe eleven thirty.'

'Is there any way of confirming that?'

'You mean she died *that* night, after I left?'

'That's what we're trying to establish. She was found on the Wednesday morning by her cleaner. We have to establish the latest time she was seen alive.'

'I can see that. But I guess I don't have any witnesses to offer. There was a receptionist on duty at the hotel, but she wouldn't remember me. I didn't talk to her. They have keycards so I didn't ask for a key from the desk. And I didn't call anyone from my room. I took a shower and went to bed, then caught the first plane out – back to Boston – Wednesday. How'd he kill her?'

'He?'

'Isn't it a he? Did she . . .? Was it . . .?'

'Did she have a nickname for you, Mr Waters?'

'Nickname? What *is* this?'

'Would you just answer the question, sir?'

'If it's that important I'm not often in the UK, so she called me her Sojourner. Oh, God!' There was the sound of a deep intake of breath down the phone and then a spate of coughing. When the voice came again it sounded croaky: 'My apologies, Chief Inspector. There was some poem or other Kara knew that said something about the sojourner returns. Kind of thing. Was it . . . was it bad for her?'

'It wasn't quick and it wasn't pretty.'

'Oh, God!' The pain in Waters's voice should have been enough to confirm his innocence, but Femur was taking no chances. 'Can you give me your full name and address and details of your hotel and your flight?'

Dale Waters dictated all his details, including his planned time of arrival the following week and promised to answer any questions the police might have then. 'I'm an attorney, sir,' he added, surprising Femur. 'I'll do all I can to help. But I need to know what happened to Kara. I can't . . . Oh, God! Why didn't I stay with her that night?'

'I don't know, sir. Why didn't you?' asked Femur, interested.

'Because I didn't want to drive to the airport in rush-hour traffic,' the American said drearily. 'It's much quicker at night. What'd he do to her when I'd gone?'

'I'd rather give you the details when you're here.'

'Come on, Chief Inspector. I have to know.'

'She was attacked in her cottage and died. But don't think too much about it, sir. However bad it was for her, it's over now. She's at peace.'

'Sure.' His voice was raw enough to make Femur wish he could let him go, but there were things that still had to be asked.

'While you're on the line, will you tell me whether she ever talked to you about drugs, or drug dealers?'

'No. I don't think so. She wasn't a user, Chief Inspector, and neither am I, if that's what you're asking. She liked a drink now and then. No more than that.'

Femur heard him gulp, cough, try to say something else and fail.

'We know she herself wasn't an addict,' he said, giving the man time to get control of himself. 'The post-mortem made that clear enough. D'you know if she had any enemies?'

'There were people at work who were difficult.' His voice was working reasonably well again, but it was thickened and ragged at the edges. As well as the pain, Femur thought there was anger, perhaps even stronger than his own. 'She put some noses out of joint trying to clean the place up and cut budgets, but nothing to explain murder. Though there was a guy called Jed Thomplon, who –'

'We know all about him. He's in the clear. Anyone else?'

'Yeah, there was a man I wished she'd cut loose from. She was sure he wasn't dangerous any more. But he sounded . . . Oh God, if it's him, I'll never forgive myself. I should've made her see how –' His voice cracked and then there was silence.

'I understand, sir, believe me,' said Femur, keeping his compassion in check with difficulty. 'Who is he, this man she didn't think was dangerous?'

'He was a colleague, kind of.' There was a pause and then the sound of a nose being vigorously blown. 'His name was Blade or Blain. No, Blair. That was his first name. I don't know his surname. She talked about him often, trying to kid herself she liked him. She didn't, I could tell. He was a creep, and he made her skin crawl. *And* he'd been in trouble with the police years ago. But she tried to see the best in him, and she used to let him come to her house and talk to her about his fantasies by the hour.'

'Have you any idea where this man lives?' Femur felt cold all over. All his theories about Spinel, about drug dealers, and about the wrong sized bruises ruling out the Kingsford Rapist suddenly seemed pathetic in the face of this news of a creepy man with a police record whom Kara had let into her cottage to talk about his fantasies. God almighty! How could she have taken such a risk?

'Somewhere in Kingsford. You'd find him in her address book.'

'Right.' Femur wanted to get straight back to the station and Kara's address book but he owed Dale Waters something, so when he'd got all the relevant phone and fax numbers, he said, 'You've been very helpful, and I'm sorry – very sorry – you had to hear the news this way.'

'It's been . . . rough. I'll call you from the airport when I get in.'

'Thank you, sir.' Femur pulled his mobile out of his raincoat pocket and rang the incident room.

As he waited for an answer, holding on to his impatience with difficulty, he looked once more around the simply furnished room, wondering how Kara's Sojourner could have left so little evidence of his existence. If they had been on the sort of terms he suggested, there should have been something, a photo at least.

'Incident room.'

'Tony?'

'Guv. What's up?'

'Have a look in Huggate's address book, will you, for someone called Blair? Now. I've no idea of the surname so start at the As and carry on till you find him. And then have a car ready. We've got to bring him in. I'm on my way back.'

'OK, Guv. I've got a girl from the drugs squad here, who wants to see you.' There was a muffled conversation, then Blacker came back on the line. 'Sorry. Not a girl. Guv, I've got Constable Bethany Deal here, who wants to talk to you urgently. She won't tell me why, says the confidentiality she promised means that she must speak to you direct and to no one else.'

The last thing Femur wanted now was any distraction from Blair. It had been a long day already and he wasn't going to be able to get his head down for hours. But he'd have to find out what she wanted.

'Tell her I'll be there within ten minutes.'

He saw her as soon as he walked back into his office, a young woman in her early twenties with a calm, sensible face and a lot of luxuriant dark hair blowing about her face. She wasn't in uniform, but wearing slim-cut dark trousers, not jeans, and a long, loose, knobbly kind of sweater of some sort of shiny wool.

'Right,' he said, as he showed her into his room. 'Now, I haven't much time. What is it that you couldn't tell Sergeant Blacker?'

'A young man called Wes Jones approached me this evening, sir,' she said, with an admirable lack of excuse and shilly-shallying. 'He works for a used-car dealer in Kingsford called Martin Drakeshill, along with several other lads who've been in young-offender institutions.'

'Like this Wes himself?'

'Yes, sir. Spot of ABH. But he's been out six months and got this job as a car mechanic's assistant. I think he's a good lad, as reliable as they ever are and – '

'Why?'

'Because of the way he talked about what was worrying him, sir. Which is that one of the other mechanics at the garage, who has always frightened him, has been strutting round the place, looking – in his words – too puffed-up and too much on the edge.'

'Oh, yes?' In spite of the lack of shilly-shallying, Femur was impatient. 'What's his name?'

'Charles Chompton, always known as Chaz or Chompie, depending on whether he likes you or not. Chompie is only for the inner circle.'

'Right. So?'

'So, Wes thinks that Chompie's scary strutting could have something to do with the social worker who was killed, sir.'

Femur frowned. That was the last thing he'd expected.

'Wes says that Chompie's eyes were glittering like he was on something the morning after it happened, and he's never stopped talking since about how she deserved everything that happened to her because she was an interfering slag who caused trouble wherever she went. Wes thinks she might have been Chompie's social worker and that, maybe, just maybe, she'd been interfering in his life so that he'd decided he had to stop her.'

'Right.' Femur felt like putting his head in his hands and giving up. To have a whole slew of new suspects dumped in his lap within half an hour and no evidence against any of them was just what he didn't need. He'd been up since six, working to no effect whatever; Cally was long gone to her actress; the rest of the team had knocked off for the night, even Steve Owler. Only Blacker was out there in the incident room, trying to get an address for this Blair character. 'And has Wes got anything to back up this theory?'

'No, sir. But I thought you ought to hear what he had to say.'

'Right,' he said, trying to recover his temper. She'd done the right thing; it wasn't her fault he felt he was losing the plot. 'Yes, and you were right to tell me. You'd better give me all the details while you're here.' Femur pulled a pad out of the desk drawer and grabbed a felt-tip.

'There aren't any details, sir: only Wes's feeling, based on the violent inmates who terrified him when he was doing time, that Chompie had committed some kind of serious assault around the time the social worker was killed and later slagged her off.'

Femur raised his eyebrows. 'Couldn't he just have been turned on by the thought of it? Some violent young men are excited by that sort of story.'

'It's possible, but I'm inclined to believe Wes, sir. He knows about violent young men from first hand, in a way that I don't, and he was scared shitless, if you ask me. He hated coming to talk about Chompie, but I think he felt it was his duty.' Bethany Deal got up to go, putting her chair tidily straight against the wall. 'You look tired, sir. I'll get out of your way.'

Just a minute. Why did this Wes come to *you* with his worries?'

'Oh, he didn't. He came looking for Sergeant Spinel because he's picked up on the fact that Drakeshill sometimes gives Spinel information he hears on the street about drugs coming into Kingsford. That's why Wes thought Spinel would be the most appropriate person to give *this* piece of information to.'

'Right.'

'But the sergeant was out,' she went on calmly, 'so I filled in for him. As soon as I realised the kind of thing Wes wanted to say, I took him out for a walk. When he got brave enough to tell me what he had, I said I'd handle it for him and the best thing he could do was go back to work and pretend he'd never come to talk to anyone. That way he'd be safer.'

Femur frowned. The constable's eyes were clear of malice and nasty knowingness. 'Safer, eh? And was that why you came to me instead of waiting until the morning to give the message to Sergeant Spinel himself, Constable?'

She opened her mouth then shut it again, before taking a careful breath and trying a shy smile. Femur didn't respond. She'd have to say it, whatever it was. Did she have the bottle? If not, he'd be disappointed in her. 'I don't know how well you know Sergeant Spinel,' she said, her pleasant voice shaking just a little, 'but I'm not sure how safe he would be as a confidant for a frightened boy trying to report the violence of one of Drakeshill's staff.'

'Ah. Would you like to sit down again, Constable Deal, and tell me more?'

'Not really, sir. I think I've probably said too much.

And I haven't any evidence in any case.'

'Is it Spinel's discretion that worries you? Or his likely treatment of the boy? I *am* a safe confidant and I have no loyalties here in Kingsford.'

'No, I know. That's why I thought I'd come and talk to you. It was a little bit of both actually, sir. And Martin Drakeshill is a . . . well, a friend, I think, of Sergeant Spinel as well as a snout, and he's sometimes been in a bit of bother, so if he thought one of his lads was grassing up one of the others, it might not go so well for the lad who's doing the grassing. If you see what I mean, Guv.'

'Clear as crystal, Constable Deal. I'm impressed all round. And that you waited here this long to tell me. You'd better get off home now, and don't worry about a thing. I'll look into it and no one will ever know where it came from. OK?'

'Yes, thank you, sir.' She sounded grateful, but not in any exaggerated way. Femur began to think quite well of whoever had been recruiting young officers for Kingsford. Between Deal and Owler, they had the beginnings of a good, honest, painstaking team. Even if Owler had cocked up the search for Kara's lover and missed Blair completely.

'By the way, Constable Deal?'

'Sir?'

'Have you ever heard of a local man called Blair something? Blair as a Christian name?'

She thought for a moment then shook her head.

'OK. What's Wes's address in case we want to talk to him?'

'He wouldn't tell me, and I couldn't force him, but you could always find him at Drakeshill's. They wear name badges there.'

'Right.'

As soon as Bethany Deal had gone, Blacker put his

head round the door. 'Blair Collons, Guv. Flat four, Holmside Court, Park Road, Kingsford. You want me to drive you?'

'Thanks, Tony. I'll fill you in as we go.'

It was still pouring with rain, but Femur's mac felt wet inside as well as out. He left it dripping over the back of his chair and made a soaking dash to Blacker's car.

Blacker listened in silence to Femur's outburst of fury that the team who were supposed to have trawled Kara's life for anyone who could have done her damage had missed not only the Sojourner but also this Collons character, who was actually in her address book, for God's sake.

'But not in her diary, Guv,' Blacker said, apparently trying to be fair. 'I checked while you were with that girl just now. They are working through her address book, but I think we've all been so hung up on the idea that it's S we're looking for, that someone whose initials are BC just wouldn't have registered. They'd have got to Blair Collons in time.'

'We don't have time,' Femur said, rubbing his eyes again. Then he blew, a great gust of frustration. 'And then again, this Collons character may be a decoy.'

'You mean if the Sojourner isn't on the level?'

'Right. It's possible he was phoning to establish the idea of his innocence in case we'd got on to the fact of his existence some other way.'

'It's a bit far-fetched, Guv.' Blacker was peering through the rain, looking for a street sign. 'But if you're right, maybe he was just frustrated. I shouldn't think any of the US papers are reporting the case, so he could've rung Kara's number in the hope that someone would answer and he'd get news of how far we've got with the investigation.'

'Bloody nowhere.' Femur knew he was sounding

morose, but he was so tired and so angry he didn't care.

'What did that girl have to say?'

Femur told him that, too, feeling as though he was trying to keep afloat in a murky pond full of oil slicks and rubbish. All he needed was one solid bit of evidence and he could climb out and start doing something useful.

'No wonder you look punch-drunk, Guv. It could still be any of them. Though I'm not sure that I'd put the overtime budget on the word of a frightened boy's assessment of the glitter in the eyes of a bully who'd always scared him. Would you?'

'No. But we'll have to take a look at them both, and Drakeshill. Can't ignore anything in a pig of a case like this.'

'Guv, I know you're hung up somehow about Barry Spinel, and you're probably right. I've never known you wrong when it comes to bent cops. But have you thought of turning him over to CIB3?'

'I'll do that if I have to. But I want to get Kara's killer first. If we bring them in to investigate Spinel's perversions of the course of justice, or bribery, or whatever it is, they'll only get in the way. We'd get the killer in the end, but that wouldn't be their priority. Still . . .' Femur caught sight of the number of a building on their left. 'This is it. Pull up as near the door as you can. I don't want to get any wetter than I have to.'

He stayed in the car while Blacker leaned on the bell for Flat 4. Failing to get any answer, he rang 6 and then, when that didn't produce any voice, 5.

'Yeah?'

'Blair Collons?'

'Christ, who wants him *now*?'

'What d'you mean?'

'There was some woman after him earlier on, ringing my bell. She got him in the end, though, and they went off together in her car. I should think he's with her now.'

Blacker looked back at Femur and beckoned. Femur picked himself out of the car and splashed through the puddles to the inadequate shelter of a shallow-tiled porch.

'May we come in and have a word, sir? We're from the Metropolitan Police,' said Blacker.

The owner of Flat 5 admitted them. On the way upstairs, Blacker told Femur what the householder had said. The first thing Femur asked when he opened the door to his flat was: 'What did she look like, the woman who came back to see Mr Collons?'

'Tall, thin, dark. Short hair. Driving an Audi.'

Trish Maguire, thought Femur, almost shaking with rage. So this is what she didn't tell me. How much does she know? And who the *hell* is Blair Collons? And why hasn't anyone mentioned him till now?

CHAPTER TWENTY-SIX

The repeated ringing of his bell didn't help, or the demanding voices, but they weren't the problem. Blair could ignore them if he tried hard enough. But Kara had gone, and there was no way he could ignore that.

He lay in bed with his limp prick drooping between fingers that didn't seem to be his at all. He hated it, and Kara. In spite of all the stories he told himself about her, her photos, and even the knickers he had stolen from her bathroom, nothing happened. Tears oozed out of his eyes. After everything he'd done, it didn't seem fair that he should have lost her now.

If she'd lived she'd probably have despised him just like everyone else. Just like Trish Maguire. He'd thought for a while that Kara might have been right about Trish Maguire, but she was as bad as all the rest. Now he had no one. He was going to be alone for ever, like he was before he'd found Kara. He'd been like other people when he'd had her. She'd cared about him; she'd talked to him, told him things she didn't tell other friends. He'd mattered to her.

But she was dead. Worse than dead. Her photo was

still behind him on the wall, but now it wasn't anything except a photo, and a stolen one at that.

He couldn't go on lying there, so disgusting, with Kara's photo looking down at him.

As he stood up, he ripped the photo from the wall and tore it in two. Then he fetched the others from his desk and tore them up as well. If she'd gone, she'd gone. He didn't want her pictures sneering at him like every other woman he'd ever met. He picked up her knickers and threw them with the torn bits of the photos in the kitchen bin.

It was Trish Maguire's fault. If she hadn't said the things she'd said, Kara would still have been with him. He hated Trish Maguire.

CHAPTER TWENTY-SEVEN

Half-way back to Southwark the rain started pounding down on Trish's windscreen like a celestial power shower. She was so tired – and so worried about what she ought to do about Collons – that she could hardly make herself peer closely enough through the deluge to see the landmarks she needed. Even when she did, it was tricky to read the road surface, so slick with rain that it threw up weird reflections. A flash in her mirror made her look away from the road ahead for a moment.

An enormous container lorry surged towards her car, throwing up fans of dirty brown spray from each of its dozens of enormous wheels. Idling as she was, Trish had clearly infuriated the driver, who was flashing all his headlights.

He could bloody well wait until there was somewhere for her to pull in safely. A bus stop appeared in the rainy distance and she turned on her indicator, pulling aside to allow the blaring monster to pass. She saw the driver mouthing something at her through his window and shrugged, sticking in her lay-by until he, his anger, and the spray from his wheels were far ahead.

Trish reached Southwark eventually and managed to park in her usual space on the opposite side of the road from her building. Her head was aching again and she felt drained of all energy and decisiveness. The iron staircase that led up to her flat was almost directly opposite her car yet in all the rain it seemed miles away.

As she tried to gather the tiny amount of strength she needed to get herself across the road and up to bed, she decided she'd have to tell Femur about Blair Collons. However much she wanted to be as kind and protective towards him as Kara would have been, she couldn't take the responsibility any longer. If he was what she feared, Femur would have to deal with him.

She took her mobile out of her bag and dialled the number he'd given her. No one answered. She rang Directory Inquiries for the Kingsford police and got through quite easily, but they couldn't raise Femur either. They offered to take a message, but she wanted to be sure it was Femur himself who dealt with Collons and so all she asked them to tell him was that she'd rung and would try again in the morning.

Feeling slightly less pathetic for taking even that small action, Trish got out and locked the car. She had to pull up her collar against the icy rain that trickled off her short hair. On her way across the road she stepped in at least three deep puddles, soaking her shoes and socks. As usual, her keys were right at the bottom of her bucket-like shoulder bag and she had to fumble through money, notes, cheque books, bills she had meant to pay, Lil-lets, makeup and all sorts of rubbish.

She wished that George was there, waiting for her, as he had once or twice waited for her to come back from an out-of-London case. The flat would have been light and warm, and there would have been saucepans full of delicious food steaming in the kitchen, and, best of all, George himself.

At last. The keys poked painfully into her cold questing fingers and she wrenched the bunch up through the layers of detritus, showering bits of paper all over the wet step.

'Oh, bugger it all!'

She got the Chubb unlocked before she bent down to pick up what she'd dropped. Most of it was already sodden and filthy. Then the keys slid out of her cold wet fingers.

Suddenly anxious, she paused, still bent over, listening. She couldn't hear anything, but she was sure she was not alone. She had to get inside before it was too late. Fumbling with the keys, her fingers feeling twice their usual size, she shook the bunch until the right Yale came to the top. It was already in the lock and she was flexing her hand to turn it, when she heard a familiar voice behind her. 'Go in. Quickly.'

She couldn't move. And she didn't dare look behind her. His arm touched her shoulder and she felt the prick of sharp metal against the side of her neck. As she squinted sideways she saw the red wooden handle of some kind of tool. Her heart stopped beating for a second and she almost fell. Her right hand was still on the key in the lock; water dripped from her hair down her face and neck, and under the sleeve of her upraised arm, almost sizzling on her warmer flesh. She felt paralysed.

'Get in.'

'What do you want?' she asked, furious with herself for producing such a high, quavery sound. The sharpness against her neck took on an added pressure and turned to pain. The sensation of trickling rain on her neck warmed, and she knew she was bleeding. A gloved hand reached over her shoulder and forced open the door.

Then the hand loomed across her face and the arm settled around her neck, not tight enough to choke her but quite powerful enough to fill her with terror.

'Get in, bitch.'

The flat was pitch dark, with all the blinds shut, blocking out the street-lights and the moon, but Trish knew exactly where everything was. She edged forward, and when she sensed the man pausing to slam the door, she wrenched herself down, away from his enclosing arm, and ran, dropping her heavy bag on the floor. As she fled towards the far side of the room, she heard him trip and fall heavily. She hoped it was her bag that had felled him, and thought she should have stayed to trample on his body.

Standing behind the chair, hearing him swear and pick himself up to come after her, she screamed, a hoarse, shocking sound that had burst out of her before she knew what she was doing.

The man started to walk heavily towards her through the darkness, swearing as he knocked into furniture or stumbled, telling her what he was going to do to her when he caught her.

She couldn't get away. Any minute now, he'd find a light and see her.

'I'll kill you, bitch.'

He was much nearer. She had to do something. But she couldn't think of anything except the huge, shrieking danger. His breathing was like a bloodhound's. It was very near now.

'I can see you, slag.'

He probably could. She could see the shape of him in the dark. He had a round, tight-looking head and big shoulders.

Then the star-like halogen spots in the ceiling flashed and spread light into every possible hiding place in the huge room. He'd found the main switch. Trish clung to the chair-back, unable to move.

He was of middle height, very powerfully built, and he had a black woollen balaclava covering his head, with rough holes cut for his eyes and mouth. His lips were very red against the coarse, ribbed wool, and they were full and slick with spit. His clothes were the muddy green and brown of all paramilitary fantasists.

It wasn't a knife in his right hand but a long, red-handled screwdriver with a tip that looked as though it had been honed to needle like sharpness. In his other hand he had something soft and black. As he came towards her, his eyes glistening and his lips moving slowly in the rough woollen slit of the balaclava, she saw that it was a sock.

The chair in front of her had a heavy seat cushion and she grabbed it. A knife, even a sharpened screwdriver, would cut through it easily, but it was all she had. It might deflect a blow just enough to give her time to get out of range if he did try to stab her.

He lunged. Trish couldn't think, but her feet took her out of the range. She clutched the cushion to her stomach and dodged to her left behind one of the long squashy black sofas.

He extricated himself from the chair without trouble, laughing. His breathing was even shorter and more excited. The spittle was collecting in the corner of his mouth, and he pushed his tongue forward, spreading the moisture all around his lips. He drove himself at her again, still laughing.

Trish caught his screwdriver with her pathetic cushion. The cover was cut as though it were made of the thinnest paper. Feathers billowed out of the wound in the fabric and floated upwards on currents of hot air. He spat out a mouthful of feathers like a fox who'd had his fill of one particular chicken and grinned through his mask.

Trish realised he was only playing with her. He could have stabbed her for real, but he hadn't even tried. Yet.

He pushed up his right sleeve with his left hand. His white skin was darkened by the thick black hairs that sprouted all over it, almost disguising a large tattoo on his forearm. Trish gagged as she saw that it was a red and blue pattern of snakes feasting on a woman's eviscerated body. He flexed his muscles to make the snakes move.

Feathers seemed to be everywhere, getting in her mouth and eyes, and tangling in her hair. She dropped the split cushion and pushed her hands across her eyes. It didn't seem possible that she would ever breathe freely again. He moved nearer, still laughing and playing his tongue about his lips. She backed away at the same speed, letting her eyes stray away from his for an instant so that she could pick up another cushion. She heard a slight noise, thought it was the creaking of the front door, and whirled round to see George launching himself forward as he yelled, 'Trish, look out!'

He smashed into the man at full stretch in a rugger tackle that brought him crashing face down to the floor. As he fell, the screwdriver in his outstretched hand slipped down Trish's leg, ripping through her jeans. Surprised by pain, she looked down and saw a long red line, with blood swelling out of it in a fat, scarlet mound that burst and poured down her leg.

'Trish, get the screwdriver,' gasped George, who was working himself up the man's prone body, eventually sitting straddled across his back and pinning his arms to the floor.

Trish nodded, but she couldn't move.

'It's OK, Trish,' George said, more quietly. He struggled to control his breathing then smiled at her, looking almost normal. 'It's OK now. I'm here. I've got him. He can't do anything else to you now. But it would help if you could get his screwdriver away from him, and then go to the phone and call the police.'

Trish nodded, but she still couldn't move.

'Come on, Trish darling. You can do it. And you've got to. We need to get his screwdriver first. Don't use your hands, just stamp on *his* hand. OK? Come on, darling. Come on, Trish. You can do it.'

Feeling as though she was pulling herself out of a viciously sucking bog, Trish forced herself away from the wall. Once she had started moving, it got easier with each step. And when she planted her still-soaked shoe on the man's wrist and pivoted the ball of her foot on it, turning it from side to side with most of her weight on it, as though she were stubbing out a fag end, she felt flooded with power. It was extraordinary: a wildly exhilarating surge of utterly shaming revenge.

The man was still cursing her, even though his head was jammed against the floor by one of George's hands.

'Shut up and let her have the screwdriver!' he yelled.

When the man didn't let go, George grabbed a handful of balaclava and the hair underneath it, picked the man's head up then banged it on the floor. And again. The balaclava came off in his hand, revealing a young, snub-nosed face covered with stubble. George flung away the balaclava.

The man's hand opened at last and Trish kicked the screwdriver well out of his reach, before bending to pick it up between her thumb and forefinger.

'Well done, darling. Now, the police. Quick as you can. Aagh.'

Trish, on her way to the phone, glanced back to see George rolling aside with his hands clasped over his genitals. The man was struggling to his feet. Trish punched 999 into the phone and was answered within a split second. The man was on his feet. Trish yelled her address into the phone and then: 'He's got a screwdriver! Quick!'

She didn't wait to hear any answer, but left the receiver on her desk. The man was running towards her again. His face was clenched into a furious mask. The screwdriver was at the back of her desk. She flung a pile of heavy legal reference books over it, and stuck out one foot, hoping to trip him up. But he dodged, ignored his screwdriver and belted for the door. Trish followed him, but she was too late. He'd reached the bottom of the iron stairs before she was half-way down and she knew she'd never catch him.

George's face was greenish white when she went back to him, and there were huge drops of sweat all over his forehead. 'Sorry, I can't chase him,' he gasped. 'Trish . . .'

'It's all right,' she said, taking his head between both her hands. 'It's all right, George. There's no point in even trying to catch him. The police may get him. They'll be here any minute. You did brilliantly.'

She managed to laugh, half sobbing, and kissed his hair.

'Aagh.' George tried to straighten up and failed. 'Christ! Trish. You're bleeding like a stuck pig.'

She looked down at her leg and then across to the trail of blood between them and her desk. 'Shit!' she said, in astonishment. At last she became aware of how much her leg was hurting.

In the distance she could hear sirens. It sounded as though there were at least three cars. In what felt like seconds there were heavy footsteps on the iron stairs and then a tremendous pounding on the front door with yells of, 'Police. Open up. Police.'

The last time the police had come pounding on her door, she had hated them. Now they seemed heaven-sent.

'Coming,' George shouted, trying to stand up again. He hobbled towards the door. Then, as the banging increased into a frenzy, he added even more loudly, 'He's gone. We couldn't stop him.'

Trish, hopelessly trying to staunch her leaking leg with the remains of the slashed cushion cover, overtook him and opened the door. After one look at the blood everywhere, the feathers sticking to her scarlet hands and leg, the first fresh-faced constable put up a shaking hand to his radio. Other men and women jostled behind him.

George caught up with her and said, gasping between the words, 'He ran about two minutes ago. Dressed in army fatigues, about five ten or eleven, tough, early twenties, black stubble, snub nose, curly hair. Did you notice anything else, Trish?'

'Only that he must have a big bruise on his face. George had him by the hair and slammed his face down on the floor. There must be a mark.'

'OK, Constable,' said an efficient-sounding woman officer to the man with the radio. 'Got all that? Call it in *now*, take the car and go after him with Thompson.' She looked back at Trish 'Will you be able to identify him when we pick him up?'

'Yes.'

'Great. Well, I can see you need a bit of help here,' she said, smiling from Trish to George and back again. 'Wayne? Call out a blood-wagon will you. Sorry, ambulance. I call them blood-wagons.'

'Fine by me,' Trish said, relieved to be in the hands of someone so breezily confident.

'Now, I'm Sergeant McDonald.' She put a hand on Trish's shoulder. 'Come on in, and tell me your names.'

She urged Trish towards the sofa. Now that the danger had gone, and even George was looking better and not as though he might pass out or throw up at any moment,

Trish felt almost hysterical with relief. A bubble of laughter emerged from between her lips and then another.

'It's OK,' said Sergeant McDonald, who had obviously seen such sights before. 'You're both OK now. Come and sit down.'

'I don't want my sofa covers getting bloody,' said Trish. For some reason her legs gave way just then and she subsided, not very elegantly, on to the floor, still laughing. But there were tears on her face, too, along with the feathers that seemed super glued to her cheeks with her own blood.

'I must look like a half-killed chicken,' she said.

'Turkey,' said George, who was wiping his hands over his face and giving his name to another officer, busily taking down the details. The young constable Sergeant McDonald had addressed as Wayne was still yelling urgently into his radio and three others stood, just gazing at the carnage. 'It's not as bad as it looks,' said Trish, working hard to get herself back in control.

'Cups of tea, Wayne, when you're ready. OK?' said Sergeant McDonald, whose hand was still on Trish's shoulder. Trish couldn't quite work out how it had got there or what she was doing on the floor. Her mind wasn't firing properly.

The sergeant was squatting beside her, talking to her, asking her questions. Heat flooded Trish's head and then her whole body, only to be followed by what felt like a cold shower. The floor beneath her tilted and flung her about. She didn't know she was going to lose consciousness until she was too far out to do anything about it. She tried to say George's name again, but her tongue wouldn't move.

When she opened her eyes again, a man in a livid lime

green all-in-one uniform was bending over her. She looked up into his face.

'Ah, there you are. D'you know what your name is?'

'Of course I do. This is my flat you're in,' she said crisply. Then she realised why he was asking and smiled. 'Trish Maguire. Is George here?'

'Yes. He's recovering in the chair over there.' The paramedic moved aside so that Trish could sit up.

She wasn't in her flat any longer. The walls around her were a dirty cream and the chair George was sitting in was one of a row full of people in their outdoor clothes. He smiled at her and stood up.

Trish frowned. She looked down at her own body to see that it was covered with a red blanket and that she was lying on a wheeled trolley. Hospital.

George, looking almost his normal colour, came towards her. She had never seen so much love – or so much relief – in anyone's face.

'God! Trish, you frightened me, passing out like that. How're you feeling?'

'Wonderful,' she said. 'Well, sore. You?'

'Ditto. They've got a doctor coming pretty soon, they say, to check you out and see if you need stitches.'

'Great.' She turned back to the paramedic. 'Look, I don't suppose I needed an ambulance really, did I? They were only grazes.'

'The cuts aren't deep, but I thought you ought to get checked out. The doctor'll tell you everything you need. He'll want to know if you've had a recent tetanus shot.'

'I hadn't thought of that. That screwdriver could've been filthy. And presumably hepatitis as well. And Aids.'

George's hand was stroking her hair. 'We can think about all that in time, Trish. The crucial thing now is to get you stitched up and on your feet again.'

'Did the intruder cut himself?' asked the paramedic.

275

'No. No, I don't think so.'

'You should be all right, then. The Aids virus can't live long without a host. It's unlikely to have been active on the screwdriver. But you can always have a test to make sure. I've got to get back to the ambulance. Will you be all right now?'

'We'll be fine,' said Trish. 'Look, you've been very kind. Thank you so much.'

'It's what we're here for. So long.'

Trish smiled at his Kermit-like retreating back and then at George. 'I'm sorry, you know,' she said. He looked surprised and his stroking hand paused. 'About what I said. About, you know, interference and all that.'

'No. It's me who should be sorry. It was a ham-fisted thing to do, my love.' His hand moved on her head again. 'Whatever I think, the way you deal with your father *is* your affair. I shouldn't ever have –'

'What have we here?' said a young woman doctor, with a face like a hurt child. 'Knife wound?' She looked suspiciously at George, then behind him to where, Trish saw, two uniformed police officers were standing.

'No, no,' said Trish quickly, reading the expression in the doctor's face. 'It wasn't him. He saved me. It was an intruder.'

'OK. Good.' The doctor waved to a porter who came over to wheel Trish's bed into a cubicle.

It turned out that the paramedic had cleaned Trish's cuts in her flat while she was still unconscious, and had also made sure that there was no arterial damage, before strapping her wounds with temporary dressings. Those had to be removed, painfully pulling the stubble from her leg.

'Teach me to let my legs get hairy in winter,' she said, seeing that George was worried by the faces she'd made.

'Nothing serious there,' said the doctor. 'I'll get a nurse

to sort you out and take some blood samples. We'll test for all the possible infections. And then you can go home. Have you got transport?'

'I think we'll get a lift in a police car,' said George, gesturing to the cubicle curtains, behind which the two young officers were still patiently waiting.

'Oh, sure,' said the doctor, whisking the curtains aside as she left, adding to the officers, 'Won't be long now.'

Only half an hour later, with the tight, comforting strapping around her leg, Trish was back in the flat, sipping tea and answering questions. At first it had been hard to persuade either George or the police that the attack hadn't sent wild persecution fantasies flooding through her brain. As she relayed everything she knew about Kara's murder, it seemed weird that George had no idea what she had been doing and hadn't even heard of Blair Collons.

Collons, she thought suddenly, pausing in her explanation of her first visit to Kingsford. Since he hadn't been her attacker, he was almost certainly innocent of Kara's murder too.

'Ms Maguire?' said the constable, who was taking notes.

'Sorry,' said Trish, flooded with relief at the knowledge that she had not been protecting a killer from the police. 'I keep thinking of other things. Look, I think you'd better get in touch with Chief Inspector William Femur in the incident room at Kingsford as soon as you can. He's dealing with the Kara Huggate case and he knows everything I know – and much more. I was with him only this evening. Oh, shit!'

'What, Trish?' George, who had been looking horrified as she related what she'd been doing, sounded as though he was in the twelfth round of a fight with a world heavyweight champion. 'What now?'

'The screwdriver. I wasn't even thinking.'

'It's OK, Trish. The police have already got it.'

'No. It's not that. Just that I've probably buggered the fingerprints by picking it up.'

'You may have. But didn't you say the man was wearing gloves?'

'Yes. So maybe that's not . . . Look, I think that's really all I can tell you.' She gazed around her flat. 'It still looks like a chicken killing shed in here. Will I be able to clean it up or will you need any of it for evidence?'

'We'd like to send a SOCO first thing in the morning so you won't be able to do any cleaning till then. Is that OK?'

'Fine. I just want to get to bed now.'

'We'll leave you to it. If you think of anything else, you will tell us, won't you? Either of you?'

They both agreed and Trish sat nursing her mug of tea while George showed the two officers out.

Later, when they were lying in each other's arms in her bed, she asked him why he had come back just then. He kissed her bare shoulder. 'I wish I could say I knew you needed help, or that I felt you calling out to me, but I didn't. I got your message and I'd come back to have it out with you. I couldn't sleep – again – and I thought we had to clear the air, tell each other how angry we felt and draw a line and start again.'

'Ironic!'

'Yes. And then when I had a foot on the bottom stair outside I heard you scream. I came up those stairs like a torpedo. I'm not quite sure what happened next. I saw your face, and his screwdriver, and I lost it.'

'You did brilliantly.' She kissed him. 'A true hero.'

The phone rang.

'It's him,' she said, as her eyes dilated.

'What? What d'you mean? How d'you know, Trish?'

She turned on the light and looked at the clock. 'It's the time he rang before.'

'Don't,' said George as she touched the phone.

'I must. We need to know who he is. Hang on, George.' She lifted the receiver, holding it a little way from her ear so that he could hear too. 'Hello?'

'You may have got away wiv it vis time, slag, but don't fink we'll let it happen again.'

That was it. The phone was banged down and they heard no more.

'That settles it,' George said, pushing off the duvet. 'We're not staying here. I'm taking you to Fulham. We'll spend the rest of the week there.'

TWENTY-EIGHT

'Chief Inspector William Femur returning to the interview room at ten thirty-three, Sunday the sixteenth of February,' Tony Blacker said into the tape, as Femur stood in the doorway holding two plastic cups of tea. He watched Blair Collons twisting his fingers in and out of each other and chewing his lips, still looking as though he might throw up at any minute. The thin plastic wasn't much protection from the heat of the tea and Femur shook his hands to cool them as soon as he'd dumped the cups on the table.

Collons didn't look up, he just sat nibbling his lips and staring at the tea stains on the melamine. His Adam's apple was working up and down in his neck as though he was being forced to swallow too much.

Watching him, Femur thought of the hour that he and Blacker had spent hanging around Collons's flat last night, hoping to catch him returning from whatever assignation he'd had with Trish Maguire. They had given up after an hour, but they'd gone back first thing this morning and had better luck. But he wasn't giving anything away.

All he'd told them in a couple of hours' questioning was that he'd met Kara Huggate on council business before he was dismissed for gross misconduct. Close examination of the events surrounding his dismissal had produced the fact that Kara had played no part in it, having no responsibility for his department, but that she had been wonderfully supportive after he'd been forced out.

When it became clear that they weren't going to be able to persuade or force him into telling them anything else, Femur had left the room to phone Trish Maguire in the hope of getting something he could use as a lever. But she wasn't answering her phone. Femur had left a message on her answering-machine and then, deciding to find out whether sympathy might trigger a confession, fetched the tea.

'Here.' He smiled. 'I got you one with milk and sugar, Mr Collons. I hope that's OK,' he said, pushing one cup across the table towards him.'

The little man looked surprised at the kindness. 'Thank you. How much longer am I going to be here?'

'Only as long as you want. As I've repeatedly said, you're not under arrest. But you knew Kara Huggate better than any of us. And you have information that may help us to get her killer.'

Collons shrugged and shimmied in his seat. 'Sergeant Blacker's been treating me as though I was your chief suspect.'

That was the last thing Femur wanted or would have expected of such an experienced officer. He turned to look at him in amazement. Tony Blacker was tugging at his left ear. He looked embarrassed and so he bloody well should have.

'While you were out of the room, sir, Mr Collons admitted that he sometimes spent some time after dark in Kara Huggate's garden, sir,' he said. 'Without her knowledge. That fitted in with everything we'd been told by the neighbours, but it seemed strange behaviour to me and I was trying to persuade him to explain it.'

And to deal with your own guilt at not having believed the neighbour, thought Femur, in irritation. He wished he hadn't given Caroline the weekend off, she'd have tackled the whole interview differently, worked to give Blair Collons enough confidence to open up.

'Right. I see.' Femur turned back to his suspect.

Collons was looking defiant but even more embarrassed than Blacker. Femur smiled again, hoping he looked a lot more kind than he felt, and tried to think himself into Caroline's skin.

'Were you perhaps watching over Kara in case anything happened to her, Mr Collons?'

Collons's red eyes began to swim. He opened his mouth but no words emerged. He shook his head and found a handkerchief to blow his nose. He coughed and then whispered, 'Might I speak to you alone, Chief Inspector? Without the tape?'

'We have to tape record all interviews nowadays, Mr Collons. It's for your own safety and protection. But we can certainly lose my officer.' He nodded to Blacker, who looked a bit sheepish and made no protest as he got up to go. Femur told the tape recorder what was happening. 'Now, Mr Collons?'

'You're right, you see I did sometimes go to the cottage to make sure Kara was all right.' He was blushing painfully. 'And I *was* there that night, the night she died. But not in the way Sergeant Blacker was trying to make out.'

A large translucent drop was hanging from the end of his nose. Femur wished Blair would use his handkerchief, but he said nothing.

'Right. Now that will help us. It's a pity you didn't come forward before this. We could've got a lot further.' Femur tried to look friendly and appreciative, and that was nearly as tough as anything he'd had to do in the investigation. 'But you're here now. So, what exactly did you see?'

'A man,' Collons whispered. 'He drove up in a big car. A BMW, I think it was. It came swishing up the road and parked as though the driver owned the place.'

'Did you get a good sight of him?'

'Fairly. He was tall and fit looking. Tanned, too, I think, as though he'd been skiing.'

'Where were you?'

'Erm.' Collons coughed again, neatly covering his mouth. He looked as though he wanted to die before he had to say anything else.

Femur smiled again, willing himself to feel kind. 'Mr Collons, we need your help here. No one else has any idea what happened to Kara that night. You may be able to give us the key that will get us to her killer.'

'I was behind the hedge, but I could see well, because there was a decent moon, and because . . . because . . .'

'Yes?'

'Kara opened the front door and the light was streaming out from behind her. She looked wonderful, prettier than I'd ever seen her. She was wearing a loose, long black dress. It sort of clung to her legs when she came out of the door. She stood there, with the wind blowing the stuff against her legs, and she had her arms out. It was very low cut.'

The torrent of words stopped. Femur thought he had the picture. Kara's Sojourner returning. Kara, having dressed herself up to receive him, waiting full of love and welcome in the moonlight.

'I . . . It was difficult for me. I was upset and I left as

soon as they'd gone inside.' Collons blew his nose again. 'That's what I can't forget. If I'd stayed, I'd have been there when she needed me. If I'd been there when she began to understand what kind of man she'd let . . . I could have saved her. I . . .'

I wonder if you did leave, thought Femur, watching him. Collons wouldn't meet Femur's eyes, and he kept wiping his hands on his trousers as though they were perpetually sweating, and yet it wasn't at all hot in the interview room. Femur put a hand on the radiator and felt no heat in it at all.

It couldn't be heat making the man sweat. But was it guilt or fear? Femur started to probe 'Are you sure you didn't stay there to watch? You sound very jealous of this man she'd dressed up for and welcomed so lovingly.'

Collons's puffy cheeks flushed a dense, dull red and his lower lip pushed out further than the top one. His eyes were half shut and betrayed nothing. Femur decided to push a little further, try out a few possible stories and see what sort of reaction he got.

'Perhaps you waited there behind your hedge, watching until her visitor had gone. Was that it?'

Collons's eyelids lifted. He looked at Femur like a rabbit in a car's headlights, terrified but unable to protect himself.

'You didn't go home at all, did you? You stayed in the garden, waiting until the man had left and Kara was alone again. And then you went in, didn't you?'

Collons didn't move or speak. He just sat there, looking as though he was being tortured.

'Was it because you thought that if she'd been giving it away to the man who'd just left, you deserved a share too? Was that what it was?'

'No.' The word was forced from between his lips in a kind of howl.

'You knew your way around her cottage, didn't you? You've already told me you'd been there to drinks. Or was that just a story to explain why we'll find your fingerprints among all the ones we took from her cottage?'

'No, she had invited me for drinks. She'd asked me there twice and the second time we had supper.'

'But she didn't ask you in that night. That night she had someone she liked better than you, didn't she? That must have made you angry.'

Collons put his hands over his eyes. Femur battled on relentlessly, hating the thought of Kara having to deal with a man like this, having him in her house, watching him slavering over her. Femur wanted to wipe his hands on something too.

'And you were left out in the rain watching them. I should think that made you very angry. Did it, Blair?'

'No.' Collons let his hands drop away from his eyes. But he didn't look at Femur, he just sat, with his shoulders sagging and his little round belly sticking out, staring at nothing.

'I think it did. I think you watched and saw what they were doing together and hated her because it wasn't you she was making love with.'

'Don't be disgusting. Of course I didn't.' The little man's Adam's apple was working again, moving up and down, up and down, and he kept coughing his short, dry coughs. He really did look as though he might throw up. 'I never hated Kara. I couldn't.'

Femur glanced quickly around the room for a receptacle to use if he had to. There was a metal wastepaper bin. That would do at a pinch. He put out one leg and hooked the bin towards him with his foot so that it would be ready when he went in for the kill.

'Shall I tell you what the pathologist has told me about

what was done to Kara that night?' Femur asked in a casual kind of way, unthreatening.

Collons looked up, his watery eyes even more scared. He shook his head.

'It was one of the worst cases he'd ever seen.' Femur leaned forward in his chair so that their eyes were on a level. As he began to describe the screwdriver and how it had been used on Kara, Collons's cheeks turned the colour of old putty. His jaw dropped and a blob of spittle appeared in the corner.

He's excited, thought Femur in disgust.

Then Collons raised his eyes. They looked as if he was in agony.

'You took your time about it, didn't you? The pathologist's told me it was a good hour before you finally killed her. Was it hard controlling her for so long? Strangling her like that, just enough to keep her quiet while you had your fun, but not enough to put her out?'

Still Collons said nothing. Femur tried again.

'You were straddling her, weren't you, sitting on her belly with your legs trapping her sides to keep her quiet? And every time she tried to throw you off, you squeezed her neck again; not enough to kill her but enough to make her lose consciousness. And then you let her come back again and again to all that fear and pain. You know, every time I think of what she must have felt . . .'

At the sight of Collons's face, Femur suddenly grabbed hold of his disappearing self-control, asking himself what the hell he was doing. The man in front of him might have killed Kara in just such an obscenely cruel way, but then again he might not. And even if he had there was no future in this kind of interviewing. No court in England was going to accept any confession bullied out of a man like this. Besides, he'd just handed a whole lot of confidential information over to a suspect.

Blair Collons was swallowing hard. His putty-coloured face had taken on a greenish tinge and he was sweating like a pig.

Femur grabbed the bin and thrust it across the desk. He was only just in time. Collons threw up. Femur had to turn away. He shouldn't have been so squeamish, but the noise and the smell, quite apart from the sight, of anyone being sick had always revolted him. Hot liquid burst into his own mouth and for a moment he was afraid he was going to join Collons in paroxysms of vomiting. Femur told the tape what had happened and that the interview was terminated.

Then he stopped the machine, and opened the door to call for a uniform. When the constable came, a fresh-faced girl who looked like a school-leaver, Femur asked her to send for the doctor and get hold of some water and some tissues and someone to clear up vomit.

Then he waited with Collons until the doctor came, glaring at Femur as though he were Herod. He left them to it, told the custody sergeant to phone through as soon as Collons was certified fit to leave or be questioned again, and went painfully back to the incident room.

'I did you an injustice, Tony,' he said, stopping by his desk.

'What, Guv?'

'I was angry that you'd bullied Collons, stopped him giving us everything he had, and then I went and did exactly the same. Only worse.'

Blacker stopped picking at his ear. 'It's the thought of him with a woman like Kara. D'you reckon he did it?'

Femur shrugged. It wasn't that he didn't care. He cared more than he could say, but he still hadn't any proof. 'Try and get me Trish Maguire on the phone again, will you?'

Femur watched him dial and then wait, his mouth half

open, before he spoke, obviously leaving a message on her machine. Femur shook his head in disgust and went into his own office. He couldn't think what Maguire was playing at.

There was a batch of phone messages on his desk, taken by the overnight desk sergeant. Femur leafed through them, then sat staring at the one at the bottom. It had come in from a nick in Southwark, informing him that Trish Maguire had been attacked in her flat by a man with a sharpened screwdriver.

Femur phoned through at once, only to be told that the officers who'd sent the message had gone off shift and no one on duty at the moment knew anything. After pulling rank and nearly losing his temper, he persuaded someone to look at the paperwork left by the preceding relief.

It took nearly five minutes, but then Femur was able to listen to an account of everything that had happened to Maguire. Half-way through, impatience got the better of him and he asked whether Maguire had given any description of the assailant. She had, the voice at the other end of the phone told him before laboriously reading it out. It wasn't much, but she'd said enough to prove to Femur that the attacker couldn't have been Blair Collons.

Having checked that the screwdriver and balaclava mentioned in the report had been properly preserved in the right sort of evidence bags, Femur arranged to have them sent directly to the lab and put down the phone, wondering whether he would ever get himself sorted.

His teeth were clamped together with a bit of the inside of his cheek between them. It was painful, but not half as painful as his conscience. He'd known Maguire was frightened of the man who'd phoned her in the night, but he'd told her patronisingly to go home and stop interfering in his case – well, words to that effect anyway. And now she'd had to face a murderous attack.

Lucky she'd had her boyfriend with her. Otherwise . . . Well, otherwise didn't bear thinking about. But why the hell wouldn't she answer her phone?

His own rang then. Expecting to hear about Collons from the custody sergeant, he simply said, 'Yes?'

'Chief Inspector Femur? It's Trish Maguire here.'

'Ah. I hear you've been in the wars, Ms Maguire,' he said, not as helpfully as he'd intended. 'I mean . . .'

'It's all right. I know what you mean. I was ringing to make sure you'd got the report. The officers promised to phone it through to you.'

'I have. I understand that you saw your attacker's face.'

'That's right.'

'What did he look like?'

When she'd given him much the same description he'd already had from the Southwark police, he said, with fake lightness, 'So, it wasn't Blair Collons, then?' There was a pause. He could almost feel her nervousness down the line. 'You *do* know about him, I take it, Ms Maguire?'

'I do. But . . .'

'Why didn't you say anything about him when you came in yesterday?'

'He's my client, Chief Inspector. I'm to represent him at his employment tribunal. I couldn't talk about him.'

'Even though he could have killed your friend?'

'I didn't think he had.' Her voice sounded strained, but that could've been the effect of what she'd been through. 'And last night's performance pretty well proved it. Have you talked to Blair?'

'We're in the process of it now, but I needed to take a break. Get some air.'

'Ah. Yes, I can see that. Has he told you about the conspiracy yet?'

'Conspiracy? What conspiracy?'

'I think you'd better get it from him. I promised him I wouldn't pass on anything he said to the police. That's why I couldn't tell you about him. And I can't let him down, specially not now.'

'Right.' It was going to take Femur a long time to forgive her. 'Before you go, had you ever seen your attacker before?'

'I don't think so.'

'Would you know him again?'

She was obviously thinking before she spoke. He approved of that.

'Yes. I'm pretty sure I would.'

'Right. Now, I gather you're not at home. Where can I find you if I need to?'

She gave him her boyfriend's phone number then rang off. Femur sat at his desk, taking deep breaths and blowing them conscientiously out again, until he felt more in control. Soon he'd be able to go back to Collons and find out what Trish Maguire had been talking about.

It took nearly half an hour for Collons to tell Femur what he thought had been happening at the council. When he'd finished writing up his notes, Femur frowned. 'You really believe all this? That Martin Drakeshill, a second-hand-car dealer in Kingsford is also a drug importer, that he's got a sergeant in the drugs squad on his payroll, that he's infiltrated Kingsford Council for some nefarious purpose of his own and, afraid that you were about to blow his cover, engineered your dismissal?'

'Yes.'

'And not content with that, he sent someone to murder Kara Huggate, to silence her, too, after she'd started asking questions about the financing of some building work by the council?'

'Yes.'

'And you expect me to believe it too?'

'Yes.'

Femur blinked. 'I suppose I can just about see how there could be a connection between a drugs squad officer and a drugs importer, even that there are people within the council who are in the pay of the same drugs-importer, but I can't see how they could be connected with the building work.'

Collons looked as though he was about to cry again. His head wobbled. 'Nor do I,' he said at last, the words coming softly between his lips like a sigh. 'I'm just sure that there is some kind of a connection.'

'I see, sir.' Femur slapped his notes into order and screwed the top on his felt-tip. He felt slightly less angry with Trish Maguire: if she'd been listening to this sort of stuff, she might well have hesitated to dump it on him and his officers. 'Thank you for telling me all about it. I'm sorry you were unwell earlier, and I expect you'll feel more comfortable back at home.'

The little man leaned right across the table and grabbed Femur by the wrist. 'But you will follow it up, won't you?'

'We'll do what's necessary. Don't you worry.'

'That's not good enough. You have to get Drakeshill in and –'

Femur removed Blair's hand and said, 'I'm afraid it's all I can promise at this stage. I'm grateful to you for telling me all about your theories, although it would have been helpful if you'd come forward earlier. But I'm satisfied that you've told us all you know now and so I'll say goodbye for the moment.'

'You mean, I've just got to go? With everyone knowing I've been here, talking to you?'

'We can hardly keep you in custody, since you haven't

committed any crime.'

Collons whispered something about 'protective custody'.

Femur got to his feet. 'Don't worry so much, Mr Collons. I've said I'll look into it. You go on home, take a couple of aspirins and get some sleep. You'll feel right as rain in no time.'

CHAPTER TWENTY-NINE

Trish had never attended an identity parade before, and, in spite of what she'd said to Femur, she wasn't at all sure that she would be able to recognise the face she'd seen only for a few seconds. But, in fact, it was easy. Walking along the glass wall with DC Lyalt in attendance, staring at ten snub-nosed, dark-haired white men in their early twenties, Trish knew him at once.

'It's number eight.'

'Are you sure?' asked DC Lyalt. 'We need to be sure you're right.'

'I'm well aware of that,' said Trish crisply, wondering how much the constable knew about what had happened to her. She didn't seem quite as sympathetic as Trish thought she should be. 'It's him. Number eight is the man who attacked me, ripped my leg with his screwdriver, and was rugger-tackled by George. I saw his face then, and again later when I tried to trip him as he ran out of my flat. I'd go into the witness box on it any day.'

'You'll have to.'

'That's fine.' Trish laughed at her expression. 'Don't

look so worried, Constable Lyalt, I'm used to standing up in court. They won't shake me.'

'No,' said DC Lyalt with a considering, half-admiring expression in her eyes. 'I don't suppose they will. OK, thanks, Ms Maguire.'

'And there is one other thing,' Trish said, staring at number eight's arms. 'I've only just remembered. He's got a vile tattoo. On his right arm, I think, about a couple of inches above his wrist on the inside of his forearm. It's a snake eating the guts of a woman, who's been half disembowelled.'

'Sure? If you're not . . .'

'I'm sure,' said Trish. 'Get them all to roll up their sleeves. You'll see.'

After DC Lyalt had given the instruction through the intercom, the men behind the one-way glass rolled up their sleeves. Number eight was obviously reluctant and Trish shot a triumphant look at DC Lyalt, who nodded, but did not look away until the tattoo was revealed.

'Well done, Ms Maguire. We'll be OK now. Thanks.'

She spoke into the intercom again and the officer on the other side of the glass told the men they could go. Something about the way number eight moved tweaked at Trish's memory, but she couldn't work out what it was. Then he bent to pick up something from the floor and she recognised the shape of his back. She turned to DC Lyalt.

'D'you know? I think I might have seen him some-where before.'

'Oh, yes?'

Trish couldn't think why DC Lyalt should look worried by that piece of news until she realised that it might be evidence of mistaken identity.

'Yes. But don't worry: he's definitely the man who attacked me in my flat.'

DC Lyalt's good-looking face relaxed.

'But I think I may also have seen him at Drakeshill's Used Cars in Kingsford. I couldn't swear to that, but I'm reasonably confident it's the same bloke.'

'That is quite interesting in an anecdotal sort of way, but if you couldn't swear to it, it's not much use to us.'

'Perhaps not,' Trish said peaceably. 'As a matter of interest?'

'Yes?'

'Did George pick out number eight, too? You won't be breaking any confidences because I'll ask him as soon as I get out of here.'

DC Lyalt smiled, revealing a much livelier, more interesting character than the efficient, passionless officer she had seemed at first. 'He did.'

'Great. And *does* number eight have anything to do with Drakeshill?'

At that question, DC Lyalt's official expression came back over her face like some kind of security shutter.

'Oh, go on. It can't do any harm to tell me, if I'm not going into the witness box on the question of where I first saw him.'

'Oh, all right,' said Lyalt, sounding much more like a friend than a police officer. 'You could have seen him there because he does work for Drakeshill.'

'Doing what exactly?'

'Come on, Ms Maguire, you know I can't tell you anything like that.'

'Pity. Let me know if you need anything else.'

'We will. But you've done OK, Ms Maguire. We're all very grateful.'

'What, just for identifying him?' said Trish, in surprise.

'No. I probably shouldn't tell you this. Actually, I'm sure I shouldn't. But since you were a friend of Kara Huggate's, I'm going to. We hadn't any evidence before you were attacked. Your quickness in getting hold of the screwdriver, even more than your identification, is the first real break we've had. You will keep that to yourself, won't you?'

'Naturally,' said Trish, taking in the full import of what DC Lyalt had said. 'Then you do think he's the one who killed Kara?'

The other woman nodded, her face full of sympathy, as Trish leaned against the wall. The thought of what could have happened to her if George had not appeared just then made her head swim again. She covered her mouth with her hand as she remembered the instant when she'd understood that she was not going to be able to get away. Looking back through the glass at the place where her attacker had been standing, she said, 'He is on remand, I take it?'

'Oh, yes. He's got enough of a record to make sure of that. No hot-shot barrister is going to persuade any magistrate to take the risk of a man like that reoffending.'

Trish's guts lurched as she wondered which of her colleagues at the bar would have the task of defending her attacker – Kara's killer. It might be someone like Jeremy Platen, whose skill at persuading juries that they couldn't convict on the evidence before them was legendary. As far as Trish could remember, he had never acted for the defence in a murder trial and seen his client convicted. Never had the barrister's perennial dilemma of giving their all to the defence of a man they loathed seemed so difficult. If Kara's killer got off because of clever arguments or a gullible jury, Trish knew she would never be able to go home after dark without fear. And if it were a friend of hers who'd got him off, she would be faced with an insoluble dilemma of her own.

Abruptly, and without another word to DC Lyalt, Trish went out to find George. He took one look at her face and put an arm round her. But he didn't ask any questions. In the car, he put a Brahms concerto on the CD player so that she wouldn't have to talk and drove smoothly back into London. As they reached Wandsworth, he turned down the volume, glanced at her and said, 'Now that we know your attacker is safely in custody, would you like to go back to Southwark? Or would you prefer to stay on in Fulham for a bit?'

Trish put her hand on his thigh. He took one hand off the steering wheel to lay it over hers.

'Southwark, if you really don't mind, George. The SOCO's finished there, and I would like to get it cleared up.'

'I thought so. And you do feel confined in my house, don't you?'

'A bit.' Trish thought about the chintz and the antiques, and the smallness of the rooms, and the fact that everything in it belonged to George. But then she thought of being alone in Southwark again if the man she had just identified was not convicted and shuddered.

'Don't fret about it. I know you like wide open spaces in a way I don't much. It doesn't matter.'

She let her head droop on to his shoulder for a second, full of all the usual conflicting emotions. He ruffled her hair casually. She got the feeling that he understood at least some of her muddle. Perhaps he even shared it.

Later, when her flat was tidy again and all the bloody feathers had been collected and bagged up for the binmen, George volunteered to get some food to restock the almost empty fridge.

'Oh, I'll come with you,' Trish said at once. 'There's no need for you to do my shopping. You've done so much already.'

'Rest your weary legs, my love,' he said, misquoting one of his favourite poems. She only just recognised it as Auden's 'Lullaby'. 'I won't be long.'

When he'd left her alone in the flat, it struck her that he was a remarkably generous man. She remembered telling him once that he was like Kara and she wondered whether, like Kara, he had a talent for seeing through people's masks of contentment to the unacknowledged sadness they carried around with them. The idea was startling enough to make her think again about their argument and face the possibility that the icy black knot in the centre of her memories of her father might not be fury after all, but something only Kara and George had recognised for what it was.

After a while, she realised she was going to have to do something about it. She reached for the phone and then, remembering she had no idea of his number, bent down to the bottom drawer of her desk for one of the unopened letters.

'Hello?' she said tentatively, when she heard his voice. 'Is that Paddy Maguire?'

'It is. Is it you, Trish?' His voice was so eager that she felt squeezed with shame.

'Yes. I'm sorry it's taken me so long to ring back.'

'That's fine, my dear. And how are you?'

'Fine. Fine. And you?'

'All the better for hearing your voice. You're not too busy now?'

'Well, no, not just at the moment,' she said, bridling a little at the mischievous laughter in his voice. It sounded much more richly Irish than she remembered.

'I shouldn't be teasing you now, should I? Although you used to like being teased in the old days.'

'Did I?' The question had come out rather cold, but she couldn't help that.

'You did. But it's a long time ago. And we've all changed. I'm well aware of that, Trish.'

'Yes.'

'I read about you in the paper, you know.'

'Yes, I'd realised that must be why you'd rung.'

'And I'm very proud of you.'

Various bitter little responses occurred to Trish, but she swallowed them all down like medicine, and tried to do what she'd intended when she rang him. 'I'm glad.' It was surprising how easy it had been to say it and so she said it again. 'I'm glad.'

'Good,' he said simply.

There had been no surprise or even gratitude in his voice; but she thought there had been an acknowledgement of the magnitude of what she was doing.

'And how are you really, Trish? You don't sound your usual brisk self, m'dear.'

'I'm not too bad. Although my leg's still sore. But that's only to be expected.'

'Leg? What leg?' Paddy Maguire sounded urgent in his concern, almost aggressive. 'What happened to you?'

And Trish found herself telling him everything, answering his warm, sensible questions as fully as she could, even explaining why she had ever put herself at such risk.

'And this friend of yours,' he said at the end, 'this Kara, was she worth it now?'

'Kara?' said Trish, as quite unexpected tears filled her eyes and trickled down her cheeks. She sniffed. 'Yes, she was worth it. And if what happened to me does help convict her killer, as the police seem to think it might, then my leg won't matter a toss.'

'And if he's not convicted? You will take care now, won't you, Trish? I don't want to . . .' Paddy paused, then said, much faster than usual, 'I don't want to be hearing that something bad has happened to you.'

Trish didn't know what to say. That he had latched instantly on to her own worst fears was at once reassuring and seemed to make them worse.

'OK. Now, do you think we might meet?' he went on, sounding more tentative. 'When your leg's better. I'd like to see you, Trish. I won't ask you to come here to my house, if you don't want to, but we could meet in a restaurant maybe.'

'Well, yes, I suppose we could.'

'And you could bring your young man if you felt like it, or come on your own. Whichever you prefer.'

'Would you be bringing . . .?' Trish wasn't sure she could bring herself to mention the name of the bimbo he'd run off with all those years ago.

'Bianca? No, Trish.' He sounded untroubled. 'She left me years ago. I'm not living with anyone now. If you'd feel easier having other people with us, I could ask a friend, but you've no stepmother so you don't have to worry about that.'

'Could I think about it, and ring you back?'

'Sure. But don't forget now, and don't take too long. I want to see you, you know. Get to know you again.'

'I won't forget. I'm . . . I'm glad we talked.'

'Me, too. And it wasn't so bad, was it?' There was so much humour in his voice that Trish couldn't help smiling.

'No, Paddy,' she said at last, 'it wasn't so bad.'

'Great. And I hope it'll get easier still. You know, I've regretted what I did every day of my life for the past twenty years and more. Goodbye for now, Trish.'

He didn't leave her a chance to say anything, which was probably just as well as she wouldn't have known how to respond to the apology she'd thought she had to have. With the sound of his voice echoing in her ears and pictures from the past flashing through her mind again, she sat wondering just how much she had sacrificed to her stubborn refusal to talk to him for so long.

She thought of another apology that had to be made and wondered whether she had the energy to put it into words. Collons had warned her that she would be at risk from the people who'd killed Kara and she'd laughed at him. She'd assumed that all his stories were the results of paranoia or an attempt to make himself interesting. Once again she had made assumptions about someone's character and reliability on the altogether unsound basis of how he had made her feel. She should have known better.

Deeply ashamed of herself, she picked up the phone receiver again and dialled his number. When she heard his recorded voice she relaxed. Leaving a message was going to be much easier than talking directly to him.

'Hello, Blair, this is Trish Maguire. I wanted to find out how you are and to tell you that I realise you've been right in so many of the things you've told me. If I'd been readier to believe you, I'd have escaped a pretty nasty experience. And I . . . I'm grateful for everything you've tried to do for Kara. I'll see you again at the tribunal anyway, but perhaps we'll meet in the meantime. Goodbye.'

It wasn't very graceful, but it was the best she could do just then.

CHAPTER THIRTY

Waiting for the luggage on the carousel at Gatwick, Sandra hated having to stand next to Michael. Katie was supposed to be their buffer, but since neither of them had told her what was going on, she hadn't realised. She would have to be told, and Simon too, when they collected him from his friend's house. But it wasn't going to be easy.

Sandra glared resentfully at Michael. She still couldn't understand why he'd fallen for a woman like Kara Huggate – or why he was still trying to pretend he'd never had an affair with her – but she didn't care any more. She just wanted him out of her life so that she could get down to rebuilding it for herself and the kids.

The luggage carousel jerked into action. Smart American bags came first, soon followed by battered old English suitcases, sets of strapped skis, buggies in falling-apart cardboard boxes, and then Katie's dirty pink nylon bag with the scrunched-up white straps. Sandra was already reaching for it when Michael's hand touched hers. They both leaped backwards as though their skin was burning then glared at each other as the conveyor belt chugged on, taking the pink bag out of reach.

Eventually they got all the bags on to the trolley, collected Katie, and started wheeling the trolley through the EU Customs channel. A slim man in his forties, wearing a pale-grey suit, appeared suddenly in front of them.

'Michael Napton?' he said, in quite a nice voice.

'What is it, for God's sake?' Michael said angrily. 'You can't seriously believe I'm smuggling something. I've been on a family skiing holiday. We've a few duty-free cigarettes, a bottle of whisky, and some perfume. But that's all. If you want to ransack our luggage, you're welcome, but you'll be wasting your sodding time as well as ours.'

'Don't swear, Michael,' Sandra said. He looked at her as though he hated her. Well, that made two of them.

'I'm not with the Customs and Excise, Mr Napton. If you would just step this way,' said the man in the grey suit.

'Why?'

'I think you'd rather do this in private, sir,' said the man, flicking open a small black plastic wallet to show a police warrant card.

Sandra stared at it in surprise, then looked back at Michael. His face was a peculiar greenish white and his eyes were quite blank. He looked as though he was sleepwalking.

'Will you come this way, sir?' said the man.

Michael nodded and opened his mouth as if he was going to say something, but no words emerged. He turned to Sandra, but he still couldn't say anything. She saw that there were tears leaking into his eyes again.

'We know about Kara Huggate,' she said quickly. 'We read about what happened to her in the paper.'

'Mrs Napton, there's no need for you or your daughter to wait,' said the grey-suited man, as politely as ever. 'We do want to talk to your husband, but there's no reason why you shouldn't go straight home. I'm sorry to put you to inconvenience.'

'That's all right,' she said automatically. 'We'll take a taxi. But what's going on? Why do you need to talk to Michael?'

'We hope he can help us with our inquiries, Mrs Napton.'

'Inquiries into her death?'

'Don't, Sandra.' The tears were now spilling down his face. People were staring at them.

For once Sandra didn't care. 'Michael, this is important. I need to know.'

'Yes,' said the police officer.

'But it happened while we were away.'

'Nevertheless there are questions we have to ask. But they don't affect you, Mrs Napton.'

'Go on home, Sandra. Take Katie and look after her. And forget about all this.'

'I'm not sure I can. What do I do about getting him a lawyer?' she asked the officer. 'He'll need one, won't he?'

'Don't fuss, Sandra.' Michael was beginning to sound his usual irritable self. In a way it was reassuring. 'I'll deal with it. Get on home and take care of Katie. Have you got enough money for a taxi?'

She looked at him as if he was mad. He probably was. He was being taken off by the police to talk to them about a murder and here he was bothering about whether she had her taxi fare. He shoved a bundle of notes at her. She could see that lots of them were French francs, but she took them all the same.

'Well, phone me if there's anything you do want me to do to help.'

His dazed eyes focused. 'You wouldn't know where to begin.'

CHAPTER THIRTY-ONE

DC Lyalt came quietly into the interview room to put a folded piece of paper in front of Femur. Tony Blacker told the tape what was happening, then dismissed her with a brief, impatient gesture. Caroline's lips tightened, but she obediently opened the door, hovering there in case Femur wanted her. He opened the note, apparently oblivious to their by-play, to read: 'Michael Napton has been picked up at the airport. ETA 10 minutes.'

'Thank you, Constable.' Femur smiled at her to make up for Blacker's irritability. She left the room, shutting the door quietly. Then Femur got back to business. 'Sorry about that, Mr Bletchley.'

'As I was saying, Chief Inspector Femur, it is outrageous that you are even intending to question my client,' Bletchley said. 'He has told you that he has no knowledge of the woman who was attacked in London last night. Still less of the unfortunate social worker who was murdered in Kingsford. That should be the end of both matters unless you're going to charge him, and I can't imagine what basis you might have to do any such thing.'

'Sorry, Mr Bletchley. Chaz has been identified by both the woman he attacked in Southwark and the man who intervened to save her.'

Poor Bletchley looked as though he was having to work like a samurai to keep his feelings out of his face. Femur knew how he felt. He was finding it almost impossible to sit calmly at the table when all he wanted to do was take Chaz Chompton by the throat and rattle him against a hard surface until he admitted what he'd done to Kara and who else had been involved.

'And the social worker?' said Bletchley, successfully sounding disdainful. Femur just looked at him with pity and was glad to see he understood. He glanced quickly at his client, then back at the two police officers. Chaz Chompton just went on grinning at the lot of them.

The fury and disgust Femur had felt when he'd been faced with Blair Collons had been nothing to what was gnawing at him now. The cocky pleasure in Chompton's face would have irritated the hell out of him in any circumstances, but reacting with his memories of the photographs of Kara's body it brought him nearer to the edge of violence than he had ever been in his life.

But Chompton was sitting beside the best solicitor in Kingsford so Femur would have to play the interview very carefully indeed if he were to get anything useful out of it. He thought of all the various calming techniques he'd ever heard of, and even tried to see himself in his imaginary garden. None of it worked. Only the thought that if he didn't get control of himself and his voice he might lose the chance of nailing Kara's murderer kept him sitting quietly at the table.

'So, I have a theory to put to you, Chaz,' he said, with a fair assumption of tolerance. But Blacker looked sideways at him. He'd understood.

'Oh, yeah?' The boy was chewing gum, squelching the

sticky plug between his teeth and his cheek. His dark eyes were hard and his lips permanently smiling, in spite of the chewing. He leaned back, so that his chair was balanced on two legs, and propped his pristine white trainers on the table in front of him.

'You took a screwdriver with you to Trish Maguire's flat in Southwark. A sharpened screwdriver, which you left behind.'

That was news to Bletchley, Femur saw, and highly unwelcome news too. Chompton opened his mouth to reveal the chewing-gum sitting bang in the middle of a very pink, very healthy-looking tongue. 'Nothing to do wiv me. I never took no screwdriver nowhere.'

'A similar home-made weapon, perhaps even the very same one, was used on the social worker who was murdered the week before last. But you knew that, didn't you?'

'You don't have to answer that, Chaz,' said Bletchley quickly.

The gum was transferred with maximum visibility to the right of Chompton's mouth.

'Yeah, I knew it was a screwdriver or a chisel. Everyone in Kingsford's heard vat. It was all over ve papers, what he done to her. Animal.' He grinned even more widely, then let his teeth close on the gum.

'And what were you doing the night she was murdered?'

'You don't –'

'No, vat's right, Mr Bletchley, I don't. I know my rights, same as anyone. But vere's no reason not to answer. I was down ve club, wasn' I? Wiv the boss and some of ve other lads.'

'They'll confirm that, will they?'

'Course.'

'Which club?'

311

'Lots. I can't remember all ve names.'

'I think that just about wraps it up, don't you, Chief Inspector?' said Bletchley, leaning forward in his chair as though he was about to get up. 'You have my client's statement that he did not go to this woman's flat in London and that he knows no more than any other newspaper reader about the murdered social worker. You say you have some identification evidence, yet you've shown no sign of wishing to charge him. Unless you're going to do that, I must assume that you're ready to let him go.'

'Good try, Mr Bletchley, but we're not ready to let him go yet.'

'I'm sure I don't need to remind you, Chief Inspector, that you have already held my client for close on twenty-four hours, and –'

'Don't worry, sir. The superintendent has already sanctioned a further twelve hours and we'll go to the magistrates after that, if necessary. I'm awaiting some information from the lab, and I can't let Chaz go until it's come.'

Bletchley sat very still in his chair. Chaz Chompton stopped chewing for a second and slowly let his trainers slip off the edge of the table. But the grin kept his lips well apart, showing off his glistening teeth. As Femur watched, he pushed the gum out from between them, spreading it around with his tongue, stretching it, then he hooked it back behind his teeth and chewed happily. Femur thought of Kara's body as he had seen it during the autopsy and with difficulty stared Chompton down.

'No doubt,' said Bletchley recovering himself fairly well, 'when you have received your information, you will want to talk to my client again. I'm sure I need not remind you that he will not answer any questions unless I am present.'

'That's fine, Mr Bletchley. Now I'm sure you'd like some time alone with your client now. Tony?'

Blacker dealt with the tape, then followed Femur out.

'Get on to the lab at once,' Femur said, 'and tell them to pull out all the stops. I need the results of the tests on the screwdriver as soon as they can get them. If Chompton used it on Kara, there's got to be something, however carefully he thought he'd cleaned it.'

'It's not going to be the same one, though, is it, Guv? I mean, come on. If you'd done what he did to Huggate, wouldn't you get rid of the weapon and make yourself a new one?'

'Maybe, but he's not so clever as he thinks.' Femur rubbed his forehead. 'If it hadn't been for Bletchley – and the fact Chompton is afraid he'll report anything said to Drakeshill – we might've got through to him. As it is . . . Still, we've got Napton next, who may be easier to crack. If so, we'll have a lever to use on Chompton.'

'How are we going to work the interview with Napton, Guv?'

'That's not your problem, Tony. I want Caroline doing that one with me.'

'But, Guv –'

'No,' Femur said, with enough force to make Blacker's face shut down in resentment. 'I need you to get a warrant to search Chompton's gaff. Take Owler with you and give it a good going over. I want anything that relates to Kara, any drugs, any offensive weapons, anything. Right? We're going to need physical evidence.'

'I'll do my best.'

Blacker still didn't look happy, but he was going to have to put up with it. He'd be much more use collecting evidence against Chompton than treading the delicate line between sympathy and aggression that Femur was sure he'd need with Napton. Caroline could do the sympathy bit, and he'd handle the aggression. Blacker's brand was a bit too fiery just at the moment.

'In the meantime, I want you to get the squad pumped up and working at full throttle. Tell them about Chompton and Maguire and the screwdriver. Tell them about our suspicions of Drakeshill, on the grounds that he's Chompton's employer, and get them on to scouring every possible source for details of his activities. But don't say a word yet to any of them about Spinel. We don't need any divided loyalties at this stage.'

'OK, Guv.' All the resentment in Blacker's face had been overtaken by anxiety.

'What?'

'When are you going to bring in CIB3 to deal with Spinel, Guv?'

'Not till I've nailed Kara's killer.'

'It's your shout, but –'

'Right,' Femur said, cutting him off. 'When you get back to the incident room, tell Caroline to come down here.'

He went without any more protest.

As Femur waited for her, he ran over in his mind what they'd got so far. The identification of Chompton as the man who'd attacked Trish Maguire was solid, and the choice of weapon made it almost certain that there was a connection with Kara's death. Chompton could not have been the original Kingsford Rapist: they'd checked as soon as they'd had Trish's identification and found that he'd been safely banged up at the time of the rapes. That left Femur satisfactorily back with his original suspicion that someone had intended Kara's death to look like the work of the Kingsford Rapist in order to hide his reasons for wanting her dead.

Femur didn't think Chaz Chompton had either the wit or the resources to have managed that on his own. The obvious source of information on the original killing was Spinel, but whether the initiative had been his or Drakeshill's, Femur was still not sure. He had no sodding evidence. He'd have to get enough from somewhere to try to push a wedge between them and get them angry enough with each other to give him everything he needed.

'Ah, Cally, good,' Femur said, as he saw her coming towards him. She was looking much better, less angry and with more colour in her face, which presumably reflected his own feeling that they were getting somewhere at last. He wished he'd had her with him when he was interviewing Blair Collons yesterday. Then he wouldn't have made such a fool of himself – or driven the pathetic little man to throw up.

'Let's go.'

'OK, Guv.' She led the way into the interview room.

Michael Napton looked up angrily and said, 'This is outrageous.'

Here we go again, thought Femur, as Caroline stuck a tape in the machine and said who they were.

'This is outrageous,' Napton said again, as soon as she'd finished. 'I've been dragged away from my family and brought here like a criminal on a charge of murdering a woman who died while I was out of the country! It's not only outrageous, it's ludicrous.'

'Have you been charged, sir?' asked Femur quietly.

'I've been arrested.'

'It's not quite the same, sir. We've arrested you on suspicion of murder, and cautioned you, but we haven't charged you. D'you understand the difference?'

There was a slight yielding in the man's angry expression. It was a good-looking face, Femur thought, if a little weak about the mouth and chin. Not that physical features were any evidence of character, as he was

315

always having to remind himself, but Napton didn't look like a decisive man, or a particularly brave one. That was all to the good: if he were the weak link in Drakeshill's chain it would break quicker.

'How could I possibly be involved in her murder? I wasn't there.'

'No, I know you weren't. Now, I understand that you have waived your right to a solicitor. Is that correct?'

'Yes. I don't need one. I told you, I was out of the country when the woman was killed, as you can check from the airline records. And if you think I slipped back here in between the flights I took with my wife and daughter, the hotel staff in Meribel ought to be able to tell you you're wrong.'

'I'm not interested in your movements or your alibi. There are only two things I want to talk to you about,' said Femur. 'One is the deal you negotiated for the council with Goodbuy's Supermarkets, and the other is your connection with Martin Drakeshill and Sergeant Spinel of the drugs squad.'

As they watched, Napton's face changed, moving through surprise to doubt and then fear, slackening all the time, as though it had been made of melting wax. So, Femur thought, Collons was right. But how the hell does it all hang together? If I ask the wrong questions now, I'll blow it. But he's ready to talk. Take it slowly, from the top.

'You did, did you not,' he went on, aware of sounding like a pompous fart, 'negotiate with Goodbuy's Supermarkets to accept a plot of land in the middle of Kingsford as a *quid pro quo* for planning permission for a megastore in King's Park?'

'We call it planning gain,' said Napton helpfully. 'But yes, yes, I did.'

'And what was Drakeshill's interest in it?'

'I don't think there was anything, was there?'

Damn, thought Femur. Got that one wrong. Aloud he said, 'But he became involved, didn't he?'

'No, I don't think so.'

'Then how did you come to be working for him?'

'So she did come to you, did she?' Napton said. 'I was afraid she would, once she realised. That's why I told them I had to stop. And I thought . . .'

Femur sat in silence. Sometimes that got better results than clumsy questions. But he assumed that the 'she' in question was Kara Huggate.

'How did she get on to it?'

Femur shrugged. 'Same way as us, probably.'

Napton nodded, but he didn't say anything else. Femur knew that Caroline was just as much at sea as he was. He thought through everything Blair Collons had said. It didn't help much. 'How did they take it when you said you had to stop?' he asked, hoping that might turn the key.

'I was amazed,' Napton said, slightly shaking his head. 'I'd envisaged all sorts of rows and more pressure of the old sort, but they were great. Spinel was quite aggressive when I first told him, but I said there just wasn't any option and there was no point him trying to blackmail me again. If I lost my job, then I lost my job. I was so . . . It had got so bad, and I knew Kara Huggate wasn't going to let go, that she'd go on probing until she'd worked it all out. I –'

'I'm just a thick copper,' Femur said. 'Lay it all out for me. How, exactly, did Spinel blackmail you in the first place?'

'By threatening to tell the council that I'd known all along about Goodbuy's land being contaminated,' Napton said, in an impatient tone. 'I thought you knew that.'

'I'm still a bit puzzled about the timing of it all.'

'Oh, I see.'

'When did the council find out about the contamination?'

'When the engineers dug their trial trench,' he said, as
though Femur were proving himself ever more stupid.
'With all the subsidence in the area, they had to be sure
the buildings were going to be secure, so trial trenches
were dug all over the site, and it became clear straight
away that something fairly bad was fouling the ground.
They reported, and we got Flower Brothers in to do the
assessment and quote for cleaning it up. And . . .' He
flushed. 'I'd forgotten, you see, in all the excitement
when everyone was pleased about the land and telling
me how wonderful I was, to tell anyone what Goodbuy's
had said about the chemicals.'

'Which was?'

'They were so casual about it – I'm still not convinced
they knew quite how bad it was. They just said they had
an idea there might be some chemical residues from one
of the factories that had been operating there and we'd
probably have to do a bit of a clean-up before we started
building. I had no idea it was so serious, and once I had
realised, I couldn't admit I'd cocked up like that. Not
when I'd been promoted on the strength of it, made head
of department, and –' He broke off, looking helplessly at
Femur.

'Right. So, you'd always known there was contamination, but you hadn't taken it seriously and then you
forgot about it. Have I got that right?'

'Not exactly forgot, it just didn't seem very important.'
Napton pushed his hands over his face and through his
thick hair. 'I'd never had experience of this kind of thing
before and it had never occurred to me that it could be so
expensive to decontaminate.'

'Right.' Femur was frowning. He'd like to have handed the questions over to Cally, but he thought she was probably quite as confused as he was himself. 'And when you did discover . . .?'

'It was too late to do anything about it. Goodbuy's had been given permission for their megastore, there'd been the usual stink from all the local greens, but the council was standing firm. Everyone had got so excited by the prospect of building the social housing right slap bang in the middle of Kingsford that I was still flavour of the month for brokering the deal. I couldn't give it all up and admit to being such a fool, so lazy, really.'

Femur was so lost that he turned to Caroline. She nodded decisively and put her clipboard flat on the table. Femur saw that she'd written three questions on it.

'Let me make sure I've got this right,' she said. 'You omitted to warn the council when you put the deal to them that they were facing an enormous bill for cleaning the land Goodbuy's had handed over as planning gain?'

'That's right.'

'And somehow Sergeant Spinel – or was it Drakeshill? – discovered that you'd always known and could have saved the council this vast amount of money?'

'Yes.'

'How?'

Napton sighed. 'I owed him one after he helped me save my son from drugs two years ago. He was picked up with a tab of E and Spinel put the fear of God into him. He's been clean ever since. So when Spinel came to me, as a mate, to ask whether there was any reason not to buy a house that he and his wife particularly liked on the edge of the land, I told him he'd do better elsewhere because the land was contaminated. That was just after Goodbuy's had offered it to us.'

'I see,' Caroline said, smiling at him as though he were

an old friend. He responded and sat more easily on his hard chair. 'So when news of the cost of the decontamination became public, Spinel put two and two together and realised that you faced a certain amount of embarrassment?'

'Not quite.' Napton closed his eyes. 'I was fool enough to go to him and ask him to keep quiet about it. I trusted, him, you see.'

Femur opened his mouth to ask a question, but Caroline overrode him. He knew her well enough to let her get on with it.

'So how did the blackmail work if it was only embarrassment you were facing?'

'That's what was so clever.' Napton looked at her again, pleading for her to understand. 'At first Spinel just asked for another little bit of information. It was about a planning decision, confidential but not fantastically important. And I felt I owed it to him for being so decent and keeping his mouth shut.'

'Just a minute,' said Femur, leaning forward. 'What about Goodbuy's? Why didn't they publicise the fact that they'd warned you about the contamination?'

Napton shook his head. 'Why should they? They'd got what they wanted, it wasn't in their interest to rock the boat. But I wish they had. None of this would have happened then. Kara Huggate would still be alive.'

Femur didn't trust himself enough to speak. Caroline smiled encouragingly at Napton.

'As it was,' he went on, 'they expressed amazement and regret that the contamination was so bad. They even offered a goodwill payment to help us out. Of course it was nowhere near enough to make any difference, only a token, really, but it made them look good.'

'Right.' Femur gestured to Caroline to go on. He was beginning to understand, and the thought that Kara

Huggate had been tortured and killed to save this weak fool a little embarrassment, even the loss of his job, was making it almost impossible to keep hold of his temper.

'So after you'd handed over that first piece of confidential information, Spinel had even more of a hold over you,' suggested Caroline.

'That's right, you see. And it got worse and worse. It got to the stage where I had to warn Drakeshill of all major planning applications, then arrange to block any that came from people he didn't want in Kingsford – you know, potential rivals or people who'd crossed him.'

'Rivals?' Femur said, in the probably vain hope of getting everything clear in his mind. 'What kind of rivals?'

'Other people trying to horn in on his monopoly.' Napton looked from one officer to the other, his eyes beginning to show suspicion.

'The drugs, you mean,' Femur said quickly, to stop Napton realising quite how little they actually knew.

He nodded. 'It was ages before I understood what they were up to, and when I did realise, I didn't know what to do. I *hate* drugs, but by then I couldn't have got away. They'd never have let me go, knowing what I did.'

'Which was?' Femur smiled. 'Exactly, I mean.'

'That Drakeshill owns all the clubs in Kingsford and uses them as major outlets for smack, coke and crack. He also supplies a whole network of smaller dealers. No one who tries to sell drugs in Kingsford for anyone else lasts very long. Drakeshill's bouncers in the clubs or his mechanics hear of it as soon as it starts. Drakeshill then tells Spinel, who has the dealers arrested and prosecuted. Anyone who protests, or who shows signs of being prepared to talk to the police, gets blackmailed or beaten up until they toe the line.'

'Or die.'

'Napton covered his face with both hands.

'So how,' Femur said, with real interest, 'did you find the courage to tell him that you were stopping now?'

Napton looked hurt, which made Femur's hands clench into fists. He kept them under the table so that he couldn't give in to temptation. Thank God for Caroline, keeping him on the straight and narrow. 'Well?'

'When Kara Huggate told me she wasn't going to rest until she'd found out who was responsible for the costings fiasco on the social housing, and then make sure that it was his budget that got clobbered in order to meet the costs so that hers could be saved for her clients. Everyone else had just taken it as "one of those things", embarrassing but that was all. Only she was interested in a witch-hunt.'

'So you went to Spinel and asked him to have her killed, is that it?' Caroline said.

'Christ no!' Napton looked and sounded appalled. 'How could you even think me capable of . . .?'

'That's what happened, though, isn't it?'

'Not like that. No, I went to Spinel and said it was all over, that I'd tell the whole truth about the contamination and resign. I'd never have got another job in local government, but that didn't matter. Anything would be better than going on, day after day, waiting for it all to come out. And, you see, I thought if I went quietly, then no one need ever know what I'd been doing for Drakeshill or what *he* had been doing. I'd look a fool about the contamination fiasco, quite rightly, but no one would know the rest.'

'I see,' Caroline said, shooting a warning look at Femur. She knew him well enough to understand everything that was beating in his brain. 'And what did Spinel say?'

'As I said, at first he was aggressive, but once he'd

talked to Drakeshill, he was very decent about it. He said they'd realised that I'd been under too much stress, that I ought to have a holiday, and that when I got back it would all be different. They'd never ask me to do anything more for them and all I'd have to do was keep my mouth shut and look around for another job. I'd probably find one before Kara Huggate got very far with her witch-hunt, and then I could move away from the area in peace and that would be it.'

'And you believed them?' Femur almost felt pity for the idiot in front of him. Almost. 'When did you realise the truth?'

'When I read in the paper about her death. When I first heard she was dead, I was relieved.' He looked at them with sickening regret. Catching Femur's expression, his own changed. 'I didn't realise then how bad it had been. I just thought it was coincidence, and that it meant I was free. But then, once I read the account in the paper, I saw it had to have had something to do with Drakeshill. And I couldn't bear it. You must believe me.'

'And what were you going to do about it?' Femur asked curiously.

Napton said nothing. The answer was written all over him. He hadn't been going to do anything. He began to cry. Caroline silently handed him a box of Kleenex.

Femur thought that Spinel and Drakeshill had judged Napton fairly well as a vain man, a coward and utterly malleable. Their mistake had been in thinking that they were the only people who could hammer him. When Napton had threatened to confess his part in the costings disaster, they must have realised that questions would be asked, questions that would uncover their own activities. They must have decided then that if Kara were silenced, Napton would be scared enough to keep his mouth shut for good and carry on doing whatever they told him.

It was Drakeshill's bad luck that he and Spinel had not judged Blair Collons so accurately. Collons had proved to be far braver than anyone, except perhaps Kara, would have expected. Without his information, they might never have worked out who had needed to destroy her. With it, they knew who and why and how: all that was left was to prove it.

'What'll happen to me?' Napton asked, when he'd got control of his tears and mopped himself up.

'That rather depends,' Femur said. 'First of all, I want you to go with Constable Lyalt to fetch all the documentary evidence you have of what you've told us. Any papers, computer disks, message tapes. Anything. She and another officer will escort you to your office and your home and then bring you back here.'

Napton nodded. 'I'll do anything, Chief Inspector. Anything. I don't want . . . I owe that poor woman . . . I want those two behind bars, you know, as much as you must.'

'Right,' said Femur, hiding his surprise that Napton didn't seem to realise that he, too, was going to be behind bars. If there wasn't enough evidence that he'd colluded with the others to have Kara Huggate murdered, there was always corruption. From everything that he'd said, it sounded as though they wouldn't have much difficulty finding something there. 'Constable Lyalt, will you organise transport, please? And take Constable Jones with you.'

Alone in the interview room, with the damp, crumpled tissues as the only evidence of Napton's remorse, Femur faced his own. It was here, at this same table, that he'd become convinced that Blair Collons had killed Kara and had treated him accordingly.

Even afterwards, when Collons had poured out his

account of the questions he and Kara had been asking and their likely effect on the triumvirate of Napton, Drakeshill and Spinel, Femur hadn't shown him much consideration, still less apologised. He'd listened and taken notes, then sent the pathetic little man away with a chilly promise to look into the story.

Now he was going to have to apologise, and that was something he always loathed doing. Still, better get it over with. It was pissing with rain again so he went upstairs to fetch his coat, his shoulders aching and his feet dragging.

The moment he pushed open the swing doors at the end of the corridor that led to the incident room, he could sense that something was happening. It wasn't just the high-pitched buzz of talk: there was something in the air, excitement and hot, pulsing anger. He could feel it all from ten feet away, and when he opened the door into the room itself, he was greeted with a roar. He stood, a little puzzled, waiting for an explanation.

'You've done it, Guv,' Blacker called from his desk. 'You were right all along. It is a copycat and it is Chaz Chompton who killed her.'

Femur let his shoulders settle. 'What did you find in his flat?'

'This,' Blacker said, holding out a flat plastic evidence bag.

Femur walked across the room to look. He saw a familiar photograph – in colour – of the real Kingsford Rapist's last victim. The print was creased down the middle as though it had been folded to fit into a pocket.

There was dust around several distinct-looking fingerprints. There was also a red-brown smudge in one corner.

'You found this in Chaz's flat?' he said, hardly daring to believe it. He and Cally must have spent much longer with Napton than he'd realised.

'We did. And the reference on the back of the print shows that it was made three weeks ago.'

Femur raised his eyebrows. 'Does it indeed?

'Sure, Guv. And the prints have been photographed. They're being checked now, but they look right.' He grinned. Femur realised he must mean that there were prints on the photograph that looked like Spinel's. Blacker must be sticking to his orders to keep quiet about Spinel. Good.

'And that's blood, I take it?'

'We think so. Owler's about to take the print to the lab to get it tested against Huggate's.'

'Good.' Femur let his shoulders settle a little. He could legitimately postpone his visit to Blair Collons until this was sorted. 'But before he goes, make a note of the reference on the print and find out who requested it.'

'Then we'll be home and dry.'

'With luck, Tony. I'll be in my office. Tell me as soon as anything comes through.'

Four hours later, Blacker picked up Barry Spinel, brought him to the interview room where Femur was waiting. They cautioned him, charged him, and offered him legal representation. He declined that and sat, as cocky as ever, challenging them both.

'It won't help you to hold out on us now,' Femur said, with a slight smile. Spinel was a fair target. He wouldn't crumple or throw up. He could take whatever Femur chose to throw at him. And he deserved it all. 'We've got plenty of evidence. We've got Michael Napton singing like a canary, and we'll have Drakeshill before long. You could improve your chances by helping us.'

Spinel leaned back in his chair, his strong muscles bulging in the usual overtight jeans. His jaw was taut and his eyes were watchful, but he wasn't afraid. There hadn't been any leaks from the incident room, even when Spinel's involvement was announced. Femur was proud of that. The local Kingsford officers had come good in the end, and stuck by the AMIP team as though they were part of it.

'Things must've changed since I last questioned a suspect,' Spinel said, in a casually mocking voice.

Femur raised his eyebrows. At his side, Tony Blacker shifted in his seat, restive as always when anyone challenged his boss. Femur nodded to give him permission to say whatever he wanted.

'You should be lucky we don't use your techniques, Spinel.'

'And what do you know about my techniques?' Spinel asked, suddenly dangerous. 'If you think I've ever held out inducements to *my* suspects, you've another think coming. Lucky for me the tape's running. You'll never get away with it, you know.'

'What I heard on the street is that you terrorise defendants, hit them, blackmail them, just like you blackmailed Michael Napton into working for Drakeshill.'

'Do I have to listen to this shit?' Spinel asked Femur, who shook his head slowly.

'You don't have to do anything, Spinel, but as you well know, if you do not mention when questioned evidence you later rely on in court, that may harm your defence.' Femur laughed. For the first time in days he could remember what it felt like to enjoy himself. 'But, like I say, we don't really need anything from you since we've plenty of evidence already. Evidence no one could wriggle out of.'

'Then why am I here?'

'Because you could help yourself by helping us.'

'Why should I? You've arrested me on suspicion of the murder of Kara Huggate but, as I've already said, I've an alibi supported by hundreds of witnesses. I was at a work dinner of my wife's in the City the night the woman was killed.'

'Yes,' said Femur, as calmly as though he was asking for a cup of tea, 'and I'm sure you can rely on everyone there to say what you want them to say.'

Spinel nodded, satisfaction all over his face.

'But unfortunately you can't always rely on everyone in the same way.'

'And what does that mean?'

'Charles Chompton.'

There was a definite movement in Spinel's face, which he tried to disguise by smiling widely and saying, 'One of Drakeshill's mechanics? The one they call Chompie?'

'As if you didn't know,' said Tony Blacker viciously.

Femur waved his right hand, palm down, as though he was trying to slow the traffic. 'That's right, Sergeant Spinel,' he said. 'The lad who kept the scene-of-crime photo of the Kingsford Rapist's last victim that you'd given him.'

He waited for a reaction, but Spinel had himself well in hand and didn't move. He didn't seem to be breathing either so Femur wasn't too worried.

'The photo Chompie used to work out how to arrange Kara Huggate's body on the floor of her cottage after he'd killed her so that it would look as much like the Kingsford Rapist's victim as possible. You were taking a risk, you know, trusting a lad like that.'

'I don't know what you're talking about.'

'I expect you told him to get rid of it after he'd finished with her – or perhaps you just assumed he would – but he didn't. I don't know whether he kept it as insurance in case we ever did pick him up, or whether he was just too thick to realise how we'd use it.'

'And how's that, sir?' Spinel was back in his favourite

pose, legs spread, head thrown back, hands splayed on his meaty thighs. I dare you, his body language said. You'll never beat me.

'To tie him to Kara's death, since there are traces of her blood on it, as well as his fingerprints.' Femur smiled. 'And yours, Spinel.'

Spinel's hands tightened, the fingertips pressing into his legs and the joints whitening. But he didn't speak.

'Yes. I don't know why you didn't wear gloves,' Femur said, sounding regretful, sympathetic, even. 'Unless you thought that would make the woman from the photo lab suspicious when she gave it to you. Or perhaps you didn't worry since you were certain you could rely on Chompie to destroy the photo. But we've two nice prints, you see, unmistakably yours. And there's no legitimate reason for you to have handled that photo. We've even talked to that poor pathetic girl in Records.'

'I don't know who you mean,' Spinel said automatically.

'The one you went to only three weeks ago to say you thought you had some more evidence on the rapist and needed to check something on the photo.'

'Bitch.' The single syllable was almost spat. 'She . . .' Spinel recovered himself and shut his mouth. But his chest heaved as though he'd been running, and his face was reddening as they watched.

'We know she owed you – and ultimately Drakeshill, no doubt – for her smack, but she's been wise enough to come clean. She'll lose her job, but that's probably all. It's all unravelling, you see, Spinel. You might as well join the angels and give us Drakeshill. We know he's always been the boss and you're only a gofer. Talk to us and we'll see what we can do for you.'

For a moment Femur thought Spinel would respond to the insult, but he didn't. He kept his mouth shut and went on smiling. He hadn't asked for a lawyer or even a Federation rep. He must have known he was in far too deep to do any kind of deal with them. He was going down, and he had a better chance of surviving what he'd have to face in prison if he were known to have kept quiet about Drakeshill.

Femur couldn't bear the possibility that Drakeshill might escape, but he had to face it. They were working their socks off to get evidence against him, but so far not much had come through. Informally Femur had been told that the CPS would bend over backwards to help – they'd been longing to go after him for years – but they needed something concrete. Napton's evidence would help, but without support from either Spinel or Chompie, it might not be enough.

THIRTY-TWO

As Femur followed Steve Owler out of the station, the dank air clawed at his chapped lips and seemed to float up his trouser legs to make the skin chafe against the fabric of his suit. He'd never realised how rough it was. He hunched his shoulders down into the coat and told himself to stop whingeing. It only seemed as bad as this because he was on his way to apologise. Most officers wouldn't have bothered, but he owed Blair Collons. He owed him for the information that had broken the case wide open, he owed him for the contempt, and for the bullying.

Owler drove straight to Holmside Court in helpful silence, as though he understood enough of Femur's mood to know that the squad's crowing triumph was getting to him. He was a good lad because it was probably his first successful murder case and he must have been fizzing with triumph.

There was no answer from Collons's flat when they rang the bell. Femur stepped into the neat flower bed that ran along the front of the building and walked along to the furthest window, which he knew was Collons's, so

331

that he could look in. The curtains were drawn, but there was a narrow gap between them.

'Oh, shit!' he said then yelled: 'Owler, get an ambulance.'

'Who are you?' came a nervous female voice to Femur's right. He pulled away from the window and saw a young woman carrying a baby in a sling against her breasts. She looked terrified as she stood by the front door to the flats and was cupping both her hands around her baby's head as Steve Owler jabbered into his mobile.

'It's all right, madam. I'm sorry I startled you. My name is Chief Inspector William Femur of the Metropolitan Police.' He smiled and held out his warrant card. Seeing some of the terror leaving her face, he walked quickly back to the path and showed her the card again.

'Sorry,' she said, letting her hands fall to her sides. But she was still breathing faster than she should have been and the baby was wailing.

'No, please. It's me who should apologise. But I need to get into the ground-floor flat over there straight away. D'you know the owner?'

'Mr Collons?' Her nostrils flexed and her lips thinned. She shook her head. Her hands were once more protecting her baby's head. 'He never talks to any of us; just scuttles in and out. I don't want . . . What's he done?'

'Nothing at all. He's been a witness for us; very helpful; I just need to get in to his flat quickly.'

'I can let you in to the front door, but I haven't got a key to his flat. None of us have. He doesn't mix much.'

'Right. Well, if you could open this door. That would be very helpful. As soon as you can.'

She got the door open and stood aside to let Femur go first. He ran. Luckily the baby's wails rose to a pitch that no one could ignore and she muttered an apology and disappeared up the main staircase. Femur fished in his pocket for a credit card.

He slid it between the door and the jamb and felt the Yale move back.

But the door wouldn't budge. Shit. There were no other keyholes in the door itself. Collons must have bolted it from the inside.

'Steve! Quick.'

But neither of them could kick the door down. The bolts must be the security type; well installed, too.

'Back to the garden, Steve. Break a window.'

This time there were no passers-by to make a fuss as Owler efficiently broke one half of the big casement window and knocked out the loose glass with his arm. Femur thrust him aside and climbed over the sill, grazing his hand and wrenching his shoulder. The curtain blew back in his face and he forced it away, pulling out two of the hooks and tearing the thin material.

It was much too late. He'd known that all along, but he'd had to try. With the sound of the ambulance siren in his ears, he saw that the slumped body, crouched and hanging from the door handle, was way beyond anyone's help. From the eyebrows down, the face was deep purple and there was a trickle of dried blood making a wobbly line from the mouth to the chin. Blair Collons must have died hours earlier.

Femur was aware of Steve Owler standing behind him, trying to say something. He shook his head and held up a hand to ward off the words. He didn't want questions or sympathy. This was his fault.

He pulled on a pair of latex gloves, but he didn't touch the body. It looked like a straightforward suicide, but it might not have been and he didn't want to wreck any evidence.

There weren't any bruises on the face or neck, just the

almost horizontal ligature at the base of the dark-purple stain under the skin. And there were no marks on the hands that he could see.

'You'd better cancel the ambulance,' he said drearily to Steve. 'And get hold of the police surgeon instead.'

'Too late, Guv.' Owler's voice was gentle. 'The paramedics are here. I'll go and have a word.'

Femur nodded and turned away from the body to look for a letter. The first thing he saw, as Owler went to unbolt the door, was a pile of creased photographs on the writing desk near the window. They looked as though they had been ripped apart and later carefully mended with Sellotape. Stirring the pile with his gloved finger, he saw that they were all of Kara. He shook his head. Beside the photographs were some women's underclothes, stained with what looked like tea leaves and orange peel. So Collons was what he'd always assumed. But it didn't make it any better. He turned away, disgust and sympathy fighting each other.

Then he saw the letter. It was propped on the mantelpiece and marked: 'Kara'.

Femur knew he should have left it for the SOCOs, but he couldn't. Still wearing the latex gloves, he opened the envelope. The single sheet inside was covered with neat black writing, just three words repeated over and over again: 'Kara, I'm sorry. Kara, I'm sorry. Kara, I'm sorry.'

CHAPTER THIRTY-THREE

'I've been worried about Barry Spinel and that poor Kara Huggate for months,' Drakeshill said, with a confiding air that didn't convince Femur one little bit. 'I didn't want to say anything, but ever since she was found, my conscience has been nagging at me. All along I've wanted to come in and talk to you lot, even though I've got no evidence. But it's the suspicion, Mr Femur. You can't think what it's been like. I tried to hold out – I mean, he's been a friend for years – but I can't. Not any longer. You've got to know about Spinel and why he wanted that poor woman dead. At first he –'

'Stop there,' Femur said. 'When's "at first"?'

Drakeshill shut his eyes and frowned, pursing his fat little lips. He looked as though he hadn't shaved in a couple of days. 'Three months ago? Four? I can't remember.'

'OK. So what did Spinel do – or say – that worried you?'

'He fancied that poor woman.' Drakeshill suddenly forgot about looking tormented and grinned as though he couldn't help himself. 'We've always had different tastes in women, Barry and me. I like 'em younger and foxier, but he's always gone for the teacher-type. Mad. Anyway, he had the hots for this one. I shouldn't talk like that about her, now she's dead, but you've got to understand, see. Barry kept making up reasons to meet her, pretended she had information on drug dealers for him to arrest so's he had an excuse to see her again and call round at her cottage.'

Drakeshill's grin turned into a brief, barking laugh. Femur battled to keep his own lips smiling. His teeth were grinding against each other like the mills of God. He knew this story of Drakeshill's was some kind of scam. He knew it was Drakeshill who had given the order for Kara's death, but finding the evidence wasn't going to be easy. And stories like this would only add to his problems. He wanted, more than anything he'd wanted in a long, long time, to get Drakeshill, and Spinel with him.

Femur had no illusions about the Job, but every time he came across a bent officer he hated him – or her. And Spinel was one of the worst he'd come across. Even though Femur was sure Spinel hadn't been the prime mover in what had been done to Kara, he'd had a hand in it. At the very least he'd procured the crucial photo-graph of the Kingsford Rapist's first dead victim, and he'd almost certainly given Chompie a map of Kara's cottage and probably a good deal else.

'And?' Femur said, still pretending to share Drakeshill's crass amusement at the thought of Spinel fancying Kara Huggate.

'Well, she wouldn't have none of him, would she?' Drakeshill settled his paunch over his belt and leaned forward. 'So after a bit he changed his tune, stopped making excuses to see her and stopped telling me how great she was. Suddenly she'd turned into a frigid bitch who was giving him grief. I knew he was angry, but I never thought he'd go this far.'

To Femur's astonished rage, Drakeshill stopped grinning and pulled a handkerchief out of his pocket so that he could mop his eyes. 'And I never thought he'd corrupt one of my lads like he's done Chompie.' Drakeshill even produced a kind of sob.

Oh, please, thought Femur, in disgust.

'I know Chompie's no angel, but he'd never have done something like this without being pushed into it.' Drakeshill took the handkerchief away at last and Femur saw that he'd managed to make his eyes red.

This was a man who was going to work a jury like an expert, Femur told himself. Drakeshill was obviously prepared to sacrifice Spinel, Chompie and probably everyone else to keep himself out of it and *he* hadn't been stupid or arrogant enough to leave his fingerprints on any of the physical evidence.

'This'll sound mad,' Drakeshill said, still sniffing and gazing at Femur as though he were a kindly uncle, 'but it's going to be harder for me to forgive Barry Spinel for what he did to young Chompie than for the poor woman's death.' He shrugged his fat shoulders and sniffed. Then he wiped his nose on the back of his hairy hand. Femur nearly gagged. 'But, then, I never knew her, and he was like a son to me. They all are, you know, Mr Femur. My lads. They've all had their problems and I know they've done things they shouldn't, but treated right they come good in the end. Over and over again I've seen it. And now this. I tell you, it's enough to make a man . . .' He whimpered again and mopped his eyes.

He can't think I'm falling for this load of tripe, Femur thought, while he said briskly, 'Right. Tony, will you finish up in here? Get a signed statement with all the details and any shred of evidence Drakeshill can offer.'

Tony Blacker, who had been staring at Drakeshill as though he was a Martian, shut his mouth. He was still explaining Femur's departure to the tape recorder as Femur shut the door behind him.

Two hours later, Femur nodded to Caroline Lyalt. She'd better ask the next question. He felt as though he was on the point of banging someone's head against the wall, probably his own.

'So, Sergeant Spinel,' Caroline said, still smiling, 'once more for the tape. You never had any sexual interest in Kara Huggate, despite what your friend Martin Drakeshill has alleged, both in a taped interview and in his signed statement. Is that right?'

'Of course it is. How often do I have to tell you? I can't think what he's playing at.' Spinel was clearly furious, whether because Drakeshill was trying to pin all the blame for Kara's death on him or whether because of the sexual insult, Femur wasn't sure.

'And he's not a friend. He's a snout, for Christ's sake. No one who knew me would think I could ever fancy an old bag like Kara Huggate. He's living in a world of his own, these days. None of his information's been any good to me for months. I should have axed him.'

'If you had,' Femur said, with wholly deceptive mildness. 'Kara Huggate might still be alive, mightn't she?'

'I had nothing to do with her death.'

'Oh, come on! You can't expect us to believe that with your prints all over the photo of the Kingsford Rapist's victim.'

'No, listen, sir, you don't understand.'

'Too right, Sergeant Spinel. So give me enough to make me understand.'

'I never thought they were going to kill her. Christ! You

can't believe I'd let myself be involved in anything like that?'

'So, what did you think?'

'That they were trying to scare her off. I understood that Chompie was going to dress up like the Kingsford Rapist and crash about in her cottage, perhaps even give her a bit of a slapping and terrify her into leaving Kingsford. That's all.'

'Leave aside what that says about your brains,' Femur said, aware of the rage that was heating up inside Caroline's slim body, 'and tell me why Drakeshill was so anxious to frighten Kara Huggate. What did he think she could do to him, a lone social worker?'

'I've never been quite sure, sir.' Spinel was spitting out the words. 'But she'd riled him from the start. He'd been picking up rumours from his mechanics that she'd been talking all over Kingsford about how she was going to get to the bottom of whoever it was putting all the drugs into local schools. She'd find out who it was then use all her influence to have him sent down for the longest possible stretch.'

'And who was he?' Caroline asked, so that they could have the admission on tape.

'Drakeshill, of course. But you knew that.'

'Sure. But we like to have it all clear.'

Spinel muttered something Femur couldn't catch. He didn't need to know what it was: the feeling behind it was obvious enough.

'Even so,' he said, 'I can't see that kind of provocation being enough for what he had done to Kara Huggate. Are you trying to make me believe Drakeshill also thought Chompie was just going to slap her? That the assault and murder were part of some kind of private enterprise of Chompie's?'

'Well, they could've been, couldn't they?'

'If that's the story you're planning to tell in court, I'm even more worried about your brains. You'd never have given Chompie a photograph of the Kingsford Rapist's body if you'd thought he was just going to give Kara a slapping. You knew all along what they were planning. You're in it up to your neck. Drakeshill's trying to make you take the rap for it. I know he was the one who gave the order. You might as well save yourself a bit of bother and tell us why.'

Spinel shrugged. The ghost of his old cockiness still hovered around him, but at last he looked what he was: a grounded bully, a fundamentally weak man who'd enjoyed terrorising other people and now didn't know where to put himself or what to do.

'It looked like it was something personal,' he said sulkily, 'but I could never understand why she pissed him off that much. Then when she started to go after Napton, I found out Drakeshill thought she had more information on him than she'd let on at first. He thought she was going to pick off his people one by one and then get to him.'

'That makes her sound powerful.' Femur was puzzled. 'No one else has suggested anything like it.'

'Drakeshill thought she was.' Spinel shrugged again. 'He wouldn't listen. I talked to her over and over again a few months back, probing for whatever she had on him, and there wasn't anything. She was an angry woman, and she hated drugs, but that was all. She didn't know his name. She didn't know he had the monopoly in Kingsford. She didn't know shit. I told him that, but he didn't believe me. And I still think it was just coincidence she got on to Napton. But Drakeshill wouldn't wear it. He decided she was just a front for someone else, someone who really did know the whole story, maybe someone who wanted to take over his empire here. So he wanted her dead, for herself because she riled him and for whoever was behind her as a lesson to keep out of Kingsford. That's all there is to it.'

'Except that you were prepared to help him. You know, Spinel, if there's one thing I hate it's a bent copper. But a copper who's prepared to go along with murder is something else again. You're going down, my son.'

'So long as I take Drakeshill with me, I don't fucking care,' Spinel said, through his teeth.

'Right. Then let's get down to it. D'you want a brief now, just to get all the formalities sorted so that Drakeshill can't wriggle out of this one?'

'OK.' The big shoulders shrugged up the leather jacket again. 'But not Bletchley.'

'Right.' Femur turned to Caroline with the first real pleasure of the investigation stretching his face into a smile. 'Get on to it, will you, Cally? And send for some tea for us all while you're about it. We've got work to do.'

EPILOGUE

There wasn't much room in the church of St Michael and All Angels when Trish and George walked through the door only two minutes before Kara's memorial service was due to start. Every pew they could see was full. Heads turned at the sound of their late arrival. Trish caught sight of Darlie, looking tearful and very fragile in her short black skirt and sweater. Just in front of her was a pewful of police officers in uniform. There was an extraordinary range of dress, from the scruffiest of jeans to formal black suits and even one or two hats. There was an almost cheerful buzz of conversation, as though the congregation was waiting for a wedding or, at least, an ordinary service.

An usher came towards them, his shoes squeaking against the stone flags. As he handed each of them a thick white order of service, he whispered that there were spaces near the front. They followed him up a side aisle to the third row.

Trish, constrained by the thought that they must be invading the family's space, smiled hesitantly at the nearest occupant of the pew, a tall, slim man in a dark

343

suit and very white, very smooth shirt. He moved nearer to the woman beside him and nodded encouragingly at Trish.

'Is this really all right?' she whispered. 'You're not expecting more family?'

'No. I'm not family either,' he whispered back, his accent distinctly Bostonian.

Trish smiled and slid into the pew ahead of George, just as the organ burst into life with a triumphant crashing sound that didn't seem altogether appropriate. There was a rustle all around the church. She looked back to see the choir processing up towards the chancel, followed by the vicar, dressed in a simple white surplice over his cassock.

The organist stopped playing as the priest reached the chancel steps, where he turned. Holding his prayer book against his heart, he said, in a voice of surprising power, 'Friends, we are here today not to mourn but to remember, rejoicing, the life of a remarkable woman. Mourning there has been for all of us, and anxiety and anger, but today we must put all that aside. Kara lit up our lives, each one in a different way. She had a gift of friendship that will live as long as the last one of us. She gave freely of herself to all of us and many others. Remember her.'

The man beside Trish shivered. She snatched a glance at him and saw such pain in his face that she had to look away.

'And now, will you join with me in singing, 'Love Divine, all love's excelling'?

As the huge congregation stood, Trish caught sight of Femur and Constable Lyalt in plain clothes in one of the pews on the far side of the aisle. She thought of the last time they'd met, in a grim little crematorium on the outskirts of Kingsford, where they were the only mourners at Blair Collons's dismal funeral.

There had been no hymns and no address, simply a hurried recitation of the burial service and some tinkly taped music as his plain coffin rolled away through the curtained doorway to the furnace. Trish had watched it go, sick at heart and full of shame.

'You mustn't blame yourself,' Femur had said, when they walked out into the raw cold outside, averting their eyes from the miserable ragged wreaths of earlier services. 'If it's anyone's fault, it's mine.'

'We both failed him,' she'd answered. 'And both for much the same reason, I suspect.'

'He didn't come across as a good witness,' Femur said. 'He didn't help himself.'

'I know, but it doesn't excuse us,' Trish answered. 'We were both sure at one stage that he'd killed her and we must have shown it. Given how guilty he already felt for not having saved her, that can't have helped him find a reason to go on living.'

Femur had nodded, but as they reached the edge of the car-park, he sent Caroline Lyalt on ahead. Standing in the rain beside Trish, his face unhappier than she'd ever seen it, he said, 'Did it ever occur to you that he could have been the original Kingsford Rapist?'

She nodded. The rain trickled through her hair, right over the back of her head and down her neck. 'But I didn't think there was any evidence.'

'There wasn't. But someone assaulted those women and killed the last of them. And he – '

'Don't,' she said urgently. 'Don't decide it was Blair just because he was creepy and made you feel ill. If you think it was him, then find a photograph of him and show it to the surviving victims, then . . .'

'Their rapist was masked,' he reminded her. 'We'll never know, since there was never anything to use for a

DNA match. But I think that outpouring of apology to Kara meant that he knew it was his fault she'd died like that. He'd got over whatever had driven him to attack the other women – perhaps it was relative success at work, perhaps it was the stress of having been driven to kill the last of them, we'll never know. But he must have come to understand that, if he'd never done any of it, Kara's killer wouldn't have had the blueprint for what he did. You and I both realised he felt guilty about what happened to her. I think this is why.'

'But you've no proof,' Trish reminded him.

'No. We'll never know.'